Sinful Salvation

Lost Royals of Transylvania

Book 4

Sinful Salvation

Lost Royals of Transylvania

Book 4

Alexa Whitewolf

Sinful Salvation
A *Lost Royals of Transylvania* novel

by Alexa Whitewolf

Cover design by Y. Nikolova at **Ammonia Book Covers**
Editing and formatting by Luna Imprints Author Services

First Edition

ISBN: 978-1-989384-23-7

10 9 8 7 6 5 4 3 2 1

Rogues Extended Universe—Reading Order

Moonlight Rogues
Flaming Rogues
Immortal Rogues
Lost Royals of Transylvania
Vârcolac Legacy (Coming Soon)

Content Warning:

This book contains scenes and themes that may be triggering or upsetting for some readers. These include:

- Ableism

- Some graphic violence, including fight scenes and descriptions of injury

- Flashbacks and descriptions of torture (non-sexual)

- Grief, loss, and emotional distress, including the loss of loved ones and struggles with bereavement

- Mature themes, including sexual content and strong language

If you are sensitive to any of these themes, please proceed with caution.

Glossary

Vampir/vampiri—vampire/vampires
Inima mea—my heart (an endearment among lovers)
Da / nu—yes/no
Ce naiba—what the heck/hell
Nu iară—not again
Babă—slang (not exactly a kind term) for "old woman"
Mulţumesc—thank you
Ai grijă de tine—take care of yourself
Nu înţeleg—I don't understand
Săpam—was digging
Sigur—of course
Frate—brother
Sorella/fratello—not exactly Romanian, but an endearment used by Silviana and her brother; it's Italian and means sister/brother.
Da, sigur—yes, of course
Ştefan—phonetically, the ş is said as sh
Scuze—Sorry
Bine—fine
Iubito—also an endearment meaning "darling"
Ţuică—a fantastic Romanian vodka-like drink :D
Castelul Corvinilor – Corvins' Castle

Creatures

Vârcolac/ Vârcolaci—werewolf/werewolves; in this book, it refers to Dominic's wolves.
Pricolic/pricolici—a smaller type of wolf, possessed by

dark magic, at the mercy of Dacians.

Voivode—an old title given to the lord of a region; similar to king.

Cavaleri Serafim—Serafim Knights; in this universe, they're knights who have become vengeful against supernaturals.

Chapter 1

Elizabeta

"Liza!"

Alex's shout comes just in time. I snap out of my mood and duck the muroni coming at me, elongated nails extended into the perfect weapon to scrape half my face off. These things are so damned stupid, and yet I nearly let one have the upper hand.

My palm rises, smacking him straight under the chin. He stumbles, and something drops out of his other hand. A stake. *Interesting. I always thought these things were too stupid to use human weapons to kill us. Guess you learn something new every day.*

I catch the stake before it hits the ground and shove it straight where its heart would've been. Then I rip one limb apart, and another, and finally elongate my nails to decapitate it. Blood gushes everywhere. The head rolls to the ground, all slimy hair and rotting body, eyes open wide.

I wipe some of the blood off my face, off my dress—the boots are going to need a good scrub. *Ugh.* I spit some blood that made its way into my mouth, and turn to Alex. "Thanks for that."

He arches an eyebrow. At his feet are four dead muroni, part of the same cluster as the one I killed. "What was that? You know better than to lose your focus around these fuckers."

"Yeah, what *was* that?"

I close my eyes, wanting to ignore the second voice. When I open them, he's not gone. Instead, he's right next to Alex, but visible only to me. Dark hair to his shoulders, he looks the same as he had hundreds of years ago. And the sight of him still sends a pang of longing to my heart.

Daniel Silva. My brother's best friend, the guard to our little clan. Silva, they used to call him. I always called him something much more intimate.

Even now, his eyes are narrowed on me. His shimmering form isn't visible to Alex, or any of my other siblings. Sometimes I think I'm imagining him and it's the grief at losing him that turned me mad. But my imagination was never this good, nor does it have a conscience. My companion, my ghost, my personal haunting lover. I gulp, averting my gaze from him, and address Alex instead. "I don't know. It won't happen again."

"Better not." To take the sting out of his words, Alex blurs closer, still in full vampir speed, and cups my cheek. "Nico would kill me if anything happens to you." He kisses my temple, then let's go just as quickly. Shows of emotion aren't really his thing, so I appreciate the gesture even more.

I force a bantering tone. "Since when do you care what Nico wants?"

"Since never."

Laughter escapes me, and we leave the cave the muroni were hiding in, heading back into the woods. At least we can return with good news to our siblings.

As the scourge of our kind, muroni live in caves, avoid the sun, and basically meet every vampir stereotype there is. The problem is, they've also been playing for the enemy.

See, as royals, we've always been targets. But since we started making moves to get our throne back? Even more so. It seems some of the clans of vampiri—used to be six, now five since we punished a particularly naughty one—who've lived on by happily while we hid in the shadows have, well, taken to wanting things above their station. Us returning to power doesn't really fit into their plans for grandeur.

Which makes it even more imperative that we get back on top. Fast.

Hence me and Alex doing our own little hunting party trips. We used to do the same in the woods around our previous castle. Now that we're in a new spot? We both know it's even more important to make sure no muroni lurch in the shadows, ready to be used against us.

And yet somehow, they always seem to.

"You know why they do," Daniel says, keeping pace with me. His form is nearly transparent today, which I take to mean his emotions are not as strong. When they are, that's when things get confusing. Because I could almost touch him—almost, but not quite.

"No one asked you," I mutter, knowing full well he's going to ignore me anyway. Lately, he's taken to giving way more advice than I ever asked for. And though he can't read my mind, centuries at my side mean he's gotten pretty good at reading my expressions.

"Liza, I'm serious. This curse on the Dracul line, it's pulling everything out of the shadows. All the darkest creatures, the most fucked up souls."

I stop in my tracks, glance around to make sure Alex isn't near—he's a blur, moving through the darkened woods—then meet his gaze full-on. "Then they've met their match, haven't they?"

Before he can answer, I take off again. This time, mercifully, he stays behind. I never know when he'll appear, or disappear. In the beginning, he was by my side all the time. He showed up shortly after his death, and never left. He's been my consolation, every time I've felt low. Every time the memory of the past threatens to pull me back in a whirlwind of darkness...which happens more than I'd like to admit.

But Daniel being around also makes things awkward when I need to have certain needs filled. Maybe that's why his appearances are less, now. *Or maybe I'm losing him.* I shove the thought away the moment it appears. I won't lose Daniel. I can't. He keeps me sane. He's the last bit of my heart, of my humanity, and a reminder of what I stand to lose if I'm ever stupid enough to give in to feelings again.

Which makes the matter of the curse he referred to even worse.

Because said curse wants me to find a consort, and act on the bond between us, solidifying a union, of all things. I'll be damned if I tie myself to anyone for the rest of my immortal existence, all to give in to the fancy of some god who had a bone to pick with Father.

I increase my speed, trying to outrun my thoughts. I love the feel of the wind in my face. The freedom of being so strong, so on top of everything else—the world. I can have everything I want, and that's how I like it.

An odd bend in the path comes, with trees clustered together. Weird. I don't remember them being this—

Shit. My dress snags on a branch, the tear of fabric follows, and I go tumbling. Groaning, I stand. That's what I get for wearing a freaking dress out on a hunt. Not that Alex didn't warn me.

I stand, dusting myself off. Then freeze. Something's wrong, here. Something—

"Don't panic."

I whirl toward the voice. A twig cracks under my heel. "I never panic."

But that voice. Who the hell is it? And why do they sound so goddamned familiar?

He steps out of the trees half a second later. In another life, he must've been a Viking—he towers over me by almost two heads, and his shoulders are broad, filling and stretching the measly human t-shirt he's wearing as though he's about to burst out of it. His head is shaved, and the last time I'd seen him he sported a thick, brown beard. It's still there, but trimmed closer to his jawline, making him look less Neanderthal and more...

No. I won't go there. When I place his features, I recoil back in horror. "*You*. You're that witch's brother!"

At the same time, my brain screams for me to run away. *Far* away. From him. As if he's something I should fear.

He nods, but something in the way he's staring toward me strikes me as odd. "Da. Ștefan Dragoș."

"He's blind, remember?"

I jump at Daniel's voice, and toss him a glare. Of course he'd pick this moment to reappear. He ignores me, as usual, instead tossing me a challenging look of his own.

To the warlock, I add, "What the fuck do you want?" Venom fills my tone, and hopefully it'll be enough to keep him at arms' length.

I still remember the first time we'd met. In the fight, weeks ago, just before our last home was burned. To say that fight contributed to us moving would be an understatement. And how I'd planned to kill him, only for my body to refuse to listen. And then running into him again at the castle, right before the attack that forced us to move… I'd done everything in my power to get away from him, fast.

Ștefan raises his hands, showing me his palms as if to placate me. "Relax, vampir. I'm not after anything shady. I've come with a question." He waits a beat, and when I say nothing, adds, "Are your siblings doing anything to help Silviana out?"

It surprised everyone that Vlad didn't take off with the Dacian witch as soon as we talked about moving areas. He's been so damned possessive of her, freaking out every time she so much as jumps because of that god that she invited into that airy brain of hers. And we're no better, fearing the void that used to overtake *him*, would return. Surprisingly, he's been fine. The same can't be said for his consort…

I roll my eyes at the Dacian. "We have other priorities, you know."

And, sure, Nico and Tassa are scouring the books trying to figure out how to break the god's hold on the annoying witch, but that's beside the point. Nor am I required to tell him that.

I turn to leave, but Daniel stops me. "Hear him out."

I glare at him strongly. "Fuck off."

Behind me, the mountain of a man snorts. "Is that really needed? All I did was ask a question." If he was any other human, I might find his rumbling, gravelly voice sexy. Might. Given who he is, I only clench my teeth at the sound of it.

"Well, you can take your question and shove it." Unnerved by his presence, I step away, then whiz through the trees. Daniel's gone quiet, as has everything in me.

Everything except the memory of when I first met the Dacian. It blurs in my mind, refusing to be shut out. The woods, Vlad losing his shit, the bodies...

Covered in blood, my sibling blinks, and comes out of his daze. He takes us all in, but it's when his gaze lands on me that he stops. Horror fills his features. Blood drips off his clothes, his hair, his face, his hands.

"What—who—"

I'm as stunned as he is. The kindest of us, the sweetest, capable of such carnage—it's impossible. Is this what the curse does to us, changes us to our core? And if it does, what else will it ruin in me and Alex? We're already unhinged as it is.

I gulped. "You did this."

At my words, Vlad's eyes widen. But then his expression twists in pain. He drops to the ground, and it's only then I see the tendrils of darkness. And from the woods, a human emerges. Tall, broad shoulders, strong jaw with a well-maintained stubble. Someone I'd fuck, easily.

Then I see his palm extended, and fury lashes through me. He attacked Vlad, from behind? Ah, hell no.

I don't think. I rush at him, ignoring Vlad's screams to stop. I slam into the warlock, and we fall to the ground. My fist connects with his jaw, then his side. Straddling him, I reach for a rock, ready to slam it onto his face before he knows what's coming.

"Liza, no!"

It's not Vlad's shout that stops me. Rather, the moment I raise the rock, I lock eyes with the warlock. Register the blankness in them—he's blind.

"Liza, don't," another voice says next to me. Daniel.

I glance at him, then back at the warlock. Even as I try to drop the rock on him, my body resists. It's like my hands won't work, refusing to budge even an inch toward his face.

"Going to finish me?" the Dacian whispers, his jaw clenched. "Go on, then. I can feel your anger, vampir."

I try to move the rock again. My mistake is staring into his eyes again. Something rushes through me. A sense of… I don't understand it, but it hurts. Like a knife into my side. I drop the rock to the side as if it burns and stumble off him, my legs shaky.

The human reaches for me, but catches only air. I'm already gone.

I shove the memory away, sick and tired of revisiting it. It's been weeks, and I still don't know what possessed me that day. Nor should I care so much to figure it out. I've got bigger fish to fry.

Determined to not give the warlock another thought, I push forth in the woods, blurring even faster, outrunning everything. Even my own personal ghost.

Ștefan

Dammit. I should've known they wouldn't do anything, but I'd hoped. It's been two weeks since I left Silviana with Vlad in the cabin. Two weeks since the zmeu Tytus confirmed what we knew. That Zalmoxis, the god we serve, is embedded in my sister's mind. When she opened the portal, hoping to channel something to help Vlad, she weakened the barrier of her aura, of her mind, and he sank his claws into her. And he won't let her go so easily.

Two weeks since I've done everything in my power to find the Oracle my people use—and the artifact I read about in Liviu's scrolls. The one that can protect anything and anyone, from *anything*. Getting my hands on that would mean Lana being safe, for good. But all my attempts have led me nowhere.

And while two weeks might be peanuts to these creatures, it's a long time for me. A long time to agonize over how to save my twin. How to help her get her happily ever after.

I warned Vlad to keep my sister away from his siblings. But over many phone calls, he admitted she was struggling, and keeping her safe would be a hell of a lot easier if he had his siblings around him. I caved. Do I regret it? Fuck yes. I still think Silviana being around the Draculs acts like a calling for Zalmoxis, drawing his attention to her time and time again. But I can't deny Vlad's plan worked. So far, she's been safe—at least physically.

I leave the woods, returning to the path leading to the vampiri's new castle. Because though I'd approached Elizabeta first, I'm not about to give up. Keeping my sister's body safe is one thing, but I also need them to take her mind's safety into account. I'll make Silviana a priority for them, come what may. These vampiri may think they rule these lands, but they've never met a brother's rage. Not like mine.

First, though, a pit stop.

"Ştefan!"

It didn't take him long. I felt the ripple in the barrier a few moments ago, and already Liviu—the Grand Master and head of the Dacian community I'm part of—has found me.

"Da, Grand Master?"

"Where were you?"

I face the direction of his voice and the air around him shimmers. People I'm connected to, whether by choice or not, they emit a glow. It's nowhere close to *actual sight*, more like a shard of light amid a sea of darkness. And when I focus on those shards, I've noticed I'm able to pinpoint people's locations better. The only cost is exhaustion if I'm overusing the ability, since it does source itself from my magic.

Still, I've gotten used to it—walking in a perpetual fog, interrupted only by people's energies. It's how I'm able to function. That, and years of practice learning to use the darkness our magic taps into for purposes other than offensive magic. Some might call it dark arts. I call it resourcefulness.

"Spying on the vampiri," I tell him.

His silence speaks volumes to his shock. Then, "Come with me."

He passes by me, and the sound of his steps on the ground orients me. Meter by meter, I follow him. It's made easier by the faint gray matter he seems to leave behind on the ground. His energy always has surprised me. As did the fact I started seeing these things, despite not seeing in the way most people think of having sight.

The night our parents were killed, darkness became my friend. I woke up blind, but my magic seemed to become enhanced. In the last few years, the auras—or energy traces—showed up as yet another element. I was smart enough not to tell Liviu about that new development. Though he's invested a lot in my teachings, and in developing me as a tool, there's a snake-like quality to the Grand Master that I've recently become more familiar with.

It's why I've stuck around, rather than left with my sister. It kills me to be away from her, especially in her time of need, but I need to know what the Dacians are planning. Liviu is neck-deep in this Zalmoxis issue—in the hold the god has on her mind—I just know it.

Once at his cabin, I pass him and enter. Stand in the doorway, pretending I'm not well acquainted with every inch of it. Like I haven't come in here every time he's gone, seeking more information in the scrolls he hides and would protect with his life.

"Now, explain it to me. Spying? Who gave you permission to do that?"

I clear my throat. "All due respect, Grand Master, no one did. They ensnared my sister and glamoured her into betraying her kin, despite the fact Dacians aren't supposed to be susceptible to that. Of course I still care for her, but ultimately I want them to fall. So I've been trying to find out more of what's going on."

"And what have you found out?"

It's a good thing I did, actually, do some spying. At least my story will be somewhat convincing. "The Dracul heirs moved to a new location, following the burning of their old castle. They've spread duties, it seems. Some are hunting muroni clusters in the area, others are reaching out to the vampiri clans. A mix of wielding steel and diplomacy seems to be their strategy to reinstate themselves as heirs to this region."

"Interesting." His tone tells me everything I need to know—he's not upset; on the contrary, he's relishing this new information.

I know the time has come to play my trump card. "Word is, they're planning a ball."

"Yes. Yes, they are. Tomorrow night."

"You knew?"

In hindsight, I should've known Liviu would be just as informed. Silviana did say he has an unhealthy obsession with the Dracul heirs. She thinks it's because he's trying to kill them, but I have a feeling there's more to it. He had plenty of chances to kill Vlad when he was imprisoned here, yet he didn't. Instead, he wanted to sacrifice his essence so Dacians' magic could continue.

Da, that's another little gem I discovered. Zalmoxis, mad at the Dacians for not finding the Draculs' sire—Vlad Țepeș himself—and hurting him before he killed himself, pulled back on his support. Meaning, the magic he gave us started having a ticking clock on it. Dacian lifetimes, which previously had been lengthy, became less so. And the price we pay for our magic has become much steeper.

Liviu knows this, and using Vlad—the younger one—was his way to fix it. By tapping into his vampir essence, which was still very much connected to Zalmoxis and more potent, he could've renewed the source of our Dacian magic. At least for a while...until the next vampir sacrifice would be needed. Given his failure with that particular plan, it's no wonder he's been keeping tabs on the Dracul heirs.

"You're not the only one spying on them," he says, once more confirming my suspicions.

Good to know. Especially if I'm going to approach them again.

"What were you going to suggest?" Liviu asks.

With composed features and a voice devoid of emotion, I say, "I thought I might infiltrate, under the guise of wanting to speak to my sister. Then, find out more information. See which alliances they favor, which they don't."

"Good. That information will come in handy, as we can then approach those same leaders and turn them, coordinate for a full attack." He pauses. "I expect a full report upon your return."

I nod and leave the room. Make a show of accidentally banging against the wall, then feeling my way out the door. Let him think I'm weak and unaware. The longer he believes that, the better.

The walk from Liviu's cabin to my apartment is devoid of incidents. The icy cold bites at my cheeks, and I rub my hands together, blowing on them. I increase my speed, until I get to the edge of the main Dacian compound.

Silviana described it to me in detail a million times. But she doesn't feel it the way I do. The power in the earth, emitting little tidbits of magic in the air. The freshness in the air. The sharp cry of an owl, and the howls of the wolves at night. I may not see the way they all do, but in my own way, I feel it all.

"Ștefan?"

I stop, turning to the soft voice. The aura in the fog shines a faint pink—Maria, one of the Dacian witches. Like my sister used to be, she's been relegated to the menial tasks of making potions, reading tarot cards for tourists, and picking herbs.

"What is it, Maria?"

"I, um, Cezar was looking for you."

That bastard. My status precedes his but the dumbass has been after my title—master of training, at Liviu's command—for too long. I'm just thankful Silviana's out of here. Because I may be blind, but I'm not stupid. And between Cezar and Victor, it's a wonder I've managed to keep her safe for so long. At least that latter bastard is dead.

"What for?"

"He didn't say."

Of course not. I run a hand over my smooth head, then try to speak as though I'm not pushing words through extremely gritted teeth. "Any idea where he is?"

"Back there." A half-second later, she stutters, "I—so sorry, Ștefan. I was pointing to the training grounds."

"Don't worry about it." I offer her a wan smile and head the way she meant.

The training grounds are always easy to find. The light shines differently here. Whereas the fog that normally surrounds me is a soft blue, the training area is a darker burgundy. Probably on account of the blood that has been spilled onto this ground.

The area doesn't seem to need us to bleed as much to tap into our magic when we're training, which comes in handy as with one cut, we can cast several spells versus only one. There's a reason Liviu chose this spot for our quarters, and this specific section to train his army. After all, he's Grand Master to win, not to take prisoners.

The closer I get to the training grounds, the louder the noises of a fight grow.

"Come on, stop pussyfooting about!"

A clash of metal against metal, a grunt of pain, followed by a yelp.

"Cezar, please! My arm!"

"You fucking—"

Metal sings in the air, slicing through it toward its target.

I don't think. I push my thumbnail into my palm hard enough to draw blood and whisper to the shadows. The air around me sizzles, and I count my steps until I know I've reached the gate—the entrance. I know what I'd see, if I could. A tennis court, refurbished as fighting grounds. Tall, thick gray walls, to stop others from witnessing what's going on. And my magic, dark tendrils leaving me.

There's another grunt, but it sounds different. It's soon followed by a curse and the clatter of metal—a sword?—on the pavement.

Footsteps scurry away, and someone runs past me, not even thanking my efforts. I'm not surprised. Cezar has that effect on people.

"Still butting your nose where it doesn't belong, huh, Dragoş?"

Chapter 2

Ştefan

"Last I heard, Cezar, beating up new recruits *is* my business."

There's a pause, and the scrape of metal against cement once more. It's got to be a sword. Liviu favors us fighting with older weapons, as he's a firm believer in the energy they carry. The damage they can do. But when it comes to training, we're supposed to use wooden ones.

My jaw clenches to the point of pain. This dumbass clearly didn't get the memo since he's running a session with a real sword. I drafted the guidelines, and he should've followed them to the letter. Not taken advantage of me being gone to do whatever he pleased.

"Tsk, but you weren't around to give permission. And Trăian's too baby-faced for his own good." He chuckles. "A little hard fighting won't do him harm."

Trăian's one of our newest members. We're all well into adulthood, but Liviu had some of his elite trusted advisors scour the country—and its surroundings—for more people with Dacian blood. Lambs to the slaughter in the war he has no qualms about starting.

I take a step in Cezar's direction, guided by the same dark gray matter as Liviu breaking through the fog. "You could've hurt him."

"How would you know?" he says from somewhere to my left. "It's not like you could *see* what was going on."

My teeth grind, making an audible sound. "Your little jibes about my lack of sight are getting old, Cezar. When are you going to give it up?"

"Why should I?" He's behind me now, taunting me. "There's absolutely no reason you should be the golden boy. What Liviu sees in you, especially now that your sister's gone, is beyond me."

He tuts, and shifts. The air shifts with him, and the darkness at my command—the same darkness I'd stopped him with before—warns me. A hiss in my ear, a gut feeling later, and the cold steel of the sword touches the back of my neck.

"It would be so easy," he whispers. "What would Liviu do, you think? Cry after you?" He sniggers. "Probably for a day. Once he sees the benefit of having me at his beck and call, he'll soon forget about all about you."

I remain rigid, mindful of the sword and whatever angle it's aimed at. But it doesn't stop my smug tone. "Maybe before you plan my execution, you should check yourself."

There's a beat, a tension-filled pause. His sharp intake of

breath tells me he's noticed the darkness surrounding him as I asked it to—crafted into a million pointed swords, all ready to stab him with a single command from me.

"Drop it."

He gulps audibly, then does as I ask, removing the steel of the sword from my skin.

I turn and face him, knowing he hasn't moved for fear of being impaled. "Don't mistake my lack of sight for weakness, Cezar. Next time, you won't be so lucky."

I walk away, leaving the dark swords in the air around him as a warning. When I cross the gate and shut it behind me, I drop the magic and force myself to keep moving. He won't get to see the weakness I feel after using that magic, so close to what I used to get the vampir to answer my questions.

It's only once I'm through the courtyard, then into the building, and my apartment, that I let my façade drop and allow myself to feel some weakness. I stumble to the couch, relying on sheer memory of its placements, and plop onto it, drained.

I should've been more careful. It's only recently I've dug into this level of magic, and my body isn't used to it. Liviu's scrolls might have provided me with the blueprint, but I need to build myself up. Still...

Since we—Silviana and I—found out the role our Dacian community played in the whole Țepeș fiasco, and our father's death, it's been harder and harder for me to keep my cool. Anger I've never felt before has taken permanent lodging in my heart. But I tell myself the time will come for vengeance. And that time is not now.

Cezar is only the latest example. He's pushing, and sniffing around me. If he gets a whiff of what I've got planned, of the dual nature of what I'm doing, he'll be the first to serve my head on a silver platter to Liviu. And whether I like it or not, he's right, in some regards. My lack of sight means I don't see everything happening. And that leaves me vulnerable.

Silviana was my second pair of eyes, my backer. And now that she's not here... It won't be easy, but I can still do it.

With a sigh, I roll onto my back on the couch and allow sleep to take me. Just a few hours. Then I'll get dressed and head out to the vampiri's new castle to carry out the next part of my plan.

So long as I can continue feeding the Dacians the wrong information, and keep them away from Silviana, it's worth my being here. Pretending. Biding my time.

Elizabeta

"You're really going to ignore me?"

I've slowed my pace from vampir-speed to regular walking. It allows Daniel to be even more annoying, maintaining pace with me and constantly pestering me. But it also hides the weakness spreading through me. I've tracked down hundreds—thousands—of muroni, but these latest hunting trips with Alex are getting harder and harder. And the weakness that follows me after...I refuse to admit it's what I think it is.

I throw Daniel a look. "I'll stop, as soon as you decide whose side you're on."

Hurt crosses his features, turning him from a faint transparent form to fully there. "Liza, you know the answer to that. Your side, always and forever."

I stop in my tracks, taken aback by the sincerity in his tone.

Daniel's the only one I allow myself to be even close to sentimental with, but that vulnerability tears through my heart, time and time again. What's left of it, anyway.

"You weren't acting like it."

"I've been by your side for centuries now. Which means I know you, and sometimes I see things that you don't. Or refuse to."

I snort. "Oh, yeah? And what did I refuse to see with the Dacian, then? Go on. Tell me."

He purses his lips, annoyance flashing in his eyes.

"Right. Well, when you're ready to tell me, feel free to do so. In the meantime, I'm going to go feed."

I've barely taken a few steps when he says, "Feed or fuck?"

I pause again. Without meeting his gaze, I toss over my shoulder, "You're best off not knowing."

To his credit, he doesn't follow me. I'd known as much. He's never around when I choose to indulge in either, though his reappearance is bound to try to guilt me. It's not even that he cares I'm fucking around—more that I'm doing it so carelessly, without even trying for a relationship.

As if anyone could compare to him. To what we could've had, and what was denied to us.

The thought sours my mood even further. First my lack of attention with the muroni, then that damned warlock, Daniel's jabs, and now this—a useless nostalgia? Ugh. *Get a grip, Elizabeta.*

My appetite gone, I keep walking to the grand castle, thinking not for the first time that Mirabela's gone and outdone herself this time. In the span of a few weeks, we went from a dilapidated castle to an old-school palace, ready for our royal asses to live in. The kicker? All the money we thought was gone, it turned out the vampiri clans were all too happy to contribute to our new residence. With some...persuasion. Not all of them liked it. But the alliance with the Munteanu clan more than helped us get there.

Of course, this means we're expecting more trouble any day now. But at least we'll fight in style.

Alex beats me to the new castle—he's always been competitive, so that's no surprise. I find him waiting by one of the benches on the massive new grounds.

"Took you long enough."

I roll my eyes. "Got sidetracked."

He arches an eyebrow.

"That witch's brother. Popped in my way, asking if we're doing anything to help her."

Alex scoffs. "She's not our priority."

"That's what I told him."

"I'm so tired of this fucking curse and how it's got everyone twisted. It's like we've forgotten how powerful we are, and that we can take over whatever and *whoever* we want."

"I know."

"Look at Nico and his blasted human. If he hadn't started this—"

"Violeta was already sick," I remind him. "I don't like it either, but I don't want her getting sicker."

His cool blue eyes rest on me. "What are you saying?"

"Nothing. Just pointing out that, like it or not, Nico, Violeta, and Vlad—their shit with their consorts—helps keep them, and us, alive. Much as we dislike that."

He mutters something under his breath. Out of my periphery, Daniel filters in and out, as though wanting my attention. I try to hide my surprise—didn't I warn him off with the two things he hates to see me do?

Alex chuckles. "Can you imagine if one of us will be next?"

That draws a full laugh out of me. "No consort for this bitch, thank you very much. Besides, I got a brand-new castle to explore."

He stands and walks on ahead. My eyes linger on the outside a bit, still in awe. The castle seems even more imposing against the dark woods and twilight sky. The dark stone walls, weathered by centuries of wind and rain, rise up like a warning to all. It has no turrets, unlike most other castles in the region, but instead the architect built in a mix of domes and minarets. High arches complete the set-up, decorated with fae-like patterns.

As my favorite time of day comes, the large windows glow with flickering candlelight. I remember how the first time Mira showed this to us at night, I thought, *This place beckons to lost souls.* And aren't we exactly that? Still, being here reminds me of better times...when we didn't have to fight tooth and nail for everything.

My feet take me inside, passing under more fae-like carvings and arched doorways. Soon, we'll have our crest etched within them to stake our claim to this place. I can't wait.

Mirabela did a good job, I'll give her that. Everything about this place screams *us—the heirs.* From the great hall I walk in, with vaulted ceilings and faded frescoes showcasing scenes from famous Romanian heroes like Ștefan the Great and Mircea the Brave, to the ancient tapestries with silver and gold threads. To the grand ballroom, with its crystal chandeliers—*plural.*

My gaze lingers on the heroes. Ștefan, much like Father, was renowned for his resistance to the Ottoman Turks. Eventually, they joined forces and Father helped him secure the throne of what was

Moldavia back then, in 1457. While Ştefan ruled at a time when this beautiful country was split into three principalities—Wallachia, Moldavia, and Transylvania—Mircea turned it all around. Under him, the principalities united into what would be known as Romania. And the neighboring powers of the Habsburg monarchy, the Ottoman Empire, and the Polish-Lithuanian Commonwealth would fail to acquire any parts of this rich and treasured land. Having their presence via these frescoes in our new household feels much like embracing our past. Believe me, the poetic symmetry has not gone unnoticed.

Da, one could say my sister has outdone herself. Not only does the entire castle speak of splendor and extravagance, but somehow, our new home has maintained a sense of mystery—a whisper of what it was used for. And, well, it does help that it comes with multiple rooms, kitchens—plural—and a library worthy of fairytales.

I shift my gaze from the frescoes to one of the glass-painted windows and the sprawling courtyard outside. Marble fountains with sparkling waters, a labyrinth of pathways, and overgrown ivy everywhere. It's...perfect. There's no other word for it. It also sends a signal to the vampiri that we're here, and we won't be ignored anymore.

I'd tell Mirabela as much and praise her for this find, if I could get her alone for a few minutes. She's been acting weird, disappearing when she thinks we're not paying attention. Oh well. At least I have Alex.

Speaking of, the devil waits for me at the bottom of our new double staircase.

"What do you think about Mirabela's idea for a ball?" I ask.

Alex shrugs. "Idiotic, if you ask me. Why bother schmoozing and manipulating the clans, all to endear ourselves to them? We could just slaughter them all. Assert ourselves as the heirs once and for all, with no contests to our power."

"Don't hold back, Alexandru. Tell me how you really feel." Mirabela pushes the big doors open, arching an eyebrow. Her dark hair is coiffed to near perfection, and she's wearing a sleeveless, V-necked black velvet dress that hits the floor. Between that and the smoky eye makeup, and red lips, she's ready for the runway.

I arch an eyebrow. "Nice getup."

"Da. Nico's meeting the Munteanu clan before the ball. Thought we'd look the part. Care to join?"

"I'll pass," I mutter. Then what she said registers. "Wait, the ball's *tonight*?"

Mirabela throws me an annoyed look. "Did you even *look* at the invitations?"

Behind me, Alex drawls, "I don't recall us having a chance to do so, only that your minions from the ex-Ardelean clan went and delivered them." But he might as well have not spoken, for all Mirabela takes notice of his words.

She shrugs. "Well, then, you can't complain, can you?" She looks me up and down. "How about you go get ready? The first guests are set to arrive in a few hours."

"You can't be serious, Mirabela!" Alex snaps behind me.

Biting back a growl, I leave them behind to argue about the ball and the pain in the ass it'll be.

"Are we not going to talk about it?"

I ignore Daniel, heading up the stairs and straight to my room, where I fall on the big divan, staring out the window. I have a perfect view of Zlatna. The city is far from our last failed attempt at a home, near what most humans know as Dracula's Castle—officially,

Bran Castle. The fools. As if Father ever would've chosen that weak and indefensible castle for his quarters.

No...this is more like it. The palatial mansion we're in is not exactly a castle—that's reserved for Peleș Castle, the old monarchical family residence of the human royals. But it *is* straight out of a book. And the view from my room? It gives onto Bucegi Natural Park. I've walked through many sanctuaries and natural parks in my lifetime, but nothing quite compares with this one's untamed beauty and wilderness.

From where I'm standing, I can see mountains shrouded in fog with snow-capped tips. Emerald forests and alpine meadows, ancient forests of pine and fir, Clear streams and a plethora of animals taking full advantage of them. But there's evil in those woods, too. Because much as every other natural landscape in every other place we've resided near, Bucegi also hides muroni. Luckily, as Alex and I have proven, they're easy enough to discard.

I shove the thought aside and turn my attention to my room instead. Gone are the worn carpet, fading wallpaper, and creaking windows and doors from the old place. Instead, velvet curtains in my favorite color—the deep burgundy of blood—cover more huge stained-glass windows. A massive four-poster bed, covered in blood-red silk, dominates the room. There are also two lamps, a vanity, and a velvet chaise lounge—all in similar shades of burgundy.

Under my feet is a thick, plushy carpet. I'm not sure if it came with the place or if Mira went around redecorating at some point, but my new favorite thing has become sinking my toes into it after a shit day of hunting. Wallpaper covers the walls, but unlike the battle scenes from downstairs, this one has an intricate pattern of roses and vines.

This is more like what we're used to. More up to our standards. Less hiding, more showcasing. More pushing back. If there's one thing vampiri understand, it's money and status. And if they don't... Well, perhaps Alex has the right view, after all.

"You can't keep ignoring me, Liza."

I growl, and face Daniel. His translucent form is hovering near the bed, staring at me with a faint glare. He can't get mad at me—never really does. But he gets close.

I keep my voice low, fully aware my siblings can hear everything going on. Just because we've all agreed to give each other privacy and block the whispers we hear, doesn't mean we don't accidentally tune in every now and then.

"Didn't I tell you I was going to feed? Or fuck? Time for you to make yourself scarce." I shoo him away.

"I don't see you doing either."

My growl grows more pronounced. "What do you want? What the hell are you on about now?"

"That warlock. Your connection with him."

"There's no damned connection."

"Isn't there? Why didn't you kill him, then?"

I give him a pointed look. "Didn't you tell me not to? 'Liza, don't,'" I mock. We both know it's a defense mechanism and a way to avoid talking about it.

Daniel narrows his eyes. "That's the first time you've ever listened to me, then. And I'm not buying it. He has to be the only human male who's crossed your path twice and hasn't gotten fucked or killed."

I scowl at him. "What's your point?"

"Maybe the curse is coming after you, this time."

A shudder runs through me, especially recalling the weakness I'd felt earlier. I stand, no longer in the mood to lounge. "The curse can suck it. I'm not giving in to anything."

My ears pick up something else. Not the dulcet tones of my siblings, but something raspier. A voice I'd heard in the woods not that long ago.

"What the fuck...?"

Ignoring Daniel, I push out the door and go to the first-floor library. I could've used my vampir speed, but Mira's warned us one too many times about the massive crystal chandelier—the largest among all of them—highlighting the wall-to-wall shelves and old editions of books. Apparently, we're not to fuck it up. And running at vampir speed through the house tends to rattle it.

So I walk, instead, barely holding on to my impatience, and round up the corner to enter the sizeable room. I find Nico facing a mountain of a man, rubbing his neck.

"Ştefan, I'm not sure where you got that impression, but I assure you we're doing everything we can to get Silviana some help."

Ştefan

I'm pretty good at figuring out if people are being real with me or not. I've had to learn, once I lost my sight, to rely on my other senses. This is why when I barge into the vampiri's newest home and question their leader, Nicolae, on why they haven't done anything to help my sister, and he assures me they have, I believe him.

First, because his tone is sincere. Second, because underneath that sincerity is also frustration, laced with impatience. Not at me, but at not having the answer to a nagging question. Which is something I can easily understand. And third, he could've responded by attacking me, yet he hasn't. That alone tells me more than I need to know.

So, I tone down my approach. "I realize I came barging in here—"

"How the hell did you even find this place?"

Her voice. So much entitlement, so much arrogance, in so few words. Clearly, Elizabeta Dracul is used to getting her way.

I turn in the vague direction of it. A faint aura of blood-red tinged with darkness—unsurprising, given the vampiric essence only came into this world as a result of Zalmoxis—amid the fog of my vision, tells me I'm on the right path.

"The same way everyone else will," I say, facing back in Nicolae's direction—his shifting feet indicate his location this time. "Invitations to your ball." Technically, I'd overheard their guards when I was following them, but the Draculs don't need to know exactly how close of an eye I've been keeping on them.

"Ball...? Dammit, Mirabela!" Nico's shout surprises me. From the very few interactions I've had with him, I'd expected a more laid-back attitude. This hands-on, *what are you doing contesting my authority* sentiment is new.

Then again, Silviana did say they infight a lot.

When his sister doesn't reply, Nicolae moves somewhere. Not quite out of the room, but out of the immediate vicinity. Judging by how everything echoes, I'm guessing I'm in some sort of sizeable room. There's a bit of containment of noise, though—shelves? In a library?

I'd been so enraged when I entered here—part of it pretend, part of it very real—that I didn't much pay attention to the layout, other than to get where the closest energy source was. Plus, the darkness that fills them is something that pulls me in like a spider's web. Not surprising, given Zalmoxis himself is the root cause of their own powers, having gifted their sire with his vampir lineage.

I tap my foot, listening to it echo. There. A few feet away, a barrier. Shelves, it has to be. I turn at a forty-five-degree angle and tap again. No barrier.

"What the hell are you doing?"

Heat creeps up my neck. Much like Nicolae's, Elizabeta's aura had also moved out of my field of vision, which made it easy to forget she was around. Unfortunately. Somehow, having her notice what I've been doing is way more intimate than I'm comfortable with. She already sees me as weak, and feeding into that is the last thing I want to do.

Still, manners. "Getting my bearings," I say, returning to my original position.

There's a pause, and Elizabeta shuffles. I'm better able to pinpoint her location. Not that it helps, with vampiri, given they can be in one spot one moment, and another the next.

As if to prove said point, there's a breeze. And then I catch the scent of ocean breeze mixed with something spicy and sea salt. My nostrils flare, taking it in. With each inhale, it feels like it's coating my throat, soothing it from an otherwise weird, dry ache I hadn't had a few moments before.

I clear my throat to mask my unsettlement. "You make a habit of interrupting conversations?"

Instead of answering, she shoots, "How did *you* come by an invitation to the ball? Mirabela only sent them yesterday." Ah. So she's in cahoots with her sister. Interesting.

"Someone must've not been that careful with theirs. It landed in my mentor's hands."

Her energy changes. That's another thing I've learned to pick up on. And right now, Elizabeta's anger whips the air. "And what, pray tell, did he ask you to do? More Dacian machinations?"

I take a wild guess and step closer. The scent becomes more potent. "What do you think?"

Someone clears their throat. Male.

"Sorry about that," Nicolae says. "Mirabela was meant to have waited. Clearly, she's got no qualms about filling this castle with vampiri."

"Not a problem."

The potent scent is gone, making me guess Elizabeta has stepped back. Is she still in the room? Or gone completely? I cast my senses to catch a whiff of her presence, but her aura is overshadowed by her brother's.

"As I was saying, I apologize I came barging in. I...find myself in a particular situation."

"Go on," Nicolae says. "If there's anyone who understands worry for a sibling, it'll be me. I have five of them, after all."

"Da. Well, you know I chose to stay behind in the Dacian community as an insider. Grand Master Liviu watches my every move. He doesn't fully believe I won't turn on them. But Silviana is everything to me, and I'll cross whatever lines need to be crossed to help her."

"Is that why you stayed, then?"

I nod. "Liviu has information. In his coffers, he possesses old scrolls, passed down through generations of Grand Masters. Some of them, like the one I passed to Vlad weeks ago, I've been able to use my magic to copy and read, but there are more." My fists clench of their own accord. I'll spare the vampiri the pains I've gone through to get this stuff. "I need more time. And in order to gain it, I offered to come spy on you for this ball."

"And Liviu agreed, just like that?" There's a hint of something like suspicion in Nicolae's tone, but it's faint.

"Yes. He asked me to infiltrate it and see what I can gather. He intends to break any alliances you make, and stir shit up." I pause. "This is but a theory, but I wouldn't put it past him to send in one or two assassins."

"I'm not surprised," Nicolae mutters. "Things just keep getting better."

"Well, this ball is our chance to showcase our power." The smooth voice isn't Elizabeta's, but another female's. Mirabela? A moment later, heels clack on the floor and someone approaches. Same blood-red aura tinged with darkness, but a different scent. "I'm Mirabela, the eldest sister. I've heard much about you." Intrigue coats her tone, laced with more suspicion.

"And how do you propose we showcase our power if you won't let me and Alex do what we do best?" Elizabeta whines from somewhere in my periphery.

I've never felt as restless as I do now—wishing that I was able to see everything, and catch all the facial expressions I'm missing that fill in the gaps of this conversation.

There's a long pause. I imagine they're exchanging eye-sparring.

Then, Mirabela says, "Ștefan, why don't you stay?"

"I'm sorry?"

"Stay. See your sister, and figure out for yourself that we're not keeping her prisoner."

Her taunting tone causes another flush to creep up my skin. Do these women see past everything? Or is it just her vampir hearing that filled her in on my purpose here?

"Besides," she continues, "the ball is tonight—"

I blanch. Liviu had said the next night...

"—*and* you might learn something good enough to take back to your...mentor," Mirabela goes on. "And by being at the ball, you would be an asset to us. Your sister is also meant to join us with Vlad."

An asset—she means because of our Dacian blood. Having two of us supporting the vampiri, at their beck and call, means the clans might reconsider an attack since Dacians are both known and feared in these parts. Vampiri aren't stupid, and they'll pick survival any day over facing the end of their immortality.

It's not a bad plan, using us. I know from Liviu that one of the reasons the other clans hate the Dracul heirs, aside from the obvious—that they're royalty and trying to assert their authority over them, after centuries of being in hiding—is that they no longer have magic or shifting abilities like their creator, Vlad Țepeș, did before them. So whatever ammunition the Draculs can use, will only be to their advantage.

I swallow, my throat thick. I want nothing more than to see Silviana. "Why... How would that not turn out wrong for me? If something happens, you'll accuse me of being involved. And what would I even tell Liviu when this gets back to him?"

"You can always tell your Dacians that you overstayed your welcome because we ensnared you. Forced you...but that you saw it as an opportunity for information gathering and chose to stay."

"Mira, are you insane?"

Elizabeta's insulted tone does it. I grin. "I would love to. But, I have nothing to wear for a ball."

"We'll find you something," Mirabela says.

"Doubt it," Elizabeta shoots from farther away. "A peasant will always be a peasant."

A breeze tells me she's gone, and the tug I feel in her presence disappears with her, as does the tension I'd been feeling. I force another chuckle to hide my discomfort. "Is she always like that, or am I just special?"

Chapter 3

Ștefan

No sooner do I say the words, that the sense of danger increases, pressing around me. Almost as if there's more of them. "You expecting Vlad early?" I ask, before I think better of it.

"Nu, why?" Mirabela's tone is full-on suspicious now.

Well. Might as well out with it. "Because another one of you just arrived here."

A breeze hits my face, presumably from her leaving in a rush to check. Meaning... I'm alone with Nicolae.

"Thank you, Nicolae," I say. "For agreeing to this plan."

He steps closer, and a moment later his hand grasps my forearm in solidarity. "No need to thank me. And call me Nico."

I nod and return the grasp. He's one of the few of them I'm comfortable with.

"Come, let me show you to a room. Hell knows we've got plenty of them."

Interesting. So their new castle is an upgrade. I'd surmised as much, but it does make me wonder how they pulled it off.

I follow Nico's footsteps, doing my best to orient myself. I sense him hesitating at first, then he seems to understand I'm not completely powerless and follows my lead. I allow my senses to guide me. I reach to my wrist, and the leather cuff holding a small athame blade. Clenching my fist makes the tiny blade slide out of the cuff, enough to puncture the base of my palm.

I use the blood as fuel for the darkness, pulling on it just a little. Not enough to be obvious—except to another Dacian—but enough to send it seeking on my behalf. Like a good pet, it feels out every nook and cranny for me, mapping out the surrounding area in my head. Ten paces to the right, there's a wall. Twelve to the left, another. Twenty up ahead, and more...nothing. Just empty space. So, we're heading into some kind of antechamber.

No sooner do we step through it, and I send the tendrils to map it out some more, that I hear more voices.

"I had to come and tell you in person," another female voice says. Her voice is deeper, yet fainter than Mirabela and Elizabeta's. It lacks their arrogance, sounding almost...human.

This must be the third sister, Violeta.

Confirming my suspicion, Nico says, "Violeta! What are you doing here?"

There's an odd pause as she—presumably—takes me in. "Is

this Ștefan, Silviana's brother?"

"I am."

"Then you'll need to hear this." More footsteps follow as she approaches. "Marcus and I have been helping Nico and Tassa to hunt for potential solutions to the curse. And, lately, with Silviana's little problem."

Little problem is an interesting euphemism for the god my sister's got stuck in her head.

"And what did you find?"

"There's rumors of a witch, in the woods. An Oracle of sorts. She's supposed to have answers to things that elude anyone, even other supernaturals."

My heart starts hammering in my chest. I try to quiet my excitement, knowing it's probably not a good idea to remind them how human I am—especially as I'm bleeding—just in case they decide to whet their appetite.

"And you think this...Oracle...can help Silviana?" Could it be the same one I've been hunting? Who has the artifact I've been seeking?

"Da," Violeta says, and there's a hint of a smile in her answer. "We've heard she lives in the Hoia Baciu Forest, but the kids who told us about it warned that only those who seek answers should go."

"I will. Gladly."

"*After* the ball," Mirabela says. "You want to see your sister, no?"

Impatience rankles at me—I want to fix Silviana *now*—but I know she's right.

"Thank you," I say in Violeta's direction. "This...is more than I'd expected."

"We're not all bad," she whispers.

"Speak for yourself." Ah. This must be the infamous Alex. Silviana's told me all about his threatening antics. I was wondering where he was hiding.

"Not now, Alex," Nico mutters. He touches my elbow, subtly turning me toward the stairs. "Let me show you your room."

Behind me, I can hear mutters, but they're too low, pitched only for vampir ears. I've no doubt Alex is expressing his dislike of me to his siblings, though.

Nico leads me to a room upstairs. Similar to before, I leverage my senses and darkness to orient myself. I also walk close to the wall, using it to keep my balance, which prevents me from some particularly nasty falls.

We emerge onto another landing, and my feet sink—a plush carpet? A few moments later, a door squeaks to the side, and I turn to it.

"It's one of the guest chambers," Nico says, "but it'll be free even if some of the...guests...decide to stick around. The last thing I'd want is you to be bothered by them."

I smirk. "You mean, serve as a snack for them?"

He chuckles. "Right." There's another beat of awkward silence. "I'm not sure if I should point out where everything is...?"

"I'll be fine. Do you mind sending Silviana up here?"

"Of course. I'll let you get settled."

Yet he still doesn't leave. His aura, if anything, seems to intensify. "Something on your mind?"

He lets out a breath, probably more for my benefit than because he needs to, and says, "It may serve more than one purpose, you attending this ball."

"Oh?"

"All types of vampiri will come, from each of the clans. Old ones. Maybe we'll get lucky and they might know something to help out your sister."

I snort. "Don't tell me you plan to explain her whole issue with a god most of them probably don't know anything about, no matter how old they are."

"No, of course not! I just... We'll poke around, see what we can find, if anything." His footsteps move a bit farther from me and pause once more. "Don't worry about what to wear for the, uh, party. Mirabela already sent one of our guards into town."

Guards. He must mean what's left of the Ardelean clan. The Draculs wiping out that particular clan created quite a noise, even in my part of the world. Rumor has it that what's left of the clan came to the Draculs, tail between their legs, and begged for jobs as soon as they were settled. Or, well, that's what Liviu's spies would have us believe.

Then another thing registers. "Town?"

"Da, we're closer to Zlatna now, in the Alba County. I guess the vampiri thought it was protected enough from tourists, but still has a strong historical foothold. Plus, this place Mirabela got—it's off the beaten path, so to speak, but Vlad says it must've been owned by some pretty powerful people because it's so well-maintained and, well, opulent."

"Hmm." Darkness doesn't give me directions, at least not measured in kilometers and time. So I'd thought we were just in the middle of the woods, but I stand corrected—we're about an hour or two from Sibiu, where our main Dacian compound is. Which means close enough for Liviu's people to get here, should he decide to send them…not good.

A few beats later, Nico leaves. And I'm left alone with my thoughts.

I make my way slowly across the room, hands splayed out in front of me. A trickle of blood runs down my palm, coating the rug—fur?—under my feet. I take my shoes off to feel better. Ah, yes, rug. Persian, by the feel of it. Interesting that they're no longer shying away from their opulence.

Then again, I would imagine with a ball coming, they need to get everything set up at its best. After all, money is power. And power is money. And if the House of Dracul is to show the other vampiri clans they're back...they can't just talk the talk. They need to walk the walk, too.

Two hours pass. I only know the passing of time because I set my watch to buzz every thirty minutes. A few times, I hear raised voices below, before they drop down to murmurs. I conclude Silviana was right, and the siblings are dysfunctional as hell. But in their own way, there's a camaraderie that binds them. Even Alex. I'd half expected him to come and try to rip my throat out for daring to enter his new house. But, surprisingly, he doesn't show up.

By the fourth watch buzz, I'm pretty familiar with the room, the polished wood and aged leather scent permeating it, the corridor outside, and the en suite bathroom. A knock sounds on the door, and I tentatively call out, "Come in." If it's Alex coming to slit my throat, I don't suppose he'd be knocking first.

The door opens, followed by a delighted squeal. I turn, just in time for my sister to launch herself into my arms. The force of her tackle sends me back a few steps—no time to prepare my balance for it—but I happily wrap my arms around her slight frame. Her hair tickles my nose, her familiar scent engulfing me.

A frown creases my brow when the flesh beneath my hands registers—it feels so much frailer than before. I let her have her hug, then slowly push her away. Cup her cheeks, resting my forehead against hers. "Sorella, how are you?"

"I'm fine." The tremble in her voice says otherwise.

Sure enough, tears seep past her lashes the moment after, bathing my fingers. I pull her back in my arms, holding her tight.

Long moments later, we sit on one of the divans by the window.

"They've really spoiled you," Silviana says.

I laugh. "Is the room that amazing?"

"Uh, yeah!" She goes on to describe it at length, giving me every possible detail. Like the massive four-posted bed with a dark oak frame. Dark brown drapes, framing the bed like "curtains fit for a prince," in her words. The fancy floor, looking like it has vines captured within it. The multiple orange and red shades of the fireplace, which I can hear crackling with burning logs. The dark leather armchair, tucked in a corner, overlooking the grounds. On and on, it goes.

When she gets to describing the tapestries on the walls, telling me how the overall vibe fits my "masculine and rugged personality," I lose my patience. I tug her hand and place it on my chest. Her pulse will be a telltale sign if she lies. "I don't care about the room, Lana. Tell me what's wrong."

"Nothing. I... Vlad is amazing. I just miss you. Miss being around people. But it's hard if I am, so I understand why I have to stay away."

The frown grows more pronounced. "How?"

"When there's people around, sometimes, *he* comes to the surface. Tries to take control of my magic. It…It's hard, pushing him back. He tries to do it here, too, but Vlad helps a lot. And that zmeu, Tytus, he came by again, reinforcing the shield in my head. Says he needs to do it at least once a week going forward."

I frown. "I don't like this. The more he pokes around in your mind—"

"He's careful."

"But still."

"I know."

I take a deep breath. "Nico says they've been looking for another way to get Zalmoxis out of your head. They haven't stopped."

"I figured as much. Vlad's kept me up to date, and they've done so much more than I'd hoped."

I don't tell her about the Oracle just yet. Not until I can get some more specifics out of Violeta or Nico. Instead, I add, "I've also found another hidden alcove with scrolls in Liviu's chambers, but the bastard hasn't been gone long enough for me to copy them into braille. There's hidden knowledge there, I know there is. I just need to break in again and see what else I can find."

"Don't risk it, please, Fane!"

"For you, I'll risk anything."

"How quaint."

I jerk upright at the voice. Elizabeta. The movement changes the air, and her scent assails me once more. And that damned reaction—as if on cue, my body tightens, and my mind blanks. I hold my breath in a vain effort to stop it, but only manage to make myself dizzy. Fuck.

Silviana shifts by my side, wariness filling her tone. "What do you want?"

There's a rustle of something, and then Elizabeta's voice sounds farther away. "From Mirabela."

Silviana inches away from me. I hear a door closing, then more of that rustling. Eventually, she says, "It's a suit. And...some casual clothes. Why are the vampiri gifting you stuff?"

I sigh. "Because I said I'd spend the night, and attend the ball tonight. I nearly begged Liviu to let me come here under the pretext I'd spy, and return home with 'information.'"

"Isn't that dangerous?"

"Poate—more than likely, in all honesty. But I needed to know what's going on, and what they're doing to help you. And besides, Nico says there's plenty of old vampiri at this ball. One of them might let some things slip, too."

"Such as?"

"Connections. Maybe someone else knows about Zalmoxis, someone we don't know."

"Hmm."

"I know, sorella, it sounds farfetched. But we might as well let them help—those who wish to, anyway. You intertwined our fates with these vampiri the moment you fell in love with one, and I refuse to let our differences get between us. I swear it. We'll find a cure for you—a way to get Zalmoxis out of your head, once and for all."

I can only hope I'm not wrong. Because I've never lied to my sister, and I don't intend to start now.

Elizabeta

Fucking fantastic. On top of Tassa, Silviana and her damned brother have also joined the ever-growing roster of humans in our fancy new castle.

"What's gotten up your butt?"

I whirl on Mirabela. "You know what. Why do we have so many humans around?"

She rolls her eyes. "You need to behave. Now's not the time to throw a tantrum, when we're going to have a castle filled with vampiri in a few hours."

"And you think it'll look good for us to show them we mingle with humans? We'll be seen as weak!"

Lighting flashes in her eyes. "Don't test me, sister dear. Nico and I are on the same page with this."

"Not that long ago, you used to not be. What changed?"

"Our survival did. I'll do anything to ensure that."

"Clearly." I turn, but she grips my arm. I grit my teeth, whirling on her and getting my face as close to hers as I dare. "Mira, watch yourself."

"No. *You* will." She searches my face, then grins. Coldly. "Matter of fact, why don't you accompany Ştefan to the ball?"

"Fuck you. I'm not taking him anywhere. I'd rather be dead rather than seen with him."

The grip on my arm tightens. "Don't play, Liza. There's a time for that, and there's a time for us to come together. This is it." She moves closer, her blue eyes sparkling red. She's been gone for so long, I've forgotten how dangerous it is to make her angry.

As if to remind me, the paintings on the walls shake. A vase nearby nearly topples over, but she catches it with her free hand.

"I'm not going to repeat myself."

"What's the point? Why would my accompanying Ștefan make any difference?"

She pauses, her lips pursing. "Some rumors might have spread about the curse. We can get ahead of them, rather than let them rule this ball. And show that for any concerned, the curse only makes us stronger. *Not weaker.*"

"Stronger?" I frown.

Behind her, Daniel flickers into appearance. "She's saying that showing up with Ștefan will appear as though he's on your side. With you."

My eyes widen, the full extent of what my sister's saying dawning on me. She wants me to pretend to the vampiri that not only is Vlad mated with some fucking human, but I am, too? Ah, *fuck no.*

I meet Mira's gaze, knowing my own has joined hers in flashing red. "I am *not* playing some pretend relationship game with that Dacian!"

She scoffs. "We all have to make sacrifices. This is yours." Her eyes narrow. "Father would be disappointed if he saw what you became."

I try to maintain my bravado, but it's no use. The words sting. She's always known which buttons to push.

I yank myself out of her grip and run off, storming into my room moments later in full vampir speed—fuck her chandelier. "How dare she? Like I'm a child, incapable of making my own choices!"

I pace, back and forth, back and forth. But Daniel's there, watching me.

"Don't you even say it."

He laughs, getting on my nerves even more. "Why not? I think it's a grand idea that you go to the ball."

Sure. With a human on my arm—or rather me on *his* arm—smiling as if I'm enjoying myself, as if all is fine in the House of Dracul, and we're not dropping like flies. Acting as if I don't have my own personal ghost—my *stafie*, tied to me more in death than he ever has been of his living—haunting me.

I don't know what's worse. Having to feign I'm on good terms with Silviana and her Dacian brother, or having Daniel in the background witnessing everything, protecting me as he's wont to do. Or perhaps it's the sole idea of *mingling* with the lesser vampiri.

A shudder runs up my back. These peasants don't seem to realize I'm royalty—well, I'll show them in a way they can't deny.

"Why? Why would I bother attending?" I bite back at Daniel. "So you can laugh at me?" My rage, as always, morphs into something else. Something that makes my heart ache. "Or so I can suffer, always at a distance? Never able to touch you, to be with you."

The mirth disappears from his expression. His eyes lose all sparkle and darken with the same haunting longing that's filling me. And it kills me, knowing I'm the cause of that.

I take a step closer, reaching out for him, then dropping my hand by my side once more when I realize how futile it all is. "Sorry."

He shakes his head at my whispered mutter. "You know as well as I do that what we had is long gone."

"What we had never had a chance to become more."

His expression softens further. "You'll have to let me go eventually, Liza."

"No." I clench my fists. "I won't. I need you."

He floats closer to me. "I can't be what you need me to be. You know that."

"I. Don't. *Care*!"

The door opens behind me, and Alex enters. "I thought I heard you—"

I whirl toward him, turning my back to Daniel. "Nothing. Let's get out of here."

I push past him and he follows, albeit bemused. At least another hunt will ease my mind. And maybe the tightness in my chest.

Daniel's wrong. I do need him. But for now, what I need more is him out of my head—and a hunt will do that. The only time he stays away from me is when I fuck, feed, or hunt, unless I'm in danger. So if the only way I can get some peace around here is by diving deeper into the monster I am, then that's a price I'm more than willing to pay.

Anything to avoid the pain, the longing...the impossibility of what we'll never have.

Chapter 4

Ştefan

"Well? How do I look?"

Silviana's quiet for a moment. Then she says, "Hot. You're my brother, but you look...hot."

I laugh. "That good, huh?"

She flicks me on the shoulder. "Yeah, *that* good. They got you a simple black suit with a white shirt, but you fill it *real* well, Fane."

The door creaks open, and I turn in its direction. "Who's there?"

"It's me, Vlad."

I sober immediately at my sister's consort apparition. I know

he means well, taking care of her, but this was my time with her. And I can't help resenting the intrusion.

As though aware of it, he says, "I didn't mean to interrupt, but we should head down. Together. Nico suggested we could both escort you." His voice lowers, though not by much. "And you look downright stunning, iubito."

I turn my back on them, giving them privacy. Even if I can't actually see them, there's something intimate in his tone that makes the compliment sound like it's meant only for her ears, and hers alone.

After a moment of whatever passes between them, Silviana clears her throat and touches my shoulder. "You ready?"

I nod, and she hooks her arm through my right one. The other, presumably, gets hooked with Vlad's. We walk in silence, me mentally counting the number of steps until I know we've gotten to the top of the stairs. I'd have expected noise from downstairs, but it's muted.

Silviana leans toward me. "They all have sensitive hearing, and the music's not as loud as we'd expect. But there's a lot of them... Holy *shit,* there's a lot of vampiri down there, Fane."

Her tone wavers and I place my left hand above hers, squeezing in muted understanding.

For the biggest part of our lives, we thought vampiri were the enemy. That they had attacked our parents, and made us orphans. It was only a few weeks ago that we learned we'd been lied to. Not only was our father, Davide, killed by the Dacian community we've been a part of all our lives, but Grand Master Liviu himself altered our memories. He made us forget our parents, and that Dacians don't just live a normal, mortal life, but can live for over a hundred years—so long as they capture the essence of a vampir. Without it, Dacians lose their magic, until it fades into nothingness. A little goodbye present from the Dacian god, Master of Death himself, Zalmoxis. Turns out the Draculs aren't the only ones cursed, in a sense.

Finding all that out—making peace with the fact we were born somewhere in the 1890s, and so are roughly one hundred and twenty-three years old—was crazy enough. Having my sister threatened by a god...that crossed the line straight into insanity. To say we're both confused and conflicted is an understatement.

Silviana's arm trembles slightly in mine. I wonder if Vlad picks up on it.

A moment later, Vlad says, "You don't have to do this," confirming that he has.

"I do, though."

That's my sister, always stubborn and refusing to show weakness. Even among Dacians, who practically expected all women to hold the traditional role, she never submitted.

"If it makes either of you feel better," Vlad adds, "it's not just vampiri down there. The wolves are here, too."

"Dominic's wolves?" Silviana asks.

"The one and only. Nico talked to him and asked them to come keep an eye on things."

"And show the wolves' alliance with the House of Dracul, I presume?" Silviana's tone is rueful. "Much like we're being flaunted around."

Vlad's tone lowers. "I hate this. Just say the word, and I'll take you back upstairs, far from everything."

She's quiet for a long moment, then takes in a deep breath. "No. No, I'm fine. I'll *be* fine."

Still, her grip is iron-tight on my arm as we descend the stairs. In contrast, her tone is even—almost too even—when she says, "I forgot to mention something."

"Mm?"

"The others, um, they thought it'd be a good idea for you to be paired with one of them."

I stumble on my next step, but Silviana's grip keeps me from outright falling and face-planting among who knows how many vampiri.

"Who?" I ask when I've regained my balance. "Didn't Vlad say we're both to escort you?"

"Yeah, but he probably got briefed by the wrong sibling." There's an undercurrent of wariness and tiredness to her tone. "And…Elizabeta."

Fantastic. The crazy sibling, and the one who hates my guts and thinks I'm a complete peasant. This should be fun.

"Is there a reason for it?" Vlad asks. "She's not the most…subtle."

I feel slightly better at the annoyance fueling his tone. At least he's also unhappy at being kept out of the loop.

"You can say that again," I mutter.

Silviana sighs. "All I know is Mirabela asked her, and she said yes. And I'm to ask you."

"Doesn't sound like I have much of a choice."

"I'm sorry, fratello."

I turn my head to the side, catching her forehead in a tender kiss. "It's a small price to pay."

Vlad clears his throat. "We're reaching the downstairs, so might want to be careful. Look less…cozy. In case Liviu has more than one spy here."

I nod and school my expression, facing forward.

We get to the bottom of the stairs. Thankfully, vampiri don't feel the need to be as boisterous as us humans, so the voices are just as muted as the music. But I pick up many. With various inflections, indicating age, and accents that hint at the region they're coming from.

"The Draculs attracted a lot of attention already," I whisper to Silviana.

"Da, we have."

Elizabeta.

I turn my head in her direction. The swirl of darkness and blood-red aura to my left confirms it's the feisty and arrogant heir. And she doesn't sound amused—at all.

"I'm told you're to escort me. So, escort me."

I bite back a smirk. There'll be plenty of time to needle her later. Instead, I kiss my sister's cheek and turn to Elizabeta, holding out my hand.

"So. Am I still a peasant?"

I can practically feel her eyes perusing me, and my skin reacts, heating to her gaze. I hate that it does, but then again, my body has a mind of its own.

"Yes," she mutters. "But you'll do."

Elizabeta

"You have to admit, he cleans up nice."

I ignore Daniel. I don't have to admit to anything. Most especially not that Ștefan looks utterly fuckable in his suit. The black jacket stretches over his shoulders, showcasing his broad back, yet also somehow enhancing his trim waist. The pants are cut just right—and the fucker has too good an ass.

But that means nothing. I'd jump anyone who looks that good. Which is why I'm not about to give in to Daniel's smug grin and admit anything.

Still, I feel Daniel's attention on me as I take Ștefan's offered elbow. I grit my teeth when my hand touches him, and jolt in surprise when the movement brings me in closer contact. He oozes heat and some musky cologne, though I don't recall bringing any to his room. The scent of him is mouth-watering, though, and in spite of myself, I lick my lips and flare my nostrils.

Enough! I catch myself and give myself a mental shake. *He's a* human, *Elizabeta. And brother to that witch. Get through this damned evening, then you'll never have to see him again. There are plenty of others you can find to fuck.*

Da, occasionally I speak to myself in the third person. It's warranted when my own mind feels like it's trying to betray me, and it works in most instances—like now. The mental chastising has its expected result. Back in control, I focus my attention on the crowd.

Vampiri have come from all over the country, here at our beck and call. And dressed to the nines. Everywhere my eyes land, I see women and men in evening gowns—all silk, velvet, or whatever fancy fabrics they got their hands on—and tuxes. Cool, assessing eyes meet mine at every turn. My scar must be legendary though, because they quickly avert their gaze. I can't help but feel a sense of satisfaction at that.

Ștefan clears his throat. "Did all the clans show?"

His question, delivered in a regular tone—*loud* for us—pulls more than a few eyes in our direction. Fuck. Damn human can't keep his mouth shut, and it's not like a Dracul answering questions is a good look for us. Especially to a human.

Unless they realize quickly he's not a regular human.

I plaster a smile on my face and ask out of the corner of my mouth, "Can you do some magic voodoo so they don't think you're just eye candy?"

"It doesn't work that way."

I turn slightly to him, digging my nails into the tight muscles of his biceps. "I don't care what it works like," I hiss, "just fucking do it. Me, next to you, is meant to show strength, not weakness."

He clenches his jaw, and my eyes are drawn to it. Somehow, it looks even sharper than before. "I'm not a puppet."

I can't believe I have to actually *convince him* this is in his best interests. I whirl on him fully, keeping my tone still low. I lean in closer, my lips nearly brushing his cheek. And inadvertently inhale a full gust of his cologne. I was right, before—musk, but also something woodsy and appealing.

I purse my lips, shoving the thought away. *Nothing about him is appealing*. Out loud, I say, "I thought you wanted to avoid getting in trouble with your precious master? If you play nice with me, it'll show him—and any other spies or assassins he sent here—that you did well infiltrating us. That we trust you."

He sighs, but then a moment later I smell the tinge of copper in the air. Which has even more eyes turning toward us. And finally, magic. Power. Its sulfur scent fills the air around me, surrounding me like a blanket.

I plaster a wide smile on my face and meet a few more eyes as we walk the perimeter of the room.

Murmurs and a buzz of an undercurrent tell me something else is happening. I glance toward the stairs, and my jaw drops. Nico's descending, Tassa by his right side, and Mirabela on the left. I have to admit, the human looks...decent. Regal, almost. She's wearing a dark green wraparound gown that showcases curves I'd never have expected under all those baggy clothes she loves. With her dark hair and fair complexion, she makes a striking couple with my brother.

I glance at Ştefan, curious to see if he finds her attractive—then remember he can't see her. "Nico and his human just came down the stairs," I mutter. Why I feel the need to keep him in the loop, I don't know.

I cast around for Daniel, wondering if he caught this, but he's gone. If I'd had a heart, it would've pounded at the realization. As it is, dread fills me instead. Where the hell did he disappear?

Nico stops just before he hits the bottom of the stairs. With a nod to Mirabela, he steps off with Tassa. Probably trying to keep her out of the center of attention in a room full of vampiri. Not that I blame him. If it had been up to him, she wouldn't be here. But since he's trying to make it clear that she's off-limits, he had no choice but to bring her along.

Mirabela, in a floor-length, V-necked, and sleeveless burgundy dress, faces the crowd. Her blue eyes sparkle like sapphires under the light, and the tilt of her chin is all royalty. "Welcome, all, to the inauguration ball for the return of the House of Dracul." The last of the murmurs dies down when her clear voice rings out, loud and firm. "It may have seemed like we were long and gone, but I assure you, we never stopped watching and caring for the clans. Each and every one of you."

Someone near me whispers, "Da, like they did with the Ardelean clan."

I wait until I catch the woman's eye and smile sweetly. "Would you prefer your clan suffers a similar fate?"

She blanches and backs away so fast that she stumbles into the next vampir.

I fix my attention back to Mira, but another voice pulls it away.

"I guess what they say about you really is true," Ștefan murmurs.

I angle my head toward him and tilt my chin up. Even with my heels, the top of my head barely reaches his jaw. "And what is it they say?"

"That you're ruthless"—I smile, about to agree—"and you never think things through."

The smile dies, replaced instead by a snarl. "Excuse me?"

"You heard me."

His gaze remains glued in the direction of Mirabela's voice, making me want to slap the smirk off his face even more.

"Elizabeta."

I whirl around to Alex. "Da?"

"I didn't realize you're fraternizing with the help."

The judgment in his eyes roots me to the spot, so much so I pull my hand out from underneath Ștefan's arm. Guess no one bothered to tell my brother about Mirabela's wondrous idea, and now he's looking at me like I'm the goddamned enemy.

"Mirabela's idea, not mine, I assure you."

He arches an eyebrow. Then snorts. "She's not even subtle. What, she told you that by being around him, you'd be showing some kind of strength to the masses?"

I shift on my heels, tucking a loose auburn curl behind my ear. "Yeah, why?"

He rolls his eyes. I've seen this look on him so many times, but it's never made me feel as dim-witted as it does now. "Think, Liza. A human—a *blind one* at that—isn't going to make much difference to our reputation."

"Da, but—"

"It's just a ploy so our siblings' little human pets don't feel threatened in a room full of vampiri." He bares his teeth in Ştefan's direction, but the latter doesn't react. It'd be impossible not to feel the rage emanating from Alex, though, sight or no sight.

I step closer to him, my hand on his arm. "Ploy or no ploy, we're meant to be united this night."

"What, like with *them*?"

I follow the direction of his glare, only for my eyes to land on two of the wolves. I heard whispers from Nico and Mira that they'd been invited to boost our illusion of strength, but they've been doing well keeping to the corners, much like our guards. Dominic and his son, though, stand out dressed in matching suits.

Dominic's is navy blue and fits his form like it was poured over him. His sharp blue eyes scan the room non-stop, even as his lips move—he's talking to his son. Out of curiosity, I break the barrier I usually erect around everything I hear and tune in to their conversation.

"—I just don't understand why you wouldn't let Mom come," the son is saying. His features are very much like Dominic's, but his hair is a darker blond hue. "Now she's going to be in a huff when we go back and *you know* how that goes."

Dominic rolls his eyes. "Luca, what's between me and your mom is between me and your mom. And I'm not about to explain why she's not here when we're surrounded by vampiri who can hear *every single word*."

Luca has the grace to appear contrite, and rubs the back of his neck, falling quiet. A few seconds later, Dominic does the exact same gesture, not even realizing it as his eyes keep scanning the crowd. His gaze falls on us, and his expression shutters.

I turn my body fully toward Alex, tugging on his arm. "Enough, Alex," I whisper. "Not now, and not here." If I don't rein my brother in, he won't be above starting a fight with the wolf. He's been against our alliance with them ever since it was struck.

Alex's angry expression falls on me, then relents. "You're right." A quick rake up and down my attire brings a smirk to his lips. "Planning to break many hearts?"

Better than most of my siblings, Alex knows that I work through my issues with sex and feeding—sometimes at the same time, sometimes not. Which is why his gaze holds no hint of surprise at what I'm wearing.

I chose a burgundy dress that clings to my every curve like a second skin. The fabric—a high-quality silk by some famous human designer—shimmers under the glow of the chandeliers. Coupled with the plunging neckline and the slit up my thigh, one could say my porcelain skin is very much on display. The dress also dips at my back, extremely low, leaving my skin bare. With every step I take, I feel the fabric ripple and flow with my movements, like liquid fire cascading over my body.

I was fully aware when I put it on of the effect it would have—that it'd send the message not of a princess, but of a seductress of the night, a black widow, someone not to be trifled with. Let's hope these fuckers get the hint.

"Perhaps a few," I say to Alex. "It feels like a while since I've had a proper...feed."

"Wouldn't want that, would we?" he teases, tucking an auburn curl behind my ear.

The gesture bares my scar—as much a fuck-you to our audience, as a reminder to me to hold my head high. Alex always knows what I need, and I sense some of the tension and anger at this entire façade seep out of me.

We're so into our bantering that I don't notice Ştefan leaving until Alex says, "Finally got rid of him."

Shit. There goes my promise to my sister. A niggling sense of unease crawls up my spine, knowing Ştefan heard everything Alex said.

And, as if on cue, I sense another pair of eyes on me. "I don't like who you are with him," Daniel says, back and more visible than ever. "Alexandru, I mean. He didn't use to be like this."

I want to tell him none of us used to be like anything, that we're all paying the price for so many centuries of living. Things he knows, better than I do. After all, he saw us in our original states.

But, it's not like I'm free to do as I wish. Not among so many vampiri. An unhinged Dracul heir is the worst thing I could project to be right now.

"Elizabeta, go *find him,*" Daniel insists. "This is a room full of vampiri and he's too freaking appetizing to them."

"Liza?"

I tear my gaze from Daniel's glare, to meet Alex's. "Mm?"

"You seemed pensive," Alex says.

"Not at all. Let's show these vampiri how the Draculs run a ball, hmm?"

A glint of mischief shines in Alex's gaze, and his previous smirk turns into a full-out grin he reserves only for me.

Ştefan

Listening to the Dracul siblings belittling me is not my idea of having fun this evening. So I walk away, secure in my powers and manhood as I cross through the throng of vampiri, head held high.

I push the athame deeper into my palm, forcing a bit more blood. Darkness leads me through the fog of my gaze. On the periphery, I see blood-red auras—much fainter ones than the Draculs'. Once or twice, I sense them leaning in closer, as though to get a whiff of me. But my power seems to keep them at bay.

And something else draws me, besides. I reach the stairs, and move up...slowly, holding onto the banister. Then, quicker. When I'm on the first landing, I pause. *What brought me up here?*

A noise to the side. A *twang* and a *click*. I head in the direction it's coming from. Stop. There—a flash of a different-colored aura. Gone, in the blink of an eye. I tilt my head to the side and turn around in a circle. Nothing. But I know I heard *something*.

"What are you doing up here?"

I face in the direction of my sister's voice, another question on my lips. "Why aren't you by Vlad's side?"

"She is," he says from somewhere nearby. "We saw you come up, and didn't want a vampir to get too...comfortable."

I snort. "They won't, believe me."

There's a muttered curse, then Vlad says, "Dammit, Liza." His footsteps move around me, in the direction of the banister I'd touched.

Silviana inches closer to me. "Her and Alex are putting on a show. Tangoing, of all things."

I snort. "Yeah, they seem mighty close, those two."

Something in my tone gives me away, and my sister picks up on it immediately. "What did she do?"

I hesitate to speak my mind around Vlad, but he surprises me by getting ahead of it.

"Let me guess," he says. "The usual Liza cold, heartless shit."

I shrug. "It doesn't bother me. Pitting her with me was probably not Mirabela's brightest idea, I'm guessing. Besides, something pulled my attention here."

Liar, a voice nags at the bag of my head. *It does bother you. It confirms you're no use to anyone, least of all to someone of her rank. You're useless, pure and simple.*

I'm well familiar with these doubts, so instead of fighting them, I flat-out contest them with the truest possible rebuttal I can muster: *Why in all hells would I want to be of use to someone like her? Her loss, not mine.*

"What was it?" Silviana asks about my previous statement. "What pulled your attention?"

I think back to the sound, to the flash of an aura—which I can't admit to. Not even Silviana knows how much I've enhanced my senses and magic, and I definitely don't want the vampiri to be aware of it. "Not sure. Nothing good, though."

"You don't think it was one of those assassins you warned my brother about?"

"If I had more information, I would give it to you."

"I know. Sorry. Didn't mean to come across that way." Vlad's steps come closer. "Why don't we go back down? Safety in numbers and all."

Not so much when the majority of those numbers are soulless, bloodsucking vampiri.

We hit the bottom of the stairs right as the last notes of a song finish. I feel the tug of Elizabeta's aura in my orbit, like a star pulling me within its orbit. It's disconcerting, to say the least. Is it because she's a vampir, a royal, and therefore unattainable? Or because she's female? Is someone else in this crowd wielding magic of a sort, trying to play a trick on us? None of my thoughts make any sense, let alone the fact I want to go anywhere near her after the conversation she was having with Alex.

"She's up ahead," a voice says.

I can't place it—but the owner is male. "Who said that?"

"Who said what?" Silviana asks next to me.

"The—someone spoke. No?" I'm reluctant to say what exactly they said, because that'd mean revealing a certain vampir was in my thoughts. And I'd rather not.

"No..." Concern coats Silviana's tone now.

I shake my head. "Never mind."

But a moment later, it comes again. "Ten steps ahead, two to the right."

I jerk again. Silviana squeezes my bicep. "You okay?"

"Fine." Who the hell is fucking with me?

"I'm not playing games," the same voice says. "Just trying to help you out."

"I don't need help."

Silviana lets go of me. "Sorry, I—"

"No, not you." I sigh and move away. "Give me a second." Despite my wariness, I step as I was directed. Ten steps ahead, two to the right.

Again, why the fuck do I want to be anywhere near her? *Maybe because she only responds to authority and I haven't spent the last years building myself up in the Dacian community so a vampir can stomp all over my ego.*

Yeah. That's right. Ego. Fantastic reasoning.

Ten steps ahead, two to the right, and...someone hurtles into me. A hint of ocean breeze mixed with something spicy and sea salt assaults my nostrils.

Before I can stop myself, I hold out my hand. My tone is stronger, more assertive than before. "I think you owe me a dance."

I can feel Elizabeta's astonishment permeating the air. "*Dance*? But you—"

Without giving her a chance to reply, knowing full well she's going to make a snarky remark about my blindness again, I grab her arm and tug her into the middle of the dance floor. Throughout it all, the male voice leads me, as does the darkness I lean on.

It's easy to make out the circle of onlookers—their aura is practically a ring around us. As for my half-assed plan? Well. I'll either succeed and gain Elizabeta's grudging respect or I'll fail and walk away in sheer embarrassment. Can't go halfway.

It shouldn't matter, gaining her respect. But it does. Because if she sees Silviana's brother is strong, capable, fearsome...maybe, just maybe, she'll stop rubbing my sister the wrong way. She and Alex, both. I'm tired of them thinking we don't belong here for whatever prejudiced notion they've got about humans.

"Here," the male voice says, and I listen.

I stop, turn to Elizabeta, and place my hand on her waist. The fabric of her gown is silky under my fingertips, like water. Coupled with her scent as I step closer to her, it's enough to make me dizzy once more.

Elizabeta has the opposite reaction. She stiffens, and when my hand moves from her waist to her lower back, touching bare skin, her spine goes full rigid.

"If you don't watch that hand, I'm going to make sure you're without it in a few seconds."

I drop my head to her ear...and drop it some more...until her hair tickles my nose. *Wow, she's tinier than her voice made her in my mind.* "You wouldn't want to show these vampiri that we're not as allied as they think, right?"

"Fuck off," she hisses. But she doesn't shove me away.

The beginning notes of a waltz start, and a moment of panic flutters through me. I haven't waltzed since I used to with my mother, and Silviana as she grew up.

But then, his voice—the unknown presence—is there. "I'll help."

And he does. Weirdly. I keep expecting the other shoe to drop, but it doesn't. Instead, we complete a perfectly good waltz—at least judging from the mutters I'm picking up on.

It should be hard, and require complete focus. Weirdly... it's not. Muscle memory plays a huge role—I would've messed up more than half the steps otherwise. But it makes it easy to lead Elizabeta. The voice—whoever he is—gives me a heads up when I'm stepping close to the "line" of vampiri. And as for darkness? It continues painting their auras.

Weirdly, there is no aura anywhere in my complete vicinity—outside of theirs—that could account for the voice. Which makes me wonder if it's a stafie. As leftover souls, stafii cling to the living for either protection or vengeance. It usually takes a deep kind of bond to establish that type of connection to overcome death, which makes me curious, despite myself, as to what this could be.

All that to say, after I get the hang of the first few rounds we waltz, I have plenty of time to register how Elizabeta feels pressed up against me. How her hair continues to tickle my arm around her waist, and spills over it. How her scent wraps around me like the headiest of smokes. And how she's so fucking soft—cold, but soft—in my arms.

On a turn, I sense Elizabeta stiffening even more, but instead of loosening my hold, I pull her flush against me.

That soon has her nearly fighting me on turns and taking the lead. But I refuse to give up—or give in. She's mine for this dance, damn it, without her siblings whispering in her ears. And I want to understand what the hell the magnetic pull is. First our encounter in the woods, and now this. She's everything I should hate, everything that should repulse me. How come she's anything but?

The ending notes come all too soon—way before I'm ready to let her go, or have figured out an answer—and I pause, breathing heavily. She's gripping my shoulders, her nails nearly digging through my suit, into my flesh, even as she's shoving me away.

"You'll pay for this," she says.

I open my mouth to retort, but then there's a *whoosh* in the air. And that voice, the man, screams, "Protect her!"

I don't think, I just act. Grab a handful of her dress, pulling her to me once more, and covering her body with mine at the same time. I drop us to the floor. Someone screeches somewhere. Then there's the smell of—ashes?

Pain radiates in my body, and darkness envelops me altogether as chaos ensues.

Chapter 5

Elizabeta

The Dacian's weight crushes me to the floor. I don't think, just react. Shove him off me, and get back to my feet, fangs extended. My furious gaze—probably flashing red with rage—sweeps over the circle of vampiri watching us. Off to the side of the dance floor, my siblings are rushing toward me.

But the circle...something's off. Dust, on the floor. Ashes. Right where I was standing.

Daniel. Staring at me in horror. Saying something, but I can't hear it. There's a roar in my ears—the thought of times past, of being attacked, of being tortured.

"Liza!" Daniel's in my face now.

I want to talk to him, to reassure him I'm okay, but—no, he's a ghost. He's here, but not really. And most of all, he can't help me.

Someone's dead—a vampir. The ashes. That's what... And he'd been standing behind me. If Ștefan hadn't pulled me down with him, if he hadn't—

I shake my head, meeting Mirabela's gaze. Vlad and Silviana drop by the Dacian, who's now groaning on the ground. It's only then that I catch it—a strong copper tinge to the air.

Blood? I didn't push him that hard.

Mirabela's saying something, but my attention is on Ștefan. Almost in slow motion, I see Vlad roll him over to his back. Shove the jacket of the suit aside, showing a red patch on the whiteness of the shirt, right under his right shoulder.

A *red* patch, darkening under my eyes...

"What happened?" Mirabela's expression is cool, composed.

Nico joins us, Tassa by his side. And, coming down the stairs, Violeta and Marcus. They take one glance at what's going on and are by my side in a blur. Vampiri move out of their way. A few head for the doors. Dominic and Luca immediately trail them, with twin determined expressions. A few of their scattered wolves follow.

"An attack," Nico says. He nudges Tassa toward Silviana. "Go see if you can help him. And do not leave their side."

I've never seen such fury in him. His normally blue eyes are a deep shade of burgundy and electrified by it. And, little by little, I see the same in Mirabela, Violeta—even Vlad when he looks up at me.

All except one. Alex.

"Where's Alex?" I ask.

As if on cue, the last missing member of our dysfunctional family breaks the circle of vampiri. His expression—I've seen *him* angry, and every shade in between. Now? He's feral. And he's got someone by the neck, dragging their gasping self.

With nary a look at anyone else, he brings him into our midst. A sheep to the slaughter, as it were. Light hair, brown hair, pale face—he's as unremarkable as they come. But Alex wouldn't have picked him without proof.

"Call it," he tells Nico, and his fingers flex over the man's neck. A neck where a pulse beats, strong and steady. Not even a flutter of nerves.

The realization hits me like a ton of bricks. He's *human.* The attack came from a *human.* And the only humans I know who attack vampiri are...

No. You can't think about it. Snap out of it.

Nico blurs in and out of our tight-knit circle. A moment later, the guards that had been positioned subtly along the edges are moving. I don't have to ask him to know what they're doing. Heading outside, to find the attendees who'd run off. Scattering across the grounds, throughout the castle, to prevent more from leaving. Blasé faces turn annoyed, then outright fuming around us. We're not making any friends, that's for sure.

"No one fucking leaves," Nico says. He doesn't have to yell, but still, his tone increases in volume. "Am I fucking clear? If you all want don't want to meet the Ardelean fate... *No. One. Fucking. Moves.* Until we know why an heir of the Dracul line was attacked." He levels his gaze at everyone in turn. Then, to Alex. "Drop him. I want to hear what he has to say."

The man falls to his knees, gasping for breath still. I get in his face, kneeling. The angle spreads my gown too much over my thigh, and the fabric rips, exposing the side of my left thigh in a deep slit. An almost indecent slit, but I couldn't care less. I grip his chin, forcing his pale brown eyes to meet mine.

"Who sent you?"

"Fuck you," he says.

"Wrong answer." With my free hand, I slash at his arm, my nails tearing through the fabric of his suit easily, and drawing blood. He screams, and a moment later, the slashes turn into cuts. He starts bleeding. "Try again."

He still doesn't.

My gaze lifts above his head, trying to see who, from the crowd, is looking suspicious. Way too many faces. I focus again on the man, this time tapping into my glamour side. "You will tell me everything I need to know."

I can feel his mind, bending to my power. The room seems to darken just slightly, less brightly lit. And the man—oh, he tries to resist. More than I'd expected. But then he relents with a low groan, and his eyes glaze over.

"Who are you?" I repeat.

"I should think it obvious, vampir. I'm a hunter."

If he thinks his revelation is about to shut me up, he's got another think coming. "And what was your mission?"

"To kill you."

I don't miss a beat. "Why?"

"To show the vampiri here that the Draculs aren't above some comeuppance."

Here's the thing about us heirs. Clans come for us. Gods throw curses at us. And somehow, people think we're weak. But when push comes to shove? We'll have each other's backs, always. It's the

Dracul way—the *only* way.

I move in closer, grasping his chin in my fingers. To the side, I hear Ștefan's hiss of pain, his mutters to Silviana that he's all right—I block it all out.

"What comeuppance? For what?"

"For being alive. Still."

I let him go. My gaze meets Alex's expectant one. He hates humans with a passion, and that hate simmers under the surface. I know what he wants. A blood bath.

I'll give him one, but first, I have one more question. "Did the hunters come up with this plan on their own, or was someone else involved? Like a vampiri clan? Or perhaps the Dacians?"

Here, he resists me. Some of his subconscious rises, refusing to answer me. As if the answer is too precious to him.

"Liza..." By my side, Daniel hovers. He got lost among my siblings, but now that I'm crouching with this piece of shit, he's there. Right there, next to me—a distraction I can't afford right now. "He's not one of them. Not from back then."

I throw him a look. *You don't know that. And I won't take the chance.*

Beneath me, the hunter blinks. I narrow my eyes on him, forcing the power of the glamour until his body goes slack again. "Answer me. Was someone else involved?"

"You know the truth."

I nod, stepping away. My heels clack against the floor, the only sound in the room, aside from Silviana and Tassa's soft whispering.

Keeping a clear voice, I say, "You entered Dracul territory and attacked me. Unprovoked. There are no second chances in my world." No sooner do I finish speaking that I rush to his side, and stuff my hand in his chest, breaking skin, and bone, and not stopping until I get what I'm aiming for. He gasps, once. I twist my wrist, and yank out his heart, still beating. He falls to the floor, and I drop his now useless organ over his corpse. Then my gaze meets Alex's smug one. "Let this be a lesson to any who try to fuck with the House of Dracul."

The guards have finished taking down everyone's name, making sure we didn't miss anyone. Later, we'll get together and tally the clans with potential suspects. For now, it's clean-up time.

Nico and Mirabela scared the shit out of the rest of the vampiri. Dominic and his wolves helped—seems it's been a while since a clan of vârcolaci has nestled close by, and vampiri in general don't want to make enemies of them. *Guess unlike what Alex thought, the wolves actually came in handy. Without their quick reactions, we wouldn't have been able to round up the few vampiri who tried to escape. Maybe it's time he cuts them some slack... But now's not the best time to die on that particular hill.*

Speaking of my dear brother, Alex didn't leave my side the rest of the night. Vlad came to check on me, then went upstairs with Silviana, her injured brother, and Tassa, while we conducted vampir business.

And now, all six of us have reconvened in the ballroom. Along with three members of the clan we've built an alliance with—the Munteanus.

"Are you saying the Hatmanus or Cazacus are the ones behind this?" Nico asks the leader.

"It's why we stuck behind and came to see you. When this happened..." He shakes his head. "There were rumors they'd aligned with...witches."

"No, not witches," another says. "They're worse."

"Fuck." Nico runs a hand through his hair, then glances at me. "Why Liza, though?"

"I don't think it was her, specifically, they were targeting. Perhaps she was just the easiest target, in the center of the dance floor."

Centre *and* distracted, by a freaking human, no less. A low growl builds in me.

Vlad clears his throat. "Ştefan heard something, a few minutes before it happened. He went to investigate, but it didn't pan out."

I snort. "You sure he didn't set the arrow himself so he could be some fucked up version of a knight in shining armor?"

"And what makes you think any knight would save *you*?" Mira asks.

It stings, more than it should. I flip her off, and she laughs at me, good-naturedly.

Violeta glances at her watch. "Marcus and I need to be going."

Nico nods, hugs her, and she walks away. Stops in front of me and leans in for a hug that I return stiffly. Violeta and I...we've spent too much time fighting for Nicolae's attention, and too little time building our own bond.

"I'm glad you're okay," she whispers in my ear, then leaves.

I watch her go, and my indifference to her thaws a little. I sense a gaze on me, and meet Alex's. Shrug, as though the hug didn't really get to me. But it did. Violeta's always been the softer sister, the kindest one. The one we all protected. When she got sick...it fucked us all up. Little did we know how bad it would get.

I clear my throat. "What, exactly, are we supposed to do next? Expect hunters to come out of the woodwork, because some vampiri clan decided they're going to make a show of power?" I will not let that thought scare me. *I will not*, no matter my past.

Nico shakes his head. "No. None of that. Mira, Alex, and I will go meet with the Hatmanus, and the Cazacus. This has gone on long enough." To the Munteanu leader, he says, "Thank you for your loyalty."

He bows low. "At your service, my prince."

He and his cronies leave, and then it's just the five of us. Before we can catch our proverbial breath, Dominic strides in, Luca on his heels. Two of his wolves wait by the door. Next to me, Alex tenses with repressed fury.

"Dominic." Nico extends his hand. "Thank you. Without your help, we wouldn't have been able to round up the fleeing vampiri. I won't forget this—none of us will."

Without a hint of hesitation, Dominic shakes his hand. "I'll make note of it." His gaze travels over each of us, then returns to Nico. "We'll take our leave now. Call if anything else comes up." To me, he adds, "Glad you weren't injured."

It's such a surprising sentiment, I'm left baffled and speechless as he strides back out the door, his son and wolves following.

"I'm going to check on Silviana," Vlad says and leaves.

"We might as well all go," Nico says. "We owe Ştefan some gratitude."

Alex snorts. "Count me the fuck out. First the wolves, now groveling to a human? Not on my watch. I'll be anywhere *but* there."

Too bad I can't do the same. A small inkling of morality tells me I do, after all, owe him a thank you.

Ștefan

"Don't move," Silviana says in my ear.

I let out a low hiss as she maneuvers my arm, removing my suit jacket. Something squelches against my skin—my best guess is my shirt, presumably wet with blood.

"How bad is it?"

Silviana says nothing, which in and of itself is an answer. A beat after, she says, "Tassa can fix this. Right?"

I might actually believe her—if it weren't for the desperation in her tone.

Someone clears their throat. "Da, uh, I'll do my best. But it'll hurt. You sure you don't want to use magic for it?"

"No, she doesn't." Based on what she told me, I know her using her magic only draws Zalmoxis out of his cage in her mind. "But I can try, with a small amount." The question is, how much can I use without Zalmoxis becoming interested in me, next? And using Lana to get to us both?

There's a beat of silence, but Tassa doesn't move. I frown, wiping a bead of sweat off my forehead with my free hand. The movement still makes me cringe in pain. "Not trying to be rude but...what are you waiting for, exactly?"

"I—"

Her aura is sharper, her emotions more tangible. Probably because of the amount of blood I'm losing and how it enhances my other senses. I pick up confusion, hesitation, and something else.

Silviana, mercifully, speaks. "I think I understand. You're waiting for him to do the healing cocoon I did, right?"

Tassa breathes out a sigh of relief. "Yes. I mean, I can bring some creams to help, if you think they would—"

"They would," I say curtly. "Bring them, please."

Tassa waits for a beat, then whispers, "Okay, give me a second and I'll be right back."

I count to five in my head, then say, "You showed them the cocoon?"

"It wasn't on purpose. My magic just...did it." Her voice lowers. "When I got attacked in the woods. That's when I drifted into this sleep-state, and saw the zmeu...Tytus."

"Lana..." I reach up, but with the wrong hand, and a hiss of pain escapes me. My chest feels wetter, too. I must still be bleeding. "This part of our magic, only you and I were ever able to do it. I've never found anything like it in Liviu's books, and..."

When I don't immediately continue, she asks, "What?"

"Part of me wonders if perhaps Zalmoxis felt that. You, that light, around the heirs. Maybe him entering your mind has nothing to do with you opening the gate, and everything to do with them."

"How so?"

I hesitate to voice where my mind has gone, but I know I owe it to her to be fully transparent. "Zalmoxis is attuned to the heirs—we know that. It seems to me he's doing everything possible to sabotage them from ever surviving this curse he's set on them. And because our magic comes from the same source as their immortality—*his* source—it makes sense that large bouts of it, used around you or them, draw his eye." I take a deep breath. "What I'm saying is I think Zalmoxis had his eye on you well before you opened that portal, and I'm starting to believe you activating your cocoon of healing around them is what caused it. Which means any further large amount of magic around you could easily break whatever thin defense you've established in your mind and give him more of an anchor...in you."

She's silent for a long moment, then her fingertips brush my forehead. "I know you want to release me of blame, Fane, but I'm very much at fault here." A breath later, she adds, "But, perhaps it's a good idea not to use the cocoon. Or much magic around me, for the time being."

The door opens then, and I hear the clang of various things. Jars with healing creams, judging by the herby smell wafting to my nostrils. Enough to make me sneeze.

"Sorry," Tassa says. "They're potent. I, uh, heard you mention you're not planning to use the cocoon."

"That's correct."

"May I ask why? It's just...the wound is serious, Ștefan. You have to know. And if you won't go to a hospital..."

"No hospitals. No cocoons. The former because of humans. The latter because if Zalmoxis is prowling for another mind to latch onto, I don't want to give him a reason." My mind may resist him longer than Silviana's, but if he gets access to the kind of powers I've tapped into, it will *not* end well for anyone—least of all my sister.

Tassa is silent for a long moment, then says, "Okay. I have some calendula herbs, that should bind the skin back together. And some disinfectant to clean it."

"Do what you have to."

She removes the bandage around the wound and pours something in. Something that burns so bad, I nearly shoot off the bed.

"Sorry! It's the disinfectant. I'm applying the cream now." Her soft touch is followed by a sensation of coolness and something being rubbed onto my skin. "Okay, done. Can you use your magic to help me with the stitches only?"

I grit my teeth and nod. Then pull on the blood, the darkness, and close my eyes. Picture the flesh tying back together with some thread, gritting my teeth more at the pain—it feels as though a needle is being inserted in my flesh, drawing a thread through it, and repeating the pattern over, and over, as darkness listens to my bidding.

"Oh, Fane," Silviana says by my side.

Panting, I let out a long exhale. "I-it's okay. I'll be fine."

Her small hand finds mine, gripping it tightly. "Why in all hells did you think it was a good idea to take this bullet for her?"

I shrug, wincing when movement pulls at the stitches. I'll really have to be careful with this. "Beats me."

Someone clears their throat. "We wanted to stop by and see how you're doing." Nico.

A moment later, I feel a presence by Silviana's side. And Vlad's voice follows. "Shit, that looks bad."

I force a smile for my sister's benefit. "Looks worse than it is."

Nico says, "Thank you. For saving Liza."

Tassa's butterfly hands hover over my chest, this time sprinkling something. And adding more bandages. The scent of herbs and spices, something warm and earthy, fills my nose. Then the ache in my chest simmers down.

"You're welcome," I tell Nico. It's not what I'd intended, but it's not like I had a choice. "Was anyone else around?"

"What do you mean?"

"It's just, someone warned me. It's how I knew."

Elizabeta's tone is biting. "No one was around."

A heavy silence descends. Makes me wonder what she's hiding, because I can sure as hell hear the lie in her voice. Am I the only one?

“Right. I’ll deal with you later, Elizabeta. I think you owe Ştefan a thank you, no?”

“Mulţumesc,” she says sweetly, her tone laced with sarcasm.

“You’re welcome.”

The door opens again and someone else walks in.

“Nico, there’s some tall guy here.”

“Mira, be a little more specific.”

“Tall, dark, and handsome. Gray eyes.” She sniffs. “Magical.”

“Sounds like Tytus,” Vlad says.

Tytus...the zmeu who helped Silviana, when Zalmoxis initially entered her mind. Without him, she would have been lost. I didn’t want to trust him when he popped out of nowhere. But the fact he did as he’d promised—and helped her—meant more to me than any vow he could’ve made.

Still, it seems the heirs are not necessarily fans of him.

“What the hell’s a zmeu doing on our doorstep?” Nico grumbles.

The siblings’ voices fade away as they disappear.

Then Silviana’s touching me. “Come with us, you might as well hear what’s going on.”

I nod and shift slowly off the bed. Leaning heavily on her, I make my way downstairs, and hope I don’t embarrass myself by passing out. Tassa’s patch-up job and my magic will only take me so far. Still, I can’t refuse my sister anything.

I enter the library on Silviana’s arm. Normally, I wouldn’t allow her to lead me, but every part of my body is exhausted, and I simply don't have the energy to familiarize myself with my surroundings or to use more magic. Plus, I might as well save myself the embarrassment around the vampiri, and Elizabeta.

"Thank you for having me," someone says. I recognize the smooth voice as Tytus.

"We didn't *have* you," Elizabeta mutters. "You showed up."

I realize from her voice that she's near me. Her ocean breeze scent mixed with something spicy wafts to my nostrils and I can't help inhaling it. And then am surprised when it makes me dizzy.

"You okay?" Silviana whispers.

I nod jerkily, even though I'm not. What is it about this vampir that's creating such a reaction in me? It wasn't so long ago I'd thought they had killed our family and been responsible for every loss in our life. And now...it turns out that's not the case. But I can't have gotten over my distaste and wariness about them so fast.

"Tell the zmeu about what you felt."

This time, I jump. The voice—it's the same person who warned me. Right before the bullet came to Elizabeta.

"Fane, what's going on?" Silviana asks.

At the same time, the zmeu breaks his conversation with the vampiri and addresses her. "How's Zalmoxis faring?"

"Fine," she says.

"Is he really?" Elizabeta asks. "Because you sure seem to be whispering a lot with your brother. Who somehow magically knew a bullet was coming for me even though he's blind."

Nico groans. "Liza..."

"No, it's fine," I say. "I did *magically* know. Someone whispered in my ear."

Elizabeta scoffs. "We already covered this. There was no one else around."

"And yet."

Someone clears their throat. A beat later, Tytus says, "I think you have bigger problems than some petty squabbling and assassins."

"Such as?"

"Silviana. She's a doorway to Zalmoxis. It won't be long until he uses her against you, or tries to leverage her more to create more havoc. If used properly, however, this doorway he's created could be key to undoing him. But you need help."

"And how do you suggest we get said help?" I ask.

"There's an Oracle in the Hoia Baciu Forest. Go see her. She...sees things others do not. And she would have a way of helping you."

"We know of the Oracle, Violeta also found out about her. But, see, something bothers me about this. Why would she help? Out of the goodness of her heart?" Nico asks.

"Of course not. There will be a price. But do you have any other choice?"

I sigh and take a step forward. "I'll do it. Just point me the right way."

Elizabeta

I let out a giggle at the Dacian's words, which soon turns into a full-blown laugh.

"Liza!"

I ignore Vlad's incensed glare and keep laughing. Too bad Alex isn't here, else he'd get the joke.

"Are you quite done?"

Mira's snobby tone finally stops me. I sober up, then toss my hair over my shoulder and level my gaze on her. "Don't tell me you don't find it funny. *Point me* the right way. As if he can actually see."

"Maybe you're just jealous I care enough about my sister to do something," Ștefan says. "Would your siblings do the same?"

Same as Mirabela's words, his jab hits too close to the mark. I glare at him, even though he can't possibly see it.

Ștefan scoffs. "Didn't think so. Well, zmeu? Where do I go?"

Tytus shakes his head. "It's not that simple. There are things at play you all don't realize. Zalmoxis' influence on Silviana is directly related to a struggle among the gods."

"We don't care about the gods. What we care about is breaking the curse," Mira says.

At this, Tytus rolls his eyes. "You're missing the point. Everything is intertwined. But to answer your question, this is a task for two people, not one."

"I'll go," Vlad says.

There's a short silence at the thought, then everyone breaks out in protest.

Ștefan's voice is the loudest. "You can't leave my sister alone. Your presence keeps her grounded."

"Then I will," Mira offers.

Nico soon counters. "I need you here. I'm not going to meet up with the Cazacus and Hatmanus alone with Alex. Your diplomacy is our strongest point, and judging by Liza's execution of the hunter, we're going to have some fires to put out if we're to find out their involvement."

I glance up from my nails. "Now, why are you making it sound like me killing that guy was a bad thing? He was a threat to us all."

Nico growls. "I'm not going to answer that unless you actually want to hear the answer."

"Try me."

"Your actions made you seem like a rogue player, and no one likes those. The vampiri don't care about some damned hunter, but they will care that it seems we're asserting our authoritarian rule onto them."

"Isn't that the whole point of all of this?" I gesture around. "To assert ourselves over them?"

"Da, but *they* don't need to know it, Liza. If we appear as more calculating and willing to form alliances, it'll be better."

"Tell that to whichever clan was responsible for that assassin, Nico, because we both know he didn't just come out of the blue."

He shakes his head, then faces everyone else who'd been listening. "I propose Liza goes to the woods with Ştefan."

"Are you fucking kidding me?" Both me and Vlad yell.

"No, I'm most definitely not. And last I checked, I'm still head of this house, no?" When no one contests him, Nico adds, "Liza, it's the least you can do after the trouble you caused. And you owe Ştefan."

"Fuck off," I hiss, then turn on my heels and leave before I give in to my baser impulses and throttle one of them.

Chapter 6

Elizabeta

I can't believe this shit. I storm through the castle, heading straight for the woods. I'm the one who nearly got executed, and yet I'm the one who has to pay now, too? And not to just anyone, but a human of all fucking things.

Tears prick my eyes. Nico knows what my deal with humans is. He *knows,* and he's still forcing me. Whatever the hell happened to having each other's backs? Or is it only with Vlad and Violeta that he cares, and not me?

Hallways blur past me, even as I blink furiously. I haven't cried in ages, and I'm not about to now. Not even if my damned brother is being a dick.

"Liza, he's doing it for your own good," Daniel says, floating a bit ahead of me.

I scowl at him, not stopping my blurring run. Annoyingly, he refuses to disappear. "I'm not in the mood, Daniel."

Fresh, cold, biting air hits my cheeks, and still, I keep running. Running, as if that alone will take me away from anything unpleasant. It worked before...why not now?

"You're never in the mood—not for the truth, anyway," Daniel says, harsher than before. "But Nico's right."

I stop in my tracks, the betrayal his words provoke harsher than the chill of the wind outside. "How can you take his side?"

"Because Nico wouldn't have asked you to do this without a reason."

"His reason is more than clear—to score points with his human whore!"

"That's uncalled for, and you know it."

The disappointment in his expression would've normally clawed at me. Except I don't give a flying fuck right now. "Get out of my way."

"No. Liza, look at me."

I don't want to. But something in his tone gets to me, as it always does. The pull of regret, of the tie between us, might as well be a lasso around my neck. I face him. "What?"

His expression is pained. "You're angry because it's easier. Easier than to admit you're hurt."

I scoff. "Why the hell would I be hurt? I'm not some soft-hearted virgin who can easily get her feelings crushed."

He floats closer to me. "True. But you *did* undergo quite a trauma. And you were taught to shove it away, to not deal with it, for the sake of appearing strong. At least…that's what you got from it."

"You don't get to talk shit about what Father taught me!"

He shakes his head. "I'm not, Liza. Well, maybe I am, in a sense. But not to hurt you. Țepeș was, and always will be, a great man, yet that doesn't stop him from having flaws. From not seeing all there is to see. And he did you no favor by pushing you to be tough after that ordeal." His gaze softens, which is almost worse than his entire speech. I hate feeling pitied. "Liza, hunters took you to get back at him. On whose orders, you never did find out. And your sire told you to *shut down your emotions*. To keep on living, feeding, existing. And then you lost me. I've watched you for centuries as this drove you to the brink of psychopathy, fueled by a thirst for vengeance the likes I've never seen." He pauses, and when I say nothing, adds, "Of course, I know what went on. Once you grieved me, once you let yourself feel, your grief created this…connection between us."

"Which is as much a curse to both of us as the real one me and my siblings are facing now."

He sighs. "You're doing it again. Focusing on something else so you don't deal with your hurt."

"There. Is. No. Hurt."

Exasperation replaces his pity. "No? Then the fact you see Silviana and Ștefan so close, him willing to die for her, doesn't hurt? That your siblings would rather send you with him, than risk her life, doesn't hurt? Or how about the fact that you can't talk to any of them about this, because you think they wouldn't hear you out?"

I open my mouth to reply. He's wrong. I know he is. But why does my chest suddenly ache?

Before either of us can say anything, I sense a shift in the woods. A heavier presence.

"Liza?" Alex blurs in front of me, coming to a stop. "Thought I heard your dulcet tones. What's going on?" He frowns, scanning me. "Were you crying?"

I wipe at my cheeks angrily. "Nico's forcing me to go on a stupid quest with that witch's brother."

A muscle ticks in his jaw. Anger flares in his eyes, turning them a blazing red. "You? He's sending *you* with a human?"

The cold fury in his tone gives me pause. Maybe telling him wasn't such a good idea. Alex and Nico are already at odds, and have been since Tassa showed up. But he's my only ally, or at least it feels like it now. If I don't trust him, who can I trust?

"Don't, Liza," Daniel begs me, his tone near desperation.

I ignore him. Taking a deep breath, I recount the entire conversation to Alex.

By the time we storm back into the castle, Nico's with Mirabela in the dining room. He's leaning against the wall, arms crossed, as she argues with him—the hand on her hip and pursed lips are a dead giveaway.

We come to a stop, and Alex wastes no time jabbing a finger in Nico's direction. "What the hell is wrong with you?"

Nico's glance flickers to me—a hint of something, disappointment perhaps, in it—before landing back on Alex. "I see Elizabeta filled you in."

Elizabeta. Guess I'm not 'Liza' anymore when he's mad at me.

Alex takes a step closer, his entire body taut, fists clenched.

Mirabela narrows her eyes on him. "Alex, now's not the time for a fight."

"No? Then when? Because all I see here is the two of you willing to roll over and play dead for the humans. And that's *not the way it's supposed to be*. It never has been."

Nico lets out a heavy sigh. "This argument is getting old, Alex. Or did you forget we have a curse on our hands? One that affects all of us?"

"Doesn't mean we need to give in."

Nico throws his hands up in the air. "Then what the hell do you suggest, hmm?" He takes a step closer, and they're nose to nose. "Tell me. You think you can lead this family so much better? Then *fucking speak* and give your suggestion."

"We could hunt down Zalmoxis."

"Yeah? And where would we find the information to do so?"

Alex sneers. "You got a dragon shifter at your disposal, no? Send him instead!"

Mirabela shakes her head. "You think a zmeu wants to get involved in this pettiness? He's a being much superior to us, Alex. Unlike you, I did my research after Vlad filled us in about him. And forgive me for being unwilling to butt heads with him. For fuck's sake, his kind used to protect *gods*. And you think he's easily ordered around like some, what, puppy?" Her lips press into a thin line. "Tytus is only involved because of Silviana. He cares nothing for us."

"*Then make him.*"

Nico snorts. "I see. So your solution is *more* conflict on our hands—and with a zmeu, to boot. As if the fact we're getting shot at and hunted by hunters and Dacians alike isn't enough. Go take a walk, Alex. Come back when you have an actual solution."

I know the moment Nico turns his back that it's the wrong move. Alex reaches for his shoulder with a rage that's been building up. "I'm not some child you can dismiss. You *will* listen to me!"

Nico whirls around, but Alex's punch finds his jaw. He staggers back, then his eyes flash red and it's pandemonium. Forget rational—I see it in both of them, and I'm not alone. Mirabela screams for them to stop, but with a yell of abandon, Nico tackles Alex.

They go tumbling into an antique table, breaking it in half. The glasses and drinks atop it shatter on the ground—so much for crystal-strength. Alex does some maneuvers that I've seen in our muroni hunts and pins Nico against the wall. But my brother's not to be underestimated. He kicks back, getting Alex in the stomach—or privates? Can't quite tell from my angle.

Mirabela interrupts my view by blurring in front of me. "Help me stop them!"

Personally, I'd prefer Alex got in a few more punches before intervening. But another presence draws my attention. In a corner, Daniel's pleading with me.

Rolling my eyes, I move with Mirabela as one. She grabs ahold of Nico, me of Alex, and we step between them while at the same time shoving them with enough force to put some distance between them.

"Enough!" Mira yells. "We don't have time to in-fight right now, not when we're so close to our goal."

"He started it!" Nico yells, like the younger self he used to be.

It almost makes me laugh. Almost. Because it's drowned out by a string of curses from Alex that make my ears bleed.

I turn to him, adding more pressure with my hand on his chest. "Breathe, Alex. Please."

He half-listens, but his glare never moves from Nico. "Liza's not a disposable commodity. She's our sister, for fuck's sake. Does that mean nothing to you?"

He might as well have slapped him, as Nico only gapes.

"What are you talking about?" Mira snaps. "Of course we know that, and we care for her as we do for each and every one of you."

"Alex..." Nico shakes his head, his tone back to calm. "We asked Liza to go with Ştefan because we know she's the only one strong enough to protect him, *and* herself. Mira is needed here for diplomacy. Vlad and Violeta are already affected by the curse, but at least their consorts can defend them if need be. And as the only one with a human consort, I can't leave Tassa behind." A muscle ticks in his jaw. "We both know you're not an option; you'd sooner kill Ştefan than help him." He turns his gaze to me. "If you thought, for a second, that it's because of something else—"

"I didn't," I quickly mutter, and look away.

Daniel mouths *Liar* from his corner, and I hold back from sticking my tongue at him. Much as I hate to admit it, Nico's reasoning makes sense.

I return my attention to Alex, somewhat apologetically. "It's settled, then. I'll go with the human, we'll get the information, then come back. It'll be easy."

"I can come with you."

"No, Nico's right—you're more likely to kill him than anything else."

He steps closer, lowering his tone to a whisper only I will hear. "Be careful, Liza. I don't trust him as far as I can throw him."

"I will be." Then add, "I'm sorry, for the fight—"

"I'll always have your back. *Always.*" He pulls me into a fierce hug, then steps away just as quickly. The whole thing was barely half a breath long.

Without a glance at the others, I mutter, “I’ll go let the human know of our plan.”

Since it’s my castle and he’s a guest, I barge right into the room—and promptly freeze. Rather than sitting or lounging around, Ștefan is on the floor…doing push-ups. Half-naked. And Silviana’s the one perched on his bed, staring at me with wide eyes, mouth agape.

“Uh…” She looks from me to Ștefan, still doing his push-ups, then back again. “Can we help you, Elizabeta?”

Ștefan stops mid-pushup at the sound of my name. He turns his head to the side, and I could swear his nostrils flare, as if he’s inhaling my scent. I must be losing it. A sentiment that’s even more enhanced when my eyes roam over his broad shoulders, his flexing muscles, and what I can see from his contracting obliques.

“I’ve come to say it’s happening. The trip, into the Hoia Baciu Forest. As soon as you can manage it, if your wound is healing.” My tone turns wry. “Unless you’re otherwise preoccupied, that is.”

With the grace of a feline, Ștefan pushes off the ground and straightens. My eyes travel up his form, taking in what I couldn’t before. The tight biceps, the smooth plane of his stomach, his well-defined six-pack. The perfection of his torso is only ruined by a nasty, raised bump on his chest—where he took the bullet from me. It’s not seeping blood as it was before, but neither does it look fully healed. Why the hell he thought doing pushups would help that, is beyond me.

"I'm going to...go," Silviana whispers. And with a kiss on his cheek, she rushes out of the room.

Ștefan is quiet for a moment after her departure. Then he heads to the corner armchair, where a worn shirt is tossed. "I'm not *otherwise preoccupied*," he says, and his tone holds a warning. "I was blowing off steam."

I snort at his explanation.

This only makes him turn in my direction. He frowns. "What, you've never had to blow off steam, in all your years of existence?"

"No. I don't get aggravated."

At this, he chuckles. Something rumbles in me at the dark, rich sound erupting from him.

"I find that hard to believe."

"Believe what you will, human. If you had half the sight I do, you'd understand I'm not lying."

I spin on my heels to walk away, already incensed. But Ștefan isn't quite done with me, it seems.

"And yet, there you go—being aggravated. Tell me, Elizabeta, why do you pretend so hard you don't care?"

Although his question takes me unaware, I try to sound unaffected when I face him once more. "Because I don't?"

His blank stare remains focused in my general vague direction, and for some reason, his words annoy me even more. How can he see so much, when he's perfectly blind?

A wry smile twists his lips. "Could've fooled me."

"I could. Matter of fact, I could fool you whichever way I see fit and you wouldn't see the difference."

"You could try."

On a stupid impulse, I move closer to him—until I'm a mere

arm's reach away, slightly to his right. His eyes haven't tracked my movement. But when I reach out with my hand for his throat, his arm comes up and deflects mine with surprising accuracy.

Not only that, but he also grabs my wrist and doesn't let go.

I stare at the hand, my jaw going slack. Then my eyes narrow on him. "Unhand me."

"No. Not until you learn some manners—such as not killing your guests."

I lean closer. "Fuck you."

Before I can even register what happens, his mouth crushes mine. It's a bruising touch, not a kiss—a punishment that doesn't last longer than a few brief seconds. Yet it's a punishment that has me frozen until he releases me just as abruptly and turns his back to me.

"You can leave now."

I gape at him, lips tingling, even more furious than before.

"Touch me again," I manage to hiss, "and I'll rip your tongue out."

Ștefan

The door slams behind her as she leaves. I don't know what possessed me to poke that particular tiger. I'd warned Silviana against these vampiri, and here I am falling prey to one's.... What, charms? Elizabeta has none. That much is clear.

But her energy still pulls me in like a moth a flame.

"This one flame can seriously burn you," I mutter to the empty room, before feeling my way over to the couch.

Elizabeta's reasons for pretending to be cold and calculating shouldn't matter. Her problems are not mine to solve. I have enough of those. Not least of which is that my fellow Dacians will be quick to hunt me down if they find out I'm actually working with a vampir.

I still haven't figured out how to lie to Liviu on this end. So, I won't. I'll simply go rogue and hope they don't send someone here to verify my presence. The trip to the Hoia Baciu Forest shouldn't take longer than a day. According to Siri, it's just under three hours from where the Draculs are living. And once the Oracle tells us what we need to do for Silviana, I can check in with the Dacians then...and figure out a lie. Perhaps even use what I learn as leverage.

It wouldn't be smart to go against my own kin. At least, not at this moment in time.

I drop my head in my hands, suddenly wary. This world was never kind, but at least Silviana and I always had each other. Now, I'm stuck in a different world. And my sister is in danger. Just how much danger...

The zmeu's words come back to me. Silviana's never been shy, but the sister I've been around these past hours worries me. But I'll be damned if I let anyone, even a god, rob her of her shine.

I stand, moving to the bathroom. Set the shower running after a few moments of feeling around, then strip and get in. The hot water makes me hiss in pain, reminding me of the bullet I took for Elizabeta. My fingers tread carefully, pressing on the skin until I locate the wound. When I do, I scrape my nails against the healing scab. Tassa did a great job with her remedies, but it's time for a little bit more. And now that Silviana isn't around me, I may get away with using just enough darkness to heal it.

Resting my head against the wall of the shower, I focus on the *thump thump thump* of my pulse, of my heart...of my blood. I dig into the threads of darkness of my magic, and pull on them, imagining the skin binding, healing, becoming one as if the wound had never existed in the first place.

When it's done, a faint throbbing persists. The phantom pain will remain much longer than I'd like, but it'll be gone, too, in time.

My thoughts wander once more, to the events of the night. To that voice. A voice no one can tell me who it belongs to, except for Elizabeta herself. And yet, she's even hiding it from her siblings. What other secrets does she hide?

Eventually, I move out from underneath the hot water and dry myself with a towel. Then I go back in the room for some clothes.

"Jeez, Fane!"

I jump, hands immediately going to my junk to cover it. "Lana, *what the hell*?" It's one thing to be working out in front of her with my shirt off, quite another to walk in naked while she's in the room. My cheeks heat up.

She tosses something at me, which falls to the ground. I crouch low, fumbling for it. A robe. Thank fuck—I quickly don it.

"Sorry, I should've yelled or something," she says, sounding as embarrassed as I feel.

Yes, she should've. But disaster's been averted. "It's fine. What, uh, what's going on? How come you're back?"

"I need to tell you something about Liza, given the whole...whatever that was, earlier. And since you're going on this quest—that I hate—with her."

"Okay..."

"There's a man around her. Someone I don't know, but he's like a ghost—black hair, pale eyes, tall. I saw him."

I think back to the voice, warning me in the ballroom to help her. It was definitely male. "Did you ever speak to him?"

"No. But, well, I thought you should know."

"Hmm. He could be a stafie..."

"What's that?" she asks.

"A leftover soul, clinging to the living."

"Like a ghost?"

"Not quite. Ghosts are the fantasized version. A stafie is the soul of the dead person, who is stuck behind and can't cross because of some unfinished business. The main difference between them and ghosts is that a ghost stays behind of their own accord until they deal with whatever unfinished business they have, whereas a stafie is tied by a deep connection to a living person who is holding them back. Either because the living haven't fully grieved, because they can't let go, or a myriad of other reasons. Their pain creates a deep connection between them, and the stafie's duty becomes one of protection."

"Like a guardian angel?"

"Something like that... Though, stafii can also be evil. In that case, they're held back by the pain of those they inflicted wounds upon during their living. And usually, they're tied to a physical location, too."

"Huh. And you think this guy could be one? The good type, I mean?"

I shrug. "If I'm right, he's the one who warned me when Elizabeta was being shot at. Clearly, he wants to protect her." Which makes me wonder who, exactly, he is.

Silviana's quiet for a long moment. When she speaks, her voice is filled with worry. "Please, be careful."

"I will." I open my arms for a hug, and she laughs.

"Go put on some proper clothes first!"

Chapter 7

Elizabeta

I drive us to the woods since the Dacian can't see, and we can't exactly use my means of transportation. It's a painful two hours and forty minutes, all spent in blessed silence. At least, from Ștefan. Daniel won't shut the fuck up with ideas for icebreaker conversations. The only thing I want to break is the Dacian's neck. But since that's not really an option...

Still, his nerve, *kissing me!*

He shifts by my side, as though sensing my rising ire, and I glance at his profile. His jaw is clenched, his gaze fixed ahead with an intense expression.

"We're getting close."

"How could you possibly—" But sure enough, as I turn around another bend, the landscape changes. Rocky mountainous palisades give way to trees. At first, they're sparse, then they thicken. Even with my sharpened eyesight, I can't see past them. An uneasy feeling creeps up my spine.

I pull over to the side of the road, abruptly enough that Ștefan bangs his head against the side window. He curses, but doesn't lash out at me. Pity.

I exit the car instead, letting him fend for himself. By my side, Daniel is quiet, finally.

Well, almost.

"I don't like this, Liza."

I shrug. The passenger car door opens and Ștefan steps out, shutting it behind him.

"I'm over here," I mutter begrudgingly.

After a second of hesitation, he joins me and pauses by my side.

I would've thought he'd wait for a bit, but he moves ahead purposefully. "Let's go. We don't have time to waste."

Getting over my shock, I blur in front of him and put my hand on his bicep. It flexes under my fingers, drawing my gaze to his bulk. And I remember the muscles hiding underneath his shirt. Muscles that strained with every push-up....

I shake my head and glare up at him, though he can't see me. "How about I lead, Dacian? Then you can follow my footsteps. You won't see a trap until it's too late."

He clenches his jaw, but nods tightly. "Fine. Lead ahead."

Scoffing, I turn my back on him and start moving. At a human pace, of course.

We've been walking for about half an hour. My flowy blue dress and knee-length boots were not the best choice for an excursion in the woods, but then again, when do I ever dress appropriately? Still, by the umpteenth time I step wonky because of the uneven terrain and my boots, I scowl and let loose a string of curses.

The woods rise around us in darkened anger. Something about this place doesn't ring right, and for the first time, I wish I had my siblings with me. Or at least Alex. Instead, all I've got is a silent and slightly sulky Dacian by my side. Sure, he may have magic. Much good it'll do me if he can't use it properly. If we get attacked, it's on me to protect my ass—and his.

"Dark thoughts, Liza?"

I glance at Daniel. He's walking between me and Ștefan, who's still trailing behind me—not far enough so I lose him, but not close enough so he can hear me breathe. Good thing, too, as I let out a sigh. In the softest murmur I can muster, I whisper, "You should've stayed at the castle."

"Not a chance. And miss all the fun?" His eyes sparkle. It's the most animated I've seen him in a while. Last time, it was with anger at me. Now, it's with teasing.

A teasing that makes my heart ache. If there was a God, he'd know this torture is killing me every day. But, clearly, I'm meant to somehow survive it, since it's been years of it.

"There won't be any fun."

"I'm sure that's what Violeta thought when she went off and found her consort."

I throw him a glare.

"Sorry, sorry. Your sister's off limits, I get it." A beat later, "And yet..."

"What now?"

"You can't tell me—honestly tell me—that you're not looking forward to this. The castle was getting...tense."

I simply grit my teeth. If I could speak without fear of the Dacian overhearing, I'd tell him that I'm not happy. That I'm afraid Alex will do something stupid. Or Nico will. Or both will. One, for me. The other, for his human whore.

Or I might just tell him about the nightmares returning. As if he hasn't heard me crying whenever I do try to sleep. We may not need the sleep as vampiri, but I used to find it a good way to recover and recharge from the day's events. Not so much nowadays.

"Don't tell me you're scared," Daniel whispers in my ear. There's a smirk in his tone, somewhere.

"Shut up."

My louder protest isn't subtle enough, as Ștefan overhears. "I didn't say anything."

I bite my tongue; the last thing I need is to let him know what's happening.

"Elizabeta?"

"You should tell him," Daniel says. "He won't think you crazy."

I glower at him, but he simply shrugs with a wry grin. "You glaring daggers at me won't make me go away, you know."

"Elizabeta." Ștefan's tone is firm this time, and I reluctantly whirl to face him. He's scowling. "What is it?"

I open my mouth. Glance at Daniel. Then close it and mutter, "Nothing."

Ştefan frowns, tilting his head to the side as if hearing something else. As if *seeing* something, past my demeanor.

Stupid. He can't see anything. He's blind.

"But not blind to you," Daniel whispers again.

A shudder runs up my spine. I hate that Daniel's so damn perceptive, even in death.

We start moving again in silence, but I feel Ştefan's attention on me, even as I take the lead once more. The reaction it causes in my body is enough to make me uncomfortable, even more so because of how primal it is.

Ştefan

I sense the power in the woods. It's in every step I take, every breath I breathe. Either Elizabeta's desensitized to it, or she's too engrossed in her thoughts to notice.

What Silviana mentioned about the man around her springs to mind. Is that why she's acting so weird? If I'm right, and it's a stafie, it wouldn't be the end of the world for her to admit she has one orbiting around her. Why keep it a secret from her siblings? Unless it's because of *who* he is...

Something from her father's journal nags at me. '*The hunters who attacked Elizabeta, they are no regular vampir hunters. Someone is coming for me, my friend, someone powerful. And I cannot tell if it is because of who I am, because of my heirs, or because of that cursed prophecy.*'

Could that be what this is about? Could the pain of whatever she went through be what bonded her to this man? If so, it makes me even more curious about who he is. His presence at the ball—

because I have no doubt now that it was him warning me—speaks of his deep desire to protect her. So was he someone she was well acquainted with? Another lost sibling? Or someone more…romantically involved?

Without Elizabeta noticing—hopefully—I slip my athame out of my wrist cuff and quickly slice my thumb open. Better to have my magic at the ready, just in case. There's something…off in the air. I just don't know what. I keep putting one foot in front of the other, trying to ignore the foreboding at the bottom of my spine.

But then everything goes quiet. Too quiet. I stop, my hackles rising. "Elizabeta?"

Nothing answers me.

And then the air around me thickens, as though pressing in on me. Breathing becomes hard. And then… whatever was pressing on me releases, and I gasp, pulling in a deep breath.

I open my eyes, so used to the darkness. And stunned when…that's not what I see, at all. Instead, a sunset's light streams through trees. A mist pulls at my feet. And in front of me, the woods. No sign of Elizabeta.

"How…is this possible?" I whisper.

"Son."

One word. I turn. The man facing me—I know him, even without the way he'd addressed me. His tall, lanky frame. Shoulder-length hair, a shade darker than Silviana's strawberry-blonde. Eyes the same color as ours.

"…Dad?"

He smiles and opens his arms. I stumble into them, holding onto him. He's shorter by a head than me, and slimmer. Smaller than the last time I'd seen him, when I was barely hip height. But I hold onto him like I'd never let him go.

And then I pull back, frowning. "I don't understand. How are you…? Țepeș's journal…"

He smiles. "Leave all that aside, my son. I need something."

"Anything."

The smile widens, and a glint comes into his eyes. The hand on my shoulder digs—right into the healed, but still painful, bullet wound. I gasp, and wince when he keeps pressing. "Dad, what are you—"

The smile widens. Manic. It's nothing like what I remember from when I was a kid. I think back to the power I'd sensed in the woods and yank myself out of his grip. I'd let my emotions get the best of me. Of course this isn't real.

"What *are* you?"

He comes at me, then. I try to use magic to keep him at bay, but nothing happens. The darkness won't respond. I move my wrist quickly and the athame slides into my palm, cutting into it deeply.

When blood falls onto the forest floor, the creature's grin widens even more. "Yessss…"

He tackles me again.

I once again try to pull on the darkness, but it refuses to heed my call. The thing—whatever it is—pushes me toward a broken branch, clearly intending to impale me on it. At a loss, I shove against him and use the newfound space to yank the athame out of my wrist cuff and stab him in the gut with it. He jerks in my hands, then looks at me…and dissipates into nothingness.

Tears prick my eyes. I know this thing wasn't him, my father, but it was still *his features* staring at me in pain. Still *his eyes* showing betrayal. Still *his hands* hanging onto my neck, before he dropped to the ground.

Get yourself under control, I tell myself, and wipe at my eyes.

When I look up, a man walks out of the mist—translucent form, black hair, pale eyes. He resembles Silviana's description of the man by Elizabeta's side. He says something, but I can't hear him past the ache spreading from my temples to the forefront of my head.

I fall to my knees, gripping it. And when I open my eyes again, only darkness meets me. It's gone. Whatever regained my sight, that fickle thing, is gone. And I'm once more left without it.

It was best not to know what I was missing. I'd gotten used to it. Now...

Footsteps crunch over the ground. Then, "There you are! Is it so much to ask you to keep up? We're already moving so damn slow." The sharpness in Elizabeta's tone turns to confusion. "What are you doing on the ground? And why do I smell blood?"

"Forget it."

I push off the ground and move past her, not wanting her to see me at my worst. I also can't deal with her tone when I'm feeling so raw. Whichever way I look at it, this weakness is not something I want around a vampir. Especially her.

Elizabeta

The Dacian takes off, stumbling through the woods like he's drunk. "What happened to him?" When Daniel doesn't answer me, I turn to him. "Daniel?"

He tears his eyes away from the trees and meets my gaze. Frowning. "He saw me."

"What?" And then I realize what he means. "That son of a bitch! He's faking it?"

Daniel grabs my arm before I can take off. “No. Liza. He *saw* me. For a brief moment. Then he shuddered, fell, and it was gone.” He lets go of me, rubbing his chin instead. “Something’s at work here. These woods…they’re unnatural.”

I snort. “Who’s scared now?”

“I’m not scared *for me*. But for you.”

“You don’t need to be. I can take care of myself just fine, remember?”

He shakes his head. “That’s the problem with you, Liza. You never ask for help, until it’s too late. Just…be careful.” He glances at the spot Ștefan disappeared through. “And for fuck’s sake, go after him before you lose him.”

I mutter under my breath. I wouldn’t mind a break from the Dacian. There’s something unsettling about his presence and the way he’s so laid back, taking what I’m dishing out.

But, fine. Daniel’s right, I might as well go after him.

Ugh. Humans and their goddamned emotions. Alex is so right.

Unfortunately, going after Ștefan soon turns into the biggest pain in my ass, because I can’t fucking find him.

“Where *the hell* has he gone?”

Night has settled now, and though I’m usually able to see past the cloak of shadows, weakness fills my bones. I didn’t feed before we’d left, and I’m starting to regret it. My strength wanes with each passing hour, as though something sapping all of it.

"It's the curse," Daniel says, appearing out of nowhere yet again.

I ignore him. The curse doesn't apply to me—or, rather, I refuse to let it apply.

As if guessing my thoughts, Daniel says, "You know that's not possible."

"Fuck off."

A moment later, Daniel says, "Over there."

I glance where he's pointing, but definitely can't see fuck all. A shudder runs through me. *Is Daniel right? Could it be the curse? Violeta said this is how it started with her...* Vampir sight, like speed, strength, and glamour, are things I've taken for granted. I'm not ashamed to admit it. The problem is, without them, I don't know who I am. And if Violeta's words are anything to go by, her experience with this crap was not fun.

Still, I shove my doubts down and try to see past the pitch-black. After a few moments, my eyes adjust and something flickers in the distance. Fire, perhaps.

"What makes you think it's the Dacian?"

"Because he's no fool. The temperature dropped, the sun is gone, and animals of prey will soon be roaming the woods."

"I don't think anything roams these woods."

"Perhaps. Shall we?"

I follow his glowing form further until the trees swallow us whole. My feet tangle in more than one tree's roots, the boots heavier on my feet than before, but I manage not to face-plant. Now that would be embarrassing.

Finally, I push past one stubborn branch. It breaks off, and ahead, something moves, blocking the fire's glow. "Who goes there?"

"Who else?" I snap, annoyed I've had to chase him down however many kilometers in a weakened state.

Ștefan shifts to the side, and the fire's light casts shadows on his features. But it also lights them up enough so I can see he's frowning. "You found me."

"Of course I freaking found you. What, were you trying to escape me?"

Ștefan turns away, his features once more cast into shadows. "And be without your gracious presence? Not even." I'm not too sure what to make of his tone—resigned, defeated, or something else? What even happened with him, earlier? And why is that nagging at me, when I shouldn't give a shit?

Daniel, in typical male fashion, gets a good chuckle at Ștefan's words. Of course, he does, the bastard—he's taken to enjoying anyone who puts me in my place lately. Says I need a dose of my own medicine.

"Whatever. Let's just go," I say, keeping my gaze averted from the fire.

"Don't you want to at least warm up?"

"I'm cold-blooded, you fool. And no, I don't want to. What I want is to find the old hag and get this done and over with."

He says nothing. Then, the scent of blood—which I hadn't noticed until this point—permeates the air, stronger. He whispers something very low, and the fire disappears. The tension in my shoulders vanishes alongside it.

"Come on, then." I spin on my heels and move forward, and he follows shortly after.

It's not long before I'm stumbling again, and he overtakes me, walking ahead. We continue on like that for another hour, by which point my feet feel like they've grown weights, and my eyes burn from straining to stay awake.

"Liza, you need to stop," Daniel says.

I ignore him.

"Liza, please. The curse is hitting you. You can't just—"

"Watch me," I mutter under my breath, keeping my voice low. Shouldn't have bothered, as the damned Dacian seems lost in his thoughts since I got him back, walking way ahead of me. Or...so I think.

Abruptly, he stops and turns to me. In the pitch-black, his glazed eyes seem alighted by a fire within. "You're tired."

I stop in my tracks, keeping my distance. "How the fuck can you know that?"

He purses his lips, then runs a hand over his shaved head. The move, so awkward, is incongruous with his large bulk.

"I feel your energy," he mutters finally.

"Come again?"

A wry smile twists his lips. So much like Daniel, that it clenches something deep inside me. Something I'd buried. Something I don't want to examine, let alone become aware of.

"Your energy. It's how I know. It's hard to explain to an outsider, but after I lost my sight, my magic...internalized. I'm able to use it as Silviana does, but I'm also more receptive to changes in emotions. I don't know which of my human senses or my magic are responsible, but I get snippets of information about the people I engage with. Especially if they're..."

When he doesn't finish, I prompt, "Especially if they're what?"

He rubs his head again and shifts on his feet. "Nothing. It doesn't matter."

If I cared enough to know, I'd push him. As it is, I settle for,

"So, what, you're saying the old adage of one sense lost, enhanced senses gained is true?"

His expression, already on the precipice of closing off, shutters at that. "Something like that." He turns his back to me again and walks away, practically vibrating tension and annoyance with each step.

Ugh, humans. Again, the thought strikes me they're always so damned full of emotions.

Still, my gaze lingers over how his broad shoulders stretch the jacket he's got on. How the dark jeans he's got on make his ass look way too good. I've always noticed these things about males of either species—vampir or human alike—but something about this particular human... I think back to my earlier thought, of how being around him is unsettling. Da, that's it. *Unsettling.*

Problem is, I don't do unsettling. And I could blame it on his emotions, and the fact I'm nowhere near equipped to babysit him. But I also know I'd be lying. There's more underneath all that, and it's enough to drive me crazy trying to figure it out. So, I don't.

"He might be an annoying human," Daniel says, reading my expression like he always does, "but this is one human whose cooperation you need. Time to play nice."

"Why should I?"

"Because you need him on your side, like it or not. I have a feeling this little quest of yours isn't going to be a one-man—or woman—operation."

I roll my eyes and, given Daniel's usually pretty good at this stuff, follow in Ștefan's stead. Time for some low-core manipulation. "Fine. You're right. I am tired, so we might as well find a spot to sleep."

He doesn't seem impressed at the fake sweetness in my voice. Or the fact I've basically gone back on what I said before, about finding the hag. Nor does he complain that he has to start up another fire.

Instead, moments later, we've set up camp in a forest nook. After I gather some firewood, Ștefan pulls out a small knife from under the sleeve of his wrist, cuts his hand, and whispers some words. It's the first time I've seen the reason behind all the blood that I've been smelling, and the sight of it....does nothing to me.

Fire blazes atop the pile of dry wood and I watch in utter fascination. *I don't understand what's going on. None of my blood thirst is sparked, yet I can smell his blood, and it smells enticing.*

"Liza, look," Daniel whispers.

I glance where he's pointing, seeing the shadows that come to the flame. Like they're being pulled to it by some mysterious force.

My gaze settles on the Dacian, wishing I'd paid more attention to Vlad and his explanations of how their power works. All I know is it comes from the same source as the god who cursed us. Which makes me wonder if there's a way to use this little—okay, *big* pawn—and get to said-god. Hmm. Something to be considered for a later time.

My gaze gets pulled back to the flames, much like the shadows do. And my memories, imprisoned in a dark corner of my mind, come at me. Other flames. The burn of my flesh, the sizzling, and then the healing. On repeat.

My hand moves up to my cheek, the one reminder left of that. Every other scar has healed, though it took a lot of feeding on humans. I'd killed every single one of the hunters I could get my hands on once I escaped, but the sect itself seems to have survived. We've been running into some of them, on and off, with no rhyme or reason for how they show up. The apparition of the latest one at the ball makes me wish I'd hunted their entire lineages and gotten a chance to exorcize some more of these demons.

Daniel is mercifully quiet, and when I glance over, he's gone. A moment of panic runs through me, the same as the other times, but then I tell myself he'll come back.

I shift my attention to Ştefan. "You should rest. Your human body needs it more than mine."

He scowls. "I'm fine."

"What's gotten up your ass?"

"You."

"Me? What did I do?"

He turns in my direction, a full-blown scowl on his features. "You're impossible, that's what. Thinking you can manipulate me with some fake sweetness and equally fake words? Keep your antics for later, Elizabeta. I'm sure you'll need them."

Then he rolls over, his back to the fire, and puts an end to the conversation.

Hmm. Maybe he has some bite in him, after all. I hate how much that sparks my intrigue.

Chapter 8

Ştefan

I wake to the sound of whimpers. For a moment, I'm disoriented. I'd been dreaming I had my sight back, and I was watching Silviana play with a doe in the woods. Waking to the damp, cold ground, and the waning heat of the fire is a shot of adrenaline to my system.

Right on the heels of that is the memory of my dad. No, not my dad. That *creature* pretending to be him. My athame, stabbing it in the gut. My dad's features, twisted in pain. That whole encounter screwed with my head, and no amount of rationalizing helped. Neither did being around the Dracul princess and her haughty attitude—hiding my vulnerability took more strength than I'd had left.

I was relieved to finally drop into sleep.

My ears perk up again at the sound of someone whimpering in pain. With a jolt, I realize it's coming from Elizabeta.

I didn't know vampiri sleep, let alone dream. But judging by the sounds she's making, she's in the throes of a horrible nightmare.

Her tone escalates. "Nu… Faceți ce vreți cu mine, dar lăsați-l in pace!"

There's a haunting plaintiveness in her words, something I never would've associated with her. She's begging for someone's life. Telling someone that she'd rather they do whatever to her, so long as they leave him alone. Who is it that inspired such loyalty in her?

I get up to my hands and knees, and crawl over to her carefully, staying far from the heat of the fire to my right. "Elizabeta?"

The whimpers pause for a breath, then pick up, even more intense. "Nu! Lăsați-l in pace! Daniel…"

Again, the pleading to leave someone be. Almost as if he's to be saved from…pain?

Daniel. She has to be referring to the stafie following her around.

"Who's Daniel, Elizabeta?"

She doesn't answer, not that I thought she would. Instead, her whimpers abate for a brief second, then pick up again. She's muttering his name over and over, her tone laced with pain.

"Is he the man Silviana saw by your side?" I pause. "I know he's a stafie."

"Well deduced," a male voice says to my left.

I turn my head in his direction, somehow not that surprised that he's engaging with me. After all, he did get me to save Elizabeta's life during the ball.

"She's having a nightmare."

"I realized as much," I point out wryly.

"I wouldn't recommend touching her when she's in such a state."

I hold my breath for a moment. Elizabeta's whimpers increase. They remind me too much of Silviana's night terrors when we were kids.

"I can't do that," I mutter, and continue crouching closer, until her scent assails my senses. I'm within reach.

I extend my hand, holding my breath, and make contact with hers. Her skin is cold to the touch, but soft like velvet. There's no pulse—obviously—but her nails move up and grip my forearm, digging into my skin. I let out a hiss of pain.

Behind me, Daniel says, "Don't say I didn't warn you."

I grit my teeth and reach out with my other hand, tracing up her arm until I find the soft curve of her cheek. My fingertips graze the silky strands of her hair and move to cup her cheek.

"Elizabeta… You're all right. It's just a nightmare."

My words don't penetrate.

So, since I seemingly have a death wish, I go one step further. I seek her neck with my fingers and move my other hand to her lower back, pulling her into a half-standing position in my lap. And then I close my arms around her, rest my chin atop her head, and rock back and forth, like I used to with Silviana.

At the back of my mind, I know this is dangerous. But the thrill in my veins, the zing of awareness I feel, is something I've subconsciously started associating with being in this vampir's presence. And to have her seem almost…human? Full of an emotion other than disdain? It's mind-blowing.

"You're all right," I whisper, my lips to her hair. "Whatever nightmare has you in its throes, you're all right."

At first, Elizabeta is still lost to me. A prisoner of her mind, in what sounds like a torturous time. Was she taken by someone?

As if guessing my thoughts, the stafie speaks. "She was held captive by vampiri hunters," Daniel says. "For a long time. They wanted to see what it would take to get a vampir to break."

"You were there?" I ask.

"I… It all started with me. The Draculs found me, freed me. I entered their employ as a guard for decades. When Elizabeta was taken, and we realized the hunters were behind it, I tracked her down. And…"

"Got captured, too." That explains her pleas to her captors, to "leave him alone"—the *him* was Daniel.

"Da. Not for as long as she'd been, but enough. A few days. They tried to use me to break her in ways they couldn't before. It almost worked, but Țepeș came. Ripped everyone he found to shreds, freed us both."

I think of Elizabeta—strong-headed, never-bending, uncompromising. What it must've done to her, being in that situation… "You helped her through coming to terms with what happened, didn't you?"

"Da."

That explains the connection.

"Why speak to me? Stafii don't generally engage with the living outside of the person they're bonded to protect."

There's a long silence before he answers. "Perhaps because I think you can be part of that protection."

I'm about to say he's delusional, but in my arms, Elizabeta's whimpers stop and she stills. Inhales my scent deeply. Nuzzles my neck, causing a jolt of electricity to run through my entire body.

When I feel her canines graze my skin, I shove her off me unceremoniously and scramble away—nearly into the fire, if the blazing heat at my back is any indication.

Her pearly laugh rings out. "What's the matter, Dacian? It's only fair I take my share of payment, for you daring to lay your hands on me."

Heat fills my cheeks too, at her accusation. "I was trying to help!"

"Oh, really?"

"You were having nightmares. Begging for mercy. I comforted Silviana when we were kids, and I thought doing the same to you would help."

She's silent at my words. Then, she laughs again—it's meant to sound menacing, but there's a hysterical quality to it. "I am not your sister, Dacian."

I push myself to a standing position, dusting myself off as I turn my back to her. "Don't I fucking know it," I mutter, and give the fire a wide berth, until I find a tree I can lean against.

I close my eyes, willing sleep to come, but instead find my thoughts focused on one thing alone. Why did it feel so good, having her in my arms—like she just fit?

The next day is impossibly awkward. And that voice keeps whispering to me. *She doesn't know any better. Give her a chance.*

Despite my own mental turmoil around that creature using my dad's features to trap me, I'd give her a chance, if she'd let me. I tend to give people chance after chance, mainly because I know I'm only relying on other senses to get a feel for them, and it's not fair.

Only, Elizabeta's too busy being a thorn in my side. Revealing that vulnerability through her nightmares was a slip-up, similar to what I went through. Except I managed to hide my demons from her, whereas she...they took over while she slept. Unwittingly, she displayed a side of her to me that she probably never shows to anyone. A big part of me wonders if she even acknowledges that side to herself.

Whatever the case may be, she's determined to be back to her cool, collected self—and in so doing, she's fucking up each chance I'm tossing her way to be amicable.

"Could you move any slower, Dacian?"

Case in point.

"Perhaps, princess, it would serve you to know we're here."

"Huh?"

I can feel her incredulity. So I let out a bored sigh and contract then expand my hand, making blood flow from the previous day's wound. There's a hiss as darkness laps at my feet, doing my bidding, and unveils...

"What the hell?" Elizabeta mutters.

"Like I said. You would've passed right by it."

Silence. Then, "How did you know it was here?"

"Magic. It has a scent." And it does. I'd been sensing it the closer we got to the barrier this Oracle-type person erected around her home.

Elizabeta sniffs the air.

"Not one you'd sense," I point out. And yeah, it feels good to finally have the upper hand.

At least until a withered voice says, "Well. What do we have here?"

Elizabeta

My gaze had been fixed on the cabin in the woods the Dacian unveiled. But now it shifts to a tiny wisp of a woman who lumbers around the corner, carrying a stack of chopped wood in her arms.

I grimace. This woman is...old. "*You're* the one supposed to help us?"

"Ah, a wraith of the House of Dracul. How unappealing."

I'm in her face in a breath. Her eyes don't so much as widen, even when I growl, "Watch yourself, old woman."

"Is that what bothers you? My aging body?" She lets the chopped wood fall at her feet and circles me. By the time she's facing me again, I'm looking into a mirror—she's transformed her features into mine. "How's this, then?"

I gape at her, and she mockingly gapes back—with *my* face.

My fingers find their way to her throat. "Cut it out."

She chokes, and the illusion disappears.

Then I sense a hand on my shoulder. The Dacian. I'd almost forgotten about him. I jerk at the spark from his fingers, one I feel through the thin fabric of my dress. It's too reminiscent of last night, and how I'd woken up cocooned into the safest pairs of arms I'd ever felt. And fuck if I want to revisit how that made me feel.

"Leave her be," he mutters, seemingly unbothered. "Whatever it is she's doing to piss you off, we don't have time for it. We came here for answers, remember? Killing her won't give us any."

Reluctantly, I let the old woman go and step back.

After a beat, where she mainly focuses her gaze on the Dacian, dismissing me, she opens the door behind her and waves us inside. The cabin, if it can be called such, is one room. Jars and potions are scattered every which way and that. Scrolls, notebooks, and papers of all kinds fill every surface. In a corner, on a small table, uneaten food has molded. And the smell—musty, like it hasn't been aired in a while. Which, judging by the two windows—each of which has a latch on, and some sticky stuff around it—is accurate.

A larger table is filled to the brim with more books, more old parchments, maps, and small bowls holding powdery substances. Another wall holds a hearth, with the remnants of a dead fire within. The rest of the surfaces have shelves of all sizes, none that match. And in another corner, as though forgotten, is a small bed with what looks like a lumpy mattress.

I stop in the middle and turn to her. "We're pressed for time, witch."

"Then ask your question and be on your way."

I glance at the Dacian expectantly, only to realize he must be waiting for me to start. "Tell her," I say instead.

He wastes no breath. "My sister and I are Dacians. We got embroiled in a curse meant for the Dracul heirs, and she's now a conduit—we think—to Zalmoxis, the god of death."

"Ah...interesting. Very interesting, indeed. The banished dark god."

"Banished for what?"

She arches an eyebrow at me. Guess my words carried too much bite for her liking. "That's not what you came here to ask me, is it?"

"No," the Dacian says. "A friend told us you could help. That you could tell us how to free my sister of his clutches. So we can win."

"And what is it you mean by winning?"

"Kill the god, of course," I butt in.

"Would that end your troubles, vampir?"

"Of course it would. His curse would be broken."

"And you know that for a fact?"

I open my mouth for another snippy retort, then pause. We'd all assumed but...

"Are you saying that wouldn't be the case? The curse would continue, even with him dead?"

"Many factors to consider, vampir. Too many to give an accurate answer."

I take a step closer and lower my tone. "Try."

She looks at me, and I swear in the space of a breath, that weakness from before hits me again. I try to pretend like it doesn't, to maintain my glare, but I'm soon swaying on my feet and stumbling into the table, barely able to hold myself up.

Ștefan moves toward the noise. "Elizabeta?"

"I'm fine!" My glare levels on the witch. "Are you doing this?"

"I am not. Your curse is interesting, but I am a simple old woman. I do not have the power to mess with it."

Somehow, I doubt that. But I've already alienated her with my anger. Before I can figure out something else, Ștefan steps until he's close to her. Towering over her. The scent of his blood fills the air. Soon after, the shadows in the corners move to his feet, and crawl over the old woman. She stumbles backward, but they hold her in place.

"Tell us something, old woman," Ștefan says in a rough voice. "I have been kind, I have been patient. But I swore to my sister I would get her answers, and protect her. And I'm not about to break that promise. Do you understand?"

"I do," she whispers, oddly subdued. "Tell them off. And I will give you the first answers."

"*All* the answers. Not just the first."

"Of course."

Something in her tone hits me as false, but I say nothing. Instead, I keep an eye on her, since he can't. And let him do his thing. The darkness disappears, and the woman steps to a wall.

"If your sister is a conduit, the only way to use her would be to get into Zalmoxis' mind and find out how he created the curse. What he used. Then, you could undo it by doing the exact opposite. Or so the story goes... Curses by gods are usually imbued by their essence, something that makes them *them*, and powers up the curse. Keeps it going, even after their death."

"Fuck," Ștefan mutters.

"But you could test something," she says. "Your vampir companion is affected by the curse. I have just seen it take hold. Your magic, powered by Zalmoxis, should mute the effects of the curse. Temporarily."

I can get rid of this stupid ass weakness that keeps hitting me? "How?"

"By feeding your magic into her. Only a little is required, but it should be enough to do the trick."

I hate to seem hopeful, and even more so to give this old hag power over me by showing her as much, but there's a burning fact I can't help voicing. "My brother, who has the same curse, says only vampir blood sated his weakness."

"Unsurprising. It comes from the same spot as Zalmoxis' magic, no?"

I narrow my eyes. "You're not saying something. What is it?"

"Nothing at all… Now, I need to get something for the other part of your answer."

We both move in her way at the same time. "I don't think so, witch."

"Can you truly stop me?" She lifts a vial of something—blood?—and opens it. Whispers something into it.

Ștefan, by my side, drops to his knees, clutching his head and screaming. I move toward her, fingers splayed and nails clenched, ready for her throat—but my weakness grows and I trip over my own feet, bumping into a chair. My knees wobble and it takes every single bit of willpower to keep myself standing.

"I will see you when I return," she says, and walks around us both, disappearing through the open door.

Motherfucker.

Ștefan

Should've known this wouldn't be easy. This woman's entire abode is filled with magic of all kinds, tugging on my senses here and there. But whatever she did, I can't think past this damn headache.

"Dacian?" Elizabeta kneels by my side, her thigh brushing mine. "Ștefan. What is it? What did that witch do?"

"Mind spell…of some sort. I need…" I clench my teeth, trying to push past the pain.

"Would blood help?"

"Mine, yes. My...athame."

She reaches for my wrist, and the athame blade in the wrist cuff. I'm not surprised she realized it where it was.

"How much?" she asks.

"A two-inch cut, but not too deep." I'll need more than a prick of blood to undo this.

The blade slashes in my palm, and I let out a hiss. Then the blood flows to the surface, and I tug on the magic. It answers—thank *fuck*—and absorbs whatever the witch did, until I can breathe without the pain anymore.

"That fucking hag," Elizabeta hisses, and it sounds like she's still crouching in front of me. Her scent invades my nostrils, a balm that soothes the last of the ache. "When I get my hands on her—"

"She's testing us," I mutter, cutting her off.

Elizabeta's quiet for a long moment. "Go on."

"The woods, the..." I pause, trying to choose my words carefully. "You're not the only one who the woods fucked with. Whatever's around here, it sparked that nightmare you had. But it also screwed with me and—"

It's then I become aware of something else. Someone else approaching. "We've got company."

Elizabeta's hand reaches for my shoulder, then slides to my elbow. Instead of what I'd expected—that she'd grip me hard enough to draw blood, only so I could finish what I was saying—she helps me to my feet.

My expression must show surprise, as she says, "We'll finish this conversation later. But if someone's coming, we can't appear weak. Whoever they are, they could just as easily be foes."

I nod. And with magic still at hand, I focus on the direction of the door. “Stand back.” Then let a blast of magic blow it open.

Elizabeta, by my side, asks in her most imperious voice, “Who the fuck are you?”

There’s a long silence, then a male voice, gruff, with some kind of accent, says, “I’ve heard of your kind. Undead.”

“Spare me,” Elizabeta says, her tone every bit the princess she is. “Again, who the fuck are you?”

Another voice—female, this time—says, “How about you answer that?”

There’s a longer silence, filled with tension. I use some of the magic to quickly scan them–there’s a sense of something more about them. Something I’ve never encountered before in supernatural beings. But before I can finish, the woman speaks again.

“Are you the woman living in this cabin?”

Chapter 9

Elizabeta

Worst damn moment for my weakness to hit me as it has. I focus on appearing as imposing and bitchy as I can, but something about this redheaded female facing off against me, and the gruff man by her side, tells me we're heading into yet another world of trouble. Maybe it's the dark glare he's leveling on me, or the bow and arrow she's aiming straight for where my heart would be if I were alive.

Or maybe I'm just damn tired of this idiotic quest.

Cursing Nico to all the gods and beyond, I push out my hip and glare at her. "And if I am, what's it to you?"

Ștefan shifts behind me, as though to join me. Did he sense something?

Then the woman steps forward. I open my arms wide, blocking the entrance to the cabin.

Her annoyed green gaze meets mine. “We don’t have time to waste,” she hisses. “So either answer my question, or I’ll—”

“What, poke me with the little arrow?” I sneer at her weapon. “Try it.”

The man behind her moves in, chest puffed out like a peacock. “Don’t bother,” he says. “Mortal folklore says you’re all gone from this realm. What are you doing here?”

The woman glances at him cluelessly, clearly not making any sense of his words. Was she dropped on her head too many times as a child?

Slowly, the man explains, “She’s a vampir. They’re dead mortals, who live off the blood of other living mortals.” Lower still, he adds, “Short of using your powers, nothing else will scare her off. And that’s not a risk we can afford, after the woods.”

As if I can’t hear him. What powers, though? And should I be worried?

His words seem to do the trick as the woman nods and turns her attention back to me.

“He’s right, you know,” I smirk. “Nothing you do or threaten will scare me.”

Behind me, Ştefan clears his throat. “I’m Ştefan, a Dacian warlock,” he says, in a voice as smooth as honey. “This is my companion, Elizabeta Ţepeş, of the House of Dracul. We’re here seeking—”

I whirl on him. Is he purposefully trying to weaken us by disclosing information? “Would you shut *the fuck up*? I want to hear what *they’re* here for.”

The damage is done. His little caveat gave the woman a stupid sense of safety. She arches an eyebrow at me. "You first."

Moments pass as we stare at each other. My annoyance rises, both at these intruders, at the stupid old hag, and at Ștefan. And it seems I'm not alone, as the woman narrows her eyes on me.

Behind me, Ștefan lets out a small noise—half gasp, half grunt.

I roll my eyes and turn to him, hand on my hip. "What is it now, Dacian?"

He grabs my wrist with unerring accuracy and yanks me inside the cabin, his expression tense. Behind us, with the way now clear, the other two enter.

The woman takes one look at the mess surrounding us and says, "Did you do this? Because I swear if—"

I snarl her way, my fangs protruding and wanting a bite. Weakness be damned. But Ștefan tugs on my wrist again. I jerk it out of his grip, and inch closer, dropping my voice so it's out of their earshot.

"You better have a fucking good reason for manhandling me."

"I thought you liked manhandling." I gape at him in shock, and as if realizing what he said, he pinches the bridge of his nose and lets out an exasperated breath. "There's something about them. You shouldn't antagonize them."

"Seriously? I'm the heir to the House of Dracul, do you really think—"

Something they're saying dawns on me. Or rather, that the male just said. *I don't see the witch.*

Ștefan, too, seems to have heard it. He angles his body toward them once more. To me, he whispers, "Shut up and let me do the talking for once." While I fume at his command, he adds louder, "You're here seeking the Oracle? But how did you bypass the payment?"

"Payment?" the man asks.

I hold back another smirk. At least one of them is easily plied for information.

His words make me wonder, though. I wasn't required to *pay* anything. I've been prancing around these woods without much of a care. Ștefan, though, speaks as if from experience. Could his payment be tied to what Daniel was trying to tell me, when we got separated in the woods?

Why do I even care? It's his sister we're here to save, so if only his payment is required, then so much the better for me.

I draw my attention back to what Ștefan is saying to the newcomers.

"So you don't know—"

Something shifts in the air once more. And before I can say more, Ștefan grabs my elbow and pulls me behind him abruptly. I curse at him, but he ignores me and addresses the others. "As you must know, this is the cabin of the Hoia Baciu Oracle. She always asks for payment, and it is rumored the woods help her in collecting it. I'm not sure how or why you were able to get this far in without providing it, but there must be a reason." He pauses, then adds, "She left, shortly after we arrived. My sister is sick and the Oracle alone can provide her help." He takes another deep breath, and a shudder wrecks his large body. "But you seem like you need it more. We will return later."

"No, we won't, I—" I move fast, blurring from behind him, to the woman. "I'm not moving until that old hag returns. I don't take kindly to people playing games on my territory."

"Your territory?" She snorts, crossing the last bit of distance until she's right in front of me. "Don't make me laugh. This entire realm belongs to—"

In a weirdly similar move to Ştefan, the man with her tugs on her, inserting himself between us until he forces me to take a half-step back. "How about you two leave?"

I grit my teeth. "I said *I'm not*."

"Elizabeta."

I turn to Ştefan. "Listen, Dacian. You may take it lying down, but I don't back away from a fight."

He bristles. "Need I remind you that you're the one who scared the Oracle away?"

"I didn't!"

"Oi!" The man yells, slamming his palm on the table.

In his anger, there's a bit of an accent that slips through—Irish, if I'm not mistaken. And more to the point... I tilt my nose up in the air, catching a faint whiff of wet dog. Interesting. As if we didn't have enough issues with the vârcolaci already.

"Get the feck out of here, before I make you."

I snarl. "I'm not going to take a mutt's orders—"

His rough threat, almost a growl, seems to be the deciding factor for Ştefan. "We're leaving, don't worry."

Something fills the air then—blood, his damn magic again—and the other man flares his nostrils by the woman's side. Before I can tackle either of them, I freeze. Unable to move my limbs. Panic flares in my mind, ensnaring it in a foggy web, but I can't do anything. Ştefan picks me up by the waist, tosses me over his shoulder, and walks away.

My last view is of the other two's flabbergasted expressions as I'm being taken away. Then, I give in to the panic in my body.

Ştefan

I move as fast as I can, putting distance between us and the other two, and disappearing into the woods. I know what I felt. Those two are trouble. Whether the old hag set us up or not, I don't know. But I'll be damned if I have a Dracul heir be harmed on my watch.

Even if she drives me crazy with her attitude.

I stop running once we're deep enough in the woods, by my judgment. My finger is still bleeding heavily, darkness nipping at my heels. But I can sense the burden of the spell weighing on me, like an actual boulder of black magic. It's a good thing Silviana is nowhere near me, as I'm pretty sure the combination of all these factors—the strangers, Elizabeta, my magic—would be enough to draw Zalmoxis out.

With one hand, I hold Elizabeta balanced over my shoulder. I try not to focus on which part of her body is brushing against mine, but what I can't ignore is her scent enveloping me, to the point of making me dizzy.

I come to a full stop and crouch to the ground, using my free hand to feel around. Soft earth, some leaves. Good enough.

Gently, I settle Elizabeta on the ground. My hand touches her hair. I allow myself a moment of feeling its texture—like silk passing through my fingers—then pull back and move a few feet away. Far from her ocean breeze scent. The spell won't let off until I allow it, so I'm safe, for now. But there's no doubt in my mind she'll be trying to strangle me the moment she's free.

I cast about for some wood, and place it in what I hope is a circle, lighting it up. She doesn't need the fire, but it's the least I could do.

Then I pull out my phone and speed-dial Silviana. She answers on the second ring.

"Fane!"

"I'm fine. We're both fine. We made it to the Oracle."

Little by little, I fill her in, leaving out the bit about the creature with our dad's features. Just because I'm haunted by that, doesn't mean she needs to be, too. Instead, I focus on the arrival of the two visitors, and having to immobilize Elizabeta.

"Oh, no," Silviana says at this.

"What?"

"Fane... That's the worst thing you could've done."

"I realize that. But she was about to rip them apart. I had no choice."

"No, you don't understand."

"I mean, the curse might weaken her, but the Oracle said I could use my magic to fuel her up. Whatever that means."

"No, Fane—listen—*stop*!"

I pause midway through another sentence. Her tone is beyond panicked right now.

"Elizabeta was imprisoned, years ago. Tortured by hunters."

I take a deep breath. "I know. The stafie protecting her—Daniel—told me."

My sister seems momentarily stunned. "You...you spoke with him?"

"Da. Last night. He... Elizabeta was having a nightmare, and needed comfort."

Silviana's voice drops an octave. "Vlad told me she still gets those every now and again. But Fane, you don't understand. She wasn't just imprisoned. She was...tied up. At their mercy for their sick experiments on how far they could hurt a vampir. Day in and day out, night in and night out, she couldn't move. They bound her with magicked ties that couldn't be broken, and tore at her flesh, tried to tear at her mind." Her voice shakes, as though she's crying. "You need to let her go right now. I may not like her, but I don't want her to go through whatever hell she's mentally reliving right now."

Her words are like ice in my veins. I drop the phone, turning in the direction of where I left the vampir. Shit. I made a horrible mistake. And it probably fucked whatever thin thread of alliance has established between us.

Elizabeta

When I think about being captured, and being *held* captive, I always remember the dark woods first. The fierce hunger for blood coursing through my veins like blazing fire. I remember it was a full moon, and I'd left my siblings. Daniel had asked to come with me, as he always did in those days, but I didn't trust myself to be alone with him when I was feeling as I was.

And then it all went wrong, in the most subtle of ways.

When I ran across a hiker with a broken ankle, I didn't think twice about it. I put on my charm, not even bothering to turn on the glamour. The way his eyes sized me up—my knee-length leather boots, burgundy velvet dress that hugged all my curves, hair down and cascading in waves over my back... I had him spelled. Or so I thought.

"Lost, handsome?" I asked in a beguiling tone.

"Jesus fuck," he whispered back. "Where did you come from?"

I laughed—I remember that, how arrogant I'd been. Laughing, when in the midst of the woods, they were all rallying to capture me. How stupid I was. How ignorant. And how harshly I paid for it all.

In the moment though, I sashayed over to him, kneeling in front of him. I ran my hand over his trouser-covered leg, and stopped at the ankle. "That's a nasty break, handsome. I live just around here. Want me to take care of it?"

He hesitated. I remember glancing up, thinking he was adorable in the way he did so. Little did I know, my touch on his leg had confirmed what I was—he could feel my icy fingers even through the fabricl. And while I was busy inhaling the scent of his blood, he was signaling the others over my head. He would take great pleasure in telling me all about it later.

"I... Da, I would appreciate that. Thank you."

I smiled up at him and made to stand. But his hands shot out, grasping my shoulders before I could straighten. "Not so fast, vampir."

The kind face morphed in front of my eyes into that of a monster. Snarling lips and narrowed eyes, filled with coldness and malice. I hissed and tried to jerk out of his grip, but already I could feel a burning sensation spreading across the areas of my skin he was touching. By the time I managed to move out of his grip, my flesh was boiling, bubbling, melting off my bones, and onto my dress.

"What—who the fuck—"

He laughed. I remember that, too, how chilly he sounded. "We're your worst nightmare, child of Dracul."

Then the others emerged, surrounding me. Six in total, holding in their hands a net—like a fishing net. I tried to get to my feet, to blur away, but it was no use. Whatever his hands had been coated in was strong—powerful enough to not only numb me, but fully destabilize me.

"Hurry," he said to the others. "The mixture won't hold as long as the vervain in the net. Let's capture her and get out of here while we can. Before she somehow alerts the others."

While I was busy trying to crawl away, they tossed the fishing net over me. And when the burning started anew everywhere the rope touched me, I screamed—I remember that, too. How loud I screamed, until one of them whacked me over the head, and I fell to the ground, unconscious.

When I woke up, minutes or hours later, I was tied up on a table of sorts—it felt like one, with a hard surface. I didn't know at the time how familiar I'd become with that table. Vervain-coated ropes held my wrists bound in a T shape, and my ankles were spread, bound as well. As was my neck, and my forehead. The dress had been left on me, surprisingly. It wouldn't be until much later that they would remove it, and even then, only to cut and slash and poke at my skin. They did many things, the hunters, but they never once tried to rape me. Whether because they were too disgusted by me or too afraid of me despite their bravado, I'll never know. But it was at least one indignity they spared me.

I remember those ties like it was yesterday. Trying to move, and being unable to even so much as lift my head or turn it to the side without a fresh wave of burning agony cutting through me. The flesh that had melted had healed, but it wouldn't remain healed for long.

Bound as I was, I couldn't see much of the area they'd taken me to, at first. But I could hear. I remember that hopeless sensation as I heard their footsteps coming closer. I remember it as they spoke, taunting me with meaningless words. Words I soon lost track of, amid the rest of their torture devices. But what I most remember from that time is being immobilized, having my freedom taken away from me, and being at their mercy because of that.

I swore to myself I never would be tied up again. Least of all by a human. Which is why it's unacceptable that the Dacian's spell has made me lapse into memories I'd shoved away. It's unacceptable that he's made me scared. And more than anything, it's unacceptable that I cower down and take it.

I refuse. I refuse to be imprisoned again!

Fury boils within me, expelling out of me. A rage unlike any other I've felt builds and builds, and I feel the shackles fall off.

I snap out of the spell with a fury, launching myself at the Dacian before he can do anything. "You son of a bitch!"

Nails extended to gouge his eyes out, I'm ready for blood. Not just because he was able to immobilize me, but because he reminded me of *that* time in my past. When I was helpless, at the mercy of the hunters' experiments.

But no sooner do I get within reach, his dark tendrils rise from the ground, binding my wrists and my ankles, and keeping me away from him.

"Let me go!"

"No," he says calmly. "I don't think so. Calm the fuck down first, and then we'll talk."

"There's going to be no *talking*. The moment I get out of these restraints, you can be sure you'll pay for it."

"I get it. Binding you like this brought back bad memories. I'm sorry for that."

"I'll tell you what you can do with your fucking *sorry*—"

Ștefan shakes his head as if I'm a child. "You're impossible to speak with when you're like this."

"LET ME GO!"

Ştefan ignores me, simply settling back by the tree. He runs his hand over a fire, and a roast comes to life. He's soon eating, and I'm no closer to escaping these binds.

I focus my anger on them. Darkness used to listen to my father, same as it listens to Ştefan and the Dacians. Surely, I can make it listen to me? I was able to break his binds, after all.

As though guessing my thoughts, the Dacian says, "You can try, but you won't manage."

"Why not?'

"Because you're not as strong as your sire."

"I did it just a few minutes ago."

"Mm, da. But once doesn't mean you got the hang of it. And there's the small matter of the curse, seeping at your energy. Your aura is dwindling, vampir."

"Fuck. You."

He chuckles, going back to his food. His dismissiveness infuriates me more. First that woman in the hag's cabin, and now this. Why did I ever let Nico convince me to get on this hellish quest?

"Because you care for him," Daniel says.

I glare at him. "You must be so happy to see me like this."

"Not really," Ştefan answers. "But I won't have you kill me before I can help out Silviana."

"What he said." Daniel smiles. "Minus the bit about his sister. What *I* can't have is you killing a great ally. Especially if his presence is activating the curse the way I think it is."

I can only glare at him, since I can't speak the words burning my tongue. Clearly, Daniel has lost his damned mind—or Mirabela and Nico's reasoning has gotten too rooted in his head. Ştefan, an ally? Beyond his Dacian magic, I don't see much use for him. And even that's debatable. As for activating the curse...

As if reading my mind, Daniel floats closer to me. "Think about it, Liza. Haven't you noticed that since you met him during that fight in the woods, you've felt weaker? Same as Violeta when she met Marcus. Same as Vlad, with Silviana."

My eyes dart up to his, even as panic clutches my ribcage. "You're full of it."

Ștefan snorts, still thinking I'm talking to him.

Daniel shrugs. "Maybe. But I see what you don't, or what you're too stubborn to. Or..." His gaze narrows on me. I wait. "Is it that you're afraid?"

I curse against my bindings, trying to escape them once more—it's no use.

"You are. Of what?" Daniel comes closer. He reaches for me, then seems to remember he can't touch me, never can again. "What is it you fear?"

I shake my head, giving him no answer. I also turn my gaze to the ground, refusing to acknowledge him again. But I feel his gaze on me, probing. He was always able to see past me, past everything.

Ștefan

Could I have handled this better? Yes. But Elizabeta's not someone you give in to, and simp at her feet. If I do that, she'll eat me alive. Yes, I feel horrible for what I did and what it brought back for her as memories. But she doesn't need to know how bad.

When I'm done eating, I clear my throat. "I am sorry, you know. About what this brought back."

"Fuck off."

“I mean it. I know a little something about bad memories.”

There’s nothing but silence coming from her. If I’m to fix this, I need to open up with something equally vulnerable, so we’re on equal footing. Maybe that’ll temper down some of her murderous urges toward me.

“What I said before, about the woods and how they fuck with us both? You had your nightmare. I… When we got separated, I was also faced with something. The woods did something to restore my sight, only to trick me into thinking my dad was here, in the woods.” A bitter laugh escapes me. “It wasn’t him, of course. It was some kind of creature with his features. But it was intent on killing me and I… I had to kill it first.” I bow my head, hating how rough my voice is getting, but knowing I owe her this, as penance of a sort. “It killed me to see my dad’s features twisted in pain, in betrayal, even though I logically know it wasn’t him. So that haunts my sleep now, too. That’s…that’s what I wanted to tell you in the old woman’s cabin.”

Elizabeta doesn’t miss a beat. “And you think your little story is, what, enough to make me forgive you for this? Fuck *off*, Dacian.”

Well, it was worth a shot. Sighing, I set aside the remnants of my dinner and face in her direction. “If I let you go, can you please not kill me in my sleep?”

“I’ll try,” she mutters, and something in her tone sounds almost…docile.

Hmm. If it’s a play, it’s a good one.

I wait another beat, but nothing else comes. So with a twitch of my fingers, I release the dark binds. After a moment, her footsteps, crunching on leaves, head closer toward me. Then, everything goes silent. I hold my breath, waiting—

Something tackles me from the side, and I roll on the ground.

Elizabeta's on me next, straddling me, her hands around my neck. I don't know if she's trying to choke me or rip out of my throat. Her knees are on either side of my hips, pinning me down with her vampir strength.

I reach up to her waist, intending to yank her off me, but the grip around my neck tightens. *Seems she's decided on choking me, then.*

"Eliz—"

"*Don't.*" She pushes closer to me, her hair tickling my face as it falls all around us. Her breath fans my cheeks when she speaks. "Did you *seriously* think you'd get away with that bullshit? *Using magic on me*?"

She has a point. In hindsight, I don't know what possessed me to spell her, other than a desire to get as far away from the strangers as fast as I could, and to take her with me. Not my best thinking.

"I'm going to enjoy—"

My movement takes her by surprise, I kick my hips upward, sending Elizabeta off-balance. It's only for a moment—her centuries of grappling with creatures of all types have clearly paid off on her reflexes—but it's enough. I throw my weight over her, knowing her body is more than strong enough to take it.

The air shifts to my left and I lift my arm in time to block her strike. I then use the momentum to grip that same hand and pin it to the ground, high above her head.

"Get *off* me!" Elizabeta mutters, her anger making her voice nearly vibrate.

I can't help a small smirk. "You started this, princess."

"Stop calling me that!"

She makes the mistake of trying to strike with her other hand, but again, I sense the shift in the air and block it—albeit a bit later this time. Her nails gauge some of the skin off my neck, but nothing too deep. Just enough that I feel the blood trailing down my neck.

Elizabeta stills underneath me, oddly docile. I'm not fooled in the least as I pin the other hand above her head, lowering my body to hers. Even while the air crackles with our anger at each other, something about this position feels too damn intimate. Maybe it's the way she's arching into me, trying to throw me off her same as I did with her. Maybe it's the fact that this close up, her scent is even more intoxicating than before, ensnaring my senses in a seductive tango, binding me tighter than the spell I'd used on her…yet I find I have no desire to escape.

"Are you done?" I ask, my voice oddly hoarse.

It's not until I do so that I realize I've leaned down so far, her lips are a hair's breadth away from mine. When she expels a sigh, they brush against mine. It's not a kiss, not really, but the tiny touch is enough to electrify me—and distract me. I jerk back, my grip loosening over her hands for a brief second.

With a growl and a swift thrust of her hips, Elizabeta propels me off her, and I go rolling, rolling, rolling across the ground. By the time I stop, I don't get a chance to get my bearings. She's back on me, straddling me once more.

This time, she's not trying to choke me. Instead, she tilts my head forcefully to the side, exposing the part of my neck that's bleeding. She inhales deeply, then lets out something akin to a moan. The sound is enough to make my body tighten, and my cock rise to attention.

Elizabeta chuckles and moves her lips to my neck. If I thought the brief touch of her lips was electrifying, it's nothing compared to when she swipes her tongue over—I'm guessing—the blood running down my neck. "Mm, you sure do taste good, Dacian. Maybe I'll have a bit of a drink, hmm?"

"Do your worst, princess. If you kill me, this quest is as good as done for, and it's not just my sister who'll suffer for it."

She freezes, as though pondering my words. The silence and immobility, her body pressed to mine, is enough to fry whatever part of my brain is linked to my cock, because instead of pushing her away, I reach for her waist once more. And this time, I dig my fingers into the folds of her dress, anchoring her to me.

Lightning crackles between us, a tangible force, drawing us inexorably closer. Her fingers loosen their death grip on my jaw, allowing me to straighten my head. Tension is hot and heavy in the air, filled with both desire and defiance—in her, in me, in us both. I don't know how to label it, other than the type of desire mingled with a lust that has no logic. It's nothing I've felt before with the few women I dated. Probably why I never went further than kisses and some heavy petting, unlike most men I know.

But Elizabeta...she rouses some primal part of me that until now was buried deep. With every clash of our wills, she tugs at the strings of my fiber, unraveling me. I'm not too sure what she'll find when she gets all the way underneath.

I take a deep breath, and move one of my hands up her back, her neck, and around it, until I'm cupping her jaw. And because I *really* have a death wish, I let my thumb trace the flesh below her bottom lip, then the lip itself.

Elizabeta's deathly still throughout this, and I'm not sure whether that means she's two seconds away from actually killing me this time, or whether she's still thinking over my words.

Time to talk before she changes her mind and lashes out again. I may be too worn out to hold her back again.

"I used my magic on you because I needed to get us out of that cabin. Those two strangers weren't just regular visitors."

That gets her moving. She shoves my hand away—my thumb still tingling from her lip—and scrambles off me. Her footsteps move farther away, crunching more leaves.

Eventually, she says, "How would you know? You couldn't see them."

I hate how steady her voice sounds. Was I alone in what I was feeling? Did that entire moment between us seriously go right over her head?

Rather than bite back with something that'll anger her again, I say, "No, but I felt their power. The woman was especially irate, probably because you kept verbally sparring with her. And she was...a force to be reckoned with."

"So, she's a witch."

"No. Something stronger."

A beat later, "Well, are you going to tell me? Or are you using the suspense to save your life?"

"I think she was...a goddess." Elizabeta snorts, but I press on, "What was she dressed like?"

She lets out a sigh. I bet she's rolling her eyes. "Jeans and a t-shirt, like a human. Had a bow and arrow. Red hair. Not as nice as mine."

Hmm. Elizabeta's a redhead? That explains so much.

"And the man?"

"Same." Impatience fuels her tone now, and I know I'm on borrowed time.

"I don't know about him, but the only goddess that comes to my mind who uses a bow and arrow is Artemis."

"The Greek goddess of the hunt? Are you shitting me?"

"No, I'm not. It's her, it's got to be. That kind of power doesn't just ooze out of a regular human, Elizabeta. And the man with her, something else was wrong about him. I felt...connected."

"Only you would say that."

"You don't understand. I sensed the same hum of energy that I do from my magic, from my Grand Master, but around him."

Elizabeta's quiet for a while. Then there's a breeze in front of my face, and I realize she's moved in front of me once more, though she keeps her distance. "Whatever. Gods or not, the point is if you ever use your magic on me again, I promise you're going to understand what it's like to be strung up by your balls."

I wince. "Noted. I suppose it doesn't matter that I was trying to protect us both from the gods' wrath?"

She inches closer, her hair tickling my face, her scent in my nostrils once more. "Not in the least."

Then she's gone, and I hear her settle in the distance.

Chapter 10

Elizabeta

Ștefan finally rolls onto his side, his back to me. The fire crackles, and though it's still daytime and there are no wild creatures to keep at bay, I still find the sound soothing. Something moves in the trees. A raven croaks in the distance. It's peaceful.

And I hate every moment of it.

I hate that he's asleep, like he didn't feel that crackling tension between us. I hate that he got to me with just some words and a touch—a touch I felt all the way to my core. And I fucking *hate* that when I responded with indifference, he let me get away with it.

I glance at him again, half-debating on rousing him to...what?

I'm not about to sleep with him. That's crossing a line, even for me. But I could feed on him. His blood sure smelled freaking fantastic, like the best of port wines.

"Crazy man." Daniel flickers next to me, his gaze on Ștefan. "Trusting you, his back to you like that? Wow."

I tear my eyes from Ștefan, equally perplexed. Keeping my voice low, I mutter, "Pretty sure he's got his magic at the ready."

"Mm. That *would* make sense. Except I sense nothing."

I'm loath to admit I don't, either. Especially as Ștefan's magic is activated by blood, and there's no way I'd miss the scent of it in the air. Not after what happened before.

Instead of answering that, I narrow my eyes on him. "What do you want, Daniel?" More to the point, how much did he see of what happened?

"To check on you."

He floats closer, kneeling next to me. He lifts his hand as if to touch me. I even lean into it. But that's all we'll ever get. As a stafie, he's as intangible as a ghost. And unattainable.

"I know the spell he did brought back memories. You okay?"

Screaming. Pulling against the restraints. The feel of blood trickling down my sides, pooling under the table I'm bound to...

"I'm fine."

His eyes shine with concern. "Liza..."

"I'm fine!"

Ștefan snorts in his sleep, jerks on the ground.

I lower my voice. "I'm *fine*."

Daniel's quiet for a long moment. Then he surprises me. "I remember what it was like holding you, you know? After that. We both went through hell at those fuckers' hands." He glances down.

"And I enjoyed every bit of ripping their heads off after. To avenge you, and me. No matter what the cost to my soul."

"You always were concerned about that."

He glances away, his features pensive. "You never wonder, Liza? Where we go, after tainting our souls like this?"

"No." A lie. I've wondered sometimes.

"Well, I do." A rueful smile. "Perhaps it's why I'm still lingering around, instead of moving on."

This reminds me too much of our conversations, back when he was alive, and the thought is like a dagger to my gut. I can't do this. Can't fall back into the routine with him, because I always end up falling into thinking I'll be okay, and then I'm not. Not when I can't have him.

My gaze flicks to the Dacian again. *Nor can I have him. And the fact I'm even considering it is a sign this fucking curse is eating at my brain.*

I turn my back to him, and Ştefan. "I should sleep."

Daniel hovers some more, then seems to understand I need space, and drops it. "I'll keep watch."

I don't sleep much. Not that I need to. Would've been nice to, though, especially as that weakness is at the back of my head, like a nagging fly. And when I roll over, Daniel is quiet, observing me. I try to ignore the pang in my heart.

As soon as Ştefan wakes he suggests we head back to the old hag's cabin. The sun is higher in the sky now; tall trees block its rays, giving us—mainly, me—some much-needed shade. I don't know if it's the light, even minimal as it is, or the slow human walk, but annoyance has me clenching my jaw tightly. To make matters worse, Ștefan's acting professional and aloof while we trudge on, like last night never happened.

I'm not about to bring it up or pretend like it was more than it actually was. Fuck. That.

"We can keep our distance in case the gods are still there," he says, "but if they're not, perhaps we can get some answers."

"Sure."

By my side, Daniel snorts. "You're awfully accommodating today, Liza. Softening up toward him?"

I throw him a *shut it* glare. Just because I'm not ripping his head off and I'm occasionally calling him by his name doesn't mean I'm anywhere near accommodating.

We reach the old hag's cabin within the hour. No sign of the visitors, which I'm weirdly put off by. I would've loved a chance to tell Artemis—if Ștefan is even right—off.

"Sometimes I think you've got a death wish," Daniel whispers by my side.

I throw him a look. Then I raise my hand to knock on the wooden door. It swings open in front of me, revealing the old hag. No sign of the other two.

The hag, for her part, is sipping a glass of wine, looking mighty pleased with herself. "Welcome back, heiress."

A snort escapes me. "If you're trying to cull favor with me, you're failing already."

Her gaze shifts to Ștefan as he enters. Smartly, he decides to stay by the door to block a second escape attempt.

"I realize we came in a bit too strongly," he says. "And perhaps it's why you felt the need to leave us to wrestle with the gods." No acknowledgment follows from her. He doesn't seem fazed, though. "May we begin anew?"

Satisfaction rolls across her features, like a cat who's tasted milk. Or its prey's blood. "We may, Dacian. I do apologize for my abrupt departure before. I didn't realize you and Liviu were so close."

I stiffen, and notice Ștefan does, too. I hate how much she knows about us.

"You seem to have us at a disadvantage," he says before I can. "Knowing so much about us, yet we know so little."

"Really? I thought your people told you plenty, given your Grand Master and I have a long-standing...arrangement."

I jerk my gaze to him, getting ready to yell. Daniel's already telling me, "Wait, Liza." But it's Ștefan's stunned expression that stops me mid-shout. Barely. "You didn't know?" I ask instead.

"Of course not." A muscle ticks in his jaw. There's something else under his expression, something akin to panic, or perhaps anger. But before I can take a closer look, he schools his features and says, "So, *you're* the Oracle he comes to."

"Indeed."

"That puts a new spin on things."

Definitely does. I've always found the Dacians seemed oddly in tune with my siblings' actions and *re*actions to their machinations. Almost as if they could see it all before it came to pass. Was that because of this old hag? If so, it'd be easy enough to wring her neck...

"Liza."

I clench my jaw at the admonition in Daniel's tone. Once upon a time, he would've joined me in hunts, much like Alex. Nowadays, he seems much too focused on saving my soul. As if that's even possible.

I shift my attention to Ştefan once more. He leans back against the wood of the door, his expression smooth. At his poker face, I feel a hint of the first admiration for him. Quickly stifled, because *he's still a human.*

"And tell me, old hag... What payment do you usually extract from Liviu?"

"A little here, a little there." Her eyes glint with maliciousness. "I have my ways."

"So long as you understand our query is apart from anything he comes to you with." He pauses. "We would appreciate some discretion."

"Of course, of course." She shuffles to a worn-out sink and pours herself some water, then turns back to us. "Your price will not be his, regardless. You are much too entertaining visitors, after all."

Something changes in her expression, something I don't like at all. So I decide I've been quiet for way too long.

"Listen, babă. We're here for answers, so whatever your price, just speak it already."

She looks at me, then dismisses me, seemingly finding Ştefan more interesting. "Very well. You seek more information about Zalmoxis and how to save your sister from his clutches, while also beating him? There is a price, yes. Something you can get for me. A ring. It is located in a monastery a bit out of your way... Or rather, a castle that now plays a monastic role. But it would help me so *very much* if you could seek it."

"That should not be a problem," Ştefan says.

"Hang on a second. Why can't *you* go get it?" I ask her.

"Because I am unfortunately banned from the premises." She says this as though she doesn't give a damn, but the pursing of her lips tells me otherwise.

"She's not telling you the full truth," Daniel mutters.

I give him a *Ya think?* look and that seems to catch her attention. Fuck. I'm slipping.

Unaware of the tension between us, Ştefan clears his throat. "Like I said, it should not be a problem. Assuming you *will* then give me the information that'll help Silviana out."

"Yes, yes. You shall get your answers—in so far as the information you require does not pertain to the curse afflicting the Dracul line. Nothing can release her from that except death." The old hag taps her chin. "I must admit, I am curious. How, pray tell, did your sister ever get ensnared by Zalmoxis?"

Ştefan hesitates, trying to figure out a politically correct way of saying it without tossing his sister under a bus.

I have no such qualms. "Because she was an idiot and opened a portal to Zalmoxis."

"In order to help *your* brother!" Ştefan snaps.

"My brother would've been fine without her help."

Waves of anger roll off him, and I'm perversely happy at having gotten under his skin.

Then he takes a deep breath, and focuses back on the hag. "Do I have your word, Oracle?"

I bristle at his dismissal. Maybe Daniel is right, and I *have* gotten too accommodating.

"Da," the old hag says. "Bring me the ring first." Then she turns to me. "As for you, your price is your blood."

I narrow my eyes on her. "Like fuck."

"Non-negotiable."

"Don't do it, Liza," Daniel says. "I've got a bad feeling about her. And she already took something from you both--or rather, from Ștefan. A second payment should not be needed, since this is only one quest."

It clicks, then. How I found Ștefan in the woods, on his knees. I was right in my assumption. That was her doing.

"You already took a price from him, didn't you?" I narrow my eyes on her. "Whatever you did in the woods. So how come we have to get a ring from some monastery next? And why should I give you yet another payment in addition to all that?"

She takes a sip of her water, eyes glittering. "The woods extract a price from any living person who passes their boundary. That is not my doing."

"Isn't it?" Ștefan mutters. Considering what the zmeu told us—that these are *her* woods—I'm tempted to agree.

She ignores him, leveling her eerie stare on me. "Seeking the ring is the Dacian's price. Yours is your blood."

"But I'm on the same quest as him."

"Are you?" Her gaze holds mine for a moment, then shifts to the side—focused straight on Daniel. She holds his stare until he's near shaking by my side. With anger or panic, I'm not sure. No one's ever seen him, at least until Silviana did. But not even that was enough to shake him as this does. Then the hag meets my gaze again and smirks.

I glance at Daniel, and read the panic in his eyes.

"Don't," he says. "Not for me. It's not worth it."

I wish I could ask him what I want. Whether she's promising to release him...or tell me how to...it's an answer I need. It's one I've wrestled with for many decades. But am I truly ready for it? To lose him by my side?

I finally meet the old hag's gaze again. "You're full of shit, *Oracle.*"

"Perhaps. But if you seek information, the price must be paid."

No amount of glaring at her changes her mind.

Ştefan takes a step in my direction. Then another. He stops right by my side and bends his massive frame, his lips near the top of my head. He hesitates, then says, "I'm not sure what it is you'd like answering from her, but be careful. We both know she's an unusual person."

"Listen to him, please," Daniel pleads.

I look up at Ştefan. Up close, I can smell his male scent, feel the heat of his body. My gaze is drawn to the pulse beating on his sturdy neck. It's with great effort that I force myself to focus on the task at hand.

I could deny the hag. Better yet, I could rip her head off—but then this whole thing would've been a waste. And I'd never know about Daniel.

Ugh.

Rolling my eyes, I move away from Ştefan, grab a knife from her table, and slice a cut into my palm.

"Here you go, babă." I narrow my eyes on her. "Don't get any fucking ideas."

She smiles. "Never would, my dear." She waves her fingers in the air in a toodle-oo type gesture, and the droplets of blood that would've fallen to her worn wooden floor float to her instead, and land in a vial she produces from who knows where. The glint of satisfaction in her eyes makes my uneasiness grow.

Then she turns to Ștefan. "Now, for the ring. You will find it at Corvins' Castle."

I jerk back, physically, at the name. Her knowing eyes land on me, and a curse escapes me.

"What's wrong?" Ștefan asks.

"I believe your companion is very well acquainted with that castle. Are you not, heiress?"

I am. Too fucking well.

Ștefan

Elizabeta's aura flares dark next to me. The mention of the castle's name seems to have sparked something in her, and it's a dangerous reaction.

"It's where she was held and tortured," the male voice from the ball whispers in my ear. "And her father was imprisoned there."

The silence grows and grows, so I finally interrupt it. "Someone care to explain?"

There's a cackle to my right, and the wood witch says, "Well, it depends. I'm only aware of the *official* story. Shall I tell him, heiress?" When Elizabeta doesn't answer, she goes on, "Corvins' Castle has a bit of a history, you could say. Vlad Țepeș, your companion's sire, was imprisoned there for quite a while. Humans believe it's where he went insane, and started to crave blood. Of course, no one is aware of the full story."

"Which is what, exactly?"

Elizabeta clears her throat. Her tone, when she speaks, is

smooth—with an underlying current of murderous intent. "Father was imprisoned there after fighting the Ottomans, captured by Emperor Corvinus. It was a coup, nothing more, with Corvinus saying Transylvania no longer wanted Father as its leader—a lie most believed. A few short years later, Corvinus came back groveling. The Ottomans were gaining ground, now that they know they had no one left to fear. So Corvinus offered Father a choice—marriage with a Catholic princess, his own widowed daughter, in exchange for being reinstated as voivode of Transylvania. Father reluctantly accepted and... was excommunicated by the Orthodox Church as a result. He hated his second marriage, forced upon him while he still grieved his first wife. You know the rest of that story. But when he was imprisoned, at Corvins' Castle, it's said a voice drove him to the brink of insanity. That it's where his powers...darkened. That when he gave in to it, he became the ruthless undead leader the world knows now."

"Da, indeed," the old hag says. "And that voice was none other than Zalmoxis himself, eager to exact revenge for his daughter's death. Țepeș believed himself saved... He thought Zalmoxis, much like him, hated what the Ottomans caused—his wife's suicide—and wanted her avenged. In his grief, he did not realize that Zalmoxis was only using him, turning him into a vampir, even while he built a curse within this *gift* he gave him." She cackles some more. "It was the perfect undoing."

Perfect isn't the word I would use, but I keep my mouth shut on that topic. Instead, I point out, "None of this explains why a ring you seek would be there."

"Tsk, Dacian, that is because you are not paying attention. Țepeș was not alone in the catacombs of Corvins' Castle. At the time he was held captive there, three humans were also imprisoned. One was a metal forger, a blacksmith if you will, who worked with the purest of metals. And legend has it, he designed and crafted a ring meant for the gods themselves."

"And what is that ring supposed to do?"

"None of your concern, vampir."

"It is if I'm going to risk my life for it!"

Unease builds in my gut, even as the witch keeps talking.

"No risk involved. The three men are no longer there. Well, not physically. They were asked to dig a well, and told that freedom was within sight once they finish it. The well was meant for water...Or so they thought. Of course, the then-owners of the castle were interested in what lay underneath—a link to Zalmoxis. None know what it was, whether a temple or something else. But, sadly, the men died in captivity once the well was dug. They only left behind an inscription. *You now have water, but you don't have a heart.*"

Interesting. And ominous. "You said they're not there *physically*?" I ask.

"Da. A stafie or two, perhaps, will be your worst enemy."

"Stafii can be plenty dangerous," Elizabeta mutters. Which makes me wonder if it's because of her own personal stafie. "So this ring... Where, within the castle, is it located? And be precise, old woman. We're on a bit of a time crunch here."

"The records of its exact location were lost."

"Conveniently."

The wood witch ignores Elizabeta's scoff. "How hard can it be to find, especially for two gifted youngsters like yourselves?"

"I wouldn't call myself a *youngster,* babă." Da, I had a feeling she'd take offense to that. I can't say it bothers me—after all, we're the ones calling her *old*—so long as the Oracle gives us what we need. A loud sigh later, Elizabeta says, “Does anyone else live there, besides these three stafii?”

“Not to my knowledge. And to be quite honest, even they may have...moved on. After all, once they no longer have something to protect or seek vengeance upon, not much holds them on this plane of existence.”

The slight hesitation when she says this makes me doubt her words. But, the deal is set already.

“We’ll get your ring,” I say. “And when we return, I want the information to save my sister.”

“As you wish, Dacian.”

Without another word, I turn my back and stalk away, leaving Elizabeta to follow me.

Chapter 11

Ştefan

Elizabeta's being odd. Well, odd in the sense that she's quiet, and I've yet to see the day when this vampir keeps her mouth shut for as long as she has. Especially when she's as angry as she seems. She followed me out shortly after I departed from the old hag's cabin, and took lead on where we were going, all in resolute silence.

But there's nothing purposeful in her silence, it's more like she's lost to thoughts. Dark thoughts. I can hear her footsteps ahead of me, keeping me on track on whatever path we're following through the woods. Yes, she's *that* distracted, that she's not blurring through the trees, but actually walking.

"Whenever Silviana's pensive, talking it out helps her," I say.

A long silence answers me, interrupted by a scoff. "I'm not your sister." Though meant to be delivered with bite, the words lack the sting they carried last night.

"Fine. Then, at least tell me you have a plan to get this ring the old woman wants."

"Da, I do. Get to Corvins' Castle, barge in, retrieve the ring, and return home."

"Only one problem."

"Which is?"

"The castle will be guarded."

"How do you know?"

"I'm only guessing, is all."

"You sure that's all there is? Because if you know something..."

I let out a sigh. "I don't. It's just... Weird. Corvins' Castle is a little over an hour away from Sarmizegetusa Regia, our Dacian sacred mountain. I know the old woman said no one else lives there, but I'm getting an odd feeling."

"What, you think we might run into your people?"

"No. Maybe. I...don't know. But a renaissance fortress like Corvins' Castle, turned monastic retreat, holding something of value? A relic tied to Zalmoxis himself? It won't be *un*guarded, that's for sure."

There's a shuffle, as if Elizabeta stumbles, then, "What makes you think the ring is a relic tied to Zalmoxis?"

"The old witch said the then-owners of the castle were interested in something underneath the castle, that was meant to be a link to Zalmoxis. Your father conveniently heard the same god's voice while he was imprisoned there. And the blacksmith 'designed and crafted a ring meant for the gods themselves'? Come on, it's obvious."

There's another shuffle-like sound. I stop moving. "Are you sure you're okay?"

"I'm *fine*." This, sounding like it's said through gritted teeth. "Has it occurred to you, genius, that the witch also said the blacksmith and the other two died well before the well was dug?"

"She said they died *once* the well was dug. And historical records won't be accurate as to the time elapsed, anyway. Which means the blacksmith could've well had the time to take whatever it is he found in the well and craft something from it. Something that could be easily smuggled out by the owners who'd engaged him."

"Something like a ring." At last, it sounds like I convinced her. "Bine, let's say I believe you. Let's say the owners of the castle at the time—which would've been the same traitorous bastard who imprisoned my father—realized the ring was too dangerous to have out in the world. Maybe Father knew and said as much, maybe he had nothing to do with it. But either way, presumably the blacksmith and the other two were killed after the ring was crafted. They didn't just die on their own."

"I would assume as much."

"Hmm. And if the castle is guarded, by your kin or others, perhaps those who are there don't know what they're protecting."

"Maybe. Or maybe they do know."

More silence grows. Finally, she curses under her breath, then says, "Bine. What is *your* plan, then?"

"Let me use my magic—"

"Absolutely not."

"You don't even know what I'd planned."

"You want to use it on me."

"Well, yes."

"And I said, *absolutely not*."

"Wow, you really have trust issues."

This time, she does blur, and the resulting wind sends a flurry of wood debris in my face. "You would too, if you had the experience I did in that castle."

That's the most she's ever revealed to me about herself willingly. And as though realizing as much, she pulls back, her scent once again disappearing.

A few seconds later, she asks, "What exactly would you use?"

"A spell to cloak your vampirism and make you appear more human. Should there be someone there, them not knowing you're a vampir would give us an advantage. And the spell would ensure we gain entrance as visitors. Once everyone's asleep, we can get what we need and leave."

She doesn't sound happy when she says, "It's not a bad plan. But before I even consider it, answer me something."

"What?" I ask, somewhat warily.

"Earlier, with the old hag. When she admitted to being the same Oracle your people go to... You had a weird expression on your face. Why?"

"Does it matter?'

"If you want me to consider your plan, yes."

"Fine." I sigh and run a hand over my head. "I've been busy for weeks diving into the Grand Master's scrolls for any additional information and tools I could get my hands on to increase my knowledge of magic. I knew after we found out what we did—about our ages—that Liviu was hiding more. But even before then, I was curious."

"Hmm. Wouldn't have pegged you for a rule breaker."

I scowl. "You want me to answer you, or not?"

"Please, do go on," she says in a mocking tone.

"Digging into his stuff, I found records of meetings he's had with an Oracle. The records were in code, painstaking to break when I'm always short on time. But I gathered enough to know this Oracle had all kinds of things in her possession. One of them was an artifact, supposed to protect anyone from anything, magical or otherwise."

"And you planned to ask for it nicely?"

"No. I was going to steal it—for Silviana."

Her silence screams of surprise. I hold back a smirk that I've managed to shock her.

"Interesting... And pray tell, Dacian, why didn't you do that now and save us this whole fucking quest?"

"Because I didn't sense the presence of any such artifact. What I did sense is the old hag's power, and I'd rather not toy with her just yet. So I figure we get the ring, come back, and then I'll ask for it. And if she doesn't hand it over, I'll take it."

"Hmm."

"But there's one more thing."

"What's that?"

"Unless geography drastically changed, we'll need a car to get to Corvins' Castle. Though most of the Dacians are in Sibiu, I know Liviu has smaller groups spread out throughout the region. I wouldn't put it past him to be out engaging with all manner of vampiri clans, so if we keep going through these woods, we might stumble into my own people. And I doubt either one of us wants that."

After more grumbling, Elizabeta says, "These stupid woods got us far enough off-course that going back to where we parked would be a nightmare, especially at your slow-ass human pace. I'll call one of my siblings. They should be able to get us a second car here in record time."

Elizabeta

"Ştefan has a good plan," Daniel says as I dial Nico's number. "Better than yours."

My glare serves as my only retort, given my brother picks up after the second ring. "We found the damned witch in the woods, Nico. And no, it wasn't my idea of fun."

He's quiet for a moment. "You sound pissed."

"Da, I'm fuming. To give us the answer we seek, she's sending us on a quest. To Corvins' Castle."

His silence lengths. Stupid, he is not. Even apathetic as he's been for the last centuries, he knows that's where Father lost part of his sanity. And where I was brought to be tortured. Where Daniel came to save me, got captured himself, and got tortured in front of me. It's where Father eventually tracked us down to, and rescued us both. That place is the reason for my connection with Daniel, and for my hate toward humans—and hunters, in particular.

What Nico doesn't know is I fear that place not just because of the memories for me—but also because of Daniel's. For a stafie, tied to me, what if it becomes too much? What if being around the place he was tortured, where I was tortured, is enough to snap our connection? Not so much a calling to cross over for him, but more...a reset for me. And I'm not ready to lose him just yet. Then again, maybe that's what the witch intended. Maybe that's the 'answer' she's preparing for me, the lying cunt.

"I don't like this," Nico finally says. "If I'd known, I wouldn't have—"

"It's fine. Don't bother. We're going." I bite my lip, then reluctantly say, "Ştefan has a good plan."

"Ştefan?" He chuckles. "Not 'the human' anymore?"

"Shut up."

He sobers up. "What do you need?"

"A car. Now."

"Can't do now, but I can do it in an hour if Alex breaks all the speed limits."

At the mention of Alex, I cringe. I can't believe I'm about to say this, but I force the words out anyway. "Uh, maybe don't send Alex. Can Mira come?"

"I suppose... Why not Alex? You two had a falling out?"

"No, we didn't. But last time he annoyed the human, and I need him on my side."

"Right..."

I hang up soon after, trying not to imagine his satisfied smirk.

True to word, by the time we extricate ourselves out of the woods, a silver car pulls up, with Mira at the wheel. "Greetings." She climbs out, all legs and hair and looking way too damn perfect.

I scowl at her. "Did you happen to bring a change of clothes?"

"I figured you'd be grouchy, so yes, sister dear." She points at two transparent bags on the backseat—I can tell one holds a pair of my jeans and a blouse, and the other, presumably...

"Gee, you even thought of the human," I mutter.

"Nico did."

I roll my eyes. Of course he did.

Mira glances at Ştefan, then back at me. "So...complicated, I hear."

"You could say that," he says. "But now that we have a way of getting there, we should be in and out of the castle. Or so we hope."

Mira laughs. "And how do you plan on getting my sister in a house of God?"

"With magic."

Her laughter increases. "This, I wish I could see." Then she focuses her attention on me. "Ai grijă."

I nod, surprised she's entreating me to be careful. But before I can say anything, she's gone, disappearing in the woods just as quickly as she arrived.

I clear my throat and tap the hood of the car. "She's gone, and left us the keys."

Ştefan steps toward the car. I move to the driver's side, and by the time I'm in, he's found the door handle and slides himself in, adjusting himself in the passenger seat.

"Ready?"

"Not really, but let's do it anyway."

A little over two hours later, we arrive at Corvins' Castle. My hands grip the steering wheel tighter, to the point the metal digs into them. I've done my best to block the memories over the years, but now it's like they're raging at the walls I erected, desperate to get out and remind me of the pain.

The castle's situated on a rocky outcrop, with faded cream walls, soaring towers, and a breathtaking view of rolling hills and deep valleys stretching underneath. With the afternoon sun shining high above, it stands out like a vision from a fairy tale—or a nightmare. *My* nightmare.

Even from where we've parked, I'm struck by the massive iron gates acting as an entrance. I know that when we get closer, I'll find their surface worn and weathered. I know because they're the last thing I remember seeing here after Father took me and Daniel away.

"You all right?"

I glance at Ștefan, surprised. There's actual concern in his tone. As if... But, no. *You would too, if you had the experience I did in that castle.* All I revealed of my own time there was that I'd had an "experience." Then I remember the witch's revelations. He must think it's Father's imprisonment that's getting to me. *Let him keep thinking that. It's safer than him knowing the truth.*

"Da," I mutter. "My father...it was a long time ago."

He opens his mouth as if to say something, closes it. After a long beat of silence, he says, "That doesn't make it any less painful."

I snort. "Don't humans go by the belief that time heals everything?"

He turns his head slightly to me, his expression solemn. "It doesn't always."

There's nothing I can think of to answer. Mainly because I'm surprised he has such dark thoughts in him, too. And, all right, perhaps a little intrigued as to why. *But he's still a weak human.*

Ștefan clears his throat. "Ready?"

A mirthless laughter escapes me and I toss his words back at him. "Not really, but let's do it anyway."

I can only hope this weakness I feel tugging at me won't affect me while I'm here. Because if it does, my fate will be in the hands of a human.

I turn to him, and already he's pulling out his little witch-blade and cutting his palm. Blood oozes out, and the scent hits me more powerfully this time. I inhale deeply, licking my lips. A low sound escapes me—it takes me a moment to realize it's a moan. What the hell?

Ștefan, frozen, waits. Then he slowly says, "Don't go getting ideas."

"I'm not," I growl. "Just fucking do the spell already so I can get out of this car."

He hesitates a beat more, then finally does as I ask. Dark tendrils seem to emerge out of every crevice of the car. From my feet, the air vents, the gear shift. They unravel from it, as if fueled by Ștefan's magic, then turn toward me.

A shudder runs through me. *Too late to stop now.*

They crawl toward me, then over my skin. There's a faint hiss in my ear, followed by...quiet.

I blink. "Well?" A second later, I realize how stupid my question is. Of course he wouldn't be able to see whether it worked or not.

Ștefan opens the passenger door. "Your reflection will still show the real you, regardless. But this will fool any human eye easily."

Great. And I only have his word to go on.

Well, worst-case scenario, if this doesn't work, we'll do it my way—which means I'll be feeding soon. Nothing wrong with that.

I take advantage of Ştefan exiting the car to quickly change into the clothes Mira brought me. Then I grab his change of clothes and shove them into a small sports bag that was buried between the seats, along with a second change of clothes my dear sister brought me. Finally, I exit the car, preparing to follow him.

But the moment I'm outside of the safe confines, my eyes riveted to the castle, I freeze.

Chapter 12

Ştefan

It's with some amount of trepidation that I walk toward the castle, following the path darkness lays for me. In the distance, though I can't see it, I can feel the power underneath the monstrosity awaiting us. It's an unknown, and those are never easy to get acquainted with. Add to it that I have an unhinged vampir with me, and the odds of us surviving this are getting dimmer and dimmer if it turns out I'm right and that damned ring is protected, after all. But, whatever price I have to pay will be worth it if it guarantees Silviana's safety.

Then I realize there's no tell-tale crunch of rocks or anything behind me.

"Are you coming?" I toss over my shoulder.

Judging by the quiet behind me, Elizabeta hasn't yet moved. For all her bravado, this place really does scare her. I never thought I'd witness the day when she's afraid of something. And I hate that this side of her makes me want to protect her, fool that I am.

Finally, a whoosh of air behind me tells me she's moved. A little too quickly, though.

"Remember, the spell may make you seem human to their eyes and hide your other attributes—like your fangs—but you can't be moving this fast."

"Ugh," she splutters, then mutters something too low for my ears to pick it up. Another whoosh of air later, her hand is in mine, fingers intertwined with mine.

I jump, trying to wrench my hand away, but she holds on tight. To make matters worse, she moves closer, too, and her scent fills my nostrils. "What better way to fool them of my humanity than by attaching myself to you?"

"I'm *not* playing some sick game of pretend boyfriend-girlfriend." Not when my body is tightening as it is at her proximity, as if forgetting she's a vampir and I need to stay far away from her.

She laughs. "If only you were so lucky. Now, come on. Let's move."

With the strength only a vampir could possess, she nudges me. Her elbow digs in my side, and an oomph of pain escapes me. But, I move. And she keeps me on track toward the castle. Hmm. Maybe she has her uses, after all.

A few moments later, the air cools around us. We must be passing the gate, and it shadows the sun. Which...is all kinds of weird. Because that doesn't explain the way my every nerve-ending rises as if in threat.

"Do you feel that?" Elizabeta asks.

"Da..." I turn to the right, then left. My senses don't pick up anything else. And yet I have an odd sensation, like I'm being watched. *Not by something human.*

"I wasn't talking to you," Elizabeta snaps.

Again, there's that feeling that I'm missing something. Is it the man Silviana saw her with?

"Then who—"

"Shush. Incoming."

A moment later, the people she's seen with her vampir senses come within distance of my own senses. And then the last voice I'd expected speaks.

"Ștefan? Brother, what a surprise."

Fuck. Cezar. Of all the people...

Elizabeta

"I smell trouble," Daniel says by my side.

He's flickering in and out, as if the very barriers of this place infringe on his spirit. Which is not a good sign. Much as I complain of him annoying me sometimes with his constant attempts to resuscitate my good side, I'm nowhere near ready to be without him. But this place, it's dangerous. If it fucks with me as much as it does... What if the evil that kept us here is what eventually tears us apart, too?

And now to top it off, his assumption that trouble already courts us. I mean, for fuck's sake, we've only just arrived!

I glance at Ștefan. The Dacian's bicep is so tense under my hold, he might as well be granite. All tight muscle and immobile...tension?

My gaze shifts to the man who'd spoken—the leader, I'm guessing, given the guy behind him is very much keeping his mouth shut—then I make myself drop it before he notices. Humans act demure and shit, right?

Daniel snorts by my side. "I don't think you can pull that off, Liza."

He's right. I can't. So instead of pretending I'm something I'm not, I raise my head and glare at the newcomers. The one who'd spoken turns to me. Narrows his gaze. I let a smirk play on my lips. After all, he can't know what he's going to be letting inside this castle-turned-house-of-God. Which means I'll have the upper hand.

"Cezar," Ștefan says. "Fancy running into you here."

"You know this guy?" I ask him.

When he doesn't answer, I tug on his arm. "Helloooo?"

"Oh, so *now* you're talking to me?"

Ah. So he does bite back.

Before I can retort, Cezar chuckles. "New acquaintance, brother?"

"You can say that. And I'm not your brother."

"Are we not from the same"—he throws me a look, his lips twitching in a smirk—"family?"

Family, my ass. He doesn't want to say witch coven. At least that confirms Ștefan's spell is working, otherwise this guy wouldn't be so careful around a "human" stranger.

"We are. And yet, we're as different as two men can be—and our training styles are only the beginning."

Cezar shrugs off his barb and shoots me a smile. "And who might you be, beautiful?"

I roll my eyes—not bothering to hide it—and smile as sweetly as I can. "I'm Lizzie, Ștefan's friend. See, he saved me from a big bad wolf, and I'm ever so grateful to him."

A rumble, not unlike suppressed laughter, comes out of Ștefan, but when I glance at him, his expression is all steel. As is his tone when he says, "We were in the area, needing some shelter, and I remembered Liviu mentioning this place. Figured we could hole up here." A pause. "It seems you had the same idea."

"Da, and on his orders, too."

"Ah."

The bicep under my arm tenses even further if that's possible. If he's trying to hold himself in check he's doing a bad job, but fuck if I doesn't make him suddenly more appealing. I did not expect this kind of strength in him. And I hate that every layer he sheds only makes him more intriguing.

"*Ah,*" Cezar mimics, a malicious glint in his eye. He glances at me again, then at the sports bag in my hand. "I see." He turns to the other dude by his side. "I believe we can accommodate them, right, Trăian?"

"Yes, we should have a few rooms left."

I snort. "Corvins' Castle is always empty, is it not? Especially outside of the tourist season."

"Perhaps. But we're running a...retreat, of sorts."

Yum. Food. For some reason, his mention of more humans around here only heightens my hunger. Which is all kinds of interesting, since I'm usually not this peckish.

"Behave, Liza," Daniel says, and then he flickers completely out of sight.

Daniel! It takes every ounce of my will not to panic and to focus back on the present and what the Dacians are discussing.

"A retreat, you say? How come I wasn't told?" Ștefan asks.

"Not sure," Cezar says. "I left before you did to carry out *Liviu's* orders, and haven't seen him since."

Tension seeps out of Ștefan, as though he's relieved. But relieved at what? Did he screw up in a way that's going to bite us in the ass here?

"Either way, Trăian here will show you to your quarters."

I give the other Dacian a quick once-over. He seems barely out diapers—which, for me, is something around eighteen human years.

We follow in silence. The area between the gate and the actual entrance to the castle—I suppose it's meant to be some kind of courtyard, packed with a mosaic of architectural styles, wilted flowers, and gothic arches—is equally chilly. And no sign of Daniel throughout. *I don't like this.*

Under the guise of hugging Ștefan, I rest my head against his shoulder as we walk and mutter out of the corner of my mouth, "Anything you want to tell me, Dacian? You seemed a bit tense."

"Nothing." A beat later, he adds, "You might as well call me by my first name. They'll find it weird otherwise."

I snort—what do I care what some puny humans think?—then quickly paste on a smile when Cezar shoots me a glance over his shoulder. When he turns his back to us again, I continue in a whisper, "Bine. But only if you're upfront with me. Whatever issue's up your ass, I need to know if I'm going to protect us."

He says nothing, but when I glance up, an amused smile is playing on his lips. "So, you're my protector now?"

"Don't go getting ahead of yourself," I mutter, and fall quiet. It's only as we enter the castle that I realize he meant the jab to make me calm down. Damn him!

My annoyance deflates, replaced by panic, as soon as the walls surround us and the door is closed behind us. I have the sensation of ants crawling up my arms, and my gut clenches as if in pain. *Muscle memory, that's all it is. My body remembers the torture we endured here. Whatever happens, I can't show weakness.*

So I grit my teeth and continue to smile pleasantly. We continue following in silence, passing a few more Dacians. At some point, Cezar swerves off, disappearing down another hallway. Only the human named Trăian is left to guide us. And if the Dacian—Ştefan—finds it odd that none of his kin doesn't talk to him, he says nothing.

Around a corner, we run into a group of nuns. Their dark habits mask their forms, and they bow their heads in subservience to the men. I've never understood women who purposefully relinquish control of their lives in favor of some deity. Then again, it's not like I ever understood the concept of faith, either.

They toss a look my way, and one visibly shivers. I wonder if they can sense the unholiness around me? After all, if Nico is to be believed, Zalmoxis' power in us is dark enough that some humans—the spiritual type—might be more sensitive to it. Too bad we can only muster a fraction of what Father used to access. If we could tap into more, I wouldn't have to put up with this charade. We could've just come in and *taken* what we're after.

When another nun glances at me, I barely hold back a wolfish grin. If nothing else, the encounter distracts me from the memories tugging at my mind.

Trăian's enough ahead of us that he wouldn't hear us talking, but Ştefan seems to be equally lost in his own thoughts. When our arms brush against each other, he freezes, then—it's not quite a recoil, but he's not leaning forward to get closer to me, either.

"What's going on with you?" I ask.

"Must be the retreat," Ștefan murmurs. "But—"

Before he can finish we turn yet another corner, and Trăian stops in front of a wooden door. He pulls an old-fashioned key ring from his belt and unlocks the door, then moves out of the way and gestures for me to enter.

I step in, and stop dead at the minimalistic display greeting me. A bed with a gray sheet. A small table and a worn chair. The tiniest window ever, barely letting in some sun.

Ugh. I'm supposed to live here for a day or two?

I turn to Trăian and Ștefan. "This is... there's nothing better?'

Trăian makes a face. "This isn't the royal hotel, miss. Take it or leave it."

"We'll take it," Ștefan says. "How about you show me to my room? Within close quarters, if possible."

Trăian glances between us. "There's no—this building is sacred. Carnal liaisons—"

I'm not sure what's more entertaining. The eyes wide as saucers, or the furious red blush creeping up his neck and into his cheeks.

I burst out laughing. "Oh, you're funny. Don't worry your precious soul, I won't be touching *him*." Then I toss the sports bag at Ștefan and slam the door in their face.

I turn around, and Daniel flickers back in. Relief spreads through me. "What's going on with you? You keep coming in and out, like some bad TV."

He shakes his head, opens his mouth. "Barrier..."

"What barrier?"

The way he's in and out makes me panic some more. I can't…this better not be my fears manifesting into reality. Him leaving me. I can't deal with that. Not now, not on top of already being here.

"I need you," I whisper, low. "You alone understand what happened to me here. How it screwed me over."

For a moment, Daniel's form gets fully formed again. "I want to be here for you, Liza. But the castle… something in here. It's beyond what I expected."

"Because of the past?"

He frowns. "It's more than that. I can feel the memories, yes, but they're almost…compartmentalized. As if they happened to someone else. But I can feel *your* pain, tearing at you, and tearing *me*…"

I take a step closer. "You…what? Tearing you where, Daniel?"

"Away from you."

"No! I…no. Absolutely not."

His pity-filled expression lands on me. "I'm sorry."

"Daniel, don't you dare!" I think fast, trying to find a solution. "Go. Just…get out of here. Go in the woods outside. I'll try to find you after we dig a bit for the stupid ring."

"Watch out for—"

Before he can finish, Daniel flickers, once, and disappears.

"Daniel?"

Nothing.

Well, fuck.

My previous bravado evaporates, leaving me to shiver in the dimness of the room. Flashes of another time come to me. Of pained cries. Anguished wails. And pleading…so much pleading…for mercy.

"You're not that helpless girl anymore, Liza," I whisper to myself. "You can do this."

I almost believe it.

I pull my cell phone out and dial Alex's number. He answers on the second ring. "Liza! Where the hell are you?"

"Out on that stupid quest," I grumble. "How's everything back at the palace?"

"The usual vampir politics. Mira and Nico are on a rampage of diplomacy. I, meanwhile, decided to do things my way."

Normally, I'd be entertained by his bloody stories. But the thought of him torturing someone just hits too close to home. "How?" is all I can manage.

"I followed the hunter's tracks, the one who attempted to kill you. Violeta told me some hunters also attacked the vârcolaci in the woods. I went to talk to them, but"—a low growl escapes him—"that fucker Dominic won't tell me much. I know they're holding back."

"Yeah..."

There's a long pause. When he speaks again, his tone is gentler. "You don't sound too good."

"I'm fine." Never mind the fact the shadows on these walls seem to get worse and worse. I glance at the oil lamp on the table and, with a disgusted sigh to myself, turn it on. The dimness illuminates the area somehow, and makes me feel better. Somewhat. "How, um, how did it go with the two vampiri clans you were supposed to visit? Did Mira manage to keep you in line?"

He snorts, and I can practically see him rolling his eyes. "It went as well as can be expected. Mira and Nico played the diplomats while I did my usual."

"Scowling and looking scary?"

"You know it."

I chuckle, picturing the scene all too clearly. "And?"

"They denied it all, blamed it on the Cazacus. When we went to the Cazacus, they denied it all, blamed it on the Hatmanus."

"So, in short, no one's taking credit for the assassination attempt. I mean, unsurprising. An admittance would be akin to signing their death warrant, especially after the message we sent when the Ardeleans stood against us."

"And yet, you'd think they would give us *something*." Alex growls, his annoyance seeping through the line. "If Nico hadn't been so keen on playing the diplomacy card, I might've gotten more out of them."

I let out a sigh. "One of these days, you'll have to release this grudge you have against him. And the wolves. You have to admit, he did good to invite them to the ball, else we wouldn't have been able to round up everyone."

Instead of agreeing—when hell freezes over—Alex changes the subject abruptly. "How's the human?"

"As annoying as you can expect. But surprisingly useful."

"I doubt that." A pause follows, but I don't join in on the derision. It would feel wrong to, after my conversation with Ștefan about this. When I don't say anything, Alex continues, "Where are you, anyway?"

I tell him what I told Nico and Mirabela about the castle, the hag, and her request we get the ring.

He pauses for a long moment. "What castle, Liza?"

I close my eyes and whisper, "Corvins' Castle."

"Ce naiba... Are you insane? Why would you put yourself through that? Did Nico—"

"It's not Nico's fault!" My voice echoes on the walls, so I lower it. "I swear it's not his doing. I chose this, Alex, knowing full well how crappy it might be for me."

"And, is it?"

"Pretty much, yeah."

His tone softens again. "If you need me..."

"I know. You're always there for me, and I love you for it."

He says nothing, not that I expected him to.

"What can I do to help?"

"There is something... You know Father's journal, that Nico and Mira have been reading?"

"Da, what about it?"

"I need you to have a look and see if there's anything in it about a ring." It only makes sense that Father might've left a clue in there, given how long he was imprisoned here for.

"You mean, the ring you're seeking in the same castle you were tortured in?"

I look at the ceiling for help. "Yes, the same one, Alex."

"Bine, bine. I know I can't get through your stubborn head. Give me a few hours and I'll reach out when I have it."

"Thank you."

I hang up and, needing some rest, move to the bed and take a seat. My vampir force accidentally forces the metal legs of the bed to scrape against the hard stone floor. The noise is loud—too loud for my sensitive ears. And with it comes the smell of leather and sweat...and blood. So much blood...

"We need to test the next bit. Gut her open like a pig, see if the tissue regenerates."

"No. If she dies, we have no one."

"We have the other one—the male who came for her."

A snort. "That one? Florin already had a go at him. He won't last long. We cannot lose either of them."

There's a pause as the two men speak some more. I tug at the cuffs around my wrists, wanting nothing more than to burst through the restraints and feast on their blood.

Then the one who wanted to gut me speaks again. "We could try it with a less important body part, then. Maybe cut open a muscle and observe the effects."

"That, I can agree upon. Go ahead."

The knife is coated with something that burns my flesh as it cuts through. I try to hold out on the pain for as long as I can, but it's useless. My human brain, still very much dominant over my vampir senses, feels the pain. And screams, and screams, and screams....

When I come to from the memory as if emerging from a thick fog, I'm curled up in a corner, like some hopeless maiden. Disgusted, I stretch and get up, moving to the window. I can barely see a hint of stars or moon in the darkening sky. It should feel peaceful. So why does it feel like I can still hear my cries echoing between these walls?

What did I get myself into? And is it too late to leave?

Chapter 13

Ștefan

After Elizabeta slams the door in front of us, I bend to pick up whatever Elizabeta had tossed at me—a bag of some sort? I can only hope it contains a change of clothes.

Trăian shows me to my room in silence. Judging by the steps I'm counting, it's close to Elizabeta's.

"Wait," I say before he leaves.

He clears his throat and I turn in his direction.

"Cezar...how long has he been here?"

"As he said, two weeks."

"That's impossible. I saw him just a few days ago, training you.

Are you telling me his doppelgänger is walking around?"

"No, of course not. I.... yes, he was at the main Dacian compound, but it was temporary. He came to get a few of us to help. That's why he was so... hard on me."

I frown. "Trăian, he was being a dick. It's okay to admit it."

"No, it's fine. He's right. I need to get tougher."

I take a step closer. "I've trained you, too, Trăian, and I never said anything of the like. I also found you and recruited you, so I feel a measure of responsibility for what's going on." I pause, trying to remove the ire in my voice at Cezar, and instead to sound open and approachable. "What is this? What's going on here, truly?"

He sighs. I can sense him being fidgety. "I'm not sure. Please—don't tell him I said anything. All I know is he did a lot of outreach to bring nuns here. It seemed important. Not sure why."

"All right. Thank you."

The door closes behind him a moment later. I take a deep breath—the woodsy scent of my surroundings hits me full-on. Bit by bit, I make my way around the room, acclimating myself with its layout. A cot in the corner, a small wooden table in another, and a large book placed on it that I'd wager is the Bible. The door is only three long strides from the one end of the room to the other.

Small. Quaint. I wonder what the Dracul princess thinks of her new lodgings.

When I'm done, I walk to the bed and sit on the edge. I might've lied to Cezar about Liviu telling me this, but there *is* an undercurrent of power in this place, something dark and nefarious. It's unsettling, even to someone like me whose powers come from Zalmoxis himself.

I briefly consider calling Silviana, but a wave of exhaustion washes over me. I pull off my shirt and lie down, just to close my eyes for a bit. Before I know it, sleep has overtaken me.

I wake up to someone roughly shaking me awake. "Dammit, Dacian, wake up!"

I blink, met by the same darkness as before. And then something—a scent. I jerk up when I recognize Elizabeta's voice. "Ce naiba... What are you *doing* here?"

"Nice. Hi to you, too. Believe me, I wouldn't be here if something wasn't seriously wrong with this place."

A sense of unease churns in my gut at her words, but I shove it away. "What time is it?"

"What do you care what—"

"Have they had dinner, da sau nu?"

"They did. I heard the clinks of utensils earlier."

"Perfect. That means they'll all have retired to their own rooms for the night." Silence answers my words, so I probe, "You didn't join?"

"Someone came for me, but I pretended to be asleep."

"Good."

If they think us too tired, that'll work in our favor.

"Time?" I ask again.

"Past midnight."

I nod and stand, moving to the door.

"Where the hell are you going?"

"To find that stupid ring. If you're right and there's something wrong here, then we'd best get it and get out, and soon." I don't tell her that I've also felt something dark. Beyond dark. It's like this place invites darkness, like the one fueling my magic, but also twists it, using it and imbuing every stone with pain and tragedy. Morphing it into...evil.

"Well, maybe put on a shirt first."

I cringe, recalling I'd taken mine off earlier, and retrace my steps to the bed. I fumble in the bag, and my fingers touch something soft.

"That'll be *my* extra change of clothes," Elizabeta says.

I toss it aside and my fingers find a thicker fabric—wool or cotton. When I pull it on, the fabric chafes a little against my skin, but the fit is pretty decent. I'm not about to change jeans in front of her, though, so that'll have to wait.

Without a word to Elizabeta, I open the door and head out the moment after. Take a deep breath, listen. No noises, no sounds other than my own breathing. I force myself to quiet it, and move to the right. Might as well get acquainted with the rest of the place.

"Wait," Elizabeta says to my left. "I've already looked there. Nothing around except more rooms, the dining hall, and boring shit."

"What we seek might be buried under that boring shit," I point out.

"Do you really think that?"

Her snarky tone doesn't take away from the fact she's got a point. Maybe.

"No," I finally admit. "Bine, where do you suggest we look, then?"

"The *other* way, duh," she says, and grabs my hand, dragging me through corridors upon corridors.

She moves—barely—at human speed, and I have to lengthen my stride to keep up. When we finally come to a stop, I let some of the anger coursing through me to the surface. Instead of yanking my hand out of her grip, I sweep it underneath hers, moving it in a semi-circle until I've got her wrist in mine, pinned to the wall above her head.

I move in closer, my body forcing hers against the solid wall behind her, and drop my mouth next to the side of her head. Her hair tickles my nostrils, and the body pressed against me doesn't feel half as cold as I'd expected.

"Let's get one thing straight here, Elizabeta. Just because I'm blind doesn't mean I'm a child who needs to be taken by the hand and led to places. Are we understood?"

Typical vampir, she only answers with more sass. "Well, maybe I wouldn't have to if you could keep up."

"I don't need to *keep up*. You can go look for things wherever you want, and I'll do my own research. So long as you don't get caught, I don't care what you do."

"Do you really?" One of her hands goes to my chest, nails pressing lightly through my shirt. "Do you *really* not care?"

I shake my head, moving out of her reach. "Enough with your games, Elizabeta. They won't work on me. Silviana already warned me off."

"Oh, yeah? What about?"

"I know what you're like, princess. All one-night stands and selfish needs to be filled. I'm not a plaything for you, so go back to hating me if you have to, but *enough with your games*." I'd like to think my words stunned her and that's why she's quiet, but I'm not entirely sure. When the silence stretches some more, I change the topic. "Where have you brought me?"

She takes a beat, and another, before finally answering, "The mess hall. There's a room beyond here, locked."

"Probably holds some treasures. Ah. I see. And you thought the ring would be among them?"

"Worth a shot, no?" Judging by her indignant tone, it sounds like for once I'm the one who annoyed her. *Good.*

"The wood witch was clear that the ring is more than likely in the well."

"And she also said there's no one else here, impeding our search. Which we now know was a lie. There's every chance these 'brothers' of yours are here for the same thing."

"What makes you say that?'

"I spoke to Alex." I grit my teeth at the mention of her asshole brother's name, but she's already continuing, "Didn't your Grand Master have my father's journal with him? Do you honestly think he didn't read every word of them, and find out about the ring from there? The witch herself says she works with him. And I find it slightly convenient that she's after a relic that was crafted and hidden when my father was imprisoned here."

"What did Alex say? Did he confirm your suspicions, since the journal is with your siblings?"

"He's looking into it," she mutters. "But while he does, do you want to risk going into the depths of this castle, into a place with probably few exits? When it's possible the ring isn't even there anymore? *And* without knowing the layout?"

If I didn't know what the stafie told me—about the hunters—I might fall for that reasoning. As it is, the slight tremble in her voice tells me she's afraid to go because of what happened to her in those catacombs. And I can't blame her for it, nor be ruthless and force her to go anyway.

Fuck's sake, when did I start caring about sparing Elizabeta Dracul's feelings? Probably around the same time I found this vulnerable side of her endearing and appointed myself her protector.

I grit my teeth. "Very well. If you insist we waste some time here, we might as well."

Without another word, I let the athame slip from my wrist cuff and cut into my palm. Then let the blood fill the darkness, draw on it, for that hint of clarity. The obscurity around me shifts to something...else. Vague shapes. It's something new—exhilarating. I've never been able to mold my magic quite like this. Is it happening here, now, because of the power I feel lying in wait?

The darkness keeps moving, enough so I can tell where there's a door. Everything has a blurry edge to it, but it's like the magic is shaping reality in a way I can see. I move to it, taking care with each step that I don't bump into something.

Clearly, Elizabeta isn't as careful.

A loud *thwack* behind me tells me she's hit something. I whirl around, ready to yell, but the last of the darkness shows me a shape—her—bent at a weird angle. "What is it?"

Elizabeta

Fuck. I'd been doing so well, too. But the moment the Dacian did his spell, that same weakness hit me.

"Liza..."

I glance to the side. To Daniel, flickering in and out. What is he doing here, when I asked him to stay away?

"Leave here," he says. "You—*danger*—leave."

Then he's gone, and the weakness in me becomes a woosh of dizziness so heavy, it makes me stumble into the wall. Gasping for breath, I claw the wall, trying to hold myself up.

Ştefan walks to me with unerring accuracy. I glare at him. "Are you *seeing* me?"

"No, it's the magic. Something...never mind. What's going on?"

"What the fuck is that spell?" I answer instead. "Weakness hit me the moment you did it."

"That's not possible, my magic has nothing to do with..."

He trails off, his expression going slack, then horrified.

"What?" I ask. "What is it?"

He grabs my arm. "Never mind, I'll tell you after. Let's go back to the rooms. Your little episode might've woken up someone."

I force myself to listen. Almost every extrasensory power of mine is dulled, but I can still hear well. "No. There's no noise. Let's keep going."

"If we're caught—"

"Between your magic and my blood lust, I'm pretty sure we'll be fine, Dacian. Now *move it*."

He hesitates. Then the grip on my arm tightens, and he helps me away from the wall. Holds my weight as I move to the door, and he whispers something to unlock it.

Inside it, there's barely any light. I say as much, and Ştefan says, "If I light it up and someone comes, they'll know we're here. We'll have to make do in darkness."

He drops me by the door, letting me slide to the floor. "Just sit here, and I'll look around."

"How do you expect to—"

But more chanting answers me. The smell of blood gets more intense even whilst the obscurity seems to thicken, densifying into a cloak that covers everything. Every shadow, every hint of obscurity in a nook or cranny, answers his call. They lap at his feet like obedient puppies, waiting for their master's command. I've seen it before, of course. In the woods. In the car, when he did the spell on me. But this is something different. It fills the air with a thickness that's all dark, powerful, unbreakable magic.

The Dacian turns his head to the side, a contemplative look on his features. Then he shoots his hand forward and the tendrils take off like snakes, slithering everywhere. A heavy sensation presses on my shoulders through everything he does, but I'm also grudgingly impressed. I've seen Silviana's tricks, yet her brother looks a hell of a lot more commanding.

And there's something about his command of this magic that makes him seem way too sexy. Must be my weakness-addled brain.

In an effort to distract myself, I ask, "Do you think Zalmoxis feels this use of magic?"

Ștefan pauses, hesitates. "I hope not. If he does, I can see him reaching out to my sister, trying to use her again. But I think the distance between us should help keep him...unaware."

I don't much care for his sister, but the god becoming a pain in our ass during this quest? That's something I don't want to deal with.

A stack of paper draws my attention. I reach over and rifle through them quickly. My vision blurs in and out, but it focuses enough so I can find a blueprint of the grounds. "I have the layout plans."

"Good." Ștefan turns in my direction, shaking his head. "Because there's nothing else of use here. No ring. No artifacts."

"Fuck."

He helps me back to my feet, whispering, "Any noise?"

I shake my head. "Nothing."

"Let's get you back to your room, then."

I pull the top of my blouse from my breast, tuck the paper with the blueprints under it, and let him lead me back. Total irony, given how I'd dragged him to begin with.

Once we're back inside my cramped four walls, I turn to him. Doing so too fast makes me dizzy once more and I sway, but grit my teeth against it. Ștefan reaches for me, and in the small confines of this place, I realize how much space he takes with his broad frame.

"Spit it out, then. What is it that you figured out?" I ask.

Through the entire walk, I couldn't get his horrified expression from earlier out of my head. Now, watching him shift his weight on his feet, run a hand over his bald head, a sense of nausea roils through me.

"You feel weak now, da? Like your brother."

A near-growl escapes me. "Stop beating around the bush."

"I'm not. Remember what the witch said? That I can help when this happens?"

My gaze drops to his neck, and the vein throbbing there. I should feel some kind of thirst, but all I feel is revulsion. "Somehow, I doubt that."

"I don't mean by feeding on *me*. But if you feed on my magic..."

I frown. "What?"

"Just try it, Elizabeta. For once, stop being so damn stubborn and listen. What's the worst that can happen?"

"How about, I snap your neck off for annoying me?"

He has the nerve to chuckle. "Maybe. Or, maybe for once, a human will save you."

"Doubtful." I still feel there's more to what he's not saying, but relent. Weakness is not something I do well with. "Fine. Try whatever it is you want to try."

"You should probably sit, if you're not already."

"I'm fine standing."

He steps closer to me, raising his hand. Blood seems to have coagulated around the wound, but he opens and closes his fist, and it comes pouring out again. And the shadows grow, and grow. I look into Ștefan's face, the concentration on his features. His jaw made of granite. The width of his muscles. The bicep, tight under his shirt, as his hand is raised.

"Ready?" he asks, snapping me out of my trance.

"Da."

He whispers some more, and the faint thread of darkness that had circled his hand now moves toward me. I watch it warily, but then it inches closer, and closer and...I inhale deeply. It rushes at me all at once, and I feel a sharp sensation in my nostrils, then... The effect is immediate. All dizziness vanishes, my head feels clear—it's as clear as if I'd fed. And I feel back to normal. Unerringly so.

"What the..." Unable to deal with the overflow of emotions, I grab Ștefan by the scruff of his shirt and whirl him around, slamming him against the wall. "What the hell did you do? What is this sorcery?"

"No sorcery." A muscle ticks in his jaw. "Earlier, I... There's no other explanation. I think the curse, the one on your Dracul line, is triggered by us working together."

I narrow my eyes on him as the full implication of his words hits me. They're much too close to what Daniel told me in the woods. "Oh, hell NO. No no no no. *No.*" I let go of him and move backward, jabbing a finger his way. "You are *not* telling me the consort bullshit bond is trying to pull us together."

His silence is my only answer.

"Hell *no.* And NO and *fuck no!*"

"Elizabeta, keep your voice down—"

"Don't fucking tell me to keep it down, not when you drop something like that on me!"

He pushes off the wall and marches toward me, cornering me between him and the desk. I'm at a weird angle, the corner digging into the back of my thigh. But all I can focus on is the insanely *tasty* smell of his blood. The same blood that previously repulsed me now calls to me. Clearly, my vampir senses are up and running again, and his words have just made him that more enticing.

He grabs my shoulders. "You need to keep your voice down," he hisses. "I don't want Cezar to see past our deceit."

I glare at him, even though he can't see me. "You've got some nerve." Then shove him away with enough force that he slams against the other wall. "We are *not* linked like that."

"Fine. I'm wrong, you're right. But how else do you explain that you got weakened *right when I used my magic*, hmm? Tell me." When I don't answer, he juts his jaw in the air. "Go on, I'm waiting."

"Vlad never had that side effect with Silviana! And I... you... *no.* There's got to be another explanation."

"Sure. Let me know when you figure it out, princess." With a final shake of his head, he feels his way to the door, and leaves.

I drop my ass on the desk, head in my hands to muffle a scream. "This isn't fucking happening."

Ștefan

What a blind fool. For someone who's been around for centuries, she sure likes to keep that wool over her eyes when it suits her. Then again, what else did I expect from a princess of the Dracul line, who's always been given everything?

Even so, I can't shake away the fear permeating her voice. She was scared. Beyond scared, she was downright close to losing it. And a part of me wishes I'd stayed to make sure she's okay.

When I get back to my room, I feel a buzz in my back pocket. A tinny, robotic voice says, "Silviana calling." I press the side button—my shortcut to answer—immediately.

"Fane! Are you okay?"

"Da, why?"

"I just... I thought something was wrong. I had a dream." Her voice drops. "I was back in the tower. And Zalmoxis was there. Only...he said something about you."

A shiver runs up my spine. "What did he say?"

"That...That you need to leave where you're at. Forget the quest. Or else he'll make sure you lose your life."

Shit. I'd hoped our distance was enough that he wouldn't feel me tapping into whatever fuels this entire castle. Clearly, that's not the case. *He feels it, all right, but at least he's not able to use Lana to tap into it, too. That's why he's trying to scare her.*

"He's bluffing, Lana."

"Is he, though?"

"I'll take the chance." At her agonized gasp, I say, "Where's Vlad? Is he around?"

"He's in the shower."

"Get him on the phone, please."

Moments go by as she shuffles around their room. I hear water running, then stopping. Muffled voices. And Vlad comes on.

"Ștefan?"

"Da, it's me. Listen... Silviana's nightmares seem to be coming back. I think my being here is triggering Zalmoxis, maybe he sees it as a threat, I don't know. But it means I'm on the right track to finding a way to free her from his hold."

"What do you need?"

This is what I appreciate about my sister's consort. He doesn't beat around the bush.

"Watch over her. Don't leave her side. As I get closer still, it's possible he'll retaliate through their link. Bring her to Tytus if need be."

"All right, I promise. But be careful. She needs you, you know that."

"I do."

I hang up shortly after, and sit on the bed, running my hands over my face. The smell of metal hits my nostrils—the wound on my hand hasn't closed properly. I mutter a healing spell which seems like it's taking a bit too long to work, but eventually it does. Even if the flesh feels tender.

Exhausted, I lean my head on the pillow and close my eyes. Sleep grabs me immediately.

The next morning, rather than leave my room as soon as I wake, I busy myself with making the bed and waiting until someone comes to get me. About half an hour after, the door opens.

Trăian enters—I can tell it's him by the shuffle of his feet and the way he quickly shuts the door behind him. "It's me," he says.

I nod, continuing to make the bed. "Something on your mind?"

"Da, it's... Cezar. This whole thing with the nuns. Tomorrow's a full moon, did you know?"

"I didn't."

"It is...supposed to be a blood moon, too."

"Really?" I wonder if I can ask him about the ring. Either this is a set-up, or he's being real. But how to figure out which is which?

"Can you do something?"

"And what is it that I'm doing something about?"

He's silent.

"Tell you what. Come to me with information, and I'll help. I promise. But I can't without facts."

Another pause, then, "Okay. I'll bring you information."

He opens the door, mutters something to someone, and then his footsteps depart. "Who goes there?" I ask.

"It's me," Elizabeta says. "I'm told we're to go join everyone for breakfast."

"Good. It'll give us a chance to get the lay of the land."

I walk out, and she blocks my way. "About what you said—"

"Like you said, I must've been mistaken."

She growls under her breath, then says, "I'm sorry, all right?

Maybe you weren't. Can you"—a pause, a deep breath—"would you *please* share the rest of your theory?"

I bite back a grin and hold out my hand. "Sigur." After a beat, she takes it, and we start walking. In a low voice, I continue, "I think the darkness I'm using will bring on more of your episodes."

"But why didn't it for Vlad and Silviana?"

"Not sure."

"Are you really not sure, or just keeping your cards close to your chest?"

I tilt my head in the direction of her voice. "Would you blame me if I was?"

She snorts. "You're not as much help as I'd hoped."

"I didn't promise otherwise, princess."

"Stop calling me that."

I chuckle, and judging by the tension in her slight frame, we've entered the dining hall.

Chapter 14

Elizabeta

If ever I wanted to go back in time, the dining hall at Corvins' Castle is how I'd do it. Broad, sweeping arches give way to an open-concept space. Dark, worn cobblestone floor. Old-school wooden tables, long enough to seat a dozen or so people. And instead of lights hanging from the ceilings, torches have been lit. In combination with the sunlight coming through the tall windows, the effect is cozy yet medieval. The smell of burning oil and wood fills the air, along with a variety of cooked foods.

Two of the main tables are occupied: one is all nuns, and the other seems to be all Dacians. Unsurprising, given they're the only males around here.

Cezar, seated between two of his kin, catches sight of us and waves us over. I plaster a smile on my face and nudge Ştefan toward them.

"Cezar and some cronies," I whisper out of the corner of my mouth.

He nods, and I sense the tension in his arm. The closer we get to Cezar, the more I become aware of a glint in his eyes. It takes me a moment to realize it's a look I've seen in Alex many times.

When we stop at the head of the table, some Dacians move to the side, making room for us to sit. I have no intention of joining these peasants. Not because I can't control my hunger, but because I'll be too tempted to ram my fist in Cezar's face. There's something about him...

Cezar smirks. "Never thought I'd see the day you rely on a woman, Ştefan."

I smile at him sweetly. "He's not relying on me."

The bicep under my arm tenses, becoming as solid as a rock. But Ştefan's expression gives nothing away. "Do I smell nuns?"

Cezar chortles. "I didn't think it was possible to smell nuns. But yes. There are a few."

"How come?"

"I told you, organizing a retreat."

"And you said this was on Liviu's orders?"

None of the smugness leaves Cezar's features, but his expression grows more intense. "You know, that's not the first time you call him by his first name. Forgive me, but I didn't realize you and the Grand Master were so...close."

"There's a lot you don't realize, Cezar."

"Yes, I suppose so," Cezar muses in a tone that's like a cobra waiting to strike. "Which is ironic, since I can actually *see* enough to realize things." His gaze shifts to me. "Wouldn't you agree, *Lizzie*?"

Oh, if I could only lunge across and rip his throat out... Now *that* would be feeding my inner bloodthirsty monster. Not just because he's so smug, but because his words infuriate me. It's one thing to hear Alex dissing Ștefan for his blindness, and even that hadn't made me exactly comfortable. But for this guy to do it, who's supposed to be his "brother"?

Nu, I don't think so. Time to put him in his place. Though my smile remains, my words are filled with a cool warning. "Oh, I don't know about that, Cezar. I think sight is like a good dick—victory doesn't lie in *having* it, but in how you use it."

Cezar flushes beet red and more than a few nuns turn their heads in our direction—I hadn't been exactly quiet in my delivery.

I don't need to glance up at Ștefan. His silent chuckle reverberates in his body, but on the outside, he keeps an impassable mask and says, "Right. Well, I'm famished. Shall we get some food, Lizzie?"

"Sure thing." I rise on my tiptoes, kissing his cheek for good measure.

Ștefan turns to leave, but Cezar isn't done yet. *This guy really has a death wish.*

"It's interesting, don't you think?" He waits until Ștefan turns in the direction of his voice once more. "If you and the Grand Master are so close, how come he didn't put *you* in charge of this retreat?"

To his credit, Ștefan doesn't miss a beat. "Maybe because the mission I'm on is more important."

"Really?" Cezar's cool gaze lands on me. "And what is that, exactly?"

Instead of answering, Ștefan says, "You must have a busy day ahead. We'll just grab some food and get out of your way."

I squeeze his bicep in warning. But I've got to give it to the Dacian, he's cool as a cucumber throughout.

Even when Cezar drops the polite tone and asks, with a more cutting tone, "How much longer do you think you'll be staying?"

"One more night."

"Good, good. You'll be able to partake in the festivities."

Something about the way he says it tells me they're going to be the opposite of festivities. But I don't have a moment to inquire further, because Ștefan is dragging us away resolutely.

"You caught that?" I whisper to him.

"Da. This morning..." He hesitates. "Are we alone?"

I nudge him toward a table in the corner. "Now we are." I wait until he takes a seat and push a plate of food in front of him, cringing at the somewhat loud noise the sole movement makes. *Guess everything in this place is old and creaky.*

Ștefan reaches for the plate—filled with some boiled eggs, cornmeal porridge, and pieces of something that vaguely looks like spinach pie—and nods in thanks. "This morning, Trăian came to see me. Said he's got information on something nefarious Cezar is doing. I'm not surprised, but I am worried. This many innocents around, in this dark a place, can't be good."

"Hmm." I tap my chin. "Tonight, then. We get this done then leave."

"Yes."

I take a seat next to him and lean forward, lowering my voice even though no one within a ten-foot radius could hear us. "Tell me more about the darkness and what you said before."

There's another hesitation as he chews on a chunk of the spinach pie. I pick a piece of it for myself and pretend to nibble on it for the benefit of the humans. It tastes like ashes on my tongue—ugh. What I wouldn't give for a fresh vein to drink from.

"What was that?" Ștefan asks, taking me by surprise.

"What was what?"

He finishes his next pie bite before answering, "You, jumping to my defense with Cezar."

"Was that what I did?" And though my tone comes out mocking, I'm inwardly kicking myself for being so obvious. Ștefan is giving rise to impulses I don't recognize, and making me do things I would never normally do—like defending a human. Because he *is* right about that, much as I'm loath to admit it.

To his credit, Ștefan waits. His infuriating patience is getting on my nerves.

"You and Cezar already seem to have issues. I didn't see why I would tip the balance in his favor by agreeing to the bullshit he was spewing."

"It's not so different than what Alexandru was saying at the ball."

Touché. "True. But Alex is my brother and, misguided as he can sometimes be, he—"

"Don't say he didn't intend for his words to cut, because he did. And your silence was pretty much agreement."

I let out a sigh. "Fine. You're right, Alex was being a dick, too." I pause, trying to find the right words. "But... we're on this quest together and to me, that means something."

"Something?" He arches an eyebrow.

I roll my eyes. "Yes, something. You had my back with the old hag and with those gods, right?"

He snorts at my words and nearly chokes on his food as a result. His hand reaches out and I push a glass of water closer to him. He takes two large gulps and, once done, shakes his head. "Correct me if I'm wrong, but didn't you threaten to kill me after that last event?"

"Mm, is that what I did?"

Ștefan shifts on the bench toward me, and his thigh brushes against my knee. The movement sends a jolt of awareness in me, much like that night, and my eyes can't help roaming over his large form. How tiny the plate and glass look compared to his hands. How strong he seems, even in a hostile environment. I think back to the press of his body against mine, in the woods, and have to shift back on the bench to put more distance between us.

Ștefan tilts his head toward me at that, as if waiting—for an explanation of my movement, or more about my meaning, I'm not sure. But that's the extent of what I'm willing to say for now.

After a beat, he seems to get it. "Fine. I'll take that at face value. We have some weird watch-each-other's-back-thing going during this quest." When I still don't reply with anything, he clears his throat. "The curse seems to be getting worse. It took only a few days for it to kick in with us, but now it's intertwining my magic with your abilities. If I use it, it drains you. Yet I can also use it to fuel you. It's almost like…" He stops, mouth dropping open at a thought.

"Are you going to finish that, or gape like a goldfish?"

His mouth snaps shut with an audible click. He rubs his jaw, taps the table, then finally shakes his head. "Fuck. He's *good*."

"Who's good?"

"Zalmoxis. Lana called me last night, saying in her latest nightmare, Zalmoxis warned that—"

"Hang on a second. Didn't you say that the distance should protect her?"

"Da, I said *should.* And it did, in a way. He couldn't do anything—use her like a conduit to mooch off me, for once. All he could do was scare her by threatening that if I get much closer, I'll pay with my life." He runs a hand over his trimmed beard. "I think this is his doing. Whenever I use my magic for something to do with getting closer—to the ring, to answers from the wood witch—he makes me pay by increasing your weakness. And Silviana's nightmares."

"And your magic fueling me is an unexpected benefit?"

"Da. Probably on account of your father and the first bargain he ever struck with the god."

"Fuck."

"You can say that again."

I drop my head in my hands, groaning. Daniel's words come back to me. Everything I'd tried to deny. But if the darkness connecting us is acting in this way... "*Fuck.*" I look back up. "But this doesn't... I mean, this doesn't mean you're my consort. It can't."

"I don't like it any better than you do. Maybe the curse is just attacking us because of our proximity." He takes another bite of toast. "It doesn't have to be *the* bond, it could just be *a* bond."

I let that slide. Daniel might have more insight. Then something else hits me. "Hang on a second. But for Zalmoxis to influence anything like this, so much easier and quicker than when the curse hit my siblings, he'd need to be..."

"Stronger. Closer."

"Which means..." I look at Cezar, the Dacians, and the nuns. A sinking feeling grows in the pit of my stomach. "This isn't a resort at all, is it?"

"I don't think so. In fact, I think we've landed smack in the middle of Cezar's plans."

Ştefan

I never would've thought having a vampir know my game plan would be reassuring. Or that I'd grow to rely on said vampir to achieve what I need to. But, there you have it. And if I'm honest with myself, there's a certain kind of satisfaction in having Elizabeta know what's going on. And the fact we're both on the same page about the curse and what it means—or cannot mean—for us.

After food, she leaves to go wander around—I suspect she's more than likely going to feed. So long as she doesn't let our hosts know of her true nature, I'm fine with that. Especially with what we're assuming about Cezar's true plans.

Instead of heading to my room, I line the wall and use it to make my way around the place, expecting either Cezar or Trăian will find me. And maybe then I'll get more information about what's going on.

As I walk, my thoughts drift back to Silviana, and the whole reason for this quest. I hope that old hag wasn't having us on by sending us on this quest, and that she does know what she's talking about. *I'll go to the depths of Hell and back for you, Lana, if I have to.*

That has my thoughts drifting back to Elizabeta and our conversation. The way she jumped to my defense, when she could've easily agreed with Cezar... It's making me wonder what else hides under that snarky attitude of hers, and whether I'm playing with fire by trying to find out.

It doesn't take long for someone to find me. I'm seated on a bench when I hear footsteps heading toward me. Then someone sits. The overpowering cologne immediately tells me it's Cezar.

"So, one more day?"

"That's what I said," I mutter. "Don't you have a resort to plan?"

"It's all being taken care of."

I turn in the direction of his voice. "What is it you're planning, Cezar? I doubt Liviu really tasked you to run a resort in his name."

"Tsk. So much paranoia. It doesn't suit you."

"Fine. Don't tell me. But we both know if Liviu knew I was here, he'd tell you to let me help."

"So why doesn't he know? You haven't called him."

I walked right into that one. "Who says I haven't?"

There's a long pause, then he says, "Ah, Trăian. What do you need?"

"Ștefan was asking earlier about the library. Thought I'd show him our selection of books."

"I doubt there's much in braille."

I can't hold bad a snort at that. "You do know braille isn't a language, but an alphabet that's used to help me—and others like me—read and write in my native language?"

"Do I give a shit?" Cezar bites back.

I'd been hoping my barb would wind Cezar up because he has a habit of letting good information slip out when he's angry. Alas, Trăian's soft voice interrupts us before anything can get out of hand.

"Ah, yes, Cezar, you're correct, none of these books have been transcribed into braille. But there are some tomes of importance I thought I might read to him."

"Fine, fine. Go off and do what you please."

I stand and head toward Trăian's voice, then follow his steps while lining the wall again.

A few moments later, he says, "We're out of earshot now."

"Don't you think it's dangerous for Cezar to see us together like this?"

"I don't care. You need to hear what I found."

We walk in guarded silence until we reach the library. A sneeze escapes me as the amount of dust brings forth allergies I didn't even know I had.

"This way," Trăian says from somewhere to my left.

I follow his voice and stop when my hip collides with something hard.

"Table in front of you," Trăian says.

"A bit late for a warning."

"Sorry, I was rifling through this book to find the spot again. I hid it, earlier, after… Anyway."

His tone is laced with something very close to panic.

"What is it? What did you find?"

"Listen to this: *Zalmoxis' followers, called Dacians, have one purpose and one purpose only. To free their god of the shackles other immortals imposed upon him, and release him onto the world once more. Though it may take centuries, the plan set forth will serve its purpose, culminating in both feeding and sustaining the god, and eventually releasing him.*"

I lean my hand onto the table, feeling like my knees have given way. "It's a blueprint. You found a fucking blueprint for the connection between the Dacians and Zalmoxis, haven't you?"

"Yes…" Trăian gulps. "With dates and suggested timelines. Someone, long ago, was very good at seeing into the future. Each Grand Master signed their name on this, and was tasked with a particular set of priorities."

"Mother of all hells." Back when Liviu was trying to use Vlad to extend the Dacians' life expectancy, I thought something like this might exist. But no matter how hard I looked, I couldn't find a single trace of it in Liviu's home. "What does it say are Liviu's priorities?"

"To speed up the Dracul curse."

Which he did with Vlad and Silviana.

"What else?"

"To...provide a sacrifice. It looks like there's one such sacrifice every seventy-five years to sustain Zalmoxis. Innocent blood, preferably of women true to another god."

"Fuck. Me."

"It gets worse... According to this, the sacrifice is best under a blood moon."

"And the next one is tomorrow night?"

"Da."

I cringe. "I told Cezar I'd be leaving tomorrow morning."

"Then you either have to come up with a way to stay, or undo all this tonight. Otherwise many will die."

Great. Just fucking great.

Elizabeta

I should feed, but Ștefan's magic still seems to sustain me. So I head into the woods instead, and as soon as I'm far away, I try to blur at vampir speed. Thankfully, it works. I don't stop until I'm deep into the woods and far, far out of sight.

"Daniel?"

There's a moment of silence, of anxious waiting. But just as I'm about to call his name again, he flickers in front of me, his expression solemn. "Liza… How are you?"

"I'm fine. Good. Managing." I bite my tongue so I don't say more.

Sorrow enters his expression, drawing his eyebrows in a frown. "It's fine if you're not okay."

"What makes you think I'm not okay?"

"Liza…" He moves toward me, arms outreached.

I snort. "I'm *fine.* That's not why I came here, anyway."

"Then why did you?"

Quickly, I fill him in on what Ștefan said. His expression never changes, as though these are things he already knew.

When I'm done, he shrugs. "That's why I said not to piss off great allies."

I scowl at him. "He's not… The curse is not…" Fuck. I can't even bring myself to finish.

"Whatever you say."

I open my mouth to argue, realizing at the last minute it's what he wants. So I bite those words off and say, "Ștefan seems to think the curse is basically doing this because of our proximity. What do you think?"

"I think you're both trying to find some other answer to something that's very obvious to anyone else but you."

"You're just seeing what you want to see!"

"And you refuse to see what's right in front of you." He steps toward me again, then runs a hand over his features, sighing in exasperation. "I love you, Liza, God knows I always will. But you are so damned stubborn. And you refuse to admit when you're not okay."

That stings.

"Why do you insist on making me be something I'm not? What,

you think because I was once tortured here, that all of a sudden I'll fall apart?"

"No, but I do think you're burying the pain of the past."

"And so what if I do? What's it to you? You're dead, anyway. You only stick around me to, what, judge me?"

Hurt flashes across his features. "That's not—"

"I don't need judgment and I sure as hell don't need any sympathy. If that's all you care for, then just leave."

"Liza—"

"LEAVE!"

He stares at me for a bit, then flickers in and out, and disappears.

I will not cry. I'm a princess of the house of Dracul, and I will not fucking cry because my ghost ex-boyfriend left me.

In this castle of horrors.

A shudder runs through me. Memories of the past, trying to force their way through. But Father taught me well, taught me how to shove them in their little compartments and ignore their existence. He was right. It made me stronger. And it *will keep me* strong. No curse will undo me.

Drained, I return to my tiny room and pace. Soon after, my cell phone rings—Alex, calling about the ring.

"Da? Did you find anything?"

He's quiet for a moment, then sighs. "No. I wish I had better news, but Father's notes don't mention anything about a ring. The entries around his stay at Corvins' mainly bitch and moan about missing his first wife—did you ever know he was so sentimental?"

I'd seen snippets of it, especially after my ordeal with the hunters, but I don't want to say as much to Alex. He'd just laugh at it. So I make a non-committal sound and try to refocus his attention on the ring. "Was there a mention of any digging? Anything at all about the catacombs?"

"Not much. Just that some young kids were forced by the emperor to dig something. But no actual mention of a ring."

Dammit. That's not much more than we've learned from the old hag. "Ugh... it's fine. It was a long shot, anyway. Thanks for checking."

"Anytime."

"It took you kind of long to get back to me, though. What's going on?"

From the scoff he lets out, I can once again picture him rolling his eyes. "What else? More vampir drama. Nico's human whore was out picking weeds in the woods and some vampiri ran across her. She freaked out, but turns out they were here to defect from the Cazacus and Hatmanus."

"Defect? Like..."

"Da. They're joining the ranks of our guards and have already sworn fealty to the Dracul clan."

"Huh. I mean, I'm not that surprised. I always thought vampiri would rally around us, but..."

"Da, I know. This close to the attempt on you, it's a bit suspicious. But Nico let me use glamour on them, and nothing untoward emerged. So for the time being, we're taking them at their word."

"At least we'll have new bodies around for the next ball, right?"

Alex laughs. "True. But I won't let anything happen to you, Liza. Not ever again."

I gulp past my suddenly tight throat, and whisper, "Thank you. You know the sentiment's reciprocated."

"I've got to go—I haven't hunted in a bit. But take care of yourself, and call me if anything."

"I will. Bye."

I hang up and sit on the bed, staring at the ceiling. I don't sleep, at least I don't try to. But eventually, my eyelids grow heavy, as that same weakness enters my bloodstream. Before I know it, I'm asleep…and in the clutches of my nightmares. Another memory of that time arises… One I'd done my best to forget, to shove aside like the rest.

In the weeks they held me captive, the hunters took great pleasure in devising new ways to torture me. More than what they pursued—ways to figure out what makes vampiri tick and weaken—they wanted to *break* me. And they did everything they could think of to do so. From slicing into me, taking out my organs and putting them back in, and cutting into my cheek with vervain-soaked knives until it scarred. Little did they know, all they'd need is to capture Daniel, and his suffering alone would reduce me to the begging mess they'd wanted all along.

Before Daniel came to rescue me though—and before his eventual recapture—they tried their best. One day, they almost got close to it.

It started with a potion. Two hunters pried my jaw open and a third poured the potion down my throat. It tasted like ashes to me, but I could smell licorice and some pepper notes in it. I had no idea what it would do. Neither, it seems, did they, because they spent an inordinate amount of time simply watching, waiting, and whispering amongst themselves.

"There," one finally said. "I think it's starting to take hold."

I don't know what signs they saw that clued them in to that because I was still very much feeling the same. But whatever it was, they moved. By that point, I was naked, save for a scrap of faded and torn underwear they'd let me keep. Dried blood marred my white skin, and scars were healing. That pissed them off the most. That they couldn't find a way to make the healing stop, nor could they harvest the same healing properties for themselves. I could've explained it was unique to vampiri and supernaturals, but it's not like they didn't know it. They just wanted to have their cake—being human, being righteous *in* being human—and eat it, too—having the powers of our lot, the supernaturals. The gain without the pain, in sum.

Well, the pain came for me, that day. And just like back then, I fall into the agony, no longer able to keep myself apart. No longer compartmentalized. No longer separate. I'm...back there.

Tied up.

At their mercy.

One by one, they unbind my limbs. Like in the woods when I was captured, I can't move. A fog has taken over me. By the time it lifts, a few minutes later—which I only realize because one of them points it out in a panicked "Hurry the fuck up, it's wearing off already, her body is metabolizing it!"—they've bound me to a new device. It's a wheel, of sorts. And for the next few days, it will become my new personal hell.

Once they double-check the restraints, they step away. One of them moves to a panel with different levers in the distance. He presses on one of them and, with a sickening whirring, the wheel under me comes alive. It seems to expand under me, at first. Then I feel the first tug at my arm, at the bindings. And it only gets worse from there.

A piece of the wheel detaches from the main body, stretching to the side, and taking my arm with it as far as it can go. And farther. And farther still. I grit my teeth against the pain that soon becomes agonizing, like my flesh is being slowly torn apart. Which, it is. The pain only stops when, with a sickening sound, my shoulder pops out of its socket. A half-grunt, half-whimper escapes me, though I'm biting my lips so hard that I'm drawing blood by that point.

"Interesting," the hunter by the panel says. He inches closer to me again and I will myself to school my expression so none of my relief shows. If he's away from the panel, it means the pain will stop—for now, at least. "I expected more sounds, for one."

"Give her until we do the rest of her limbs, then it'll come."

"Perhaps. Or perhaps the dosage we gave her dulled her pain." His cool eyes linger on mine for a second, filled with hate and malice. "Go bring me the vervain tincture."

"Won't that scramble the results?"

"No. We need the creature's senses to be alive, so we can get an accurate read of the pain level. The vervain will shock the thing's system into action, which means more accurate results, not less."

"Yes, sir," the other hunter says. "I'll bring it over now."

When he leaves, the third hunter, quiet until now, moves closer. "Might I suggest something?"

"Mm?"

"Since we've ascertained the creature's body still functions as a human's—with the blood they feed on landing in their stomach,

and thus fueling the body and other senses—I suggest we pour the vervain directly in the area."

The main hunter glances up at his accomplice, then looks back down at me. And smirks, slowly and psychotically. "What an astute idea."

He pulls a knife out of his belt, and this time I can't school my expression. My eyes widen, and I bite through my lip when the knife digs into my gut.

Stay strong. Stay sane. Don't let them break you.

By the time the other hunter returns with vervain, my stomach has once more been cut open. I'm staring at the ceiling, feeling out of my body, in a way. If I'd listened more to Father, I could compartmentalize better. Shove the pain to the side, not let any of this get to me. But I didn't and so, I can't.

Stay strong. Stay sane. Don't let them break you.

The hunter uncaps a small bottle and the smell of vervain fills the room. I jerk against my restraints, but only further succeed in weakening myself. Which is a really stupid idea, given what comes next.

From the first drop hitting my insides, my eyes roll back in my head in pain. The fire in my belly spreads, invading my veins, and traveling up my throat. If I was human, I would vomit the contents of my stomach. As it is, I can only gag on nothing.

More of the tincture is poured into my opened gut, and I thrash against the restraints, muffling my cries as best I can. My best is not enough, judging by their smug expressions.

Finally, the hunter sets the tincture away and returns to the panel. "That should do it. With the thing's senses fully aware, we can get a proper read on the pain levels. Let's see how fast it heals now."

Then, he pulls on the other lever.

Stay strong.

The wheel moves under my other arm, the unharmed one. Like with the previous one, it pulls, tugging at my muscles, my skin.

Stay sane.

The tension intensifies. My flesh rips. The second shoulder pops out of my socket.

Don't let them break you.

And then the piece under my left leg moves.

Don't let them break you.

The right follows.

Don't let...

I scream. It'll be the first of many.

I wake up, sweating, panting, from the nightmare. Screaming. There's screaming. Only, now it's gone. Was that me? Did I scream in real life, or just in my nightmare?

I jump off the bed, suddenly unable to handle the clothes on my back. I chuck them all away, ripping them off me, eager to feel a cool breeze on my skin. To forget—

"Elizabeta?"

The door opens, and I freeze. Ștefan walks in, head tilted as though listening for me. He can't see me, can't see I'm naked. But suddenly, he's more than just the Dacian I'm stuck with. He's a tool. One to make me forget what I've just seen.

"Here," I whisper.

He turns toward the sound of my voice. "I heard screaming. Are you..."

"Fine. Wasn't me."

Neither of us points out that I'm the only female in this castle who's sleeping within hearing distance of him. Before he can overthink it, I walk over to him and close the door behind him.

"Did you have a bad dream?" he asks.

"I don't get bad dreams."

And then I press myself to him. He may be wearing a shirt, but there's no way he can mistake my body for anything other than what it is—naked. He reaches for my hips as though to push me away, but I arch my back, pressing my breasts into his chest. My hand, up his nape. Toying there. Scraping the skin, gently.

"What are you—are you *naked*?!"

"So what if I am?"

My free hand reaches between us, lower and lower still. Ah, there. The evidence is there—he wants me. Every man does.

"Looks like *he* doesn't mind."

I rise on my tiptoes, preparing to kiss him, but his grip on my hips tightens and he manages to push me away—barely. "What's gotten into you?"

"Nothing."

"Bullshit. You're throwing yourself at me, and you don't think I'm going to find it a little weird? A few days ago, you wanted to rip my head off."

"A few days ago, you used your magic on me!" I lower my tone. "If you don't want what I've got to give, I have an entire castle of men to choose from."

When I push past him, he grips my arm. Like I knew he would. A muscle ticks in his jaw. "Are you so easily swayed? You'll just pick any of them?"

"Da...unless you want to volunteer."

"You'll blow your cover. And mine."

"I'll glamour them to forget."

He shakes his head. "Do you really have no limit?"

"None that I care to find out."

In a whirl, I flip our positions and push him on the bed. It creaks under his massive frame, but I soon straddle him, my hair a curtain around us.

"Elizabeta..."

My name rolls off his tongue, ending in a groan when I press my naked mound onto his erection.

"Mm?"

"This is—"

I shut him up with a quick peck, a brush of the lips. "A distraction, nothing more."

I feel it the moment he drops the pretense and gives in. His hand goes to my hair, digging in. I let him hold me, pretending I couldn't pull myself out of his grip. When we both know I could.

His lips hover over mine, and I wriggle onto his lap, annoyed at the teasing. It's not a kiss I want.

"You want this?" he asks, and his other hand shifts to my hip, pressing me down until I moan at the friction between my legs. Fuck, it feels so good. "My price is a kiss."

I scoff, then stop struggling. "Fine, then." I don't make a habit of kissing my human conquests, but I'll make an exception just for him.

His lips press against mine, and I do my damnedest to not respond. But it's impossible. I should've known because of how he kissed me the first time—frustrated, and to prove a point—or how our lips hovered and barely touched in the woods. Something should've clued me in, should've warned me to keep my distance. Only, would I have truly listened?

Because when his lips touch mine this time, it's with neither the frustration from before nor the hesitation that came in the woods. Rather, there's a determination behind the press of his lips to mine, a question in the way he parts my lips, and a decision made in how he slowly but purposefully slides his tongue to dance with mine.

His being a good kisser doesn't explain what comes next.

It doesn't explain how my knees buckle, despite me already straddling him.

It doesn't explain how my hands find their way to his neck, hanging on for dear life.

It most definitely doesn't explain the whimper that escapes me when the kiss softens, as if he's determined to take his sweet time to know every inch of me.

I can't anymore. Tears spring to my eyes, and the moment they do, I jump out of his lap with an almost violent force. I don't stop until my back is to the wall, and I've left a few feet of space between us. "What the fuck was that?"

Instead of apologizing, fucking Ştefan leans back on his arms, a very-unlike-him smirk on his lips. "A kiss."

"That wasn't *just* a kiss."

"Then maybe you haven't been kissed before, princess."

I haven't. Not like that. *Never* like that. But I refuse to admit as much.

A beat later, he stands. Walks over to me. I press myself further against the wall, wanting to be as far away from him—and this connection between us—as possible.

"Make no mistake, princess. If it's a fucking you want, I'm yours. I'll give you whatever your cold heart desires. But..." He tilts his head, the smirk falling off, the Ștefan I'm used to shining back through. "I don't think a simple fucking is enough to satisfy what you're after. The way you answered my kiss shows me the side you hide from the world—even from yourself. That kind of vulnerability deserves tenderness, not just passion." He takes a step closer, and a stupid sound like a half-whimper escapes me again. It's enough to give him pause. But not enough to stop the words passing his lips. "When you're ready, I'll show you something that goes beyond the physical, something that worships *all* of you as you deserve, princess."

"You—I—"

Ignoring my stammering, he walks out of my room, leaving me even more infuriated than before. Who the hell is this man?

Chapter 15

Elizabeta

It's been days since I returned home. Home, to a castle in the midst of nowhere. To my siblings, who are occupied with their lives. I should feel safe—Father assured me nothing will ever happen to me again. That I am *safe.*

But I don't feel it.

And that's why I'm wandering the halls, in the middle of the night, hoping to find peace. Hunger fuels me—for human blood, but also for vengeance.

And then I see the orange flickers outside the library and know I found someone even more awake. As I near the doors, murmurs of voices float to me. Father and...Silva?

"I beg of you, Lord Dracul. Let me seek them out, find the vengeance your heirs deserve."

"No, Silva. My word is final. The best way you can serve us is by protecting the heirs, period." Father exits the library in a blur of black clothing, without ever noticing me.

I wait a moment, then approach the library and enter through the wooden doors. Daniel's back is to me, his torn expression lighted by the flames. He looks...defeated. In a way I never once witnessed on him—not even while he was held captive with me.

"S—Daniel."

He whirls on me, and something shifts in his expression. "Elizabeta. What are you doing awake?"

"Couldn't sleep." I take a step closer, drawn to him by the weight of the pain uniting us. "I heard what Father said."

"He's right, I suppose."

"Is he?" I move closer still. "Because I agree with you. It's vengeance I need, not protection." Within reach now, I lift my arm and touch my fingertips to his cheek. "You gave me plenty of protection when you rescued me, Daniel. And since, as I've hovered between existence and letting go." He's the only one I've ever admitted that to. And it fuels my blood with more rage that I was ever so weakened. "Now I need their blood."

Determination fills his gaze, tightening his expression. "Then I will get it for you."

I hesitate. For the first time, I hesitate. I've always been confident in myself, but the raised scar on my cheek is a reminder that I am no longer the beauty I once was.

As if guessing my thoughts, Daniel cups that cheek and runs his thumb over the scar. He steps closer and kisses my forehead. Then my cheek. His lips move over the scar lightly, until they finally find my own. A rush of desire fills me, and I throw myself in his arms, completely and utterly destroyed by the power of his kindness, his understanding...

I wake to a damp pillow. Touch my cheeks, finding them wet—with tears for Daniel. Guilt gnawing at my gut, I wipe them furiously.

Last night was a mess. Between Daniel and Ștefan, it's no wonder I've woken up so conflicted. Goddammit! No human should be making me feel this crappy.

Not now. Not ever. I swore to myself I wouldn't be vulnerable again. Not when all it does is lead to pain.

And yet...

Groaning, I stand. Run my fingers through my tangled hair. My thoughts go to Daniel. It's so weird not having him next to me. Or being able to reach out to him whenever I want to.

Our romance could have been the stuff of fairytales, if fate was kinder to me. He saved me, both from the hunters and from myself afterward. Thanks to him, I didn't fall into a well of despair. He protected me. He alone figured out where the hunters held me. Not once did he give up, not until he burst through to rescue me. He didn't account for so many of them, nor for himself getting captured again. It almost broke me, for good, seeing him in so much pain. It almost broke *him.*

And even after—once Father himself tracked us down and finished the rescue attempt—it was Daniel alone who understood what

I'd been through. To be reduced to a weakened mess, to the point I didn't recognize myself... Daniel saw the pain I carried and hid after that.

We got close. So close. He was my everything, but none of my siblings knew. Nico, perhaps, given he was like a brother to him. But he never said anything to me. And Father... Well, if he knew, he didn't let on.

For a while, things were good. I even helped Daniel track down some hunters, on the rare occasion he let me. But then Nico killed that stupid human, and the vampiri clan whose territory she lived on came after us... Their retaliation ended with Daniel's beheading. He'd stayed behind, protecting me for the last time. And I can't say I ever truly forgave Nico for it. Which is why his happiness with that human trash feels like a slap to my face.

In many ways, losing Daniel was harder than losing Father. The night I saw his decapitated body, any hope of joy and romance disappeared for me. Which is why I'm not interested in the curse afflicting my family, nor will I play into it. Why open myself up to something only to get hurt once again?

I touch my lips, remembering Ştefan's kiss, the night before. How it unraveled me. Got to me in a way nothing ever has, not even Daniel's touch. It scares me. I should be running far, far away from him, but this quest has us joined at the hip.

And his words... *'When you're ready, I'll show you something that goes beyond the physical, something that worships* all *of you as you deserve, princess.'* That shouldn't be half as tempting as it is to me right now, like the proverbial forbidden fruit.

My thoughts are interrupted when I see a flicker out of the corner of my eye.

"...Daniel?"

I turn fully to it, but it's gone. Then it reappears by the door. I move to it, and...nothing.

Open the door. Down the hall, there's a flicker again.

I blur to it without a thought. It disappears again.

On and on, it continues, drawing me deeper through hallways and darkened corridors. There's no one around, probably on account of the early morning. *I* shouldn't even be here, especially blurring like I am at vampir speed. But I can't seem to stop, driven by an irrational need— desperate for a sighting of Daniel after that dream. Maybe then I could make sense of my turbulent emotions.

I don't realize how deep I've gotten into the bowels of the castle until something slams shut behind me. I turn, and the door I'd entered through is closed. I move to it, trying to open it again, and...nothing.

"What the...?"

A shiver creeps up my spine. I look around me then, *really* look around. Feel the press of the earth above me. I'm...down. Underneath the castle. In the...

"No."

Fuck.

I'm in the catacombs. The place Father was held captive in. The place *I* was held captive in. The exact place I've avoided like the plague since our arrival here.

"Welcome back, vampir."

Trembling, I face the voice...and it all rushes back.

Ştefan

I wake up with Elizabeta's taste still on my lips. Goddamn, but that kiss—it took every ounce of strength in me to pretend it didn't affect me nearly as much as it did her. When the truth is, I went to sleep hard as a rock, with my mind in turmoil.

She's a vampir. Everything I've been told to detest since I was young.

And yet the chemistry, when we let it blaze between us, is scorching. I'm no fool. She wanted to fuck me to distract herself from whatever nightmare woke her. But I'll be damned if I let her use me like she's used every male for centuries. Siren though she may be, I won't lose my head over her. I've waited long enough for the right woman and I can wait a little longer.

Thoughts in turmoil, I get dressed and head down to the dining hall. I'd told Cezar we're leaving today, but that remains to be seen. I have to first find out if what Trăian hinted at is true.

I slow down by Elizabeta's door. Her scent permeates the entrance, as if she were just here. Despite myself, I knock and lower my voice. "Elizabeta?"

No answer. No sounds from within, either. Odd.

It's a mystery that'll have to wait, though. I'm not made of steel and I fear if I walk into her room again, we'll end up in a repeat performance of last night. And much as I enjoyed it, I don't think I'd have the willpower to walk away again.

So rather than land myself in an impossible situation once more, I head in the direction of the dining hall—at least, what I recall it to be. I pace myself, lining the wall for a better direction compass, while keeping my ears alert to any sounds.

When the clanging of dishes and murmur of voices breaks the silence of the hallways, I know I'm close. A few moments later, my hand moves from the wall to a door, and I pull it open. I'm not even surprised that when I step through it, Cezar calls my name.

"Ştefan!"

What is surprising is the hint of harshness in his tone. He can't have figured out why I'm here, could he?

I head in the direction of his voice, counting the steps to the table—the same one Elizabeta led me to the last time. With each step, I keep an eye on the gray aura emerging from the fog of my lack of sight. It figures Cezar would be holding court in the same spot.

"Yes?"

"Did you hear what happened to Trăian?"

My stomach roils, all thoughts of breakfast forgotten. "I've only just woken up. What happened? Where is he?"

There's a pause then, "Dead."

Blood rushes to my ears, and my jaw hangs open. "What? How is that possible?"

Cezar clears his throat. "Tell him, sister." He must have called a nun over.

A soft, elderly female voice says, "Brother Trăian was found dead, outside. His head was bashed into the stones. Some say he was pale, paler than he'd been. After a thorough inspection, we believe he was exsanguinated. There were no marks on his neck but we have sensed evil enter this place."

"You wouldn't happen to know anything about that, would you, *brother*?" Cezar asks.

"No," I nearly growl. "How would I? I was asleep all night."

Fucking hell. Trăian was a mentee, someone I liked. Did Elizabeta do this? I have a hard time thinking she'd be so obvious about her needs. But the way I left her last night... Would her anger be enough to cause her to lash out like this?

And if not her, could Cezar have done it? Yes. But why? If it was to get back at me or somehow entrap me, I would've thought he'd be more subtle.

Whichever way the truth lies, one of them is responsible. And Trăian, an innocent, is dead.

"Unfortunate, really," Cezar says. "Such a bright soul."

I clench my fist, then unclench it. Trăian's blood is on my hands as much as anyone else's. "Has his family been notified, back home?"

"Not yet. But I presume the Grand Master will, once I write to him."

"What is this, the 19th century?"

"Well, the report I have to send him can't be put into emails, brother. Not when everything is trackable and hackable these days."

"Right." A beat. "May I see his quarters?"

"Of course. But why would you want to? His body is already being taken care of."

"You forget I trained him. I wish to say goodbye in my own way."

"Very well. Sister Andrea can take you."

I sense movement to my left, then the same sister who had spoken says, "Please follow me."

With each retraced step toward the entrance, the tension in my body only heightens. And the entire time, I feel Cezar's eyes on me.

The sister must be on the older side, as I hear her shuffle her footsteps ahead of me. Her steps are a beacon to my senses, and they make for an easy stride to Trăian's quarters.

She unlocks the door, and it creaks on its hinges as it opens. I step over the threshold.

"Thank you, sister. May I have some time alone?"

I wait until the door closes behind her. Then, same as I did in my room, I walk the perimeter of. After a moment, I touch my wrist cuff and slide the athame blade enough to cut into my palm, using darkness to assure myself I'm alone, truly. When I'm satisfied that's the case, I go to Trăian's bed, and start searching. As I'd expected, I find a small box hidden underneath the mattress, close to the wall. I open it and touch the item inside—a piece of paper.

"Dammit, Trăian," I whisper. "Was death the price you paid, then, for whatever it is you found?"

Muttering under my breath, I cast a spell. Darkness does my bidding as it has many times before in Liviu's office, and the paper's writing soon translates into familiar raised dots. My fingers move over each one with purpose. Then I retrace them again, unsure I understood.

When I'm convinced of Trăian's meaning, I pocket the paper and exit his room, heading straight for Elizabeta's. My heart thuds in my chest, each step fueled by urgency. Ignoring my earlier qualms about being in her presence, I burst through without knocking. "I know where the ring is."

Only silence answers me.

I do a quick walkthrough, and even use darkness to confirm what I already figured out—the room is as empty as the one I just left.

Elizabeta's gone.

Elizabeta

This entire time, not once did I ever think I'd be laying eyes on one of the hunters who imprisoned and captured me. Tortured me. Watched my screams with relish.

Yet here I am, faced with one's specter.

He's not the one who carved my skin, but the one who gave the order to. And observed, taking notes from afar, as it was done. As I bled and cried. As I was broken.

My vampir mind knows I'm in the present. That I'm stronger. Faster. *Safe*. Yet the memories shudder through me, nonetheless, wreaking havoc on my concentration.

It's with a pasty mouth I finally speak. "How... are you here?"

"The same as your little savior, vampir. Oh yes, I've been watching you." A dark chuckle escapes him and he floats closer to me.

I back away, so fast that I slam into the wall.

The chuckle turns into a full-blown laugh. "Glad to see I left an impression." His gaze purposefully lands on the scar on my left cheek and he smirks.

That snaps me out of my irrational fear. I push away from the wall and slowly, deliberately, move toward him. "You didn't. And I asked you a question."

When he doesn't answer, I turn to leave. But the door won't budge...not even under my vampir strength.

A smell of sulfur fills the air. Magic. Someone's using magic. But whom?

I face the hunter again. "You're a stafie. That translucent edge around you proves as much, so I know you didn't do this. You can't *touch* anything."

"Perhaps. Or perhaps I did."

He's lying. Focus. "What do you want from me?"

A darker chuckle follows. "You know what I want, vampir. To finish what I started."

He's lying. He's lying he's lying he's lying he's ly—

And then the weakness hits. So hard, so fast, my knees buckle. I manage to lean against the wall to hold myself up. I know, rationally, he can't be the one behind the weakness. That's the curse. It's Zalmoxis. But seeing his smirk, his sheer enjoyment of my pain, of my dread, has me blurring the lines between past and present. "What.... You can't. You're dead. So who's doing this?"

He only gazes at me. And his translucent form seems to solidify, not break.... Not like Daniel's.

"Don't bother calling on your little ghost, if that's what you're thinking. I've got someone else keeping an eye on him."

I clench one fist, forcing my nails to pierce the skin. Perhaps the pain will ground me—or at least keep me from losing consciousness. "What do you *want*?"

"I told you."

Here's the thing. Anyone else, I could rip apart. But how can I do that to this piece of shit when I can't even touch him?

I think back to Ștefan. To the darkness he'd fed me. I wonder if I can force it to help me, same as Father did.

I dart my eyes to the shadowy corners, forcing it, willing it, and... nothing.

The hunter draws closer. "You were rescued before I was through with you. I will remedy that."

The weakness pushes on me like a physical weight and, this time, it has the added pain of a thousand blades being stabbed into my skin. I scream. It takes me only a few seconds to realize I gave him everything he wanted.

With one last burst of strength, I rush to the door, and pull on it with all my might. This time, it opens.

I burst through it, running, stumbling, running again. I'm unable to blur, the weakness worse than anything I've felt. But I run, not paying attention to where I'm at.

I turn a corner and walk right into a solid block of wall.

"Woah."

Hands reach for me, but I already know his scent.

I nearly jump into his arms, ashamed of how relieved I am that it's him I collided with. "It's me," I whisper in his neck, tightening my hold on him.

Ștefan hesitates, then his arms come around me. "What's wrong?"

"Nothing. Just...fucking hold me."

He does as I ask, and his strength is what I need. His solid muscles against me, his heartbeat thundering by my ear. His scent filling my nostrils.

Like it did last night...

Belatedly, it hits me that every inch of me is surrounded by every inch of him. Standing, he towers over me, and I can feel the heat emanating from his body even through my jeans and shirt. It's a reminder of everything he is—alive, warm, *human*—and everything I'm not. It's also a reminder of just how little that mattered last night, when he was kissing me the way he was.

"Are you sure you're okay?" His chest rumbles as he speaks. "You're shaking like a leaf."

The words are enough to snap me back to myself, and I pull

away abruptly. "Da, I'm fine." Wiping at my cheeks, I'm thankful he can't see me. "What, um, were you doing here?"

"Looking for you."

I look at him, perplexed. "Why?"

"Because I found something. Something that can help us get the ring and get the fuck out of here at once."

Chapter 16

Elizabeta

The thought of leaving this cursed place is enough to refocus my attention. "What do you mean? What did you find?"

Ştefan grabs my arm and tugs me around a corner, away from prying eyes. Instead of putting distance between us, he pushes closer to me. In spite of myself, his proximity entrances my senses all over again, and I don't pay attention to much else.

The bulk of his body is pressed up against mine, delivering that very human heat. It's enough to melt the ice filling my veins since my encounter with the hunter, and *almost* enough to re-energize me. Almost. My gaze flits to his strong neck—his carotid artery would've had me salivating any other time. But I find myself swaying on my feet, using the strength of the wall to support me.

My eyes drift lower, and that's when I see it. The piece of paper crumpled in his hand.

I take it and unravel it, finding a piece of paper with some nonsensical jumbled dots. "What is this?"

"I found it in Trăian's bedroom. It's a note—to me. Well, part note, part map. I used my magic to translate it to braille."

"Why would you—"

Ștefan doesn't even let me finish before he interrupts. "Cezar told me at breakfast that Trăian was killed."

"What!?"

"Apparently, they found his body outside." He pauses, as if there's more, but only says, "I asked to see his room, and found this hidden. I think it's Trăian's last attempt to help me, to point me in the way of what's going on."

"But why do you think this leads to the ring's location?"

He lifts his hand and a drop of blood falls onto the paper. It's only then I catch the faint hint of metal in the air—he bled himself already.

"Trăian's note was simple. *'If something happens to me, this place will hold the key to the answers.'* How much more obvious could he get?" Ștefan mutters something under his breath and when I look down again, tendrils of darkness disappear off the paper. Instead of the jumbled dots from before, I see the words Ștefan had just spoken, written out. And next to them is a small map. "I have a feeling what you're holding is a map of the catacombs of this place. Meaning close to the well where the ring was originally crafted and then hidden. Am I right?"

I glance down at the map. My vision is blurry, something I'm not used to, and there's a tremble in my hands. Fucking hell. I might have to ask him for his ... *No. I refuse to beg for help.*

"Well?"

I swallow hard. "Da, you're right. It's a map to the underneath." *'Underneath'* being the same underground tomb where a vengeful specter awaits me. Fuck.

He nods, oblivious to my torment. "Thought as much. Here's the thing. The ring, I'm assuming it's one of those old relics that needs to be recharged every once in a while. With any magical object, the easiest way to do this is by leaving it in its place of conception. And, if someone wanted to enhance it, then they would also do this at the place of conception."

"Enhance it, how?"

"By adding more darkness to it. To make its powers...stronger."

I shake my head, the words floating in my head. "I don't understand."

Ștefan frowns, tilting his head down toward me. "What's wrong with you?"

"Nothing." There's a bite to my tone. "Just start making sense, Dacian."

He tilts his head to the side. For a moment, I think he'll push it, but all he says is, "To add strength to a relic, you need to recreate some of its original elements—basically, whatever circumstances led to its creation. For a Zalmoxis relic, that would be death. Or sacrifice, given the fucker loves his blood oaths."

I glance at the map. "You're saying...the Dacians have the ring. Not only that, but they're trying to recharge it. And they're doing so with a sacrifice or something tied to death, at the spot this map points to?"

"Yes." A beat, then, "And they're more than likely doing it tonight. Trăian said it was a blood moon."

"Fucking hell. You and wolves and goddamn full moons."

He frowns at my curse, but I wave him off. Then remember he can't see, so I shove the piece of paper at him again. And in the process, wobble again.

"Fine. What's your plan, then?"

"I want to go check it out."

"Now?"

"Yes, now. You got better plans?"

I do. I want out of here, and away from him so I can stop being torn in two. Not to mention I don't want to be anywhere near the basement. Not after knowing that hunter stafie is in there. And it's not like I can tell Ștefan about it, because that means opening up about everything with the hunters and what happened to me. And I'm most definitely *not* doing that.

But getting the ring also means leaving... And that, too, means leaving the stafie behind. He's got to be bound by this area, after all, same as Daniel is bound to me. I hope.

"Fine. Let's do this."

I go to move past him, but Ștefan grabs my arm again. "Not so fast."

"What now?"

He raises his other hand. Magic is already swirling, the darkness stronger than before—when did he cut himself again?

"Take it," he says.

"I don't need your magic."

"You do. You need to be at your strongest and, right now, you're nowhere close."

I hesitate for only a beat, before leaning back against the wall and nodding. "Fine. Do it."

He rests one hand on the wall above my head, and with the other, he cups my cheek. I open my mouth to say he didn't need to touch me last time to refuel me, but darkness washes over me in quick waves. I close my eyes, lulled by its power and how, with every lick of it, my tremors ease. The iciness disappears, replaced by warmth. My strength returns. When I open my eyes again, they're clear, all blurriness gone.

I look at Ştefan, waiting for him to speak. Wondering how the hell he even knew I was that weak again. Wondering whether he's going to remove his hand from my cheek now that it's over, yet dreading the moment he will.

For a few long seconds, he doesn't move, barely even breathes. It feels like we're stuck in a frozen moment—an unreal, impossible moment. And then he drops his hand from my cheek and steps back.

"Better?" Ştefan asks.

"Da." I pause for a beat. "Thank you."

Those two words are ripped from my throat, and I hate how hoarse my voice sounds, like I've been put through the wringer. I think about asking what happened to cause this, especially given it hasn't been that long since he last gave me a boost. Did he use magic in a weird way again? Is it just the curse, getting worse? Did our kiss have anything to do with this? And does it even fucking matter, in the end?

Ştefan, to his credit, maintains a complete poker face. "Let's go. I'll need you to lead the way, but so long as you walk, not blur, I can follow."

In my haze of the stupid curse, I'd thought the facts Ştefan laid in front of me made sense. My mind is clearer now. I see the dots Ştefan connected between everything he found out, but also get a sense of unease. And the deeper we get in the bowels of the earth, the more that sense of dread rises. Especially as we don't run into anyone—Dacian or nun.

I pause in the middle of the corridor after we come down yet another flight of stairs and turn to him. "Are you sure about this?"

"I am."

"Let me see the paper again."

He hands it over to me, then pushes past me. The scent of his blood is in the air, and I'm assuming he's using the same spell he had before—or whatever he calls what he does that helps him better orient himself.

I follow behind him for a bit. The thing is, I hold the one sense that truly confirms none of this is right—the walls are tainted with darkness, similar to Ştefan's, but it's not dormant. It's swirling in a way that's most definitely not friendly, but as though it's wild and raw and ready to strike.

"Ştefan, wait."

He doesn't listen, so I blur in front of him and put my hand on his chest. "Listen, I'm not one to back away from a fight, but isn't it a bit weird?"

He snorts impatiently. "What's weird?"

"This paper. The way you found it."

"The time to raise objections is long gone, Elizabeta. We need to get this ring so we can get back to the hag and I can help my sister. The longer we stay here, the more Zalmoxis gives her nightmares and makes shit worse and we lose our element of surprise."

"I know that! Don't you think I know that? But this smells weird."

"No weirder than anything else that's happened here."

"How do you explain Trăian being killed?"

"I don't know, Elizabeta. How *do* you? They said he was found with his head bashed in and totally exsanguinated."

"I didn't—" I narrow my eyes. "You didn't mention that before."

He stays quiet, jaw clenched.

"Hang on a second. If you're thinking… I *didn't* do that."

My denial seems to be what he needed for the torrent of words to escape him. "I know you came in here with an agenda, Elizabeta. Because of the hunters who held you captive."

I reel back, stunned, feeling way more exposed than I'd like even though he can't see my expression. "How much do you know?"

He opens his mouth as if to lash at me, to say something hurtful, then seems to think better of it and mutters, "Enough. I know enough."

"No. *No.*" I move closer, feeling my ire rise like a volcano on the brink of eruption. "*What* do you know and *who* told you?"

After a beat, he opens his mouth to say something, but stops himself again, as though he's reassessing. "Let's talk about this later. Not now—not when we're close to getting that ring and getting the hell out of here."

"And you think we can do that, when you clearly don't trust me?"

He sighs. "I didn't say I don't trust you."

"You implied as much!" I hate how much that bothers me, too. I thought we'd been building on something, but maybe that's just been in my head. For good measure, I add, "I'll say this one more time—I didn't kill Trăian. I had nothing to do with his death."

"If you say so."

"I more than say so, you fool! I think they're playing you and you're too blind to see it."

The words register once I've said them, but it's too late. His jaw is rigid.

"No one said you have to listen to me."

"Ştefan, wait—"

He pushes past me, stumbles into a wall, and then feels his way back on the path. Which only makes me feel shittier.

Fucking hell.

I watch him go, torn. And torn that I'm being torn—damn his unreliable human emotions!

I'm fairly sure this is a trap. What he said about Trăian being killed confirms it. Which means I can go after him—and he won't listen—or I can go after the dickwad who set the trap first and stop all this from happening.

With one last glance at where Ştefan disappeared to, I head in the opposite direction.

No one's in the dining hall. And there are too many rooms to search, even with me feeling at my peak. Besides, I very much doubt I'll find what I'm seeking within the walls of this place. Which leaves me with one other choice—Daniel. He may not be allowed past whatever barrier is around this place, but as a stafie, he sees things. He always has, even if he hasn't always been upfront about it. No better time than now to pick his brain.

I blur outside, to the entrance of the castle, and again feel that odd sensation as I pass under the heavy metal gates. I glance back at the castle. I could leave Ştefan in there. Return to my siblings. They wouldn't know the truth. And I'd be spared the agony of facing that stafie awaiting me—because I know he is. If I left, I wouldn't have to face it. I wouldn't have to relieve that time from my past any more than I already have. I could just...leave. Alex would understand.

But the truth is, I couldn't live with myself if I did that. It's got nothing to do with the bond or whatever the hell is going on here. It's got to do with the fact I refuse to give the upper hand to a specter that's already dead and who already harmed me so much of his living.

Get a move on, Elizabeta. If you want to help the Dacian before it's too late, you need help.

I'm barely close to the woods when I see the translucent form of that help, pacing as though he's been waiting for me.

"Daniel!"

"Liza!" He floats to me, a panicked look on his features. "Are you okay?"

I frown at him. "I am...as good as I can be."

His expression of pure anguish roots me to the ground. *He can't be this broken up over our last fight. It wasn't our first one, and it won't be our final one. Sure, I was a bit harsh, but he was being so—*

Suddenly, it dawns on me exactly why he's so agitated.

"The stafie. You know about him?"

He nods. "He came out there. Sought me out. *Banished* me from entering. That's why I haven't been able to come warn you."

"I don't understand. How can this be possible? You said..." I try to master the panic in my voice before I continue. "When you told me what you are, what happened to hold you back, the protection linking us—you said stafii stay behind because of a personal bond. To a person or a place. Obviously, this hunter is tied to the horrors that happened here but—stafii can't leave, can they?!"

"They...we...shouldn't be able to. The ties binding us are solid in a way that's hard to explain. It's more spiritual than it is physical. A set of limitations on our souls that cannot be broken no matter what."

"But you've always been able to move as you please."

"Da. Because of *you*. You're my tie."

His words should make me happy. The inevitability behind them is as good as a promise to stay forever. But they don't. I've known Daniel for a long time. I've grown to understand his every expression, every shift in his features, in his voice. It's how I hear the faint longing behind what he says. And for once, this is beyond us. My thoughts shift to Ștefan. To Silviana, whom he wants to protect just as much as Daniel wants to protect me. Just as much as I want to protect him. Maybe we're not that different, after all.

"So what do you think is happening here?"

Daniel shakes his head. "I'm not sure. The only thing I can think of is someone broke the hunter's spiritual tie to this place. But if that's the case, you won't be safe anywhere until he's gone."

I close my eyes to get ahold of myself. I am Elizabeta Dracul. I have fought vampiri clans and every manner of creature on this earth. I will not be taken down by a stafie—especially not a hunter one.

"Liza?"

I open my eyes again. "I'll be fine. There's something else." Quickly, I fill him in on Ştefan.

When I'm done, Daniel's eyes widen. "Was the Dacian Trăian a blond man, young, with a beard?"

"Da..."

"Then you're right, because he's as far from dead as a human can be. I saw him cross into the woods, not that long ago! You can still catch him if you hurry." He points me in the direction and I take off.

The further in the woods I get, the more I catch a whiff of blood. Human blood. And sweat. And fear. So much fear. Oh, yes. This is the person I'm looking for.

I catch up to him a few minutes later. His slow pace is no match for me.

"You slimy piece of crap!"

I slam him against the tree trunk and practically hear his teeth rattle. And maybe a rib or two crack.

I turn him around, and his eyes widen. I'm not sure if Ştefan's spell to keep my real features hidden is holding or if it disappeared but whatever the case, there is shock in his eyes. "You're not.... human...."

I twist my lips in the scariest grimace I can muster. "Funny. For a dead man, you sure are funny."

He whimpers. I slam him again. Out of the corner of my eye, I see Daniel hovering, but he doesn't intervene.

"What. Did. You. Do?"

"I—I don't understand—"

I shake him again. "Stop lying! Why does Ștefan think you're dead? Why did you leave the clue about the catacombs?"

"N-nothing. He just… Cezar, he—I had to."

"Did you, now?" Anger fills me, roiling in my gut like a snake waiting to strike. I loathe weak humans and this one is no better.

With a growl, I tear into his throat. His blood tastes foul, but I still drink enough to satiate my thirst. When I pull back, his neck has a gaping wound as I haven't soothed the skin into healing.

"Why does Cezar need Ștefan down in the catacombs?"

"I—I don't know!"

"Liar!" I tear into the other side of his neck, and he thrashes against me, becoming weaker by the second.

Daniel floats closer. "Liza, stop. You're going to—"

"Kill him. It's no less than he deserves."

I go back to Trăian's neck, and feed. And feed. With each slurp, the blood reinvigorates me. And it's tainted with more—with darkness. Like a potent mix of Ștefan's magic and regular blood.

I pull away from his neck, blood dripping from my chin. At least now I'm ready for what's coming.

"Liza—"

"Don't."

I blur away from Daniel, off to do something I never thought I would—save a human.

Ștefan

Darkness empowers me to move. It helps that the corridor slopes, so all I have to do is hold close to the wall and I know where to go. I don't need Elizabeta Dracul, or her jabs. I can do this on my own.

The deeper I go, though, the more I get the sense I'm being watched.

Stop being ridiculous. You're fine.

Step by step, I keep making my way. Lost in the haze of my determination, of my anger. Cezar will pay for this. Liviu may have taken a liking to him, but when I explain that he killed one of our own, he won't let it go without punishment.

My foot catches on something on the floor and I trip, going down hard. I expect to hear the crack of bone onto the hard floor, but instead, I land on something soft… I use my hands to feel my way around, and the first thing they touch is something wet. And coppery smelling.

"Help…"

Something latches onto my hand. When I cover it with a hand of my own, I sense frail skin under my fingertips. And a pulse that is quickly dwindling.

A sinking sensation weighs me down. "I… Sister?"

"Help…"

Still holding the person's hand, I shift onto my knees and move my other hand up her arm, touching a lined cheek, and then…a coif.

I fall back onto my heels, shock filling every area of my body. *I screwed up.*

"You're a little late, but still in time for the fireworks," a voice says from my left.

Cezar.

Chapter 17

Ștefan

Slowly, I get to my feet and turn toward the voice. "What are you really doing here, Cezar?"

"Come see and perhaps you'll understand."

I follow the sound of his footsteps. When he stops, I do, too. Every nerve of my body is buzzing at the power in the room he's brought me to.

Cezar laughs. "Let me paint a picture for you, since you can't admire my masterpiece. We're in the old chapel. And instead of the pews, I've added sturdy wooden posts. Thirteen of them are placed in a circle around the room." He takes a deep breath, a sigh of satisfaction escaping him. "And from each one hangs a nun."

My stomach roils. I can imagine the scene all too easily. The darkness in here feels stifling, not at all at my command. There are no auras to see, nothing to orient me, because I'm surrounded—submerged—by it.

"You—"

"They're not dead, don't worry," he interrupts. "Not yet, anyway. I have bled them, ensuring their blood pools into a drain that goes deep into the bowels of this castle."

"Why, Cezar? This can't be at Liviu's behest!"

Cezar chuckles darkly. "You clearly don't know our master, then. All he has ever wanted is the return of Zalmoxis. It is a task passed on to him by other Grand Masters before him, but he alone has come close to achieving it."

I try to play dumb, but that part at least, Trăian told me. I remember him reading much the same off that book he had. Still, I play dumb. "The return of... What are you *talking* about?"

Cezar snorts. "Our god was imprisoned long ago by weaker ones. It took many Grand Masters to understand how, and where he is. And how to release him."

"And the deaths of thirteen innocent nuns is how?"

"Of course. Their sacrifice will not be in vain."

"You're sick," is all I can come up with.

"I doubt that. Not sicker than someone who affiliates himself with a vampir. And one of a royal house, at that."

"How did you—"

"I knew since you entered, fool! But I was curious what you were here for. And when you weren't very forthcoming with that information, well, I had my clerks dig into what this place holds."

His footsteps sound closer. "Imagine my surprise when I found out about Zalmoxis' relic." He grabs my hand. and I feel the cool metal of a circle-type piece of jewelry being placed in my palm. "This is as close to it as you'll get, *brother*." Another dark chuckle. "I must thank Trăian for his part in this."

The dread in my stomach amplifies tenfold. "...Trăian?"

Cezar laughs outright. "The beauty with your lack of sight, is it never occurred for you to ask to see the body. Because of course, there isn't one."

A sense of betrayal courses through me—Trăian was my mentee, my friend, or so I thought!—but I quickly squash it. "What is it you need me for, then? You seem to have it all under control."

"Not quite, no. See, with your presence here and this newfound ring, I can speed up the process. Amplify the power of the sacrifice. And so, my dear Ștefan, it seems you have your use after all."

I step back and toss the ring in the air. It will buy me a few seconds, but it's all I need. The athame slides from my wrist cuff and cuts into my palm. I use it to slice in my other hand, too, then pull on all the darkness around me. Luckily, there is no shortage of it.

"If you thought I'd roll over and play dead so easily, you're sorely mistaken, Cezar."

From somewhere around me, he replies, "Ah, but who says I underestimated you? You can come out, now, brothers. Time to dole out our punishment and teach our brother the price of turning his back on the Dacians."

Dammit all to hell. Elizabeta was right, and something tells me if I survive, I'll never hear the end of it.

Elizabeta

There's noise in the dining hall this time when I return, but when I poke my head around the corner, I find only a few Dacians. No sign of Cezar. No sign of the nuns, either.

I blur all the way to the basement doors. Into the bowel of the earth I go. Torches on the walls light the way somewhat; what should have been enough brilliance, is dimmed by the same malevolent darkness I'd felt before. One that has thickened, taken even more of a life of its own.

Where the hell is he?

If Trăian was the bait, then Cezar must be behind this. But where would he have taken Ștefan? I could be too late if I spend much more time searching for him.

Dammit, Ștefan!

And then it dawns on me. Daniel's words. His insistence of a bond between us. If it's true...

I close my eyes and focus inward. It's a long shot, but at this point, I might as well try it. And sure enough, there's a warmth in me that tingles when I focus on it. Within it, I can almost sense Ștefan's touch. And his smell, permeating the air, as if he was right in front of me. I follow it down corridor after corridor, until...

Pandemonium hits—a Dacian being tossed out of a room. I blur there, and a quick glance at him shows me cuts over his chest. Nail-like gauges that have cut through his clothes, digging into his skin, much like the claws of a rabid dog.

"What the hell?"

I glance inside the room, and my eyes widen. The first thing I register is the blood. So much blood. The nuns, hanging from wooden posts, their skin deathly pale. Dacians, at least twenty of them, creating a circle around someone.

Magic is everywhere—its sulfur scent nearly choking me. Before my very eyes, someone in the midst of the Dacians releases a curse. It lashes out at the nearest Dacian, slashing into him like a sharp sword. He flies back, bleeding onto the stones. And the sulfur scent grows and grows.

That's when I glimpse who's in the midst of it all—Ștefan. Alone.

Something stutters in my chest, but I ignore it. Instead, I grab the closest Dacian—who's oblivious to my presence—and dig my teeth into his neck, tearing it half off. The one next to him turns to me, and I do the same.

"Vampir!" someone yells.

Then I tear into them, too. Over and over. Until I've made myself a path in their midst, next to a now panting Ștefan.

"It's me," I say with a light tap on his shoulder.

He nods, jaw clenched. Now's not the time for *I told you* so's, even though it's on the tip of my tongue. Instead, I say, "How can I help? How do we get out of here?"

"We can't without the ring. Cezar has it."

"Cezar?"

Ștefan stops mid-toss of magic to tilt his head toward me. "Is he not here anymore?"

I do another quick scan, though I'm pretty sure I wouldn't have missed the prick. "Nu, he's gone."

"Dammit. He has the ring, Elizabeta!"

"All right, take a breath." I lunge at a Dacian getting too close, and rip his head clean off. Blood sloshes at my feet, staining my jeans and boots dark red. I turn to Ștefan. "I'll find Cezar after this. For now, let's get through these fuckers."

Ștefan looks like he's about to argue, but I say, "Behind you."

And just like that, we're back-to-back, fighting the attacking Dacians. And boy, are they persistent. With each passing moment, the nuns are getting paler and paler, and I know they won't survive this. But Ștefan and I can.

The scent of blood hits me, then. *His* blood. In quantities way larger than normal.

"What the—"

I whirl around. Ștefan's got one Dacian by the throat, but his unoccupied arm is bleeding—heavily. Dammit, this fool took another fucking bullet for me!

Only, it's not a bullet. I realize it after a great shudder goes through him. The last of his magic leaves him, and he drops to the floor. I tackle the Dacian who'd been about to strike him, and rip into his throat, no holds barred. Then wipe my mouth and turn to Ștefan. He's on his knees, panting, a sheen of sweat covering his entire body. His jaw is clenched, pain radiating from his tense posture.

"You fool!"

His teeth chatter. "Couldn't very well let you take it, could I?"

"What was the spell, curse, whatever the fuck hit you?"

He shakes his head jerkily. "D-doesn't m-matter. G-get the r-ring."

I rise, angrier than before. Angry at him, angry at myself, angry at these fuckers. "You think you can just do whatever the fuck you want? Not here. Not with me. Not under the same roof I was tortured."

A heavy silence descends on the room. But I soon realize it's got nothing to do with my pronouncement. Rather, with the person who has re-entered.

"I see you've finally let the illusion drop and shown your true colors, vampir."

I turn to face Cezar, and freeze. He's not alone—of course, he's not. Next to him is the stafie of my nightmares.

With a smirk, Cezar says, "Looking for this?" and lifts his hand.

In it is a ring. I can't be sure it's the one we need. For all I know, he's fucking with me. But in that moment, with Ștefan bleeding behind me, and faced with the creature of my nightmares, I know I'll do everything in my power to get it.

Cezar glances behind me, and his smirk widens. "Ah, I see our dear Ștefan went and got himself blood-cursed. It's no wonder he's not even attempting to heal himself—the agony alone would be worth death itself."

So that's what happened... Explains why he's not healing himself.

"We can help him, you know."

"I'll help him myself. *After* I take your head."

Cezar laughs, and the rest of them titter. "You're so sure of yourself, Elizabeta Dracul."

I toss my hair back, leveling as imperious a gaze on him as I can. "As I should be. You forget perhaps that you're standing in the presence of royalty. Kneel, Dacian, and I may yet forgive your impertinence."

The laughter dies off his features, replaced by anger. "I serve another master, vampir. I bow to no one."

"Really? Is that what this whole display is for, here?" If I keep him talking, then maybe a miracle solution will occur to me. Because right now, between Ștefan bleeding behind me, and these fuckers ready to attack me.. *I wish Alex was here. Or Nico. Fuck, I'd take any of them right now, if it meant I wasn't alone.*

The stafie by Cezar's side is keeping his eyes on me. But impatience fills his features. He wants to finish what he started, I know he does. Question is, why hasn't he?

As though guessing my thoughts, Cezar turns to him. "You can have her, as I promised. But only after the portal is open. I need the Dracul line to finish the spell."

The stafie bows his head, but I read in his dark gaze that he's not happy. Huh. That makes two of us.

I back away toward Ștefan, and chance a glance over my shoulder at him. He's on the floor, still breathing, but I don't like the sound of what I'm hearing. His heartbeat is faint.

Shit. "Don't you fucking give up on me now, Dacian," I mutter to him. Then face the others...only for the worst fucking thing to happen.

The weakness of the curse hits me.

Ștefan

Elizabeta's muttered curses are the background to my pain. Thousands of knives are coursing through my blood, feeling like they're destroying my arteries, aiming for my organs. I know it can't be true—if it were, I'd be dead already. But the pain is enough to keep me on the brink of consciousness.

Coolness fills my limbs, and I can barely open my eyes. All I catch, a brief flash, is Elizabeta's aura in front of me, protecting me. Who would've thought it? But there are many. Too many of my brethren...how can she face them all? Especially when I sense in her that weakness from before.

The curse. It's got to be. With me on the brink of death, it's come to take her, and the rest of them. Which means somewhere in the Dracul palace, the other heirs are also feeling it. Perhaps it'll jostle them into action, send them our way. But it may be too late by the time they get here, and I can't take that chance.

So I do what I swore to myself I wouldn't do, and ask for help. I close my eyes, letting myself fall deeper into a meditative trance, then look within for the sacred twin bond I share with Silviana. As kids, we used to take advantage of it. As adults, we learned to give each other the space we needed. And since the thing with Zalmoxis, I've dreaded tapping into this, for fear of giving him yet another way to get to her.

But I have no choice—this isn't for me.

Silviana... Sorella. If you can hear me, I need your help.

There's a long pause, then a shocked, *Ștefan!?*

Da. I don't have much time. We're at Corvins' Castle, and los...ing.

Already, I can feel the faint thread stretching, waning, like a bad phone connection. I'm too late. And I shouldn't be trying to drag her in this, period.

Ștefan—

There is no time, Silviana. I take a deep breath. *I love you, sorella.*

Ștefan, no! What—

I close the gateway, shutting her out. I've done my part, but I can do one more thing.

Vaguely, I can hear the sounds of a fight. Elizabeta, cursing up a storm. Cezar, the smug bastard, saying she should settle in and enjoy the show. And even more, I sense her weakness, hitting her with even more strength. And her fear...

I dip my index into the blood pooling out of me, to get a tangible link to darkness. Then I send it to Elizabeta, like I had before. If nothing else, this will give her enough of a boost to survive until her siblings get here.

As for me… I can hear Father and Mother calling my name.

Elizabeta

Between one blink and the next, Cezar's got Dacians flanking me. Taking advantage of my weakness, one strikes forward, grabbing my right arm with a tight grip.

I try to yank my arm out of his grip, but it's no use. This weakness isn't like before. It drags my body down, as though wanting to send it to sleep. I glance again at Ștefan, remembering what Daniel warned me against. If it's true, if he's my consort, then him being on the brink of death is what's precipitating this. Which means I don't have much time. For the first time, it hits me *hard*. His death won't just equal mine, but all of my siblings', too.

"You're going to regret this, Cezar!"

"No, I think not, *princess*," the stafie mutters, and I hate how Ștefan's endearment sounds on his lips—harsh, cold, and unfeeling. The realization that I only like it when he says it throws me for a loop. When the fuck did that happen?

Cezar turns his back on me. The ring glows in his hand—guess that's my confirmation it's the right one—and he lifts both hands in the air. "Sisters, I thank you for your sacrifice, it has not been in vain."

When he drops his hands, the nuns' necks sag forward. He's killed them…he's fucking killed them like puppets!

Lips numb, I toss out, "You're a monster."

"Says the bitch who's been hunting the lineage of vampiri

hunters," says the stafie, moving next to me.

"Not all of them," I say. "Just your descendants. And the fuckers who helped you."

He moves in front of me and reaches for my chin. I'm used to Daniel being unable to touch me, but this man, his cool fingers reach my chin. He smirks at the surprise I'm not quick enough to hide.

"Oh, yes. My hate toward you spans centuries, vampir. It gives me physicality, at least temporarily." He glances at Cezar, and it hits me—whatever he's done, if I can get rid of Cezar and the ring, then the stafie will be gone, too. Daniel was right. Everything has a tether. "I cannot wait for him to be done with his games. Then, you and I can finish what we started centuries ago."

He holds his hand out to another Dacian, who passes him an athame. My eyes widen. No. Not this again! Then I grit my teeth, trying to stay strong. I will not break. Not again.

The stafie grips my chin tighter and, with his free hand, places the blade of the knife to my other cheek. The non-injured one. "Let's see if we can give you matching scars, hmm?"

When the tip of the blade digs into my skin, I force myself to stare into his eyes. Jaw clenched, eyes unblinking, I refuse to shed a tear. And when he's done, and I feel the blood drip down my cheek, I still refuse to cry. "Is that the best you've got?"

The stafie narrows his eyes, but whatever he's about to say is interrupted by Cezar's chanting. The blood around his feet bubbles, almost frothing. The ring he's holding glows brighter. Or perhaps it's only brighter because of the darkness taking over everything, including the torches, in this chapel.

And then something else hits me. A burst of power, filling me.

I sneak a glance over my shoulder, knowing it's coming from Ştefan, only to find him even paler than before. His heartbeat is almost nonexistent.

Damn you, Ştefan!

I need to get to him, but first, it's time to speed this along. "I didn't take you for a slow mover, Cezar," I mutter. "Open the goddamn portal already, since it looks like this hunter and I have business to finish."

The stafie turns to me and slaps me. I hiss, but force myself to remain demure enough. I need them distracted by the portal. Then, and only then, will I be able to strike.

Thankfully, Cezar seems spurred on by my words. Perhaps he doesn't want to look bad in front of his kin. Whatever the case, his chanting cadence picks up, and the frothing at his feet bubbles more. Rises. Forms...a gate?

It shouldn't be, but it is. And in front of my shocked eyes, a door forms—made of solidified shadows, gleaming like the darkest obsidian, with a golden glow around something that looks like a lock. A circular lock... the kind a ring fits into.

If he inserts the ring in there, that's it...they'll get Zalmoxis out.

"Her blood. Give me her blood!" Cezar yells over his shoulder.

The stafie moves to him with the knife he used to carve me up, and I know that's my cue.

I rise from my crouch and smack the back of my head against the forehead of the Dacian who's holding me. Before he can utter a cry, I whirl on him and snap his neck. Then blur to the other three behind him.

Cezar turns at the noise, his eyes glowing dark. "Get her!"

But I'm too fast. They may have magic on their side, but I've got my vampir speed thanks to Ştefan, and I intend to put it to good use for as long as it'll last.

My speed, ironically, seems not to be the only thing I have. Because as I move, I notice darkness cloaking me, same as it did Ştefan. And in the depths of the gate—the place I should fear for what it holds—I feel a pull. A familiar one... It almost distracts me from a Dacian.

I don't... What is this strange sensation?

Then, the impossible happens. Another voice rings in my head. *Focus, Elizabeta! I taught you better than this.*

Chapter 18

Elizabeta

I stumble in my blur, and though I catch the Dacian I was aiming for by the throat, we both tumble down. Pinning him to the ground with my knee, I whirl toward the gate once more. *Father?*

FOCUS, Elizabeta!

That's him, all right. I don't know how, but I'm not about to question it. Instead, I do as he commands me, and concentrate all my attention on eliminating the threats. With darkness as my ally, I clean the area, leaving bodies everywhere. By the time I'm through with them, in mere moments, only Cezar and the stafie are left.

I move toward them, this time at a slower speed. "I'll take that ring now, Cezar."

"I don't think so." He turns to the stafie. "Attack her."

"With pleasure."

But before either of them can do anything, the gate behind them shudders, groans, and creaks. I stop, and they freeze.

Cezar glances behind him, an awed expression on his features. "Master, I..."

Whatever he sees, it's enough to distract him. I blur into him, clasping my fingers around one of his hands—the one holding the ring. With the other, I shove him straight into the gate. His resistance is futile to my vampir strength, and he loses his balance, releasing the ring into my palm as he does. But instead of falling *through* the gate, as he'd presumably been wanting to, he disintegrates upon touching it. The smell of charred skin burns in the air.

I look around, but the stafie is also gone. *Fucking hell. Is he gone for good, though?*

"Father?"

Nothing. *Was I imagining it all?*

I glance at the ring in my hand. At the gate, still standing. At the bodies everywhere. And for the first time in my life, I'm nauseous at the level of carnage surrounding me.

I palm the tiny ring and return to Ștefan's side. Slide the golden ring into his closed fist. "There. It's done. But there's a portal, and I need you to do your Dacian voodoo magic and make it go poof."

For a long moment, he's silent. The beat of his heart is almost impossible to hear.

I shake him. "Ștefan, did you hear me?"

At last, he nods, weakly. Clenches his fist around the ring, and shudders. "The magic in this....it's strong."

"Can you close it, yes or no?"

"I'll...try."

Every word seems to take a lot out of him. But eventually, the gate shudders and disappears. Only the blood and corpses are left.

Ștefan's hand falls open. "T-take i-it," he says, teeth chattering once more.

I try to close his fist, shocked at the coldness emanating from his skin. "Didn't you hear me? We can return to the old hag now. Hell, I'll even let you keep the damned ring."

"F-funny. Y-you g-go. I'll b-be r-right b-behind."

I scowl at him, slapping his cheek lightly. "No, I'm not falling for that bullshit. Wake the fuck up, and let's go. Your sister needs you, remember?"

"C-can't m-move."

"Fucking hell!" I lift my wrist to my mouth and tear into it, then press it to his lips. Instead of latching on to it, he turns his head away, lips closed firmly. "Drink the damn blood, Ștefan! It will heal you, not turn you."

His words are so low, I have to lean closer to hear him. "Blood...addiction..."

Of all the stubborn mules! "You're not going to get addicted by drinking from me *one time*. Those are rumors, nothing else."

"S-seen i-it..."

"Argh!" He's not going to make it easy, will he? Of course not. Humans never do. Damn principles and all.

So I rise, surveying the area, listening for—there. I flash to the Dacian on the ground. He's still breathing, but barely. I shove my bleeding wrist at his mouth and, unlike Ștefan, he latches on and drinks like a starving man.

"Enough," I mutter and yank it away. Then slap him awake. I want nothing more than to use my glamour, but it won't work on him. So I do the next best thing and put on my angriest face. "Wake the fuck up. I got a job for you."

With the Dacian's help, we get Ștefan back to his room. As soon as he's settled on the cot, I whirl on the Dacian.

I shove the man against the wall, nails wrapped around his throat and ready to rip it off. "One of your brethren cursed him. I need to deal with something but if I come back and he's dead, you'll wish you were, too. And I assure you...I'll take my sweet-ass time in killing you. Are we understood?"

He gulps, eyes filled with fear. "Y-yes."

My nails dig into his throat. "Yes, what?"

"Y-your M-majesty."

"That's more like it. Now make yourself useful while I'm gone, and fix him. Then maybe I'll spare your life."

After waiting a few more moments, I walk out. There's a chance he could try to hurt Ștefan, but it's in his best interest to work with me rather than against me. After all, healing Ștefan could mean freedom for him. Maybe.

The last boost from Ștefan is still coursing through my veins, so I blur outside, seeking Daniel. I'm not even past the courtyard when I see his shimmering form—and it's drawing closer. I stop dead in my tracks until he reaches me. "How are you here? What about the stafie's banishing?"

Daniel shakes his head, his brow furrowed. "I was about to ask you the same. I felt an energy whirlwind, earlier, and then the pressure keeping me at bay was gone."

I tap my chin, thinking back to the battle. The stafie disappeared, but I know he's still around. There was too much vengeance in his eyes, he wouldn't leave without getting it. Which is just as good, since he has some information I need.

"Liza?" Daniel draws closer.

"Come with me, and I'll explain on the way." Without waiting for his answer, I turn on my heels and head back into the castle.

Daniel is soon floating by my side, keeping pace. "Well?"

"There was a battle. Ștefan fell into a trap. Cezar—the Dacian in charge here—appeared with the stafie and the ring we needed. I… I'm not sure how to explain what happened next."

"Try," he says, his voice softer.

I throw him a glance, then do as he asks. After all, if anyone could understand the emotions rising in me at the sound of my father's voice, it's Daniel.

It takes me a moment to realize he's stopped, once I'm done. I turn to him.

"Are you saying Vlad Țepeș is…alive?"

"I don't… I don't think so. How could he be? We saw his body. But I don't believe he's fully gone. It sounded like he was where Zalmoxis is…wherever the hell that is. Which is crazy, in and of itself."

"But not impossible."

"No. Not impossible."

I turn and start walking again. He's back by my side within moments.

“Where are you going now? To Ştefan?”

“No, he’s being taken care of by a Dacian.”

“And you trust him to come to no harm?”

“If he does, that’ll be him dead.”

“Liza...”

“*Anyway*. What I’m trying to do is find the stafie. See what he knows. Because Cezar wanted that ring for a reason, and I’ll be damned if I don’t find out why. The old hag in the woods never did tell us why she wants the ring.”

“Is that really so important right now?”

“It is. It didn’t seem to be before. But it is now that I’ve seen what the ring does. What if I hand her something that can be used as a weapon against us?”

He throws me a look. “Are you sure this isn’t about getting an upper hand over the stafie?”

“So what if it is?”

“Liza.” He floats in front of me and, out of courtesy, I pause in my steps. “It’s dangerous. You said yourself Cezar did something to make the stafie more tangible.”

“Da, but Cezar is gone. Which means the stafie is just a regular stafie once more.”

“Are you sure about that?”

“I guess we’ll find out, won’t we?” Without waiting for his answer, I take off again.

Getting to the depths of the castle means passing by the chapel, and pretty much every dead body in between. Daniel's gasps permeate the air, somewhat getting on my nerves.

"Liza..."

I roll my eyes. "What, Daniel?"

"You... Did you do all of this?"

I whirl on him. "It's not like I *wanted to*. I was defending myself—and Ștefan! Something you've been on me to do."

"But Liza, some of these, they were innocents."

"And they didn't die by my hand." The look in his eyes says he doesn't believe me. And that guts me. "Fine. Don't believe me." I turn away and throw over my shoulder, "Matter of fact, why don't you go watch over the Dacian? He's more worthy of your compassion, anyway."

"Liza, that's not—"

"Just *go*, Daniel."

And I blur away, much faster than before. He doesn't follow, which is just as well.

"Come out, come out, wherever you are..."

Not even my sing-song voice is drawing the stafie out of the bowels of the earth. And that's pissing the hell out of me. I know he didn't vanish for good, so *where* is he?

As I finish inspecting the last of the area below, a nagging thought hits me. What if the pressure Daniel felt didn't just release the banishment on him, but also whatever was keeping the stafie here? And if it did, he could go anywhere...

"Shit. He'd go to seek the other hunters." My eyes widen in the darkness. I need to warn my siblings.

Just as I head toward the exit, a faint light draws my attention. It's coming from behind a canvas that's been glued to the stone wall. Only, when I step closer, I realize by the way it's fluttering that it's not, in fact, glued. Rather, it's a gateway to something.

I peel it back and duck under, inhaling a wave of dust in the process. I wave my hand in front of my face to clear it, then squint. "Who's here?"

The faint brightness I'd seen is gone. Or so I think. I see it again in another corner.

"Hello? Show yourself."

"Nu…nu înţeleg," says a faint voice. "Where am I?"

"Come out and I'll tell you. Then you'll understand."

He finally does. It's a boy, barely out of his teens. Scrawny, lanky…and transparent. Another stafie?

"Did you die here, kid?" Blunt, granted, but I've never been known for subtlety.

"I…" He scrunches up his face, as though to remember. "Da, I believe so. A long time ago. Săpam…I was digging."

Alarm bells ring in my head. "Digging for what?"

"Metal. To—" He makes a shape with his fingers. A circle.

"To craft a ring?"

He nods. "Da. *Inel.* A ring."

Holy shit! He's one of the craftsmen behind the ring's creation. Well, at least this'll give me answers about the ring even if I don't find the hunter stafie.

"I need your help," I say, softening my voice like Daniel does whenever he wants me to listen and do something. "Some very bad things happened here, and that ring you helped create is at the center of it all."

A shudder passes through him. "I…should not speak of it."

"Please, kid. A lot of lives hinge on this."

He looks at me. "Can I trust you? Not like…the other?"

I frown. "The other? Do you mean the stafie? Face like the Devil incarnate, evil eyes?"

He nods. "I should have not told him anything."

No, you shouldn't have. I don't say that out loud. "I promise you can trust me." I point to my scar. And the other, fresher one. "He did this to me."

His eyes travel over the scars; he even comes a bit closer. Then, he nods. "The ring…it opens portals."

"Portals? As in, more than one?"

"Da. To the realms of the gods. So long as the one wielding it holds something born in or tied to that realm."

That explains Zalmoxis…though I'm not entirely sure what Cezar was using for the link. But what would the old hag want with it?

"Thank you," I say. "You helped a lot."

Then I turn to leave.

"Is he…gone?"

"The other stafie?" I ask over my shoulder and he nods. "For now, yes. But I'm not sure where, or if he'll try to come back. I promise if I cross paths with him again, I will make sure he disappears for good."

The kid nods, but something in his features gives me pause.

"What is it? You look like you want to say something else."

"Only…there is but one I knew who could eradicate stafii."

I have a feeling I know where this is going. "Let me guess—Vlad Țepeș?"

His eyes widen. "Yes. The dragon's son! He was...formidable. And so sad."

Yeah, that sounds like my father.

I give him a weary smile. "He was a great man. Do you remember how he eradicated the stafii? Was it with some type of magic?"

He shakes his head. "A stafie is only strong so long as its energy keeps being fed—for someone good, with love; for someone bad, with evil."

I tilt my head. "So this hunter, he was being fed from all the evil that was happening here." That's why he was solid! It had nothing to do with Cezar's powers after all. And it explains why this kid, who's a good soul, is so translucent.

"Da, exactly. The son of the dragon could create stronger energy than any other stafie, and therefore toss them out of this plane and into the next. But if that cannot be done, the stafie needs only to be brought to a place that is the antithesis of its base soul." He glances down at himself. "Like me. I will not be around much longer."

"Thanks, kid. This helps—a lot."

I leave him behind and head back. Time to collect Daniel and Ștefan and get the hell out of here.

Daniel's waiting for me outside Ștefan's door, looking worse for wear.

"Tell me. How is he?"

He glances inside. "He'll be fine. For a human, he's strong." He meets my gaze. "He's in this suffering because he saved you. Again. You didn't mention that before."

I roll my eyes. "Whatever." I'm not about to admit to him that he was right.

I enter the room, and find the Dacian by Ștefan's bed, looking exhausted. "Well?"

"He'll live. I've removed the curse and—"

I snap his neck without a second thought.

"Liza!"

I ignore Daniel hovering at the door. "He did his job. Don't need him anymore."

Ștefan

When I gave in to the exhaustion pulling me at me, I didn't know what I was doing. The world faded away into darkness—not the friendly kind, more of an abyss. I felt suspended, held by invisible threads designed to inflict agony upon agony on me. Pain surged through me like a relentless storm, each wave crashing against the fragile shores of my consciousness.

This is the hell I remain trapped in. Nothing rouses my magic. Nothing frees me from the void.

Only agony blazes through me, fueled by a sinister force, as crafty as it is evil. I scream, I fight, I rebel against its hold. It doesn't matter what I do. I remain powerless, trapped in a suffocating embrace.

With each minute—hour?—that I spend unconscious, I'm hit by more and more waves of pain, of suffering. Always different, never attacking the same spot. Never able to protect myself against them. Shadows that were previously my friends now lap at my feet like eager piranhas. And my mind, my sanctuary, the one thing I've always had going for myself, fills with despair and hollowness.

When the pain finally lessens, leaving echoes of my surroundings to pierce through, I'm too weak to do anything other than hope, faintly, that I'm about to be freed. That I'll emerge out of this unconsciousness and into something—*anything*—better.

And...I do. Finally. I come awake to the sound of a neck, snapping.

For a moment, I fear it's mine. But it's not. With my senses, I take in everything. I feel more perceptive than normal, perhaps on account of nearly dying. But I also feel the essence of the dead Dacian on the floor. Elizabeta, and her anger. And another—a presence by her side. Not malevolent. Familiar. *Her stafie, Daniel.*

"What happened?" I ask.

Chapter 19

Ştefan

Hmm. It's not like Elizabeta Dracul to be so quiet. Yet that is who's in the room with me—her scent betrays her. "Well? I know you're there."

My relief at the fact she survived—and that I somehow did—is only dampened by her silence. "Never would've pegged you for the quiet type," I throw out as a last resort.

"Fuck off, Dacian," she mutters. "You know full well what happened."

Is that...remorse I hear in her voice? I hold back a frown, keeping my features schooled to an impassable mask. Clearing my throat, I say, "I meant after I passed out. When I was hit with—a blood curse, was it?"

"Da," she says, still in the same tone.

I push myself off the cot, half-standing, and put my feet on the ground. They touch a body, and a cooling one, at that. I freeze.

"Might want to watch your step," she says. Even after our kiss, she didn't sound like this. Monotone. Cool. Detached. She seems even more afar—physically *and* emotionally—than before.

"Let me guess. Body at my feet?"

"Mm."

The voice from the ball then says, "More than just this one. Elizabeta's been on a rampage."

I can't answer his words without her knowing he's speaking to me, so I remain quiet. But even if I could, my only answer would be, *Did you expect anything else from the daughter of Vlad Țepeș?* Because, really, Elizabeta's bloodthirst is nothing new. It's how she keeps herself in control *and* how she controls everyone else around her. Fear acts as a potent detraction from anyone wanting to get close to her.

And given what I just went through, I have a much better understanding of why she needs that shield to protect herself. *How did she even survive her captors for days, survive the pain and the hopelessness? I can't have been under for more than a few hours, and I feel like I'll never have a peaceful night of sleep again. No normal person can be whole after undergoing such pain.*

Then again, Elizabeta is anything but normal.

As if to prove it, she speaks again. "You might as well know the entire castle's filled with dead Dacians."

"Huh. Something to do with what happened after I lost consciousness?"

"Da. Well, somewhat between when you did pass out, then came back to help me close the portal, then passed out again. Basically, Cezar was trying to bring Zalmoxis through. I tossed him in the portal instead, but he disintegrated. And the rest of those fuckers wouldn't stop attacking."

I nudge my foot against the body on the floor. "This one, too?"

"No. I coerced him into undoing the blood curse. Once he did, I had no use for him anymore."

I want to tell her she's probably right in doing what she did, but I don't want to add to her homicidal tendencies. Moreover, I don't trust myself not to ask her everything else I want to—why did you come back for me? How did you find me? Why were you begging me not to leave you? Why, after all that, are you still here?

So, I say nothing.

Clearly, that's the wrong thing to do because she soon comes closer, her scent assailing my nostrils once more. "What, now, I'm not even worthy of a word? You're just going to be all righteous because I killed a couple of your people?"

"I never said that." I've known her to be many things in these few days we've been together, but not fly off the handle like this. And something's telling me it's got nothing to do with me and more to do with that voice—the stafie—and what he said to me.

"You didn't *say* anything, either." A pause. "Go on, I know you're dying to. I'm a monster. Say it."

I stand then, turning in the direction of her voice. "I sense nothing that would justify that."

I take a step closer, and find myself brushing up against her. She hasn't moved. I raise my hand to her cheek. I know from Silviana's description this is the cheek that's been injured. And I know from what I overheard the stafie say that she has a matching scar now—that should heal, soon—on the other side. Mindful of that, I keep my touch soft, but firm.

"You are a princess of the House of Dracul, and everything in these lands is under your domain. You did what you were born to do—defend your lands, your kingdom. Do I agree with you taking so many lives? No. But I'm not in your shoes, Elizabeta. No one is. So I don't see the point in judging something I don't fully understand."

I feel her jaw go slack at my words. I let go of her, wishing for the first time I had the sight to witness her full shocked reaction.

"Now, let's see what we can do about hiding this evidence, shall we?" I ask and move past her. "We don't want any humans to fall upon this."

It takes Elizabeta a long moment, but then she says, "What did you have in mind?"

Hours later, we're outside of the castle once again. I breathe in the fresh air, crisp with the night's coolness, and the first hints of smoke. Inside the castle, the darkness threads I've set loose are hard at work burning everybody in their sight. Ashes alone will be left of them. And even that is not enough.

I push the athame from the wrist cuff, slice a deeper gash in my hand, and close my fist, letting the droplets fall onto the ground. It rumbles under my feet.

"What are you doing?" The man's voice, again, this time with a quiver in it.

Though I don't feel Elizabeta's aura near, I keep my voice low, nonetheless. She still hasn't opened up about him, and I doubt now's the time to bring it up. "Making sure no one can trace this back to the princess."

"You're supposed to temper her bloodthirst, Dacian. Not encourage her."

I let out a low chuckle. "What makes you think I'd ever try to do that?" The rush of the magic escaping me fills me, and I let out a deep sigh. "Like it or not, Elizabeta Dracul is set in her ways. And this time, I don't think she's wrong at all."

He says nothing. Then a red-tinged blob nears my periphery—Elizabeta's aura. "Did you say something?"

"Just muttering to myself." Satisfied when I hear the rumble of rock, followed by the crack of walls, I turn in her direction. "Ready to go?"

Behind us, Corvins' Castle is giving its last breath.

Elizabeta

I follow him back to the car. But while Ștefan's stride is sure, I'm stumbling every few steps because I keep turning and glancing behind. Every time I do, another piece of the castle has fallen apart. The flames within blaze high, but no smoke emerges. No authorities will be coming to put them out. And by the time the castle crumbles, the ashes of the corpses will be just part of the rubble.

I can't say I feel sorry for it. These men were going to kill us. They *did* kill—innocent nuns. The least they deserve is to rot in Hell for what they did. Then again, maybe so do I.

As for the stafie I met in the castle's bowels... A kid, and a dead one, at that. I try not to let myself feel guilty. He wanted to leave, and he was already fading. Perhaps the destruction of this place will finally set him free. Nothing else anchors him around, after all. Unlike the vengeful hunter that has conveniently vanished.

My eyes linger on Corvins' Castle one last time. It was the place of my torture. My father's imprisonment. But it was also the beginning of my and Daniel's story. Is this the closure I've been needing all along?

With one last sigh, I follow behind Ștefan and try to push the resurfacing guilt away. Soon, we're on the road, with me driving again. The drive is silent—and I still don't understand why he is the way he is. Why hasn't he called me the worst of names yet? What more does he need me to do, to confirm his assumptions that I'm a monster? Daniel seems to have arrived at that conclusion all on his own, despite knowing the other side of me. Yet this infuriating Dacian hasn't. On the contrary, when he held my cheek, when he spoke those words, it was like he *saw* me. It unsettled me even more than his kiss did a few days ago.

"The nuns," Ștefan says, breaking the silence, "did Cezar kill them all? None escaped?"

"None did."

He nods. "I'd expected as much. I'm sorry I didn't listen to you. I fell right into their trap. Trăian was a good actor, I guess." He pauses, and his jaw clenches. "I need to get to the Dacian compound before he does."

"I wouldn't worry too much about him. I caught up with him in the woods and killed him, after getting what information I could from him."

Ștefan is quiet for a moment. Then he says, "Thank you."

"*Thank you*?" I jerk the wheel to the right and pull over on the side of the road, then turn to face him in the car. "Okay, what gives? What's with this whole attitude?"

"What attitude?"

I poke his chest. "You. Being okay with who I am. How I am. And killing your friend. Just hours ago, you were mad at me over the same thing!"

Ștefan, infuriatingly, only shrugs. "What do you want me to say, Elizabeta? I don't have to agree with your motives to understand where you're coming from. As for Trăian, he wasn't a friend, clearly. You gave him a quick ending." His tone darkens. "Much quicker than I would have, in the same situation."

I stare at him, waiting for more. But nothing else follows. It really is that simple in his head, and I don't understand it. *None* of it. Not why he can see me as I am, and not be repelled. Not why he's so calm. And definitely not why Daniel seems to feel the exact opposite.

I shake my head, annoyed by the pull of the connection between us. It can't be what Daniel says it is. Even if it helped me find Ștefan, amid the Dacians. Even if it helped him give me strength when I needed it. *It can't.*

One-handed, I pull the car back on the road. "Fine. Let's just get this over with."

Two hours of silence—and rumination, on my end—later, Ștefan speaks again. "The ring. Did Trăian or Cezar let anything else slip about it? What it does, for example?"

For a short, petty moment, I almost don't tell him. Then I sigh and say, "Da. Well, not so much them, but there's a stafie I ran into underneath the castle. It, umm, explained the ring opens portals to the gods. One only needs the ring and something crafted in the god's realm to open that portal. Well, and sacrifice, I'm assuming, given the nuns."

Ștefan rubs his beard, deep in thought. "No, I don't think so. If I'm right, the sacrifice was all Cezar. But he wouldn't have had anything crafted in the god's realm, because even the Dacians struggle to get ahold of Zalmoxis' relics. But...." He slams his palm on the car's dashboard. "Fucking hell! The nuns. Their deaths, in that castle, create a conduit of darkness—and darkness *would* be crafted wherever Zalmoxis is. That's why Cezar needed them." He shakes his head. "The bastard. Instead of using his own magic to summon enough darkness to pave the way to Zalmoxis, he chose to kill innocents."

"And your Grand Master supposedly agreed with that plan."

"Hmm."

I tap my fingers on the steering wheel. Ahead, I can see the bend in the road signaling we're close to the woods. "Why would this old hag need the ring, though? Don't you think it's weird?"

"Perhaps. But I don't care. Whatever it is, it's a price I'm willing to pay if she tells me how to help Silviana."

I bite my lip, unsure of anything but the dread piling in my gut. "What if the price you're paying is more than the hag revealed?"

Ștefan shrugs. "Again, I'll happily do it. If it means Silviana will be safe."

"Wow. You really care for her, huh?"

"She's all I have," he says, as if that alone explains it.

I guess it does. My siblings are all I have and, despite our differences, I know the same applies to us. Love for them alone is what decided me to help Ştefan and to save him so I can save *us* all. I never would've done that before. The idea alone is laughable. Which is why once this hag is taken care of, I need to warn them about the hunter stafie, and then go and find him.

As if on cue, the Hoia Baciu Forest emerges in the distance. I pull the car over once more. "We're here."

Ştefan

Once more, the power of the woods fills my senses. Only this time, carrying the ring in my coat pocket, it feels stronger, somehow. Like it's equally pulling and pushing at my senses. Elizabeta doesn't seem to be affected, which makes me think the ring is behind this development. That, in turn, brings my thoughts back to what Elizabeta said—about the ring, and the old hag's use of it. At the end of the day, it's not our problem. This is a currency we're paying in exchange for information we direly need. But a voice at the back of my head says I should care at least a little more.

Ahead of me, Elizabeta curses. By the time I reach her, she's in full-on raging mode about the old hag.

I reach in the air, shocked when I actually grasp her arm. "What's gotten you so twisted up?"

"Not what, *who*! That old hag isn't here!"

"What do you mean, she's not here? She has to be." After all the work—

"She *was* here. We're within reach of her cabin and I can't smell her. Which means she's gone off somewhere, and we're stuck waiting until she deigns to come back."

I clench my jaw in an effort to not lose it like she is. "It's fine. We'll just wait here for her."

"It's not *fine*! None of this is fine!"

I don't get it. Just like before, when I woke up, she's overreacting. But why? Before I can question it, she says, "I just want this done and over with so I can go back to my life. So I can be away from here." *Away from you*, is the subtext she surprisingly doesn't voice. It still stings.

At a loss on what to say that won't rile her up more, I settle for, "Elizabeta. Let it the fuck go."

If the hag is watching us, if this is another stupid test, then the last thing I want is to annoy her. Not when I need her knowledge way too much.

Time has passed, I've got a fire going in the woods, but there's still no trace of the hag. Nor is there any trace of that male stafie who's always around Elizabeta. Which has me wondering if he's gone permanently, or just for now?

"What are you holding back?" I ask abruptly.

"What do you mean?"

"You've been quiet and introspective. And I never thought I'd see the day when Elizabeta Dracul feels remorse for killing."

"I am *not* remorseful."

"Say that again, but with more truth this time."

She growls, then her scent fills my nostrils. Fabric whooshes over my legs, and suddenly she's there. Her cool hands cup my cheeks, and her breath is over me. "How about we focus on something *much* more fun, hmm?"

And then she kisses me.

Like before, the moment her lips touch mine, they detonate a whirlwind of emotions. My hands seek her hips, pulling her until she's straddling me fully, and her hair cascades over my face like silk. I dig one of the hands into the long locks, tugging on them slightly to angle her mouth toward me.

Elizabeta gives a half-sigh, half-moan, and the sound is enough to make me even harder. My cock jerks at her response, and then it's all I can do to keep my hands to myself. I want nothing more than to lose myself in her. But I can't.

As gently as I can, I stop the kiss, tearing our mouths apart. Panting, I say, "I can't."

"Why not?" Elizabeta whispers, nuzzling my neck. The sensation of her nose, her lips, then her teeth grazing my skin, is almost too much.

I close my eyes, trying to rein in my emotions. "Elizabeta. Enough."

She pulls back, and I can practically feel the shock rolling off her. No man in his right mind says no to her.

"What's wrong with you?" she accuses, shoving at my chest. Since I'm already sitting, all it does is leave a bruise. "Why can't you just.... Give in to your desires, like every other man before you?"

If she'd tried to douse me with cold water, she wouldn't have been as effective. "Because I'm not *every man before me*, princess."

She scoffs. "Da, clearly. Or maybe you just don't *function* like them."

"I assure you, I do. And everything in me does as well." As if she can't see the evidence of my desire.

"Have you thought perhaps..."

I grit my teeth. "I guarantee you, nothing is wrong with the way I *function*. Have you thought that perhaps not all of us go around having sex every day? That maybe, just maybe, some keep their purity for a special connection?"

If I wasn't so hard, I would laugh at the curses escaping her at my admission.

Elizabeta

I stumble back in shock. "You...what?"

A wry smirk twists his lips. "You heard me. I'm a virgin. Never had sex."

"But...*why*?"

"You say it like it's the worst thing."

"Because it is! It's unheard of, in your day and age."

"Well, call me a unicorn."

I move toward him again. "Let's remedy that, then. Right here, right now."

"Do you really think I would cheapen myself like that?"

I reel back this time, in anger. "Excuse me?"

Some of his bravado fades, and he winces. "I didn't mean it like that. But I don't want my first time to be meaningless. And you don't do anything but meaningless sex, right? What was it that you said—*why can't I just be like every other man before me*?"

He's got me with my own words. The bastard...

"Fine." I head opposite him around the fire. "Suit yourself." He can sleep with all the blue balls he wants. I'm still hot and bothered, and I don't intend to get through the night like this.

Chapter 20

Ștefan

I should've known the moment she backed off so easily that Elizabeta wasn't done with me. Just as I settle in to take a nap and recharge my energy, a soft moan fills the air. Follows by the rustle of fabric. And then another moan, louder.

It's a keening cry, followed by a softer pant, like she's bringing herself to the brink of pleasure. I can almost picture it... Her long hair, spread like a crown around her head. Leaves coating the ground underneath. And Elizabeta, all silky-smooth, ivory skin, arching her back, fingers caressing the bundle of nerves between her legs, bringing herself to ecstasy, moaning into the night.

You could be right there with her, the nagging voice at the back of my head sniggers. A sentiment reinforced by my hardening cock.

Another moan breaks the air.

Fuck, but she wants to kill me. Or break my resolve. This is a game to her, but I'm not going to give in. So I turn my back on her instead, and go to sleep. With a bit of luck, it'll be morning soon and we can go to the old hag and get this over with.

Except... Elizabeta's not done.

Whatever she's doing, it's increasing the sounds she's making, until I can't stop but palm my own erection. Jesus, if she keeps on going, I might just explode alongside her.

Finally, one last cry splits the air. Followed by a happy sigh, and more rustling. Blessed quiet.

Too bad all thoughts of sleep have evaporated from my mind.

"Well, well."

I open my eyes at the voice, immediately sensing a presence over us.

Next to me, there's more rustling, followed by Elizabeta's growl. "You! What's with the smirk, babă?"

"Now, now. You shouldn't be so angry I was absent, vampir. From what I can tell, you've had an interesting night."

"Were you *watching us*, you perverted hag?"

The old woman snorts, and I take advantage of their bickering to rise slowly to my feet. Every muscle aches and my eyes burn like they've had sand shoved in them. To say I've had a mainly sleepless night would be an understatement.

"Why ever would you think that, vampir?" The old hag taps my arm. "You have something for me, I presume?"

I reach into my coat pocket and palm the ring. Elizabeta's warning crosses my mind again.

"What do you intend to do with this ring?"

"That's no concern of yours."

"It is if it means my sister will escape one type of danger only to run into another."

The hag is quiet for a bit. "I swear that your sister has nothing to fear from me."

"Call me paranoid, but that's the vaguest promise I've ever heard," Elizabeta interjects.

"I agree. I'm going to need something better than that, witch."

She sighs, taps the ground, and finally says, "Your sister has nothing to fear from me—now, or in the future. None of my actions are intended to cause her harm. This, I swear by the force filling me." A moment of silence. "Does that satisfy you, Dacian?"

"It'll do."

"Still vague," Elizabeta mutters.

I pull out the ring and hold it between my middle finger and thumb. "Tell me what I need to know first, then it's yours."

"Smart man," the hag says, and cackles. When she's got a hold of herself again, she clears her throat. "A bargain is a bargain. As I told you before, nothing can release your sister from the curse afflicting the Dracul line. If the heirs do not consummate their consort bonds and relationships, they will all die. As for the bond between your sister and Zalmoxis... Your sister invited him in. Only she can push him out."

My jaw drops, and I tighten my grip on the ring. "You better have more for me than just that, or else I swear—"

"My, but we are impatient today! Of course, there is more, young fool. Shut up and listen." A breath later, after ensuring I'm keeping quiet, she continues, "What do you know about Decebal?"

"The last Dacian king?" Elizabeta says from somewhere closer.

"No one asked you, vampir," the hag hisses with more venom in her tone than I'd expected.

I wonder what's got her so antagonized over Elizabeta?

Elizabeta doesn't seem amused in the slightest. She bites back just as harshly. "Watch your tone, *witch*. I can still rip that wrinkled old head of yours off."

"And then neither of you would have any answers. Are you done with the empty threats?"

"If you want the fucking ring," I growl, "speak already."

"Very well. Yes, *that* Decebal. The last Dacian king. His was one of the first records of Zalmoxis' worship. As you can imagine, he needed quite the godly backing to win his three wars against the Roman Empire." She sighs. "A great man, as far as mortals go." Again with the odd phrasing... "There is an area, south of this country. Cazanele Dunării. Do you know it?"

I frown. "At the border with Serbia? Yes... We—" I stop, stunned at the vivid images lurking in my memory.

The Danube River, slithering between towering limestone cliffs. Crystal-clear waters. A gorge where cliffs draw closer, becoming a corridor of more rugged cliffs and ancient stone—nature's masterpiece. Birds of prey cutting through a night sky. Wildflowers clinging to the cliffs. A rustle of leaves, the gentle rush of water...and a young girl's laughter.

I know the place, but not *how* I know it. "I guess we used to go there, when we were young." It's the only thing that would explain that girl's laughter, so like Silviana's.

"I would imagine so. Decebal's statue, carved in stone from the mountain? It has recharging properties for all Dacians. It is imbued with the essence of many kings, many sorcerers, and *many* Dacian Grand Masters."

My heart picks up its pace. "How will that help my sister?"

"Take her there, along with her consort. There is a cave that goes underneath Decebal's statue, and it leads to a bunker of sorts made by your kin across the ages. Let her stay there for a few days to soak up the energy of the earth. When she is strong enough, she can put in place the barriers she needs."

"That...sound doable." Doubt coats my tone.

Elizabeta picks up on it. "And almost too easy. What are you not saying, witch?"

"Well, the territory *is* outside of the Draculs' control. And there may or may not be muroni nearby."

This time, the growl comes from Elizabeta. "Nothing is out of our control." There's a softer touch on my hand, followed by her lowered tone. "I'll come with you. Between Vlad and I, we can take care of whatever's there."

Her offer seems to take both me and her by surprise, judging by her sharp inhale.

"I mean"—she quickly backtracks and removes her hand—"it would be a shame if you were to both get killed after all this fuss."

I bite back a laugh. If this wasn't Elizabeta, I'd say she's almost endearing.

An impatient voice interrupts me. "Well? Can I have my ring now?"

I yank my hand out of the old hag's presumed reach and say, "One more thing. How long will this little patch-up solution last?"

"Ah, you're not as dumb as you seem, Dacian." If I was the type to punch women, she'd be the one to drive me to it. "Until Zalmoxis is alive, your sister will need to go there periodically. How long depends on how much she uses her magic in between, I suppose. And other factors."

"Such as?"

"Such as how strong Zalmoxis gets. And now, my payment."

At a loss, I hold out my hand. Her nails scrape my skin in her haste to get ahold of it, and that dread from before fills me up again. Was Elizabeta right? Should I be more wary of giving her the ring? But... it's too late. A bargain is a bargain, like she said.

I can practically hear Elizabeta rolling her eyes. "All this, to be told your sister needs to be put in a reinforced building so she can fix herself with whatever that zmeu shifter already told her to do. Wow."

"It's more than we had."

"It is," the old hag says. "And I'll do you one better, Dacian."

Her nails scrape my palm and leave a heavy weight on it. When I close my fingers over it, I can feel some kind of stone and a chain.

"It's an amulet," she says before I can ask. "Black tourmaline, designed to keep dark energies at bay." Her voice turns amused. "It's not quite the artifact you planned to steal from me..."

I gape at her. "How did you—" *Was she listening in the woods, when we left her cabin the first time?*

The old hag cackles. "I have my ways. In any case, this amulet is charged with a little extra something that should extend the protection of that cave... Assuming your sister doesn't go and try to play heroine again."

"She won't," I mutter. I'll make damn sure of that.

Elizabeta

Leave it to the wily hag to try to outrun us the moment she's gotten her ring. Only, I'm faster than her. So with a single blur, I block her path. She stares at me as if she knew I was going to do this, which only serves to piss me off even more.

"Yes, vampir?"

"You owe me some answers too, no?"

She taps her chin. "Do I, now?"

I move in closer, raising my hand, nails extended as if I'm about to gouge her eyes out. Which, I'm not above doing, if it comes to it.

Her eyes flash. "Careful, vampir. Has no one ever told you it's easier to catch flies with honey than vinegar?" She cackles, and the sound grates on my nerves. "As I recall, you never even laid your terms."

"You know what information I need. You saw him."

She smirks. "Saw who?"

"Babă, don't test me—"

She holds up a palm. "Ah, yes. Now it's coming back to me. The stafie by your side. An old friend or...lover?" Her eyes twinkle with malice. "And yet, he's nowhere to be seen right now. I wonder what happened in between..."

She glances over her shoulder straight at Ștefan, and I grind my teeth together.

"He's got nothing to do with it. Tell me what I want to know!"

"What you should be asking is how to release him, how to let him go into the beyond. But that's not what you want to know, is it, Elizabeta Dracul?" She takes a step closer to me, and this time, the entirety of her power hums from every fiber of her being, stunning me. “You want to know how to *keep him*. Don’t you?”

I gulp, and lower my gaze, taking a step back. She’s unnerving me, and I don’t know how or why. “Yes.”

For a long time, she says nothing. Until I look back up at her, and find her staring in the distance, a pensive expression on her features. An expression that, oddly, makes her look much younger.

“You cannot keep someone who wishes freedom, heiress. Not forever, not without a cost. Your stafie is bound by your side because of his love for you, a love you both shared. But your heart is being pulled apart by another, and it is time you release your stafie. Much like it is time you release your past and let go of old wounds.”

“But—”

“That is all you paid for. Anything else will require more blood, and I doubt you wish to do that.”

As if on cue, the weakness from before hits me, and I lean against the closest tree to catch my breath. Since I’m unable to stop her now, the witch bypasses me and disappears through the trees. When I get the energy to glance over my shoulder, she’s gone.

And so is my chance for more answers.

Though if I were truly honest with myself…what kind of answers would I still seek? She told me what I’ve always known, deep inside. And her answer, which I’d dreaded, doesn’t fill me with panic as much as I thought it would. That’s the downside of immortality, right? Always losing people. Daniel won’t be the last one. But for now, I’ll enjoy the moments we have left. If he ever talks to me again…

“Elizabeta?”

Ștefan’s moved from his spot, and he’s slowly turning in a circle. For a moment, I debate leaving him here. The quest is done. I can always send Vlad back to help him. But the more I'm around Ștefan, the more it fucks with my head.

And if I'm quite honest, I hate and fear the stirrings of desire and feelings he's been causing in me. Last night was just the tip of the iceberg. I shouldn't be around him—period. But something in me won't let me leave. Not yet.

So I clear my throat and whisper, "Da, I'm here."

He follows my voice and walks to me until he's towering over me. "What happened?"

"Nothing."

"Your entire demeanor has changed." He hesitates, then raises his hand, reaching for me.

I shouldn't, but I find myself tugging on his shirt until he stumbles a few paces forward. The hand he'd been reaching with palms the tree bark above me. His other one finds my waist, holding on. The bulk of his body presses against me and I take a moment to breathe in his scent—all earthy tones and pure male.

"Elizabeta..."

I look at him, finding his face tilted down to mine. All it would take is one press on my tiptoes, and I could feel those lips against mine again. It's insanity to even think it, and complete loss of control to actually act on it. And yet, I'm powerless against the urge, like a tidal wave cresting over me and wrapping me in its whirlwind.

My hand, still clutching his shirt, releases it, and I move it slowly up his chest, to the back of his neck. I rise on my tiptoes, my own body arching against his, despite the weakness coursing through me.

"What are you doing?" he asks, breathless, and a little choked.

"Chaos," I whisper against his mouth, and then I press my lips to his.

It shouldn't feel nearly as good as the last kiss did. But somehow, it does, even while the intensity of it is racked up by this tension between us.

Using his neck as leverage, I pull myself even closer to him, refusing to leave any inch of spare space between us. Ștefan groans against my mouth, then returns the kiss in earnest. It leaves me with a very different feeling in my knees, even while it electrifies all of me.

The curse...it's the curse...

I pull back so fast, I smack my head against the bark of the tree. I let my hands drop to my sides, pressing my back flat against the tree once more. Ștefan follows my withdrawal, burying his face in the side of my neck, his lips pressing on my skin.

"Stop," I whisper, and this time, I shove him off me.

He staggers and rights himself, his expression filled with confusion. "What...?"

"We shouldn't do this."

"Interesting you say that, when you're the one who started it." He steps closer once more, as if the curse—the bond—between us is a thread and he's just pulling on it until he's back in front of me, his hands once more pressed on either side of my head, palms flat against the tree bark. "Tell me, do you enjoy toying with me, princess?"

"I'm not toying with you," I whisper.

"Could've fooled me," he says, and this time there's an underlying current of frustration in his tone. At me? At himself? "You seem to take great pleasure in making me lose my mind, all while keeping the upper hand."

Not as much as you do with making me lose mine, I think, but don't say it. Instead, I duck under his arm and step around him, no longer willing to entertain this closeness between us. It's too much, and it won't lead anywhere good.

Once I feel there's enough of a safe distance between us—a few feet—I whirl on him, and find he's taken my spot and is leaning against the tree, facing me. His expression is once more blank, all hints of frustration and confusion gone.

"Upper hand?" I laugh, almost maniacally. "If you want to talk about an upper hand, how about you tell me *what the hell* you know about the hunters and my captivity."

This elicits a minimal response out of him—a frown. "What are you on about now?"

I clench my fists. "Don't play the fool, it doesn't suit you. Before you went down in the castle's bowels and got attacked, you were implying I'd had something to do with Trăian's death, because I was there seeking vengeance. *Who told you that*?"

He's silent for so long, I think he won't answer me. When he does, I almost wish he hadn't.

"You know who told me." A beat later, when I say nothing out of sheer shock, he sighs and runs a hand over his face. "Daniel. Your stafie. He's the one who offered that tidbit of information."

"That's not..." I shake my head. "That's not possible. He wouldn't betray me like that."

Ștefan shrugs. "I don't think he was betraying you. He was *protecting you*, the way he knew best. By telling me something you never would've. Something that ensured I could at least be more aware of our surroundings when we were at Corvins' Castle."

"It wasn't his story to tell!"

Ștefan pushes off the tree and walks toward the sound of my voice. "Then *you* tell me. In your own words. Go on." He waits a beat, then shakes his head. "But you can't, can you? *That's why* he said it. Because he knew you never would."

"He doesn't know you! That's..." The idea of the two of them, talking about me, it's almost too much for my head to wrap around. "Has he talked to you since then?"

"Da. Many times. Each time, only to say enough to protect you."

He's close to me now, but I don't realize how close until he reaches for me. I try to move around him, but his hand grips my elbow, then moves lower, grasping my wrist instead. His touch is soft, as if he knows I'm unraveling.

"Who's Daniel to you, Elizabeta? Is that what this is all about—your push and pull?"

"If you think I'm about to answer that..."

He raises his other hand to cup my cheek. I almost lean into the touch, but the heat of his palm is enough to keep me still, rigid. "I *want* you to answer that. I'm tired of turning the matter over and over in my head, wondering if he's the reason behind the way you're acting. If he's the reason you refuse to trust anyone."

I jerk my head away from his touch, and my wrist from his grip. "Yeah, well, it's none of your business, is it?" I push past him, elbowing him in the process, and avoiding his touch like the plague—because I'm afraid of what it'll do. "I think that's enough deep talk. Let's get out of here and go bring the happy news to your sister."

I'm annoyed, yeah. Annoyed at my lack of control around him. At how much I wish for *more*. At my inability to keep my hands off him lately. And even more annoyed that this entire time, Daniel was talking to him. What the *hell* was he thinking?

Betrayal, desire, and longing for something more fight for dominance in my head. No single emotion wins—though I'm starting to doubt there's a winner in this at all.

Some hours of walking later, my mood is nowhere improved. It's bad enough we've wasted yet another day with all the driving and waiting for the old hag and, admittedly, getting some answer. But by the time we head out of the woods into an early sunset, we find an entire pack of wolves surrounding our car.

"What the—"

Only one of them is in human form—a young one with light-blond hair, piercing blue eyes, and a lanky build that's slowly filling out. "Evening, House of Dracul princess."

He's got manners, I'll give him that. And I haven't forgotten that he and his dad helped my siblings round up the vampiri who'd tried to leave the ball, when I got shot at. But he must have me confused with Violeta, only I'm nowhere as friendly. "Cut the shit, little pup. What are you doing here?"

His eyes flash, but he holds himself under control. I'm almost disappointed when he speaks with an even tone. "We have a problem. Two of our pack have gone missing. We think they were taken by vampir hunters."

"And why is that my problem?"

"Your clan made an alliance with mine. We can go after them alone...but since it's hunters, your sister thought you'd want first dibs. She sent us your location."

Thanks, Violeta.

I turn to Ștefan. Debating. I really should call Nico, and fill him in on everything. But the opportunity is too good. What if this brings me to the hunter stafie, and I can settle my score with him?

It can't be a coincidence that the wolves were attacked so shortly after the damned ghost disappeared from Corvins' Castle.

As if sensing my unease and indecision, Ștefan takes a step closer, and lowers his head. His hand twitches by his side as if wants to reach for me again, but all he says is, "Go. It'll do you good."

It kills me on a whole other level that he knows me this well. That he understands my need to run, to get away from the intensity between us. But despite our earlier row, the indecision lingers. As does the unease at leaving him alone in the woods. "What about you? How will you get back to Silviana?"

"I won't. Leave me your cell, and I'll call your siblings and get a ride back to the Dacians. I've been away too long, it's time to head back home."

"And the information about—"

"I'll fill Silviana in on the phone, and you can give them a better account once you return." He reaches into his pocket and pulls out the old hag's amulet. "Take this, too. Give it to my sister, okay?"

I nod and tie the leather string around my neck. The black stone it holds settles between my breasts, emitting an odd warmth. It's weirdly awkward, saying goodbye—and so suddenly, too. But I do, and hand Ștefan my cell phone. Then I follow the wolves across the street, and into a different set of woods awaiting us on the other side.

Chapter 21

Elizabeta

The run—for it is a full-on run, as if the Devil himself is chasing at our heels—is fast, and it's exhilarating to be able to go full speed and not have to hold back. Exhilarating and bittersweet, all in one. Because Daniel *still* hasn't shown up. Where the hell is he?

I try to focus my thoughts on the feel of the wind in my cheeks against my ripped clothing, my tangled hair. As soon as I'm back at our home, I plan to luxuriate in the longest, hottest bath until my skin turns pink. Like it used to, as a human. Wishful thinking. There's no such thing as a flush in this body, not anymore.

Luca comes to a full stop ahead of me, and I pause, too, my

heels digging into the ground. The rest of the wolves spread in a semi-circle on either side of us.

"What's with the sudden stop?"

The wolf turns, becoming once more human. One of the wolves tosses him a pair of jeans, and I avert my eyes from his lean muscles and other...assets... Instead, an odd sound catches my attention, and I freeze. I know that sound. The scraping of metal against metal, muffled groans, and rushed footsteps.

"You've caught their scent, then?"

I face Luca, who's dressed once more. "Scent?"

"The hunters." He frowns. "Don't vampiri smell from far off, same as us?"

"Uh...da, but—" Jeez, I'm flustered in front of a young kid. It's not like I want to admit to the weakness coursing through my veins. It comes and goes, but it won't be long before I need another fix. Too bad I couldn't step on my pride and ask Ştefan before I left him...

Understanding dawns on Luca's expression and he nods solemnly. "I get it, say no more."

It's my turn to frown. "What do you get, exactly?"

"Your sister, she had the same thing when she came to us. The..."—he gestures at me—"that weakness, whatever you want to call it. Loss of her powers, of her senses. Until Dad gave her vrykolakas blood, filled with the same darkness that fuels muroni, and is part of your sire's lineage... And then she was fine."

I scowl. "That's not what this is."

He arches an eyebrow, unperturbed. I must be losing my scary glare. "Whatever you say, vampir."

I push past him and take a step closer to the noise. "What am I hearing, exactly? Is that..."

"Hunters." Gone is the young kid who'd greeted me. His features darken with anger, making him seem way more mature than his years. "We've been coming across their...leftovers. Muroni shred to pieces. Other wolves, their guts pulled out. I suppose they thought them shifters and when they didn't live up to the expectation, they killed them." His hands curl into fists. "I can't wait to get my hands on them."

"I won't disagree with you there. So what are we waiting for?"

He points to the sky. "A little darkness. Most of us have dark coats, so it'll give us a bigger surprise effe—"

He doesn't get to finish. Because a bloodcurdling scream tears through the woods, making every bird within the vicinity take flight.

"I don't think you'll get your wish, Luca," I mutter.

Without waiting for an answer, I take off. Behind me, I hear him curse, and then his wolves are trampling the ground in my wake.

Whoever the hunters are torturing, I refuse to let them suffer as I have. I know hunters and their bloodthirst, and I—

I'm not prepared for what I emerge into. A makeshift camp of sorts, with three tents laid out to one side. A large fire in the middle.

And on the other side of the fire... six crosses, each with an occupant. Two muroni, two vampiri, and two wolves. Shifters, in their human form.

"What the fuck is going on here?" I demand as I straighten out of my crouch. My eyes widen with every second as I take in the sorry sight before me.

One muroni is missing a limb. Which, judging by the long nails and dirty clothing, is now attached to one of the wolves. Most of them have blood around their mouths—tongues cut off would be my best guess. All but the two wolves and one of the vampiri. Who, as I'm watching, has a hunter headed toward him, armed with a scythe.

"Ah, fuck no," I growl, and then I'm moving. Blurring straight for him. Whether it's the widening of the vampir's eyes or something in my movement that gives me away, I'll never know. But the hunter whirls at the last second, his scythe raised high, and I only have a mere second to duck to the side and avoid the strike.

He grins at me with red eyes. What. The. Utter. Fuck. Violeta mentioned them using muroni blood to strengthen themselves but I thought she was mistaken. This goes against the very grain of the hunters' existence!

"Welcome, Dracul heiress," he says. "We had hoped you would show. He'll be happy to have been right."

"Oh yeah? And who might that be?"

"Princess…." A voice says behind me.

Fucking hell. Of course it's the stafie from Corvins' Castle. So this is where he rushed off to…

I whirl on pure instinct, which is the stupidest thing I could've done. The hunter behind me doesn't care that I'm having another moment with the stafie. He's just here for the kill. And when he swings the scythe again, I'm too slow. He catches my back, and I stumble a few steps forward. When I look behind me, I see a trail of blood.

Then the stafie speaks again. "I had hoped to have the pleasure of witnessing your death."

"Well, you're going to be sorely disappointed, because that won't happen today."

On cue, the wolves emerge from the woods and tackle the hunters. I only get a quick glimpse of Luca at their head, probably aiming to run and save his two wolves.

I know I need to get a move on, to watch his back. A dead wolf heir will do us no good in keeping the alliance. But my limbs are jelly, weakened to the point I fall to my knees.

The stafie nears me. "That was fast acting," he muses, and turns to the other hunter. The only one who's stuck near us. "Make sure the others know. It could be the weapon we've been looking for all along, to immobilize the vampiri long enough and speed up our kills."

I blearily glance at the scythe. It was poisoned, or coated with something. Something they've been working on. My gaze goes back to the prisoners. What the fuck did the hunters take from them? What ingredient made it finally work?

And then my gaze lands on the muroni. What was it Luca said about the blood....

I don't think. With the last vestiges of my strength, I push to my feet and go toward them. I can't blur, I can barely run at a human pace. But it's enough.

"Finish her!" I hear behind me.

Two more steps, and I fall into one of the muroni. Its eyes open—dead of any feeling, beyond acceptance. Begging for mercy. One I am more than happy to grant.

I tilt its head to the side and dig my teeth into its neck. The first wave of its blood hits my taste buds, and then the next. And the next. But also something else.

I pull back to look at the muroni, and see a faint malice in its eyes. And then it turns those eyes to the hunters. In a flash, its message becomes clear, so I feed some more. By the time the hunter's reaching me, I've taken my fill. And if I'm right...

I turn to face the hunter. He wields the scythe high, preparing to strike me once more. I raise my hand. And the shadows at his feet answer, spiraling around his ankles like snakes. But they don't stop there. They keep going higher and higher until they reach his mouth. There, they force their way in past his lips... I watch him gag, impassable. It's like someone else is doing this, not me.

Another hunter—a female one—detaches from the fight with the wolves and runs at me next. The same happens to her. From across the field, I see some of the wolves toss me looks—awe, concern, disgust, I can't tell. Nor do I care.

Whatever this is, it won't last long. My father may have been able to handle darkness in a similar way to Ștefan, but my siblings and I never could. Only the muroni, because of what they willingly sacrifice, and the evil they let into themselves, are able to. Yet somehow—maybe through the curse, maybe because I'm at my weakest, maybe something else entirely—feeding on the muroni loaned me the same power. But it *is* a loan, and it will not last.

I might as well use this power to eliminate one more before it vanishes.

I find the stafie tucked behind a tent, observing the fight. "I'm surprised you didn't slither away like you did at Corvins'," I say, though I barely recognize my voice. Dark, hoarse...otherworldly.

He whirls on me and his eyes widen. "You—"

I lift my hand and toss all the darkness at him. It pulls at him until he's torn apart, disappearing into nothingness, just like Father used to do to his enemies. It's satisfying seeing him break apart until he is no more. And with him gone, maybe I'll be able to do what the witch said. Let go of the past.

I reach up to my cheek that used to be unharmed until he cut it, and find the flesh smooth once again. Huh. I'll take that as a good sign.

As for the hunter stafie? I may have just condemned him to a fate worse than death. But I'm okay with that. Even while I sway on my feet, and feel the power leave me at once. *Looks like I was right about it not lasting*.

From around the tent, I hear shouts so I head toward them. The wolves did good with the other hunters. They've also released the vampiri, and the two wolves, around which they're gathered. The muroni are dead. They had their use, but I can't say I'm sad to see them gone.

I approach the two vampiri first. They're barely standing, but I recognize them from the ball. I focus on the one with no blood around his mouth, hoping he still has his speech. "You're from the Cazacu clan, yeah?"

"Da, princess," he says.

"You would do well to mention to your leader that it was I who saved you."

"Yes, princess."

The other nudges him, opens his mouth to speak, but only a trail of blood comes out.

His companion nods and holds up a hand to calm him down. To me, he says, "We... may we show our gratitude with some information?"

I gesture for him to go ahead, and he's only too happy to do so. "These hunters, they were in cahoots with those responsible for the attack on you."

The ball when Ștefan saved my life...

"Did they happen to say who ordered it?"

"They said more than that. Thinking that we would be dead

soon, they didn't censure their words."

"Tell me."

"They mentioned someone called Liviu—he sounded like a witch."

"I know of him." Ștefan's Grand Master, behind the attack? Why am I not surprised? "What else?"

"They mentioned a...curse." He shifts on his feet. "That you and a Dacian were mated because of it. Your death was to mean the eradication of the last Dracul lineage."

I don't know how Liviu found out about Ștefan, but this sounds like part two of the plan he had with Vlad and Silviana. Fuck.

Drawing closer to the two vampiri, I dig deep for one more bit of power—my glamour. "Forget everything you heard about the curse, but you may share the rest with your leader. Go now, and may we meet again under better circumstances."

I don't have to ask them twice before they take off. With the vampiri gone, I realize one of the wolves who'd been captured is standing, albeit appearing disheveled and more than a little worn down.

The other—with the muroni arm attached to him—is lying on the grass on his back, writhing and whimpering. I slowly approach him, and with each step notice the black veins popping out of his white-as-a-sheet skin. Agony is painted on his features.

Luca looks up at me, tears streaming down his cheeks. He makes no effort to hide them. Normally, it'd be a sign of weakness to me. It still is. But something about their suffering—one physical, one emotional—hits me. Hard.

I kneel next to the distressed shifter, showing him my good side, without the scar. "Shh..."

He looks at me, fear in his eyes, spittle at the corner of his mouth. "I'm...scared."

"I know."

"I don't...want....to die..."

I lift my hand to his cheek, gently caressing him. "I know. Don't look at it as dying, but as a new beginning." I let my hand drop to his neck. "Take a deep breath with me."

He does—and as he closes his eyes, I snap his neck.

On some level, I'd known what I was going to do. I've killed thousands. But this...feels different. I don't care to dig deeper and find out why, exactly.

Luca lets out a sob by my side, then slowly rises. Wipes at his cheeks, and forces a stoic expression once more. With that forced gesture alone, he seems to have aged. Fucked up shit will do that to you.

"Thank you," he whispers. "For doing what I couldn't."

I tilt my head in his direction. "You're welcome." Another glance at the body, then him. "I need to tell my siblings what happened here." And what the vampiri said.

"I understand. Thank you for your help."

I don't bother with goodbyes, only take off into the woods. The vampiri's revelation about Liviu bounces around my head the entire way home. A part of me wants to go to Ștefan, to warn him. But ... no. I don't like what this connection between us is. What it does to me. How it's changing me. His well-being is none of my concern—he's proven he can take care of himself, after all.

Ștefan

The feeling of dread doesn't leave me after Elizabeta disappears with the wolves. I want to go with her, but I've felt her pull away and I know she needs this. Or thinks she does, probably in a vain attempt to escape the connection between us. If only it were that easy.

It's probably about as easy as me avoiding the flashes of the despair I felt when that blood curse hit me. I've never felt so cold, so out of control. Frustrating as last night was, listening to Elizabeta's moans, at least I wasn't subjected to those reminders.

I turn my attention to Elizabeta's phone. It feels sleek and thin in my hand, with no home button, but it has the telltale two left-side buttons and one right-side button I've come to associate with iPhones. Out of most devices available, they're what I'm most familiar with, so thank *fuck* she didn't go for an old-school flip phone. I mean, considering how old they all are…wouldn't have surprised me.

After flicking the tiny button on the left side to enable sound, I try to swipe at the screen, but the whoosh I'm used to—indicating the phone has opened—doesn't happen. *Fucking hell, I should've asked her to unlock the phone before leaving.*

I pace a few more times, then another thought hits me. *If she doesn't have great security settings, I may be able to just use the virtual assistant speech-mode and get it to call Vlad. It better work, cause I sure as hell don't have time for this.*

I place my thumb on the right-side button and hold it, hoping this works. After the required one-to-two seconds of waiting, I say, "Hey Siri, call Vlad."

Nothing.

Couldn't be that easy. I run a hand over my head. *Think, think, think. Maybe it's not an iPhone after all? If it's not, could it be another virtual assistant? Fuck! What other popular virtual assis-*

tants do smartphones have? The list could be endless.

I try to think back to when Silviana did some research before getting me my new phone. I press on the button again and say, "Hey Google, call Vlad."

Nothing.

I only know of one more. "Hi Bixby, call Vlad."

Nothing.

I smack my forehead with the phone, at a total loss. What am I missing?

After a few more minutes of pacing, I stop again and feel every inch of the phone. It *is* an iPhone, dammit. It feels like an older version of the model I have. Which means the virtual assistant should be Siri.

Unless... Unless it's not Siri's name that's the problem.

I hesitate, then figure what the hell, might as well shoot my shot. I press the right-side button again, and simply say, "Hey Siri."

"*Hello*" comes the robotic response.

I punch my fist in the air—finally! Now, how do I go about figuring out how Elizabeta's got Vlad saved in her phone?

I try, "Call sibling."

"*Calling Sibling #1...*" comes the response.

Elizabeta saved her siblings as *numbers?* Is that in order of how they were turned, or in order of favoritism? Because if it's the latter, then her favorite brother is...

Shit. I panic. "Hey Siri, cancel the call!"

"*Call canceled.*"

I let out a sigh of relief. The last thing I need is to talk to Alexandru right now, if that's who Siri was calling.

Okay, let me try again. If Alexandru is "Sibling #1" then no one afterward will be as bad. But just in case he's not number one, and instead he's number two after Nico... Let me go for a midway number.

"Hey Siri, call Sibling #3."

"*Calling Sibling #3...*"

While the line rings, I pace back and forth. The air grows chillier, and I shiver.

Finally, someone picks up. "Liza? What's going on? I haven't heard from you—"

I let out a sigh of relief. I've never been so happy to hear Vlad's voice. "It's me, not Elizabeta."

"Ștefan! Is Liza...? Silviana was hysterical, talking about some message from you, needing to send help—"

"Elizabeta's fine. We're both fine. It's taken care of. Please, tell my sister I'm okay."

A pause follows. "Are you *sure*? We couldn't figure out if it was another trick from Zalmoxis or worse, something from your people designed to break your cover. But we *can* come."

"Like I said, it's fine. I'm fine. And Elizabeta just left with some wolves. There's some kind of attack or wolves missing or whatnot. Violeta sent them to get her, and she took off."

"What about your quest?"

"We ran into them just as we'd finished. I have the answers we need."

There's a note of almost urgency in his tone. Quickly, I relate what the old hag told us about Decebal and Cazanele Dunării.

"And this will fix her? You're sure?"

"It won't fix her forever," I mutter. "But for the time being, yes. Please, can I talk to her?"

A moment later, "Fane? I was listening in. What do you mean 'for the time being'?"

"You'll be going there periodically until Zalmoxis is taken care of. To recharge and fight him back."

Something like a sob escapes her. "So this is to be my life now? Always fighting him?"

"No, Lana. I won't let it be like this forever. He *will* be defeated, make no mistake. But for the time being, do what the old hag said." I pause for a beat. "Elizabeta is returning home with an amulet, too. Something meant to enhance the protection while you're away. You'll need to fill it with earth from the caves whenever you go, and add your blood to it—after you're recharged. And never take it off."

"I understand."

"And tell Vlad.... Tell him Elizabeta's coming home with more information. About their father."

"Țepeș? But—" She stops. "Wait, aren't you coming with her?"

"I need to go back to the Dacians."

"Fane, it's too dangerous. They'll know what you've done. They'll try to kill you!"

"They can try, but they won't succeed. Liviu has more information and I intend to get it." Then kill him. She doesn't need to know that part.

"Fane, please...."

"I'll come back as soon as I have it. I promise. I've never broken a promise to you and I don't intend to begin, Lana. I love you."

"I love you, too," she whispers, and I click the side button to hang up.

Since I have no car, I'll have to use some smaller teleportation portals. It's a little trick I picked up in Liviu's scroll, but not one I'm fond of leveraging. They'll waste energy and probably give me away before I even get there—two of the main reasons I hate using them—but I've got no other choice.

I exit the third portal and feel the vibration in the air. What Lana was talking about, last time she was here. Liviu and his damned protection spells.

No sooner do I cross it, that voices yell, "Halt!"

There's a cacophony of noise, of darkened auras and hands tugging at me. Followed by grips firming up on my forearms—two Dacians, judging by their strength.

"Ştefan Dragoş," one speaks in a voice I don't recognize, "the Grand Master would like to see you."

"What the hell is the meaning of this? Let me go!"

They don't listen, and instead drag me none too gently to Liviu's home. By the time they let me go, my shoulder joints ache from the journey and I have to roll them back a few times.

"The proverbial Dacian returns," a voice says to my left.

I stop my movements, more than a little uneasy that he was observing me in silence. "Liviu. What's with the welcome party?"

"You've been gone for so long, can you really blame an old man for being wary when you *finally* decide to return?"

"I was doing your bidding!"

"Really.... Last I heard, you'd stepped in and taken the bullet meant for Elizabeta Dracul."

How does he know about that?

"I did it to endear myself to them. So they would trust me." I really hope what I'm about to say doesn't screw me over. "We both know the Draculs have access to alliances and other types of magic. I wanted to know how entrenched they'd become in the area since."

He's quiet for a long time. "And?" His tone doesn't reveal much about his state of mind, but I can't stop now.

"They have an alliance with the wolves. A strong alliance. They trusted me enough to send me, alongside Elizabeta Dracul, to them. That's where I've been. I couldn't leave without drawing attention to myself."

"Hmm. A plausible explanation. And what else have you learned?"

I tell him what Silviana shared with me. "The wolf leader, Dominic, has ties to Țepeș as well. His wolves are part vârcolaci, part vrykolakas." None of this information will give him a leg up over the heirs, but at least it makes me seem useful. For now.

"Interesting.... And can the wolves be swayed away from him, be convinced to turn their backs on the pack and join a better cause?"

I have no fucking clue, but the lie comes easy. "Yes. They're not happy with his leadership."

"That information holds its weight in gold, Ștefan. With the wolves on our side, we would have the perfect army to attack and eradicate the Draculs once and for all."

Over my dead body. "Good." I force myself to loosen my fists. "Can I go wash off and rest, now?"

"Da. But I expect you to resume training. I'm awaiting news from Cezar and once his task is complete, we can put our plan into motion."

I nod, bowing my head slightly. "As you wish, Grand Master."

Then turn on my heels and walk out. I'm not sure how much he believed me, but one thing is clear—Liviu won't leave us alone. He knows too much and he's toying with heavy dark stuff. I need to eliminate him if I want Silviana and I to be safe. And I don't have much time to carry this out.

Elizabeta

A sense of peace fills me when the palace comes into view. Piercing the night, it's a beacon calling me home, and I couldn't be happier to have finally returned. When I cross the threshold, the flighty energy within me finally calms down.

"I'm homeeee," I yell.

Silence answers me at first, but then something tackles me from the left. "Finally!"

I laugh, turning into Vlad's arms to hug him properly. "Glad to see you, too."

Movement up the stairs draws my attention. Nico, Tassa, and Mirabela are coming down.

Nico smiles and holds out his arms, and I run into them. His hold tightens on me. "Glad to have you back," he whispers.

If ever I had any leftover resentment over the quest he sent me on, I know it's long gone the moment I hug him. I'm glad they're safe—all of them. And they'll never know how close they came to the end.

When I step back from his arms, Mirabela yanks a leaf out of my hair and shakes her head. "You need a bath." Then pulls me into her arms for a quick hug—unusual, but I don't hesitate to return it.

"What about me? Don't I get a hug?"

I whirl, and find Alex leaning against the bannister at the bottom of the stairs. A huge smile on my lips, I run and tackle him. He laughs and whirls us around until I'm dizzy, then sets me down but doesn't let me go. "About time you got back. Things were so dull around here without you."

I smile up at him and lean further into his hug. I missed this. My kin. My family.

But as much as I'm enjoying it, I know there's a lot to say. "I...it's good to be back. But I have a lot to tell you."

Nico nods. "Let's head to the library."

An hour later, I've caught them up on everything that happened at Corvins' and in the woods—including the stafie and the wolves. The only thing I leave out is the bit about Ștefan and our bond.

Which is why it's no surprise that Nico picks up on it. "But why? Liviu doing all of this, *why*? What did we ever do to the Dacians to trigger such rage against us?"

I shrug. "That's the question of the decade, I guess."

Vlad says, "I'll check with Silviana and see if she has any idea beyond what we already know. Which reminds me—Liza, the amulet."

I slide it out from between my breasts and hand it to him.

"Thanks," he says and takes off to his consort, leaving me with Nico, Mirabela, and Alex.

"I'll fill Violeta in," Nico says. "It might be a good idea for her and Marcus to come stay with us for a while. They're too isolated and an easy target in the woods."

I toy with the fringe of my blouse, biting my lip. "I'd thought as much, too. Especially given what I saw with the hunters."

He grabs his cell and jabs her number in, then disappears to talk to her.

Mirabela inches closer to me, and cups my cheek. "How are you? Going through that again, it must've brought back some unpleasant memories."

I gape at her. I've seen her frustrated with me and downright angry, but caring like this? Never. *Maybe this curse does have a good side, if it's making us tap into our human side.*

The moment the thought enters my mind, I shake my head. *What the hell?*

Aloud, I can't quite find my words. "I'm..."

Alex slaps my back. "Of course she's fine! This is Elizabeta we're talking about. She's tough as nails. Right, little sis?"

I force a grin and nod. But when I look back at Mirabela, I can tell she's not fooled.

"I think I'll go take that bath now," I mutter.

I'm barely at the door to the library when Alex calls out. "Food, after?"

"Hell yes." Nothing like a good hunt to bring my spirits into focus. And stop thinking about the damn Dacian.

Chapter 22

Elizabeta

Two days go by. Though hunting feeds my need for blood, it does nothing to quiet my mind. I thought putting distance between me and Ștefan would calm me down, calm these *feelings* I don't want rising within me. That being back home would ground me. But it's only made things worse. Not even the plush carpet under my feet, which previously gave me such comfort and joy, is enough to make me smile.

It can't be what I think it is. Ștefan himself said it—it doesn't have to be *the* bond the curse forces us to form, it could be *a* bond. *But if that's the case, why hasn't it gone away? Why is it getting stronger?*

When I wake up on yet another morning thinking of him again, with still no sign of Daniel, I seek Alex. "I want to hunt."

Alex puts down the book he was reading, arching an eyebrow. "Uh huh... didn't we feed yesterday?"

"I didn't say I want to *feed*. I said I want to *hunt*. So find us a cluster of muroni and let's go already." I cross my arms over my chest and tap my foot impatiently for good measure.

The eyebrow arches higher. "My, you're in a mood today."

"Don't you start."

He stares at me a moment longer, then shrugs. "As you wish, little sis. I'm sure I can find us something."

Standing, he holds out his hand for me. I take it, trying not to show the relief I'm feeling. There's a reason I'll pick him over the others any day. And it's that he never contests my moods, nor does he care, ultimately. In short, he's the perfect partner in crime. And he'll provide the perfect diversion to muffle my conscience.

"You were distracted," Alex says as we're exiting the cave of muroni.

It took us the better part of a day to hunt them, and even longer to stalk their lair until we were sure no surprises awaited us. Once that was done, the kills were almost too easy.

Yet even as I went about a task I used to enjoy, my mind wandered to the muroni in the hunter's camp. How their power had felt coursing through me. Wondering if I was to feed on another, if the same thing would hit me once more. It wouldn't be a bad side effect...

And then I shudder at the thought and dismiss it. Alex would throw a fit if I did, that's for sure.

"Liza?"

I glance up at him. He's stopped walking smack in the middle of the forest path, watching me with a peculiar expression. "What's going on with you?"

"Nothing, I—" I pause. I can't talk about Daniel with him, let alone Ştefan. But Alex understands dark impulses, so maybe there's one topic he'd hear me out on. "I didn't tell the others this. But when I helped the wolves"—his jaw clenches at their mention—"hunt down the hunters, there were two muroni in the camp. I was so weak, I did it on instinct. I....fed from one. But it wasn't just the blood I soaked in. It was his essence—his power."

He frowns and shifts his stance. His curious mind, the side that's been buried for so long and that I've seen only hints of over the centuries, is intrigued. "Are you saying you were able to wield powers like Father's?"

"For a short time, yes."

"How short? And what type of powers? What did they feel like?"

I give him all the details I can remember.

When I'm done, he seems almost excited. "Damn, Liza! We need to tell the others."

"Why?"

"Because! Don't you see? This entire time, we've been hunting the muroni. But we don't need to just destroy them. We can extricate their blood, and use it as a tool to defend ourselves. It'll be yet another weapon in our arsenal, similar to what I—" He stops abruptly, and his expression shutters.

"Similar to what?"

"Never mind. I'll go ahead to the castle and tell them. Unless you have any objections?"

I wave him onward, and he's gone in a flash.

I'm not ready to return to the castle. Not yet. So I let my feet lead me aimlessly instead until I find myself a ways away.... And in woods that are familiar for the wrong reasons.

Shit. My *aimless* brain brought me into Dacian territory.

"Great job, Liza. Now if you run into that damn Dacian, he'll think you're here to check up on him."

"Or he might think you miss him," says a voice behind me.

I whirl, only to find Ștefan pushing off from a tree. Its bulky trunk had hidden him from my view, but the moment he emerges into the light, he's all my eyes can focus on.

The strong jaw underneath the beard. The muscles stretching his shirt. The way his thighs look, clad in his dark jeans. A hot lick of desire runs through me at all the missed opportunities. Fuck. I'd been lying to myself when I thought that if I ever ran into him again, this thing between us would be gone.

"Miss you?" I snort, trying to keep a smooth tone. "Unlikely."

He takes a step closer. "You haven't killed me yet. Or threatened to."

I jerk my chin back. "There's still time."

With one more long stride, he's almost within arm's reach. "And yet..." He crosses the last inches, putting us within touching distance. His scent fills my nostrils. The tempo of his heartbeat, my ears. I can't see, or breathe, without being surrounded by his essence.

"And yet...?" I breathe.

Ștefan reaches for me, his fingers trailing my wrist, my arm, my collarbone, and up my neck, leaving goosebumps in their wake. "And yet, I don't think you will. Threaten or actually kill me." His thumb comes to rest on my lower lip.

"And why's that?"

His only answer is to lean forward and kiss me. His lips press against mine lightly, but at their soft touch, a fuse detonates in me. A shiver runs up and down my back, sending tingles to my extremities.

Before he can sense it, I grab the collar of his shirt and shove him back a little. "I warned you what would happen if you touched me again."

He laughs darkly. "Do your worst, Elizabeta. Because I already can't sleep, can't think without being around you."

The admission leaves me bereft, removed of retorts or anything to do...except yank on the collar of his shirt until he's catapulted toward me, and I can crush my lips against his. He moves his free hand to my lower back, pressing until I'm flush against him, every inch of me touching every inch of him it can reach.

All I'm aware of is his lips on mine, his body against mine, almost holding me up. I'm weak at the knees. *Me!* But I find myself hanging onto him, inhaling his scent, wanting to soak myself in it. In him.

Ștefan pulls away, barely, but I let out a growl and dig my nails into his shirt, tearing through the fabric. "Don't you dare put a stop to this again."

His laugh this time is low, almost self-deprecating. The scent of blood fills the air. "Wouldn't dream of it, princess."

"Then what—"

I don't ask him what changed. I'm not stupid enough to, not when the itch to be with him is so strong it feels like ants crawling through my veins.

The air around us whooshes with his magic, and the next thing I know, I'm not in the woods anymore, but in a rather human—and bare—looking apartment.

I arch an eyebrow. "I don't recall your sister being able to do this."

Something like a smile twists his lips. "My sister is a great witch, but she hasn't studied under the Grand Master for all these years. I have a few tricks up my sleeve. Shall I show you?"

"By all means, Dacian..."

I'm curious. Given what he'd confessed to me about being a virgin, I don't expect much in terms of skills. I've had many lovers, good and bad alike, over the centuries. There's nothing I haven't felt or seen or tried... But the way he carries himself hints I may yet be surprised. Underneath the shyness, the inexperience, there's a sense of quiet confidence. Something, I realize, I've come to associate with him.

As if I guessing my wandering thoughts, Ștefan kisses me again. Except it's not a soft kiss, like before. Not even just a passionate one. It's a soul-consuming attack on my senses. And if before I was electrified in his arms, now my knees give way under me, unable to hold me up. His sheer presence is overpowering, and I need to lean against the wall to hold myself up.

He's right there in front of me, pinning me with his body. Everything I'd previously ignored, that I'd tried to tell myself I didn't find attractive, I'm faced with tenfold. Find it pressed against me. And combined with our desperate, heady connection, it's as potent to my enhanced senses as the sweetest blood.

He trails his lips down my jaw, to my neck, to the valley between my breasts. "Your scent..." he murmurs. "It's intoxicating, Elizabeta."

I swallow past the lump in my throat. I was wrong. So wrong to think there was nothing he could show me that I haven't seen before when it comes to sex. I should've known from his kiss that it wouldn't be that simple.

"Liza. I..." I can barely speak. "You've earned the right to call me Liza."

"You'll always be Elizabeta to me—a princess worthy of the name, and all the worship that comes with it."

He lowers himself to his knees, and pushes his hands under my dress. Reaches for my knee-high boots, feeling every inch of the leather. A grin graces his lips. "Knee-high leather boots, princess? I wouldn't have taken you for the type."

"What can I say.... I like a bit of leather with my outfits."

A chuckle leaves him at that, and he pulls off one boot, then the next. The sound of the side zipper is loud in the otherwise silent apartment, and Ștefan seems to be enjoying taking his time with it. It's so unlike every other encounter I've ever had, that I'm once again left bereft and at a loss of words.

When the second boot is off, Ștefan doesn't let go of my leg. Instead, he turns his head toward it and kisses the side of my knee, then the soft flesh behind it. A gasp escapes me at the pleasurable sensation his kiss causes. And then he does it again. Followed by a nip of his teeth that has me reaching for something, anything to hold on to. Nothing—nothing—explains the fierce desire that pools between my legs at his touch.

"What are you—how are you—-how did—"

He stops his sensory assault and chuckles against my skin. The vibration only fuels my fire.

"I said I was a virgin, Elizabeta. Not a monk."

"I...don't understand."

He gestures vaguely behind him. "I read. A lot. You'd be surprised at the sheer amount of information about the female body."

For the first time, I notice the bookshelves adorning his small living room. The plain granite countertop in his kitchen, only a few feet away. A curved navy sofa, and equally dark-blue stools. A corridor and an open door further back—probably a bedroom.

Before I can assess his living quarters, Ștefan's grip on my ankle tightens, but only enough so he massages the sole of my foot with his other hand, in a way that has a low groan escape me. "That being said, princess, be sure to let me know if anything I do is not...satisfactory. I'm a very, very eager student."

"I..." I lick my lips. "I'll be sure to tell you."

He nods and places my leg on the ground, only to take up the other. It doesn't escape my notice that he's placed it slightly wider than it was before, basically ensuring I'm more and more open to his touch.

With painstaking care, Ștefan does the same thing to my other leg. The kiss behind the knee, followed by a nibble, and the slightest massage of the sole. Then he moves his hands further up, pushing the skirt of my dress at the same time. Though I don't need to breathe, I find myself panting, as if reverting to human impulses from the thrill of his touch.

When his hands reach the apex of my things, Ștefan stops. He avoids the area I most desperately need him at, and instead pushes the dress up my stomach, and over my chest, coming to stand once more.

When he's gotten it off me, I once more pull him to me by the fabric of his shirt. "Ștefan—"

His lips cut off my protest in a desperate, sloppy kiss that's unlike the previous one and shows me he's at least as affected by what we're doing as I am. Just as desperate. Just as needy.

As he's kissing me, his hand moves between my thighs, finding my center. I gasp in his mouth when his questing fingers bypass my underwear and find my clit, then my swollen lips. I flat-out moan when his fingers slip ever so slightly inside me.

"Christ, Elizabeta," he groans, breaking our kiss. "You're so damn wet for me."

"Ştefan, please, stop fucking around."

I wish he could see me. That he could read the desire in my features and understand that I'm so close to losing it. But he seems to get it even without, because he lowers himself to his knees once more, and presses a kiss where I most desperately need him to. Then he shoves the front of my panties to the side and kisses the bare flesh beneath.

His lips soon find a rhythm. Kissing in slow, exploratory kisses, until he finds a spot that drives me crazy. Alternating between gentle sucks and flicks of his tongue that leave me burning with such need, I nearly scream.

He keeps me on the precipice, whether on purpose or accidentally, until I'm left with no choice but to beg. "Ştefan, please. I need.... I can't come from just that. I need your fingers. Inside me. Please."

He hums against me and presses two fingers inside me and... I lose it. That saying humans have, of seeing stars? It's not stars. It's an abyss, a black hole, consuming every inch of me, igniting my senses, and surrendering my soul—if I even possess one—to an inferno of passion. The flames engulf me, scorching my very essence, until I explode into a supernova of pleasure...only to be pulled into the void of desire once more.

And that's when I know I'm well and truly fucked. In the literal and figurative sense. There's no way I can stay here. Not after this.

I know with the clarity only a fantastic orgasm can give me that if I stay, being with him will tear me apart even more than Daniel's death did.

Ştefan

Elizabeta screams, and it's the culmination of her moans and pants that I've been waiting for. The way she clenches around my fingers makes my chest swell with pure male pride.

I did that.

She lost control in my arms, no one else's.

When she starts swaying on her legs, I pick her up in my arms and carry her to my bedroom, more careful than ever to count my steps to make sure I don't trip and send us both sprawling onto the unforgiving floor.

I end up making it safely to the bed, and sit with her in my arms; we're a tangle of limbs and, in my case, one overheated body.

Elizabeta moans, nuzzling my neck. The scent of her arousal is everywhere around us. "I hope you don't think that's all there is to fucking," she whispers against my skin.

I frown at her use of the word, but bite my tongue. If that's what it takes for her to be comfortable with this thing between us, then so be it. By the time I'm done with her tonight, Elizabeta won't be able to deny that what's between us is a hell of a lot more than simple fucking.

"You mean, there's more?" I tease.

That draws a chuckle out of her, and I feel her pull back slightly. Then she's rearranging herself until she's straddling me.

"Let me show you, this time," she whispers and presses her lips to mine.

Her hands deftly undo my belt and I lift my hips so she can slide the jeans off me. When she straddles me once more, there's nothing between us—nothing except her heat against my hardness.

"Elizabeta..."

I grab hold of her hips to steady her, to slow her down, but I'm not fast enough. She presses down on me, taking my full length inside of her in one fell swoop. The moan escaping her makes me even harder, and her tightness is enough to have me close to blowing my load.

"Fuck," I mutter, dropping my head against her chest.

And then she slides up and down my cock, her heat engulfing me into a maelstrom of sensations. All breath leaves me, and my chest feels tight in a way it shouldn't possibly. I can't hold back anymore. I need her to come with me again. So I press my hand between her legs, seeking that elusive bundle of nerves that'll send her off into a climax.

When I touch its slickness after a few fumbles, Elizabeta cries out. "Gentle! I.... Fuck, I'm so sensitive."

I slow down my touch, circling instead of outright touching her clit. And her moans pick up in pace, as does her bouncing on my cock. I won't last.

I won't....

And then I feel it, erupting from deep within me. But I don't stop my movements until Elizabeta comes right along with me, my name a mantra on her lips.

Elizabeta

I've never cuddled after sex. Given most of the time I used the men I slept with for sex and then fed from them—sometimes killed them if they were from a particular hunter lineage—it's not that much of a surprise.

What is a surprise is how much I enjoy it. Everything from laying down my head on Ștefan's chest, his heartbeat under my ear, to the heat of his body permeating my cold skin. He runs his fingers through my hair, then massages my scalp, and it feels intimate. Close.

"Do I pass muster, then, or is any of that grounds to maim me like you threatened?" Ștefan asks.

I tilt my head back so I can see his features and the wry smile on his lips. "I think you know the answer to that."

He chuckles, but cuts off abruptly. "Will you tell me what really happened at Corvins' Castle?"

Just like his mood altered, mine does, too. I rest my head on his chest again, finding it easier to speak without looking at him. And I want to speak, for once. "I was a fool, long ago. Stupidly walked into the trap of a so-called hiker with a twisted ankle, and got myself captured by hunters."

He tugs on a lock of my hair gently. "Don't call yourself a fool, Elizabeta. You couldn't have seen that coming, surely."

"But I could've. Because decades before, we'd rescued..." I shake my head, not ready to go there. "We'd rescued a dear friend," is all I say, "from their clutches. And we knew they were hunting us. But I was...young, innocent, head in the clouds with my new power.

And they took advantage of that, and captured me." I gulp past my throat, which feels suddenly clogged. "It wasn't pretty. I'll spare you the details."

The hand on my hair tenses and Ştefan tugs on it, a bit more insistently this time. "I want you to tell me everything. I'm not some ignorant human who can't handle it, Elizabeta. And if we're going to have a shot at this, a *real* shot, then I need you to trust me to handle the shit that comes our way."

I tilt my head once more. His expression matches his words—determined, tense, eyes narrowed. I spread my hand on his chest and run it up and down his skin. His jaw clenches, but he's not taking me up on the offer to get distracted. Which is just as good, because for once, I don't fully mean it. I'd intended the touch more as a way to connect with him and have him feel that I'm listening to him.

"Is that what we're doing, then?" I whisper. "Giving this a shot?"

His taut expression falters at that, and then softens altogether. The hand on my hair shifts to cup my cheek. "It's what I'd like."

I clear my throat, refusing to get choked up on emotions. "Then maybe you should first hear what you're getting into."

So I dive in, and tell him everything. Even parts I never told Daniel or my siblings—the fear I'd felt, the hopelessness, the awareness of my mortality *despite* my immortality. The rage at my own stupidity, the yearning for vengeance when I was freed, the fire in the pit of my belly that ensured I joined Daniel to tackle every single hunter he found.

I can't tell the story without mentioning Daniel, but Ştefan doesn't stop me when I do. He lets me get it all out, and only at the end does he move—to wrap an arm around me and hoist me higher up on the bed, and against his side, until our heads are touching.

"I hate that you had to go through that," he says, and his voice is rough with emotion. "I'm glad you had Daniel to understand, because God knows your siblings aren't exactly sentimental."

His words send a zing of awareness through me. I tense against him, which I know he feels. But rather than call me out on it, he rolls to his side, so we're facing each other fully. His arm never leaves my waist, as if he needs to hold on to me to make sure I'm not ready to bolt.

Which, to be fair, I'm considering. I didn't expect how his gentle nature and understanding would make me react. I didn't expect the sheer panic roiling in my gut. The need to get as far and as fast away from him as I can. The sense that while I'm safe, I'm also on the precipice of something major...like opening my heart to him.

"He never meant to betray you, you know," Ștefan says. "When he spoke to me, there was always a reluctance in what he was sharing. But he knew I needed to have the information so I didn't dismiss you—so I could help out." He pauses and draws in a breath. "What happened at Corvins' when we went? Tell me everything."

Once more, I do, though my words are softer. I tell him how I ran into the stafie, and how he taunted me. How the nightmares came back in full force. How when he'd interrupted me that one time, it was after one of them. How Cezar's barrier kept Daniel away, and I feared I was losing him. I tell him how the fight went—everything the stafie said—and why I had a feeling he wasn't truly gone after Ștefan destroyed Corvins' Castle. And finally, I tell him what happened with the wolves—all of it.

When I get to the bit about Father's powers, and how good it felt to be able to use the darkness like that, Ștefan nods. "I can relate to that. It's what I feel when I go deep into it, past a simple cut.

When I let darkness feed on my blood, it allows me to wield it like the weapon it is. It's a powerful feeling."

"It is," I agree.

"What happened after?"

"I went back home. The wolves went their own way. And..." I hesitate to tell him the truth, that same fear gripping me. But I've never been a coward, and I don't intend to start now. "I couldn't get you out of my mind."

A smile plays on his lips. "Is that right?"

Before I can formulate a proper answer, he erases the remaining distance between us and finds my lips. The way he kisses me is different, as if to erase the memory of everything I've told him. And it rocks me to my core, much like our kiss at the castle.

I pull back, that sense of flight taking over. "I should go."

Ștefan ignores me, instead lowering his head to my neck. He rubs his beard against the skin, then follows the roughness with a trail of his tongue. Goosebumps rise on my arms, and the fight in me is real—to stay, and give in to what he's promising, or leave, and protect my heart.

"Ștefan..."

His mouth travels lower, kissing past my collarbone, and lingering onto my breasts. He grabs a hip and gently pushes me to my back, never once interrupting his kissing path. When his tongue tangles around my nipple, I arch into his touch, and move my hand to the back of his neck to hold him there.

He chuckles against me, and shifts his attention to my other breast. "I take it you're staying, then?"

I wrap my legs around his waist and, with one thrust of my hips, force him to his back. Straddling him, I bend at the waist and kiss his neck, his chest, in a downward trail down to his cock. "I think I can be convinced," I murmur, and wrap my hand around his length.

Ștefan's groan is music to my ears, and I smile as I lose myself in him.

I watch him sleep, exhausted from our multiple orgasms—again, a completely new sensation for me. It makes me wonder if I even enjoyed all the sex I've had previously, because I sure as hell can't remember ever feeling this languid and...vulnerable. *Maybe it's because you were never emotionally involved with any of your lovers.*

Hmm. Good point.

I trail my finger down Ștefan's chest, grazing a nipple, but he doesn't move. *That's my cue.* I kiss his chest, his cheek, and then rise from the bed.

It wasn't my intention to use sex to exhaust him, but I knew he wouldn't let me go otherwise. And I *need* to go. The gentler he is, the more understanding he is, the more that yearning to escape rises. I can only fight it for so long before giving in. Even if, in the end, it makes me a coward.

Once I'm dressed, boots in my hands, I take one last look at him. Tears fill my eyes—I could have this, if I let myself. But I know I can't, not when I'm this broken, and he's everything but.

Ștefan

I know the moment she's gone, because the weight in my arms has vanished and so has her energy. She's running away. Again.

I sit in bed, running a hand over my head, then my face. She's the most confusing being in existence. She enjoyed what we just did, didn't she? I may be new to this, but even I couldn't miss her signals. Just the thought of how responsive she'd been, how explosive we'd been together, is enough to get me hard again.

Forcing the sentiment down, I focus instead on something else. Her. Running away. Which means despite everything I told her, everything I tried to communicate, she still thinks this was just fucking. She's so damned afraid of what's between us, she'd rather hide away in her palace than face it.

Too bad for her, I'm persistent. I've never had someone to care for besides Lana, but now that I do, I'm not about to give up so easily. I hit the mattress, letting out a long growl. Then I stand.

I let her go last time because the wolves needed her. *She* needed that closure, though I hadn't been aware of the details back then. But I'll be damned if I let Elizabeta Dracul walk out on me again without calling her out on her shit.

It's a piece of cake, catching up to her. What we did seems to have enhanced the bond between us, acting like a straight-up thread to her. All I need to do is create a portal, focus on it, and I emerge somewhere where her scent is potent, and fresh.

Ahead of me, branches break—a telltale sign of her escape.

"Running away?"

There's silence, then a shift in the air as she faces me. Twigs and other things snap under her feet when she inches closer, then stops, as though annoyed at herself for doing so. "I'm going back home. To my siblings."

Her voice is even, devoid of its usual bite. Perhaps it's because of that that I clue in to her barely held control. A control I want to snap until I have her moaning, breathless, and needy in my arms again. Preferably for days. Until I can get it through her thick skull that regardless of what she thinks, this thing between us is real. Curse or no curse, we have a choice.

Unfortunately for me, Elizabeta doesn't respond well to declarations and feelings. So I opt for another tactic. "While you still smell of me? I would've thought they'd frown at that. Especially Alex."

She's closer now. "Are you purposefully trying to provoke me?"

"Even if I managed to, it would be useless."

"What's that supposed to mean?"

"You don't give anything you're not ready for. And everything you do give is half-assed and superficial." It's a lie—she was plenty honest with me before. But I need to hear her say it.

She's in my face now, the air moving with her scent. "Is that so?" She runs a hand up my chest, her tone cool and collected. But I know her better now—I hear the hitch in her voice, the little bit of something that tells me her walls are shaking. "Was it half-assed and superficial, what we just shared?"

I catch her hand in mine. "You tell me."

She tries to yank herself out of my grip, but I hold on tight. Use my other hand to wrap it around her waist, tugging her into me. Refusing to let her go.

"What are you doing?"

I call on the magic then, adding another element to bind us together. In my arms, she bristles even more, fighting me at every turn.

"I want to know why you keep running."

"Let me the fuck go, Ștefan, or else—"

"Or else, what? You'll chop off my head, like you do most everyone who annoys you? Go on, try. I dare you."

"This isn't fair. You know how I feel about being bound."

"Do I?" I pause, trying to regain control of my emotions. I'm not this person, with uncontrollable emotions. This isn't me. "What I do know is that you run. Always. And this thing between us, the emotions you're feeling—"

"What makes you think I'm feeling *anything*? Maybe you're just another conquest."

"Is that why you said you couldn't stop thinking about me?" I pause. "You can lie to me, you can pull up your walls again, or you can be honest, Elizabeta." I soften my tone. "I know things about you, things you refuse to see in yourself, and I love those glimpses of vulnerability as much as the strength you put forth in front of everyone else. But you don't have to with me, princess. Let yourself go, and *be with me*."

"You don't understand! You wouldn't."

"Try me."

She says nothing. Instead, her body shakes—it takes me a moment to realize she's crying. And when I do, I drop the magic, and pull her into my arms. Properly. She holds onto me, and the tough, cool, psychotic vampir side within her seems to melt.

Then, just as quickly, she shoves me away. Hard enough that I stumble, and fall to the ground. Elizabeta doesn't try to help me up, but I can feel her energy around me.

"You *don't* understand," she repeats.

And finally, I think I do. "It's about him, isn't it? Daniel. His stafie, haunting you."

Only silence answers me. She's gone—for good this time.

Elizabeta

Damn him and the high horse he's on! I don't run. I face my problems head-on! Just because I have other ways of facing them than talking about them... No one person is the same, and it's idiotic he expects me to fit some mold.

I run back home, trying to get as far away as I can from the biggest mistake of my life. The entire time, I shove away the flashes of our time together. Of the gentleness of his touch. The way he worshipped my body. The sheer desire and kindness in him.

When I finally get there, I ignore Mira at the entrance and storm straight into my side of the castle, and into my bedroom.

No sooner am I in, that Daniel appears. I gape at him. "You! Where the hell have you been?"

He shakes his head. "Around. I needed to...think."

"And you didn't even bother to let me know? I thought you'd left me!"

He sighs and floats a bit closer. "You're angry."

"Damn right, I'm angry!"

"But not at me."

"No," I say, softer.

"At Ștefan?"

Fury erupts within me again at his name. "How dare he say all those things, and act so—so—"

"Like he cares?"

I scowl at him. "Like he knows exactly what's in my mind."

Daniel looks at me with something like pity in his eyes. He says nothing, which drives me even more crazy. I storm around, screaming and shouting, refusing to listen to any bit of truth that's on my mind.

Because Ștefan doesn't know what he's talking about. He can't. He can't have seen past my walls and in such a little time that we spent together.

And yet everything seems to indicate that he did.

"He's right, you know."

I turn to Daniel. "What the hell are you talking about?" Only then does it dawn on me what his words mean. "You...saw? You were there?" Shame courses through me. "For how long?"

Daniel tilts his head to the side. Watches me. "Enough to hear the fight. But no, I wasn't there *before*, if it's what you're worried about." A sad smile. "I stay away when you feed or fuck, remember?"

I jerk my gaze away from him.

"And you know what? He's absolutely right. You do run away from all of your problems. You always have. It's your way of dealing with things."

"That's not true."

"Liza... You ran away when you got turned. You ran away from the torture those hunters inflicted on you. You ran away from my death by losing yourself in mindless cruelty and promiscuity." He pauses as I gape at him. "You can lie to yourself as much as you want. But at the end of the day, you' ll just be proving him right."

I stare at Daniel in shock. I can't believe that he, out of everyone, is actually on Ștefan's side. I never would've expected it. Something rolls in my gut, and before I can analyze it, I spit out two words. “Get out.”

“Elizabeta, don’t do this.”

“No, get the fuck out. I need you out of my life. All this time you’ve leeched on me, all this time you’ve been around, all this time you’ve held me back. Get the hell out. I don’t need you anymore.”

He opens his mouth as if to say something, but only shakes his head. “If that’s what you wish.” With a shimmer, he disappears.

And I’m left alone. As I’ve always been.

I grab the nearest pillowcase to stuff my face into and scream. I don’t know how else to deal with everything coursing through me. And for the first time, I wish that Father was still around. He would know what to do.

A few hours later, Alex comes into my room. “So, this is where you’re hiding.”

“I’m not in the mood, Alex.”

He gives me a piercing look. “Mira did say you were acting weird. What’s gotten up your butt?”

“I told you, I’m not in the mood. Can’t you just go find someone else to play with?”

“So I take it you don’t want to go hunting then?”

I give him a look. “No. I don’t want to go fucking hunting. Just leave me be for a little bit.”

“Fine. I will. But keep in mind that our dear siblings are having another political party tonight. You must be on your best game.”

And then he leaves. For the first time, I'm actually glad that he has. Because I don't know how to act around him right now, given the thundering emotions running through me.

Ştefan

There's an ache in my chest when I head back to the compound. Too much. Too deep. I've let her get inside me, and she's torn out my heart and stomped all over it.

Fucking hell.

I run a hand over my scalp and let out a deep sigh.

"That sounded pensive."

I start and whirl toward the voice. "Liviu? What are you doing here?" Shit. Did he see us? He couldn't have, I made sure to put protection spells around my apartment.

But...his timing can't be coincidental.

"Taking a stroll, much like you," he says, and his tone is measured. Too measured. "Come, walk with me."

I swallow, racking my brain for an excuse to decline.

Before I can voice anything, he says, "It wasn't a question."

So I grit my teeth and follow in the wake of his echoing footsteps. Whatever this is about, I need to get my head out of my ass and focus. Else Elizabeta may get her wish after all and I'll end up dead.

Chapter 23

Elizabeta

His head is between my legs, his tongue doing sinful things to me. My back arches off the bed, moans escaping me. I reach down for him. "Ștefan ..."

He does something with his tongue, around my clit, and I push off the bed with a cry. His hands go to my hips, pressing me down.

"You're fucking magic." He groans against me and looks up. His chin and lips are glistening with my juices, his eyes unfocused. "The taste of you, Elizabeta..."

I moan, reaching for him again. "Please...."

"Please, what?" He pauses and I don't give in. A smirk tugs at his lips. "I can hear the need in your voice, princess. Tell me. Tell me what you need, and I'll give it to you."

His other hand joins the first between my legs, tantalizingly close.

"Yes, *princess*, tell him..."

I freeze. *I know that voice!*

An evil power fills the space with menacing shadows, and I shiver, curling myself into a ball.

"Tell him exactly what you need. From that bond. Finalize it. Then I can break it, break you, and finally own the Dracul heirs."

I come awake with a start. My body feels flushed, though that's impossible. Yet there's a yearning within me for Ștefan's touch.

It's been two days since I left him, and this yearning for him is like a flame that won't be extinguished. But being immortal has its perks—a great memory, among others. And I'll be damned if I stay awake, wound up like this. With trembling hands, I reach between my legs and close my eyes once more, pulling up the memories of our time together.

An insistent knock on my door wakes me right as the sun rises. I roll out of bed and open it, finding Silviana standing there. She barges past me.

"Something's wrong."

"By all means, enter and feel right at home," I drawl.

In a corner, I notice Daniel watching us. When did he come back? And why, when I told him to fuck off?

Silviana tosses him a glance, then focuses on me. "I don't care about your little hideaway ghost or how much of a bitch you are. My brother's in trouble."

A flicker of unease rises in me at her words. I remember the woods, what the vampiri said. The piece of information I chose to dismiss, in a vain attempt to convince myself I don't care for her brother. Instead of revealing anything, I force a cool expression and ask in a bored tone, "And I should care, because?"

"I know you're mated to him."

I'm in her face the moment after. "You don't know what you're talking about."

"I do." She meets my glare full-on. "I dreamt it. And I feel it in Vlad. Every time you reject Ștefan, that sickness threatens to come over him all over again. And when you don't, he's fine."

Shit. The last thing I need is her spreading this around the castle. Or figuring out that two days ago, I was in her brother's bed.

I point to the door. "Get out."

"No. I told you, I dreamt Ștefan's in danger. Our twin bond is strong—you have no idea how strong. He reached out to me when you were in trouble, wanting to get you help! He faded away before I could respond. But I know he's in trouble now, and only you can help him."

"I. Don't. Care. *Get out*!" Without waiting for her to leave, I grab her arm and yank her to the door, push her out, and slam it behind her.

Then rest my forehead against it. *Ștefan, what the hell did you do?*

No. I can't. No matter what it is, it's not my problem. If Silviana knows about him being consort, then she can piece the rest of it together. I'm already dealing with enough confusion, I don't need more added to my plate. Not when I should be working toward being the Liza everyone knows, nothing more.

Behind me, the air changes as Daniel approaches. And it's too much. Him. Ștefan. This fucking god, laughing at me in my dreams. My shoulders curl inward. For the first time, I understand Violeta's need to leave. To hide in the woods. Away from us, from prying eyes, from....

Without moving, I croak, "Why are you back, Daniel? I told you to leave me."

"You said many things, Liza. You always do when you're angry. But I'll always care enough to come back."

"I wish you wouldn't."

"And I wish you'd stop fighting it."

I turn to him. He's so close, his eyes so sad. Tears fill my eyes. I want to deny them, but I can't. Because this story, it was supposed to be ours. He was supposed to be my forever.

"You know he's who you belong with."

"Because of a fucking curse. If it wasn't for some god pulling strings, I wouldn't ever have fa... I... None of this would've happened!"

Daniel shakes his head, clearly no longer willing to let me delude myself. "That's not true. The curse is real, da. But how it ties all of you to different people? It's like it knows....the deepest, darkest part of your yearnings. And gives it to you. The person who can make you whole." He lifts his hand as if to touch me. "And that's not me, Liza."

Tears flow down my cheeks for real this time. "Don't say that."

"It's true. It was never meant to be me."

"That's *not* true!" I scream, no longer caring which of my siblings hears me. "You were there when.... Without you, I'd have fallen apart after the hunters took me captive. No one recovers from something like that easily."

"You did."

"Da, because of *you*."

He shakes his head. "No, Liza. You healed yourself. I was merely the tool to help you do it." His expression falls once more. "But then it became your ongoing motto. Using physical release to hide from everything else. And I'm... in a way, I'm glad I died when I did."

"If you hadn't, I never would've gotten this bad."

He laughs. "As if I could've stopped it? You would've gotten bored of me eventually, Liza."

"Stop it," I whisper.

"I can't. I have to say these things, because you'll never let me go otherwise."

"I don't want to!"

"You'll be better for it, my love. And he'll take good care of you. But right now, you need to find him, and help him. He's in real danger, which means you're *all* in real danger."

I wipe at my cheeks, take a deep breath I don't need, and open the door. Behind me, Daniel flickers in and out, and finally disappears. I don't know if it'll be the last time I see him, but I know I need to act on the information he's given me. After all, he's right—our fates are impossibly intertwined, like the most intricate of vines.

On leaden feet, I make my way to Vlad's area. When he opens the door, I'm met by his incensed glare. Silviana's heavy sobs coming from somewhere in the room explain the glare he's leveling at me, completely at odds with how he greeted me only a few days ago.

"You have some nerve—"

"Shut up, frate. I'm here to help." I barge past him in the room and stop in front of Silviana, snapping my fingers. "You've got my attention. What's going on with Ștefan?"

Ștefan

I wake up, groaning. Darkness and lack of sight greet me like old friends when I open my eyes. My heart thumps against my chest, but I force myself to remain as immobile as possible for the time being until I figure out my surroundings.

The last thing I remember is Liviu asking me to walk with him, saying it wasn't a request, then.... Nothing.

My ears peek at the sound of footsteps nearing me. Then, "Good. You're awake."

"Liviu." I grit my teeth. "What's the meaning of this?"

He laughs but it's nowhere amused. Harsher. "Please, Ștefan. Did you think you were fooling me?" Another laugh. "Oh, it was entertaining watching you try. As if your poor planning could actually fool me."

"I don't know what you're talking about."

"I think you do. I think you know exactly what I'm talking about, darling boy. And it's all right. I'm not mad, not really." A pause. "Well, maybe a bit. You didn't need to kill Cezar, but I suppose I was running that risk when I let you run off free. Still, no matter."

A sinking feeling rises in me, weighing me down like a proverbial weight over my chest. Breathing becomes harder and I have to force myself to a half-sitting position in an effort to draw a breath.

"Hold out your hand," Liviu says, and I hear the crinkling of plastic.

When I don't do as he says, his calloused hand yanks on mine and he shoves something in it. My fingers automatically clench around it. It's a slender, cylindrical container made of plastic. I run my fingers over it and feel the gentle curving, the ridges of a cap, the pliability—a water bottle.

"I'm not stupid," I say, dropping all pretense of being friends. "You could've put something in it."

That laugh again. "Something like what, dear boy? Poison? Don't make me laugh!" And yet it seems I do—again. "I didn't bring you here to kill you. I need you alive."

Hmm. Did not expect that. Reluctantly, I feel my way to the top of the water bottle and twist the cap off. The sound it makes and the slight resistance tell me it was, indeed, untouched.

I take a few deep gulps and it helps both to clear my head and my breathing. "What do you want, then?"

"Your agony."

And then the fire begins, blazing a path within my insides, tearing everything apart, and I scream.

Elizabeta

Silviana wasn't clear on what, exactly, the danger was. What was apparent was that it had to do with the Dacians, and Ștefan was alone in fighting them off. So that's how I find myself with my brother and his witch in the woods. He's got her wrapped over his back like a monkey as we blur our way through the trees and toward the Dacian compound.

And throughout it all, I'm a mess like I've never been. All I can think of is how I was too late to save Daniel, and I can't be too late to save Ştefan. But it's not because I'm in love with him. It's for my siblings. With him dead, the curse wins and takes us all with it. That's my sole focus—to save all of us.

"Slow down," Silviana says at one point and I catch the scent of her blood in the air next. "We're nearing a barrier the Grand Master put around the compound right about here."

I glance at the sky—we must be reaching midday. No way to use the cloak of darkness to hide, which means we'll be even more exposed. *Should I have let Vlad bring everyone else with us? But...no. It would've put them all together, and there's no way in hell they'd miss the bond between me and Ştefan. I'm not ready to tell them yet. Hell, I'm barely able to admit it to myself.*

When I lower my gaze and take in our surrounding, the dread in my stomach doubles. It wasn't too far from here that Ştefan had stopped me when I'd run away. "Did... Do Dacians patrol this place regularly?"

"I'm not sure," Silviana says and throws me a look. "Why?"

"No reason." I tap the side of my nose. "Your magic—whatever it is you're doing now—will they feel it?"

"Yes. But I can't avoid it. I need to make sure you can pass through the barrier without issues."

"We can," I say. "I was here earlier."

And without further explanation, I blur a few meters ahead. When I whirl, Vlad and Silviana are staring at me with mouths slightly agape.

"When were you here, Liza?" Vlad asks.

"You want to talk, or go find Ştefan?" I toss back instead.

He watches me for another moment, then nods, and we blur further in, Silviana still atop Vlad's back. We slow our pace once more when we get toward a large apartment complex-type building.

"Ştefan's apartment is there," Silviana says. "Maybe we can check there first?"

I don't get to take much more than a step before I lose my footing and slouch against the wall, weakened at the knees. Not just weakened. *Hot.* In the worst way possible. My mouth opens in a vain gasp for air that *I shouldn't need*, and the loud thumping in my ears blocks Vlad's words of concern.

It takes a few minutes for the attack to stop, and when it does, I see Silviana. She lets her hand drop. "I was able to pause whatever it is but..." She frowns. "What the hell is going on, Elizabeta?"

I shake my head but my mouth runs off without me, my panic fully obliterating in its path any other thought but Ştefan. "You were right. I think Ştefan is my consort. The curse activated.... I don't know when. When he saved my life or when we were away or when he screwed my brains out two days ago. But..." I close my eyes as the rush of anguish overwhelms me again. "He's in pain. He's being tortured. Where would they take him?"

Though Vlad's eyes are filled with shock, he speaks without holding back. "Where I was, probably, underground—"

"No." Silviana's eyes fill with tears but although she seems on the brink of losing it, she's still able to hold it together long enough to say, "Liviu's house. It has to be."

"Lead the way."

Ştefan

I'm clawing the ground. Losing my mind. Frying. Dimly, I'm aware of my nails scraping concrete, not wood. Of my screams echoing back to me. Meaning I'm somewhere underground. More than likely in Liviu's own torture chamber. But then the fire takes over and all I can do is scream.

When the attack abates enough for me to gasp, Liviu speaks again. "Reach to your right. There's another water bottle. You'll need it."

"Fuck you."

"I wasn't lying, dear boy. The water isn't poisoned. The fire inside you is something else, something much better. But I'm getting ahead of myself. Drink."

I don't want to. I really don't. But my throat feels like sandpaper and I know I'll need every bit of strength to fight back. He doesn't have me bound, but it's not like he needs to. However, that means I have a tiny chance. If I can identify a pattern to the pain I could... Try...

Dizzy, wordlessly, I reach for the water and drink.

"Good, good." He seems placated. "You know, I always knew you were strong, Ştefan. From the moment your father held you and presented you to us. But this year, you truly showed how powerful you are, much more than your father, Davide. Thankfully." Another laugh. "Oh yes. I did kill him. I know you've been wanting to know, so I give you this gift of truth unconditionally. See, Davide was much too strong and beloved. Others would have followed him, his leadership. And I couldn't have that."

A different kind of agony fills my chest. "You..."

He shifts somewhere to my left and then his hand touches my shoulder.

"Don't touch me!" I jerk back, tossing the water bottle in his direction. The movement makes me lose my balance and I fall backward, disoriented for a moment. "Because of you, my sister and I grew up orphans. Orphans!"

"I don't know, dear boy. I dare say I've cared for you well enough, no?"

I grit my teeth. "What the fuck did you do to me? Why can't I reach my magic?"

"All in due time. The first thing you need to know is if there was a different way to do this.... Well, who am I kidding? I would do it all over again."

"Do *what*?"

"Bring Zalmoxis back, of course."

"You're deluded. Elizabeta fucked with that plan when she killed Cezar."

"Not quite. See, Cezar did manage to bring the portal into this realm, to open it... You were weakened. His soul needed somewhere to latch on. So a teensy bit of it did. Meaning you're—"

The dread, the fear in the pit of my stomach suddenly feels like a boulder. Nausea crawls up my throat. "His anchor."

"Very good.... And, of course, with your sister almost here to save you like the great sibling I knew she would be, I can use her as the conduit to finally bring Zalmoxis forth. Two lives lost to give him another life. Seems a fair trade."

Jesus fuck. He's insane.

And I'm beyond screwed.

With every ounce of my being, I focus on my twin bond with Silviana and send one single thought. *Don't come for me.* Liviu may get me, but I refuse to let him have her. Not when I've spent so much trying to keep her safe.

Elizabeta

We're not lucky enough to stay under the radar. Right as we move past the apartment complex to head to the woods, Dacians emerge. The scent of blood fills the air and slithers of darkness shoot toward us.

I'd had those same tendrils aimed at me by Ștefan, but they weren't this vicious. Only now do I realize how much he held back, even when he was using his magic against me.

This should be fun.

Vlad positions himself in front of Silviana, his stance tense and wild. His fists clench and I recognize the emotion running through him because it's one I'm unwillingly becoming reacquainted with—fear. He throws me a panicked look.

"Keep her safe," I mutter, on some level not believing the words coming out of my mouth. "She—"

I don't finish, because the air shifts. The earth trembles. And the little blonde next to my brother is to blame for it.

"Silviana, don't!" Vlad says, reaching for her.

She tosses her hair over her shoulder and glares at him. In her features, I can see determination, love, and a good dose of resignation. "Go get Ștefan. I can handle this."

Vlad hesitates, so I blur toward him, ducking a fresh wave of dark curses from the Dacians.

"Stay with her. I'll go get him." When his eyes widen in surprise, I add, "If she dies, we're screwed regardless."

He takes a step in my direction. "Liza—"

I don't wait to hear what he's got to say. Instead, I push forward, running into the woods toward the connection tugging at me.

A Dacian emerges from the trees, and I promptly duck his assault and slash his neck with my nails. A few feet further, another shows up and I break his neck without even pausing.

Then it's a straight shot to a cabin in the woods. And the screams I hear from within.

The moment I get to it, I wrench the door open and find myself face-to-face with two more Dacians. I jab my fingers in the eyes of one, then grab him by the throat and use him as a shield against the other's curse. When he collapses against me with a groan, I turn my attention to the other Dacian. The smell of blood fills the air, followed by the sulfur of his magic.

"Where is he keeping him?" I snarl.

"B-basement."

Fucking basements.

I snap his neck, too, and blur the way he pointed.

By the time I finally make it down, Ștefan is writhing on the ground, and some fucktard is staring at me with a pissed-off expression on his face. *Must be Liviu.*

"You're not the one I was expecting."

"Sorry to disappoint, old man." My gaze flicks to Ștefan. "Hey. Can you stand? *Ștefan.*"

He groans at the sound of my voice and manages to lift his head—barely—off the ground. "You have to.... Go. Get Silviana and *go.*"

"Not likely. Your sister's as stubborn as you are, I'm afraid." My glance shifts to the old man who's simply watching us. Unease coils within me. With his dark gaze, he reminds me of a snake. And yet he's not striking. Eyes glued to him, I speak to Ștefan. "Let's go, Ștefan."

He tries to push off the ground and falls on his face with a sickening crack. I take a step toward him, then change my angle at the last minute and rush at the old man, slamming him against the wall. "*What* did you do to him?"

He laughs and then his palms come up to cup my cheeks. To my annoyance, he doesn't even seem surprised by my outburst. "Nothing as bad as what I'll do to you, vampir."

When his fingers move to my temples, I scream. Images of my torture—sensations of those times—fill me. Run through me like the iciest of showers and the hottest lava, all at once. I drop to my knees, but he's still holding on to me.

"Elizabeta!"

Ştefan's voice, attempting to ground me.

I'm no longer in Corvins' Castle.

We destroyed it.

I'm freed of the past.

Just as I push up, trying to snap Liviu's control of my head, there's an explosion behind me. His hands drop from my head and I sneak a peek over my shoulder.

Silviana's there, surrounded by darkness.

And Liviu grins as if Christmas came early.

Chapter 24

Ştefan

I feel my twin's presence even before she speaks, crying out my name. "Ştefan! Elizabeta, get to him!"

"No…" I crawl over the ground, trying to find the source of her voice while I can. "Silviana, *LEAVE*!" I roar. "It's a trap."

But it's too late. Darkness fills the air, stripping me of the ability to breathe. And then *she's* there—her hands on my cheeks, on my shoulders, and my body jolts.

"Elizabeta…" I say, softer. The echo of her cries seems a tangible force around us. "Are you all right?" I hate that I was unable to protect her—Liviu planned this to perfection, and I've given him not just my sister on a silver platter, but my second half, too.

"I'm fine," she mutters. And I would believe her, were it not for the tremble in her voice. "Let's get you up."

"No." I push her away, or try to, but my weak muscles are nothing compared to her vampir strength. So when she reaches for me again, I fumble until I grab a handful of her hair, sheer desperation seeping out of me. "*Listen to me*! Liviu planned this. Cezar… when he hit me. It's an ongoing curse. The healing was fake."

"…what?"

"They meant for me to return here. There's—" I collapse again, releasing her hair as yet another wave of fire fills me.

"Ștefan!" Elizabeta shoves her shoulder under me, and then it's not just her. Someone else is next to us, and an arm thick with lean muscles wraps around my waist, yanking me up. *Vlad.*

"Help me with him," she tells her brother.

He grunts, seemingly unsteady on his feet. All three of us topple back to the ground. I know it's the curse even without them saying anything.

"You have to…. Listen to me, both of you! Vlad. Silviana needs to leave. She's in danger."

"I know," he says. "That magic you feel is hers—and it's much darker. Zalmoxis must be having a field day, and I have no idea how much longer she can hold him off in her head. The more she uses this, the more in danger she is. But it's our only hope of getting you out of here alive. Now let's move! She won't be able to hold off Liviu for much longer."

They try to lift me again and, on wobbly knees, I finally stand. I let them drag me away, sensing the cracking of opposing forces to the side. Darkness isn't telling me much, but Liviu is muttering under his breath, and the sharpness in the air becomes near unbearable.

Then Elizabeta staggers, too. "The curse..."

Vlad pauses and leans me against something—a corner, judging by the walls on either side. "Can you help her? The way Silviana helps me?"

In a beat, I realize what he means—and what he knows. About us being bonded. I shake my head tightly. "Liviu did something to me. I can't access my magic."

"Try," Vlad says.

As if it's that easy.

To my side, Elizabeta moves. Shifting against me. Her lips brush my ear and a zing goes through me at her touch.

"Hurry!" Vlad yells, and his voice seems to have weakened by a couple of octaves.

Elizabeta

I don't know what's possessed me, when I'm already so weak. But I know I need to do *something*.

"Ştefan..." I glance over my shoulder at the barrier Silviana put over us. Liviu's angry snarl, the concentration on his features, tells me we're running out of time. "Listen to me. Silviana's holding Liviu off on her own. She needs help, and it's not the kind we can provide. We don't have the magic to stand up to these guys. You do. I've seen it!"

I give him a little shake and a muscle twitches in his jaw. "I need something to break the hold. Whatever he did has my magic trapped."

"Something like what?"

For all answer, he reaches for me. I go to him willingly—who am I kidding?—more than eager to have his arms around me. Our lips clash with a frenzy fuelled by the danger we're all in. He groans into my mouth at the kiss and, to my surprise, nibbles on my lips. Then he bites down—hard. I jerk away, touching my lips only to see them bloody.

"Sorry," he mutters, sounding very not sorry. "I figured if anything would work, it'd be your blood."

"So much for not getting addicted to it."

He shakes his head. "I'm already addicted to you, princess. Nothing can undo that."

Oblivious to my shock at his words, he brings his hand up and the athame in his wrist cuff cuts into his palm. His steps grow more measured and the Dacians across from us seem to notice it, too. They back away, sharing a look, but seemingly don't dare to leave Liviu.

No matter. Now, I'm ready for a fight.

As if on cue, Silviana drops the shield.

It doesn't take long after that for the battle to engulf us. I lose track of Ștefan, of time, of anything but my one and only goal—survival for myself, and my siblings. Dacians shoot curses everywhere, and despite my swift attacks, they're slippery eels. The more I kill, the more pop up.

I blame them for not noticing Liviu run off when he did. But all of a sudden, the oppression around us lessens a little, which has me glance around. *That's* when I don't find his smug face anywhere.

"Stop!" I yell to the twins and Vlad. "Where's Liviu?"

Vlad and Silviana quickly scan the area, muttering curses. The remaining Dacians seem split into two factions—one still tossing curses at us; the other, backing away to observe.

I blur to Silviana's side, startling her. "Can you do that shield thing again?"

Despite the sweat beading her forehead and weariness I read in her posture and eyes, she nods. "Of course."

She clenches and unclenches her palm, swaying a little on her feet. Behind her, Vlad rips the head off another Dacian. The scent of Ştefan's blood fills the air even stronger—how much is he using? *More to the point, how long can he last?*

I shove the thought away, forcing myself to focus. We'll be fucked if we lose control of this situation any more than we already have. "Hurry."

Silviana takes in a deep breath and closes her eyes. Blood flows at her feet, stronger than before. It's enough to draw Vlad's attention. He pulls the arms out of a Dacian's sockets and blurs to us, stumbling a little.

I step in his path, placing my hand on his chest. "We need a shield. Something to help us get out of here, to find Liviu. We can't let him escape."

Vlad's expression fills with anguish, and his being practically vibrates against my hand as he holds himself back. Barely. The moment Silviana's shield flickers around us, I let him go, and he rushes to her. Pulls her into his arms.

The remaining Dacians hold off on further curses, watching us instead with wary gazes.

"Why is Silviana's shield blasting off again?" Ştefan asks behind me.

I turn to him. In the chaos surrounding us, I hadn't heard him approach, yet he must've easily been drawn to me by the same bond I feel between us. A tether. Much like the bond between him and Silviana, which is probably how he felt her shield. An unbreakable connection.

Unbreakable...until one of us dies.

No. I can't think like that.

I reach for his hand, allow myself a small touch. "Silviana's shield is up because she's got our backs, so we can go after Liviu."

I expect him to fight me on this, given the love he has for his sister. But his features settle into a mask of determination and a muscle ticks in his jaw. "Let's go. Darkness can pick up his trail."

So, we do, following the trail at a measured pace. No Dacian comes after us, which is a small measure of comfort. But with each step away from Liviu's house, the woods close in around us, filled with an unnatural obscurity. The air feels thick with anticipation—or dark magic.

It's too late by the time I hear the first twig crack behind me and realize Liviu's retreat was a trap. A sentiment that's soon reinforced when I whirl, crouching, ready to attack and... the Grand Master himself steps out from a dense thicket of coniferous trees.

"Fuck," Vlad mutters.

Ştefan, looking decidedly pale from the day's exertions, grits his teeth. "What is it?"

My eyes take in the black-clad forms emerging from the woods behind Liviu, armed with crossbows and stakes. I move to his side. "Hunters. Behind us."

It's amazing how something can go wrong in such a short period. Liviu says something, or does something, that makes the ground tremble. Silviana cries out and loses control of the shield, which shatters. She tries to fight back with another spell, but it hits a tree behind me rather than its intended target. By the time I rise from my crouch, the hunters have Vlad immobilized, crossbows pointed at his chest. And Silviana's being held by two Dacians a few feet away.

Only Ștefan is still tossing curses, determined to win. And then my vision blurs as a hunter sneaks up behind me and whacks me over the head.

By the time I come to, it's to find myself bound, yet again. Only this time, the hunters took great pains to make sure I can't move by shooting arrows through my wrists, effectively nailing me to a tree stump in the ground. The pain is dull, not yet a full ache. I don't know what's keeping it at bay—maybe because I'm so close to death already, via the curse?

Zalmoxis must be ready to celebrate. All it takes is one of us dying, and he'll have all our souls.

I can't see Vlad or Silviana anymore from my vantage point, nor hear them. But Ștefan...

Ștefan is still standing. I don't know how—with all the tears into his clothes from arrows, with all the lashings of curses on his skin—but he's still standing amid a circle of Dacians. "Ștefan..."

He turns to me, as though hearing my pained whisper. I jerk against the holds binding me, only to remember the arrows embedded in my wrists. I glance from them to Ștefan. To the hunter lifting his crossbow, ready to kill him. And in a moment of utter clarity, I know what I have to do. And it's not for my siblings.

It's for him.

I headbutt the hunter guarding me, and he groans. In a whirl, I yank my wrists out from the arrows. The fresh blood spewing through my veins gushes out like a geyser, spraying him and his companion in the face.

I claw their throats, slicing into the vulnerable human skin quickly, then rush to Ștefan. In time to see the arrow fired. In slow motion, I see it coming for him. I tackle him, but not before I feel the arrow hit me. Enter my chest, and find my heart.

I look up in Ștefan's eyes. Even though he can't see me, his features twist in pain. Does he realize what happened? Worse—does he *feel* it?

Everything rushes at me then. Everything I should've told him. Everything I should've done. Or not done. But it's too late. Humans only get one chance at a good lifetime. I got plenty. And I managed to fuck up every single one. In the next life, perhaps...

Daniel, I guess I'm following behind you, after all.

Ștefan

"Liza!" Vlad screams.

I drop to the ground, knowing Elizabeta is somewhere nearby. I crawl for her, hands outstretched. Eventually, I touch her arm, then her shoulder, and my fingers move over her back. She's lying face-down on the ground, not moving. And...I find the arrow. Embedded in her back.

"No, no, no, no, no..."

I touch her face. Nothing. She's...

No.

"*NO!*"

I rise. Fury uncoils within me, the likes I've never felt. I'd thought Elizabeta unhinged, for how quickly she kills, how ruthless she is. Now I understand that ruthlessness on a level I never have. Because what I feel is so beyond normal anger, it can't be contained.

It's boiling rage at her being taken from me. Ire at what we could've had, but that's denied us now. And complete and utter refusal to accept any of it.

I want blood. My tether to Elizabeta is there, but barely. If I'm to act to bring her back, to do *anything* to fix this, I can't be having the Dacians trying to kill me, too. *Should've known it was going to come to this.*

"You want a show of power, Liviu? All right. You'll get it. You shouldn't have fucking touched her."

I move my hand off Elizabeta's back and bow my head, bringing my hands up in a prayer-like gesture. All around me, there's noise. So much noise. I take a deep breath and let it out slowly. Already, the cuts over my body are fueling the darkness, pulling the magic to me.

When I open my eyes, darkness is my sight. The shadows convey dark gray blobs are the enemies, with white blobs as the innocents—two of them only. The darker a person is, the more likely it is I have to kill them.

And I have no qualms about doing that. At all.

So I let the darkness loose.

"Fane, no!" Silviana cries from somewhere.

I know what she's afraid of. Thinking the same thing that happened to her, will happen to me. But it won't. Because *I know* Zalmoxis is waiting, on the other side. Waiting for me to ask for power. Waiting for me to open the portal.

And I won't.

But I *will* use everything he's gifted us with to bring this to a swift conclusion.

Without hesitation, without mercy, I aim the darkness at every single dark blob in my path. It shows me flashes of things—curses thrown at me, more likely—but nothing touches me. Each curse, each spell, is deflected by a faint mist permeating the air around me, and around every other aura. I don't know if it's there in reality or just in my head, but it doesn't matter.

Darkness continues to swirl around me, tendrils of raw power nipping at my fingertips. The air crackles with tension, the echo of betrayal ringing in every whispered incantation.

This man killed our father.

He injured Elizabeta.

He hurt my sister.

Enough is enough.

"Time to pay the piper, fucker," I mutter.

With a roar, I unleash the full force of my magic at Liviu. The shadows writhe and twist as they surge toward him. The impact with his shield is thunderous, and his responding attack creates thunder like a clash of titans.

"Fane!" Silviana cries again.

This time, when I turn toward the sound of her voice, her white blob is surrounded by two darker ones. I open and close my palm, letting more blood pool, and send the emerging darkness to aid her. The dark blobs are tossed away from her.

Moments later, she's touching my arm, panting in my ear. "Liviu isn't going down, Fane. What the hell *is* this?"

I don't understand what she means until I turn my attention to the spot I'd last focused on. Despite my previous onslaught, the darkest of blobs is standing, unyielding.

"I don't like this, Fane," Lana says, a tremble in her voice.

"Where's Vlad?"

It takes her a moment, then she says, "He's tackling the other Dacians. I'm not sure how much longer he can last—it's one against five. I never should've forced him to come here alone, without more backup from his siblings. No one—"

I reach for her hand, closing my fingers around her smaller ones. "Trust me, sorella. I won't fail you."

She takes a deep breath and squeezes back. "Together, then?"

I nod. "Together."

Letting go of her hand, I once more reach for my athame and slash into my left palm. With blood pouring from each wound, I cast yet another curse, sending it to Liviu. Silviana's own magic follows mine, both of us hitting him in tandem. The resulting clash, this time, sends us both flying backward.

"Lana!" I yell, desperation clawing at me. If she's hurt...

I push to my knees, crawling in the direction I think she was thrown. I'm disoriented, barely able to catch the sounds of a fight further off—Vlad and the rest of the Dacians?

Elizabeta. Is her body... No, I can't think like that. I need to finish Liviu, then I can get back to her and fix this. And I will fix it.

"Looking for something?" comes a voice ahead of me.

I freeze, every muscle locking in me. *Liviu.* And when I focus darkness on his voice, my heart sinks—there's a white blob right next to him.

"I have something of yours," he says, confirming what darkness is disclosing to me. "And for clarification, by *have something*, I mean I'm holding a knife to your sister's neck and have no qualms about slashing it."

I swallow past the lump in my throat. "Don't do that. Please."

"Then call off the watchdog."

"Vlad..." I try, but it comes out weak. I clear my throat, and roar, "*Vlad!*"

The air itself seems to stop. A second later, the silence is shattered by Vlad screaming my sister's name. There's so much pain, so much anguish in his voice, I have to steel myself against it.

The sounds of a struggle follow. Vlad is shouting throughout it all, trying to get to my sister, from what I can tell—but it's useless. Liviu countered every single one of our assaults, and now his evil threatens to consume us all.

My thoughts fly to Elizabeta. *I can't give up. I can't...* But how do I go on, when I've tried every trick in my arsenal, and none have been enough to beat this fucker?

"Good," Liviu says, as if sensing my defeat. "You're finally coming around to it. Now, then. Time to finish what I started, don't you think? Don't worry, I'll do all the work. I'm sure everything you just used has exhausted you."

The mocking tone in his voice rankles at me, but I don't retort. I think back to what he'd told me, and true horror fills me at what he's about to do. "Lana..."

Liviu laughs. "Yes, I see you've caught on. Don't worry, you'll have plenty of time to say your goodbyes. With you as Zalmoxis' anchor, and Silviana as the conduit, this will be a walk in the park."

"Aren't you forgetting something?" I ask. "You don't have innocents to sacrifice."

Liviu laughs, and the sound of that laughter—sure, mocking—is enough to increase the horror coursing through me. "My boy, Cezar was an amateur compared to me. I don't need innocents to sacrifice. These woods hold enough evil for that. Watch and learn."

I hear his footsteps move away from me, followed by muttered incantations. The air is charged again, filled with something... Not darker, but more malevolent. Something raw, primal, something that doesn't answer to *anyone.* I shudder at the sensation, at the goosebumps rising across my skin.

"Fane..." Silviana whispers. "I'm scared."

My knees buckle as the weight of the responsibility bears down upon me. Keeping her safe, keeping Elizabeta safe—I've failed at both. If Liviu does what he wants, the entire Dracul line will be wiped. That will most assuredly bring about our own deaths, mine and hers, due to the bond created between us and the vampiri.

The air crackles, and I lift my head a little, trying to figure out where it's coming from.

"Fane, the trees," Lana whispers. "They're... He's filled them with...I'm not sure what it is, but it *feels wrong*. And they're *moving*."

I have a feeling I know exactly what he's done, given the scrolls in his cabin. Liviu isn't seeking to just open a portal here—he wants to obliterate us. Which means he's using the regular Dacian magic, fueled by Zalmoxis' darkness, to call forth something more obscure, more sinister, than anything we've ever dealt with. A primordial type of corruption that existed way before Zalmoxis did, back when the pantheons themselves were still being created.

That force is something I've been trying to tap into so I can fight him off, but now he's gone and beaten me to it. *It's not too late, though. If I can just reach into it, make the evil understand that I, too, am at its command...*

The incantations taper off then, and Liviu chuckles again. He sounds closer, like he's walked back into our vicinity. "Yes, that is correct. I've leveraged the sacrifice in these woods to awaken a force you could never dream of. And now that it's alive, I can continue with my plan. This, my dear, is where we must say goodbye."

Every instinct screams at me to retreat, to run from the power pulsing around me. But I can't. I have people to fight for, people to save. *And you don't give up on those you love.*

In the depths of my soul, a spark of defiance flickers to life. With a silent prayer to all the gods, I press the athame into my flesh, drawing blood once more. Then I yank it from the wrist cuff and turn it toward me, pointing at my solar plexus.

"What are you doing?" Liviu asks.

I don't answer him. Instead, I take a deep breath and shove the knife into my gut. Pain the likes I've never felt before fills me. My life force, my very essence, seeps out of me. Fast. Too damn fast. *I'll be dead before I can do what I...*

But darkness answers. It hasn't deserted me. It stirs, as if hearing a call from its master. One of them, anyway. *I just need to be quick, before my life evaporates along with this magic.*

Tuning everything out, I delve deep into my being, drawing on reserves of power I never knew I had in me. *Help me,* I plead with darkness. *What Liviu is doing is unnatural. Help me set things right. Take my blood payment, but heal me throughout. Help me overpower him.*

It doesn't hesitate. It doesn't linger. Darkness surges through me like a tsunami, a torrent of raw energy that defies reason and logic and any laws of the universe. My entire being vibrates with it, healing from my wounds, yet filling with power. I'm a beacon for it, a conduit to set things right.

With every fiber of my being, I channel my essence into a single, unyielding purpose—killing Liviu and saving Silviana and Elizabeta. I dig my hands into the earth, feeling the evil force that's in the trees, the one that scares my sister, and pull on it.

It resists me, refusing to surrender. Somewhere, Liviu is cussing at me. But I'm not about to give up. With a defiant cry, I let loose the full force of my darkness, drawing on the trees' obscurity as well, toward Liviu.

Everything stops.

Everything goes quiet.

Then Lana screams for me. Vlad yells her name. Dacians' shouts ring out.

Seconds later, Silviana's tiny form hurtles into my arms. "Fane, you did it! He's down!"

"Down, but not dead," Vlad says, his voice hoarse. "He's close, though. Faint heartbeat."

I nod and step forward, drawn by Liviu's pulsing power. Or rather, the power that's exiting his body, spilling into the air and earth.

With each step, I don't feel the pain in my gut. I do, however, hold out my hand and call my athame to me. From somewhere on the ground behind me, it flies handle-first into my palm, and I hold it there.

"Ştefan ..." Liviu croaks, somewhere to my left.

I turn to the sound of his voice, take a few more steps, then crouch down. "You're done for, old man. Your plan failed."

"How... How were you able to do that? You don't have the power of a Grand Master."

I shrug. "Maybe I don't have the power, but I have more of a soul than you do. You forgot one important thing in your quest to bring Zalmoxis back—nature will always seek to balance itself out. I just gave it a helpful nudge to do that."

He gasps, as though in pain, and I allow myself a smile.

"Don't be so smug," Liviu tosses back. What I did—what Cezar started—cannot be undone. Zalmoxis' prison is weakened, and nothing you do will reinforce it. He *will* be freed. And when he is, he'll come for all of you."

Dread tries to pool in the pit of my stomach, but I'm too fucking exhausted to care. "Yeah, well, guess we'll deal with that when it happens. Same as we dealt with you. Enjoy the Underworld, Liviu. I doubt you're going somewhere nice." I stand and whisper to *my* darkness, "He's all yours. But make sure his life force feeds the evil he awakened, and puts it to rest."

The air pulses again, and Liviu grunts, groans, and whimpers. He gives a few shallow breaths, like the life is being squeezed out of him. When the last breath leaves him, I walk back to Elizabeta.

Footsteps around me tell me Vlad and Silviana have reunited, and their soft murmurs pass my ears. But all I can focus on is Elizabeta.

And her lifeless body.

"Fane..." Silviana says, to my side. "I—"

"No. She's not dead."

"Fratello..." Her tone is filled with pity.

"She's not! Don't you see?" I yell in her general direction. "Else you'd be dead, too. And Vlad. And all the Draculs!"

There's a stunned silence and Vlad whispers, "He has a point."

"But...how?" Silviana asks.

"I don't know, but I'm going to make sure she comes back. You need to leave. Go to the Cazanele Dunării. *Now*. Before shit gets worse."

"I'm not leaving you!"

"Lana..."

"*I'm not*."

I feel her as she drops next to me, our shoulders brushing against each other.

"Use me," she says.

"What?"

"My connection to him. If you think she's not truly dead, then use me." She places her palm in mine.

"No. I'm not putting you in any more danger."

She removes her hand and when it comes back on top of mine, it's wet now. With blood, I'd bet. "I'm offering."

I don't want to, but I also couldn't live if Elizabeta were to die. And not just because of the curse. The depth of my feelings for her scares me, even as it fills me with purpose and a sense of calm. A contradiction. What isn't with her, though?

Indecision, however, pulls me in two different directions. I've spent the last days—and weeks—trying to keep my sister safe from Zalmoxis. Doing what she's offering, using the channel she has to him, could undo all of that. But taking her up on her offer would also mean saving Elizabeta. And if I don't, all the Dracul heirs will die. We'd be equally doomed.

"Lana..."

"Do it, Fane. Please. All this time, you've kept me safe. Let me do something for you."

I bow my head in resignation, and give a faint nod, squeezing her hand and intertwining our fingers. "I'm not letting you die," I mutter to my consort. And then, louder, "You can't fucking have her, Zalmoxis!"

With my free hand, I reach for the arrow embedded in Elizabeta's back, and yank it out. I call forth more darkness, using its strength to roll Elizabeta over, so her chest is facing the sky. Once she's in position, I place my hand above her chest, moving it over her until I feel it's roughly where her heart would be, if it were still beating. Though it's dead, that heart is the shell of her soul and contains her essence as a vampir, her livelihood.

I lean on darkness some more. The physical barrier of her chest—the flesh and ribs keeping her chest hidden from me—ripples and parts, making way for my hand. I squeeze Silviana's hand once more with my other hand, then reach inside Elizabeta with the other. And I close my eyes.

You can't have her, Zalmoxis. You can't have either of us.

Chapter 25

Elizabeta

It's no surprise, almost, that when I open my eyes, Daniel is there. We're surrounded by a faint green fog, in what looks and feels like the antechamber of a place.

He holds his hand out to me, and I take it mindlessly—then gasp when our fingers touch. My eyes fly to his. "I can touch you!"

He smiles, a sad look in his eyes. "You can."

"After all this time..." I hesitate, then throw myself into his arms, relishing the way his arms come around me, holding me to him. Tight, like he never wants to let me go. Tight, like he's been yearning to do this for centuries. Tight, like he knows it's the last time.

That thought has me pull back, enough so I can see his features. Sure enough, his cheeks are bathed in silent tears. "What...?" The light around Daniel flashes, wavers, and flashes some more. That alone is warning enough for what's about to happen.

"Are you..." I can't make myself ask him if this is where he leaves me. Instead, I ask something else. "Am I...dead?"

He looks at me with a mix of exasperating love and pity. "It's up to you, Liza."

He reaches his hand up to my cheek, caressing it with his thumb. I've waited centuries for this, to be able to touch him.

But the intimate gesture feels like a betrayal to Ștefan.

Ștefan ...my consort.

My siblings.

The curse.

With my death, they will suffer, too.

A lone tear falls down my cheek. "You want me to go with you. To be with you, in whatever follows after death."

"No, Liza. You don't belong here. And you haven't been mine in forever." His smile, this time, is a little less sad. "He'll take care of you. You just have to let him in. Stop fighting him. He's not the enemy." His eyes fixate on his hand cradling my left cheek, but I'm aware what he's examining is my scar. "Let go of the past."

"You know I can't do that. Let him in, maybe. I can try. But the past is the past, it's a part of me. And I don't plan on forgetting it."

He sighs. "You always were stubborn."

"How do I even get back?" I sniffle. "Doesn't look like there's a button I can press."

"You're going to have to do something a bit unlike yourself, and reach for help. Think of him, of your bond. It'll bring you back." The smile falters. “Can I kiss you? One last time, for good luck.”

I nod, tipping my head up. I almost expected him to peck me softly, but instead, his lips brush my forehead. And linger.

Then Daniel steps back, ever the gentleman. “Goodbye, Liza. Maybe one day we’ll meet again.”

“I doubt I’m going in the same spot you are.... But maybe.”

As the brightness around him intensifies, he fades away into nothingness. Leaving me alone, and more than a little forlorn.

With all my willpower, I shake myself out of it. If I’m not dead, I need to get back to the surface—to the living?—and fast. Who knows how much longer Ștefan and Vlad can last without backup?

Ștefan. Daniel said to think of Ștefan. But as I tap into the bond, into everything I’ve denied, a shiver runs through me.

Something’s wrong.

I open my eyes—no longer surrounded by light, but by a shadowy mist. And out of it, another form appears, dressed in black. His hair falls to his shoulders, long and jet-black like a raven's feathers. Other things register—a goatee, rugged features, that he’s taller than me. Yet, it's his eyes that catch my attention and keep it.

Eyes as blue as mine.

“Father!” I take one second for the shock to course through me, then I don’t wait, I run to him. Slam into his chest, and his arms come around me—solid. Safe. Warm.

“Oh, Elizabeta...”

I look up into his face. “I don’t understand. How....?”

His expression is a mix of frustration and fear and pure paternal pride. “You’re in limbo, same as I am. The only difference is you can go back.”

“Are you not dead, then?”

"I am. I just never reached wherever I was supposed to reach."

Tears fill my eyes, unbidden. "Your death shattered us."

"I know. I've seen snippets... what he'll show me. But you've grown stronger."

"What do you mean, what he'll show you?" And then it hits me. "You said you never reached.... He stopped you, didn't he? Zalmoxis? But how?"

Father shakes his head. "My foolish arrogance. I thought I could entreat him, beg for his forgiveness. When that didn't work, I gave him my soul, to save you all. But he lied. He didn't uphold the bargain we made because the curse he had already exacted was in motion. He only wanted my pain, my suffering. Cursing you was a way to ensure he had that, over and over again."

Holy fuck. This entire time, he's been seeing what we're being put through, unable to help us. Watching this god toy with us.

"Father..." My eyes well up with tears, ready to spill over.

"No. Do not cry for me, Elizabeta."

"You don't understand. I've fucked up so much."

"Shhh," he says and moves closer, pulling me into his chest for another hug. "You've done so well, my dear. So extremely well. You and your siblings, *you* are my crowning jewel. And no one, not even Zalmoxis, can take that away." He pulls back to look at me. "You are great—all of you—in spite of me, not because of me."

I struggle to hold back the tears, but they break free regardless. "Come with me. Let's get out of here."

"I cannot leave. You alone can. I only wanted to see you, to tell you.... That I'm sorry. I should have done a better job, preparing you all for what was to come."

"Father..." Those damn stupid tears keep on streaming down

my cheeks. "I'll make sure you get to your final resting place. I swear it. Even if I have to fight Zalmoxis myself."

Father opens his mouth as if to say something else, but a sinister laughter fills the air. "Is that so? And to think, you came to me on your own."

Panic fills Father's face. "Leave, Elizabeta. Return home, *now*!"

"Too late."

And then *he* emerges from the mist around us. Over six feet tall, with a long, dark beard and glinting onyx eyes. His voice is rough—a voice of the Otherworld, I recall Silviana saying. And it is. But more fearsome still are the shadows clinging around him, like an aura of darkness that shimmers and shifts with his every step. This darkness isn't like Ștefan's, which I've learned to love and respect, just as it has learned to accept me. It's pressing, potent, *ancient*, and feels as if it could obliterate me at any moment.

I gulp, forcing bravery into my voice. "Zalmoxis, is it?"

Although I ought to be scared, I'm consumed by rage when I see him. Rage at how much he's put us all through. Rage at what he's made Father suffer. Rage at his entitlement—that his escape is worth all of our pain. In true me fashion, said rage comes out in the most undignified way possible.

"You *dickhead*!" I yell, and despite Father trying to hold me back, I rush forward. "All this time, you had him imprisoned? For what! What did he do to you that he doesn't deserve even a moment's peace!"

Zalmoxis' eyes flash with warning. "He took my daughter."

"Your daughter took her own life. Love—losing love—can do that to someone. It wasn't his fault!"

"He should have protected her."

Even though he sounds cool and collected, I've struck a sensitive chord—the darkness intensifies, making us feel as if we're enveloped by a heavy shroud.

His words make me think of Daniel. "You're wrong. Yes, a partner should always protect their own. But sometimes that's impossible. They have to want it. And sometimes life gets in the way."

I can't believe I'm trying to reason with a god who's certifiable—even more so than I am. And for a moment, it looks like he can't believe it, either.

Then he laughs. Bitterly. "I am not interested in your excuses, but in your soul. Now."

He lifts his hand, and the malevolent force around him becomes more oppressive. Behind me, I hear a gasp and I glance over my shoulder—tendrils of darkness have bound Father.

"No!" I whirl on Zalmoxis again. "Let him *go*. He doesn't deserve this!"

"He deserves this and more. As do you."

Suddenly, he extends his hand in my direction. I try to move back, but I can't. I'm immobilized. And real fear grips me this time, because I don't want to die. I want to go back.

Back to my Ștefan.

Back to my siblings.

Back to the rest of my immortal existence...

'You can't fucking have her.'

I look around. *Ștefan? How...?* It's his voice, but as if from afar. Or did I imagine it?

And then I jerk. Because it feels like he's inside me...inside my *heart*.

Zalmoxis growls and his gaze intensifies with pure malevolence. "Back off, you stupid Dacian."

His power whips the air, creating a crackling sensation that crawls all over my skin. Behind me, Father groans. I want to turn to him, to do anything in my power to free him. But I also know what he'd want me to do is the exact opposite. If I stay, if I give in, Zalmoxis wins.

I can't let him win.

For a moment, there's silence. It feels as if the fabric of air itself is immobilized, waiting to see what will happen. Then, Ștefan 's voice grows louder, and I sense his presence as though he's beside me. "You can't have her, Zalmoxis. You can't have either of us."

I don't quite grasp his words until a faint light splits the darkness, creating an opening. Zalmoxis's features contort with rage. He's *not* all-powerful, not yet. Perhaps that's my salvation.

And then...I'm yanked out.

Ștefan

Elizabeta comes to with a gasp. "Father..."

Pulling my hand out of her chest, I release Silviana's hand. Next, I lean my entire torso over Elizabeta, and help her up to a half-sitting position, leaving my palm on her back. Coaxing darkness to heal the wound.

When it doesn't, I press my wrist to her lips. "Drink from me. Heal. Fast. We must close all avenues to him."

She hesitates only a moment, but does as I ask. I ignore the trickle of desire when her lips close over my flesh. We'll have ample time for that later, to calm both the fear and adrenaline rushing through me.

When her mouth lifts from my wrist, she rests her head against my shoulder. I allow myself a brief respite, pressing my forehead against hers. Relishing the feel of her in my arms. "I'm glad you decided to stick around, after all."

A strangled laugh escapes her. "Would you have let me go?"

"Never."

I press my lips against hers, tasting the remnants of copper from my blood. Elizabeta lets out a soft noise and wraps her arms around my neck. We're interrupted by the sound of footsteps getting nearer, stealing my chance to fully savor the moment with her.

"Fane..." Silviana kneels by my side—I hadn't even realized she'd left us be—her voice a whisper. "The Dacians...remaining ones... They had us surrounded and now they're looking at you like you're their messiah."

I jerk my head up, wishing I could take my measure of their expressions, too. Instead, I ask, "Why would they do that?"

Though I try to keep my tone low, Vlad overhears. "Because of what you just did—you yanked my sister from the clutches of death."

Silviana's hand on me tightens. "Something no Grand Master had ever done, Ștefan. You know that."

Suddenly, everything clicks and the puzzle falls into place. My strength in magic, my magical capabilities growing these last months, and what I've just done. Later, I'll tell them all about it, but for now, I can use the momentum to ensure my sister is safe from our kin once and for all.

I rise then, offering Elizabeta my hand, and turn in the direction of the Dacians. "My brothers and sisters.... You all followed Liviu. I understand seeing me kill him has shifted your loyalties. As must have the fact that I am joined here not by one, but by two vampiri. And my sister, whom most of you know as a traitor."

Mutters rise in the crowd. I move my wrist, intending only to stretch it, but the movement stills all speech. Interesting. They're afraid of me.

"This is not a coup," I say slowly. "But I will be transparent with you, if you give me a chance. Whether you stay or leave after is entirely up to you. Are you ready to hear me out?"

After a short silence, more mutters—of assent, this time—follow.

"Thank you. The truth is, we are at a turning point. We have been for a while, pawns in a game bigger than us." I reach for Elizabeta's hand. "She is my consort, and I am hers. This means we are bound by magic older than time. Where does Liviu fall into this? It has nothing to do with our relationship, if that's what you think. See, Liviu had his chance to do the right thing, but he messed up way before today's events. The Dacian way of living is to protect our kin at all costs. He broke that vow. He killed my father—those of you who helped him capture me earlier can vouch for this. This means he took not only my dad from me and Silviana, but he also stole a potential leader from you."

"Davide collaborated with the vampiri! Clearly, the apples didn't fall far from the tree."

I clench my jaw and tilt my head in silent acquiescence to the man who'd spoken. "You are correct. My dad did work closely with the vampiri—to bring us peace! To understand our magic, all facets of it. And what did he get in exchange? He was killed in cold blood by someone he trusted. So, I did what I had to do—I stopped the corruption in our midst. Not for power, but so we can all have a chance at a better tomorrow."

I pause, anticipating more naysayers. No one speaks.

"I'm not asking for a throne. I'm offering change. My dad's legacy means everything to me. He'd want us to let go of the hate. He'd want us to move forward. He'd want... if not Dacians and vampiri liking each other, at least co-existing peacefully." I draw a deep breath. "Elizabeta is with me for peace, not chaos." She snorts by my side, but thankfully it's quiet enough no one else hears. I hope. "We're all Dacians, tied by more than blood. Let's not dwell on the past. Embrace this bond between me and her that brings our worlds together.. or at least, don't hate on it." I lower my tone to a near growl. "And do not mistake my kindness for weakness. If any of you come between us, I will not hesitate to take you out."

Silence follows my words.

Then, a voice emerges. Female, and a tad familiar. "You said you don't want a throne."

"I don't."

"What does that mean? If we stay, who will lead us?"

I shrug. "Choose. That is the gift I offer you—choice. Choice of a leader and choice of a path forward."

"What if we choose you?"

By her words, I can recognize her voice at last. Maria. My expression softens. "I would be honored. But I don't expect it."

Without hesitation, I swiftly turn away from them and stretch my arm to the side. Elizabeta releases my hand and moves closer, snuggling into my warmth and resting her head on my chest. Finally, I can catch my breath.

Elizabeta

The Dacians disperse one by one, leaving us four alone. They toss glances at Ștefan, more than a few admiring. He did good. Not so long ago, I'd have been loath to admit it. But now...

The maelstrom of emotions within me has me on edge. I'm still shaken by Zalmoxis, and everything that happened. Father, trapped in a state of limbo. But the words are stuck in my throat, no matter how much Vlad asks me, begs me, to tell him what happened. How I feel.

In the end, he embraces me tightly. "I'm glad you're alive."

I push him away with a derisive laugh. "Are we, even?"

"We have our souls, Liza. We have our immortal existence. It should be enough." He frowns. 'Don't go seeking answers that aren't there."

I wave him off in my usual dismissive way, refusing to acknowledge how bothered I am. But through it all, the one constant is Ștefan—and how he hasn't left my side. His hand in mine, his touch, in some measure or other, on my body. And for once, I have no desire to distance myself from him.

Silviana seems to be similarly glued by Vlad's side, and exhausted.

"You're going now? To the Danube?" I ask.

My brother nods. "Da. We have to. It's time, and when better than now?"

Silviana glances between Ștefan and me. It's weird to see her so accepting. At the back of my mind, I'd always thought she'd have an issue with us. Perhaps because of how we all reacted to Vlad and her. But she doesn't. And that... I'm not sure what to make of it. I guess I have many years ahead to figure it out.

"Please take care of each other," she says. "Zalmoxis..."

"He won't touch us," Ștefan says, his voice filled with warning.

Vlad narrows his eyes. "You know as well as I do that he's not the only danger we face."

"Meaning?" Ștefan asks.

I tense, not quite understanding why they're bickering. We won, for fuck's sake, we should be celebrating.

"*Meaning,* something occurred to me while I was battling those hunters and trying to stay alive. When we first met Tytus, you said hunters are able to transfer knowledge from generation to generation, because of their invisible masters."

Silviana looks between Vlad and her brother, as puzzled as I am. For a moment, I think Ștefan might even snap.

But then he exhales heavily. "Da. And I understand your suspicion, because I remember theorizing that the Dacians were these invisible masters, which has now turned out to be true. But I can honestly tell you I didn't know anything about what was going on. Let alone that Cezar and Liviu were working with the hunters and planning to open that portal. If I had, I would've done things differently."

Vlad stares at him but, at an elbow jab from Silviana, ends up nodding. "Bine, I believe you. But I would appreciate it if you could let us know if anything else comes up. I don't think this is the last we'll hear of the hunters—let's hope I'm wrong." He kisses Silviana's forehead. "We should go, beloved."

She approaches us, giving Ștefan a lengthy hug, but hesitates when it comes to me. I offer my hand to her and she responds with a soft, gentle smile.

Vlad arches an eyebrow my way when he sees I'm not moving from Ștefan's side. "Liza?" Somehow, with one word, he's asking a million questions.

"I've...I'll stick around, for a bit. Make sure things with the Dacians don't take a turn for the worse."

He frowns, questions swimming in his eyes. But something in my expression must have told him he'd get no answers today, as he nods slowly, and they leave.

Ștefan holds out his hand to me, and, seconds later, we find ourselves in his apartment once more. I stumble and let go of him, trying to regain my senses. The weight of the battle and the events that unfolded after have finally taken their toll on me, leaving me feeling weakened. Untethered.

Behind me, Ștefan asks, "So, am I still meant to be your dirty little secret?"

"No, that's not—"

My protest is silenced as he spins me around, pulling me close in one swift motion. His lips collide with mine in a messy and chaotic embrace.

"Because I'll have you any way I can, Elizabeta."

I hold on to him, for once pausing his kiss. My body is buzzing with the adrenaline of the fight, of almost dying. I'm also sore in places I didn't think I could be. That weakness from the curse is gone, for now. Barely. Replaced instead by that odd sensation of being untethered. Although his touch sets me ablaze and keeps me grounded, my mind remains restless.

"Wait, I... that... Zalmoxis. What was that?"

Ștefan nuzzles my cheek, then my neck. The scrape of his beard against my sensitive skin has shivers racing up and down my spine.

"You really want to talk about that, right now?" He presses against me, his hardness a clear indication of where his mind is at.

And I don't blame him. This is how we relate, this is how I work through my shit. So I yank him closer to me, almost climbing on top of him. In one smooth movement, he picks me up in his arms, taking us from the living room to the bedroom, and finally, into a shower stall.

I barely have a second to wrap my legs around him, before water starts spraying everywhere around us. I gasp, half-shrieking in surprise.

He chuckles against my skin. "It's motion-activated, pre-set temperature."

"Fancy," I mutter, then our tongues clash once more.

Bit by bit, he pulls off my soaked clothes. Then I do the same to him. And when he's finally inside me this time, nothing else matters except how he makes me feel. Like I'm safe. Cherished. Loved. *Tethered.* And despite all my centuries of existence, and all the knowledge I've amassed, I know it's not a sensation I've ever truly felt. It feels... like my soul has finally found its haven.

So I toss my head back, giving in to the ecstasy, to the peace, to the joy of being alive and free.

After, my eyelids grow heavy, no matter how much I attempt to fight off the fatigue. I wouldn't have thought my body could get tired, but tucked under Ștefan's arm in his massive bed, the beginnings of exhaustion pull at me.

There are so many things I need to tell him...so many questions I have. Only one pushes past my lips. "Zalmoxis...Why was he so mad when you yanked me out of that place?"

Ștefan's fingers, which had been trailing down my bare back, stop. When he speaks, his voice is pensive. "I think he realized he'd fucked up. His power fuels Dacian magic, but in creating this bond, this curse between us, he amplified it. I doubt he ever thought the curse would attract Dacians as potential consorts for the Dracul heirs—let alone Dacians like myself and Silviana. I'm not sure the force of connection will ever show up in this way with Silviana and Vlad, but with you and me? Zalmoxis basically made sure I could follow you wherever you went...even if that meant right in his clutches."

I'm silent, pondering his theory. *He's probably right. Now would be an ideal time to tell him about Father, and what Zalmoxis is able to do. But I'm so fucking tired, and we've been through so much. Is there even a point in bringing that up right now?*

Though my mind is foggy, I can still grasp the severity of Ștefan's revelations. All that he risked. And for what little payout.

"Thank you," I whisper softly. *Tomorrow. I'll tell him tomorrow.*

He kisses my forehead, and that's the last thing I remember before sleep pulls me under.

Chapter 26

Ştefan

Elizabeta has fallen asleep by my side. Unable to join her, I stay awake. My watch buzzes to let me know it's twilight time—no wonder Elizabeta's dead asleep. Between the fight and the aftermath with my sister and Vlad, and then our own conversation, an entire day has passed.

I suppose I'm equally exhausted and sleep could help, but I'm not in the mood to deal with flashbacks. The pain I suffered at Liviu's hands, the fear of losing either Elizabeta or Silviana, the sheer desperation to fight off and win against someone whom I'd thought of as a mentor... Those would be nothing compared to the hollowness and despair I felt while under that blood curse. *At this rate, it'll be a miracle if I ever have a peaceful night of sleep again. I wonder if that's how Silviana feels?*

Thinking of my sister brings my mind to focus. My entire life, I've been dedicated to one thing only—protecting Silviana at all costs from anything bad that might happen. Losing our parents was traumatizing enough. Losing her was never an option. Ever.

My sister has been everything to me, and I to her. And then she fell in love. Now I've gone and fallen in love—nothing else can remotely encompass the strength of my feelings for Elizabeta. And it's not that this has made our connection lesser, but it's definitely changing.

Elizabeta is strong, stubborn, and absolutely relentless in everything she does. She's a pain in my ass and fuel to the blaze in my veins all at once. And despite all this, there is a vulnerability under the surface that pulls the rug under my feet when she shows it, and makes me so damn grateful to be hers and have her be mine. It has me determined to protect her with every fiber of my being, same as I've protected my sister. But will she let me?

I stay up all night, listening to the sounds outside, and turning the question over and over in my head. Perhaps because I'm so in tune with the fabric of the air around us and how it should be, I feel it the moment darkness shifts—like a shadow cast over the moon.

Something's coming. *Something big*.

Without a word to Elizabeta, I stand, pull on a pair of pants, and step outside my apartment. Down the hall I go, then to the elevator. My fingers tap my thigh, impatient. When the bell rings and the elevator doors open on the ground floor, I rush out of the building.

Then, I pause. I was right. Something *has* changed. Magic permeates the air—magic the likes I've only felt around those visitors at the Oracle's house. But it's not quite the same. It's…

"Who goes there?"

Nothing answers me. At first. After a short pause, a familiar voice speaks. "It's me. Tytus."

I frown. What the hell is the ancient zmeu doing here? "Is someone else with you?"

"Da. Lucrezia."

My jaw drops a little. I'd met Dominic's mate, and Luna to the vârcolac pack in the Transylvanian woods when Zalmoxis first got ahold of Silviana's mind. Sensing her pain, her agony through our twin bond, I'd sought out the only two people who—I'd hoped—could shed some light on what was going on. I'd only heard murmurs from Liviu and Cezar at the time, of course, so I didn't know what to expect.

But instead of being greeted with suspicion and attitude, Lucrezia had been kind and understanding. She hadn't hesitated to drop everything and follow me, even entreating her mate to listen to her. Without her and Dominic, I never would've met Tytus. Without them… who knows what would've happened to Silviana?

I slam my jaw shut. "I… I never got a chance to thank you for helping me with Silviana."

"I didn't do much, Ștefan. It was all Tytus, my mentor." Her voice is still as soft as I remember.

I snort. "A human, mentee to a dragon shifter? How does that work, exactly?"

"Not peacefully, I can tell you that much."

I take a few steps closer to them, wondering what this is leading to. "All right, I'll bite. What brings you both here?"

Lucrezia—her soft scent assails my nose as she approaches—

reaches for my hand. She places my fingers on her pulse, slow and steady. The move is so forward, I almost yank my hand away. But then she speaks and her words give me pause. "Hear my words, because they're the truth. And I need you to trust me."

"Trust is earned." I swallow past the lump in my throat, forcing my dread at bay. "But for you, I'll make an exception."

"Thank you," she whispers. "The truth is, we don't have time for earning. Months ago, Tytus suggested that Dominic and I move into these woods. He felt something was coming, but he didn't understand what. Twenty years ago, he and his brother Declan were in Hades' Underworld when shit hit the fan. Bad." A pause. The pulse in her wrist flutters, picking up with her emotions and the anxiety coursing through her. "I was there, too. See, a bit before that, I died. The only thing that brought me back was Tytus' protection."

His tone is hoarse at the memory. "As a zmeu, my magic is strong. Too strong, sometimes having a mind of its own. It used my connection to Lucrezia and gave her my protection. I didn't even realize what I was doing. When she died and came back, she returned as a Solomonar—a previously extinct type of witch, whose magic is now tied to mine. To my dragon from. That's why she's mine to train, to teach—the only one left of a witch clan that vanished long ago."

"So she's a dragon rider, of sorts, then?"

"Da," Tytus says. "And as our fates became intertwined, we started sharing certain things."

Lucrezia says, "I feel things like when he's in danger. Or sometimes, if he gets a vision, it hits me, too. Or some version of it does, like an echo." Her pulse, this time, is strong and steady.

"I don't understand. Why come to me, and now? What does any of this have to do with me?"

"The gods," Tytus says. "You met them, didn't you?"

"I met...someone." At their disappointed silence, I give in. "Fine. I did. I'm not sure who they were, but based on Elizabeta's description, I'm guessing one was Artemis. Not sure who the other one with her was."

"Fenrir," Tytus says. "The wolf god of the Norse pantheon."

I frown. "Why would they be traveling together?"

"Olympus sent Artemis to hunt him down. Eons ago, way before Hades even had an Underworld, Fenrir attacked him. No one knew why. It turned into quite the international pantheon incident. The gods' council sent Artemis to track Fenrir down but he hid here, in the earthly realm. Presumably, she finally found him."

"I'm still waiting for the punch line."

"Show him, Lucrezia."

She moves her hand out of my reach and I can hear tapping. A phone, maybe? Then a news reporter's voice rings. '*Reports of damage in Ireland's Dingle town are incoming, with the world watching, trying to understand whether it was a terrorist attack, or something worse. Stay tuned for more.*'

"The attack they're referring to isn't a coincidence," Tytus says. "As far as I've been able to piece together, Fenrir lived in Dingle. The town was attacked by creatures, left burning. A few days after it took place, Artemis and Fenrir were in these parts. And the creatures? They seem to be hunting the gods."

"Okay... And the humans don't know what they are, judging by that clip. I can see how that would be an issue if humans realize we exist, that magic is real, and so is the supernatural. But I'm guessing the rest of the gods are aware of this, and will do something to hide it?"

"Presumably, yes," Lucrezia says. "But it's not just about the supernatural world being unveiled. It's about the creatures themselves, and who's sending them."

"And...?" My mind whirs. There's only one reason they'd be here. "Zalmoxis? That's who's sending them?"

"Da," Tytus says. "That's what I believe, anyway, given a recent vision I had. The only one who could confirm—who has the power to tap more into this—is Hades."

"Right. Because he's also a god of death."

"Precisely. The problem is, I can't go into Hades' Underworld to speak to him anymore. Every portal into the realm of the gods seems to have been sealed shut. I tried all the locations I was aware of... Nothing. And not even my source—Hades' old guardian—can pierce them."

I run a hand over my beard. "So... you need the Dacians to break one of the portals open? Because I can tell you, given the last turn of events I just went through, that's a bad idea."

"Not exactly. In my vision, I was focused on Zalmoxis. But Lucrezia, who received an echo of the same vision, mentioned having picked up on someone else being there. A female someone—someone she was familiar with."

"Who?" I ask.

"Me."

Elizabeta. I whirl toward the sound of her voice, but she moves to my side fast. Her hand slides into mine, its coolness almost a relief.

"You?" I ask. "What do you mean? How could you be in Tytus' vision?"

Elizabeta

I survey the black-haired man, and Dominic's mate, my features schooled into a neutral mask. I could easily fuck them over, take Ştefan and leave here. Pretend I have no idea what they're talking about. But I'm starting to think there's a reason they're getting a piece of the story, and me, the other.

"Because when I died—for that brief moment—I wasn't just in a random place. I was in limbo. And I saw my father...as well as Zalmoxis." I squeeze Ştefan's bicep, softening my tone. "You came to get me at the end, but I didn't get a chance to tell you the rest."

A muscle ticks in his jaw but, if he's annoyed, he says nothing.

Lucrezia, however, looks at Tytus with a panicked expression on her features. He only shakes his head, his gaze never leaving mine. "Tell us everything."

I bristle at the order. "Want to rephrase that?"

Lucrezia snaps her gaze to me. "Listen here, princess. This affects us all, not just your precious family. It affects my mate and my son." Lightning builds in her gaze with every word. "You can tell us peacefully, or I'll have—"

"Lucrezia, breathe." Tytus clears his throat. "What she means is we can hate each other all we like. But we need to work together on this." To Ştefan, he adds, "You remember what I said when I met you all in the heirs' new home? About Zalmoxis' influence on Silviana being directly related to a struggle among the gods? Believe me, I wouldn't be here begging for scraps of information if I had any other choice."

Ştefan turns to me, cupping my cheek. "You can tell me."

I take a deep breath, and let it out. "Bine. I'm not sure exactly what happened, but one moment I was fighting, and the next I was somewhere...else. In limbo, is the best I can explain it. My father appeared out of nowhere."

"And by father, just to clarify, you mean Țepeș? Not your human father?"

I scowl at the zmeu. "Do you really think after centuries of existence I'd remember my human father? The only parent who ever mattered to me was Țepeș. So yes, that's who I mean."

"And then what happened?"

I'm not about to relate the intimate details of my conversation with Father. "We talked. And toward the end, he tried to warn me off, but he wasn't fast enough. Zalmoxis came, emerging out of some mist that was surrounding us."

"You saw him? In full form?"

I frown. "Yes. Why?"

Tytus shakes his head. "That's not good. It means he's gaining power." At my arched eyebrow, he adds, "I protected the gods for eons. Way before any of you existed, way before this world was as it was. I know their true forms, and how they lose power when they're imprisoned. He should have been mist and magic, but nothing to the extent of what you've seen."

"Zalmoxis didn't act imprisoned," I tell him.

"No, I don't suppose he would." Tytus turns to Lucrezia. "We have what we need. Let's head back."

"Hang on a second," Ștefan says. "My sister. What does this mean for her?"

"Hell, what does any of this mean for any of us?" I add.

Tytus clenches his jaw. "It means we're about to be pawns on a chessboard for beings way more powerful than any of us. The best thing we can do is defend ourselves. So take your loved ones, warn them, and prepare. It won't be long now."

"What are you going to do?"

I ask boldly.

Tytus stares at me, then shares another glance with Lucrezia. "What I can to help the gods. Lucrezia may be able to set some wards around this area, but if shit comes to shove and there's a battle of the skies, there *will* be casualties."

"And we're supposed to.... What, exactly?" I add. "Let things be?" I take a step forward. "This is our family you're talking about. Give us something more."

Tytus throws his head back and stares at the sky for a long time, tension radiating from msg being. Finally, he straightens and nods, as if to himself. "The best you can all do is strengthen yourselves. Magic. Blood. Whatever it takes. And...figure out what's going on with that curse. Something sparked it in the Dracul line. One of you did."

"Why's that important at this stage?"

"It's obvious, isn't it?" Lucrezia gives me a look like I'm stupid and I hiss back in response. She doesn't seem fazed. "Hmm. Perhaps it takes an outside view. Don't get your panties in a bunch, vampir. All I mean is whoever sparked the curse clearly hasn't followed through on it. The more the curse affects you, the stronger Zalmoxis gets. You have to weaken him and the only way to do is that for all of you to find your mates and accept them. And have them accept you. Then Zalmoxis has no hold on you any longer, and at the very least he'll stop getting stronger with every day that passes when you all are suffering."

"None of my siblings would be stupid enough to put us all in danger like that."

"Clearly, one did. It's up to you to figure out who, and fix it."

I watch Tytus and Lucrezia leave, though part of me wants to yank either of them by their hair and force them to come up with a solution. Then, I scoff, turning to Ștefan. "We don't need them. Let's figure something out."

He cups the back of my neck, then my cheek. "I won't lose you."

I reach for his hand, covering it with mine. "You won't." His expression seems pained, though, so I ask, "What is it?"

"Your siblings won't let me in your life."

"They will."

"Not Alexandru. Not Mirabela. I know from Silviana."

I bite my lip. I could lie and hide this from him, but he's right, after all. "You're right. They might take a while to get used to the idea."

"And are you okay with that?"

I move closer to him. "Haven't you learned by now, that I don't let go of things that matter to me? I'm like a dog with a bone."

He chuckles. "And I'm your bone."

"Something like that."

He chuckles. But even as I take in the sight of him, and glance back at the silent woods—no trace of Tytus or Lucrezia—I feel a nagging sense of guilt. I clear my throat. "There's something else I need to tell you."

Ștefan stills, and tilts his head to the side. "Go on."

"When I was... when I was in that limbo place, Father isn't the first person I saw. Daniel was." Nothing changes in Ștefan's expression, but his muscles seem more defined, as though he's holding himself tightly together. "We... He... I could touch him, this time."

Ștefan's tone, when he speaks, is almost impersonal. "Makes

sense. You were on the same plane of existence, in between realms, so the limitations around a stafie's form didn't apply any more. Over here, our bodies work on a certain frequency and once the shell dies, being corporeal is impossible."

I bite my lip, feeling as unsure as I've ever felt—an unwelcoming sensation, to say the least. Part of me wants to run, same as I've always done, but I force myself to continue. "Nothing happened. I want you to know that. He hugged me, kissed my forehead... We said goodbye, in short."

Ștefan nods, but that tension still doesn't leave him.

"He's gone," I add for good measure.

He nods again.

I wait for more, but nothing ever comes. Impatient, I snap, "Will you say something already?"

He seems to think this over, and eventually straightens and speaks, his voice barely a whisper. "Do you still have feelings for him? If... without the curse, would you have—" He stops, as though unwilling to continue.

But he's said enough, and I get it. All the impatience fizzles out of me, leaving only relief in its wake. "No. Ștefan, I... Daniel will always have a place in my heart. But the moment you came into my life, you threw me in for a loop. Everything I thought I believed in, everything I was, was put into question by your mere presence. And when you touch me, the way you make me feel *alive*, and grounded, it's inexplicable. I've lived centuries, and I can't find the words. Kind of silly, right?" I step closer. "Curse or no curse, you're the one I want. You saved me from myself, saw past my bullshit, and gave me strength when I was weak. I..." I pause, almost withholding the rest. *Don't be a coward.* "I love you like I've never loved another before, and never will again. *That* is the honest truth."

The tension finally leaves him and he reaches for me—I'm already moving before his fingers make contact with my skin, launching myself into his arms. My arms wind up around his neck and I kiss him with everything I've got. He groans against my lips, his arms coming around my waist, pulling me even tighter against him, and kissing me like the world's on fire and our time is numbered. Which, in some ways, it really is.

When he stops, he's breathless. "I love you, princess. More than you'll ever know."

For the first time since my first vampir kill, I feel something like butterflies spread through me. I grin wide at the sensation, surprised by the intensity of it. "Thank you. I needed to hear that, I guess."

"I'll say it as many times as you need me to."

He presses a soft peck to my forehead, then intertwines our fingers. Hand in hand, we head back to his apartment.

Chapter 27

Ştefan

A knock on the door wakes me and I slide out of Elizabeta's arms. If anyone had told me days ago that this was how I'd wake up, I'd have thought they'd gone bonkers.

Bare feet, I pull on a pair of sweatpants and pad to the door. "Who is it?"

"It's me."

Maria. Hmm. This can't be good.

I open the door and she does a weird little sharp intake of breath. It's only then I remember I forgot to put on a shirt. "What is it?"

"I, uh..."—she stammers—"they want to see you."

"Who?"

"The rest of us. Who stayed."

A day passed since Tytus and Lucrezia's visit. And though we spent it in bed—for the most part—Elizabeta did sneak glances every now and then at the outside. That's how I found out that some Dacians packed up and left, as I knew they would. It was a relief, really, knowing there were less of them around. Especially as I don't know who I can trust.

But Maria...

"Okay. Give me a minute and I'll be there."

"I...I'll wait here."

Closing the door, I walk back to the bedroom.

"I'm surprised you didn't invite her in."

Startled, I jump slightly at Elizabeta's voice. "I didn't realize you were awake."

"Mm."

There's something in that tone, some kind of tension. Despite me, I'm pulled like a magnet to her and find my legs gravitating toward the bed. "What's that 'mm' mean?"

"Nothing."

"Elizabeta..." I sigh. "They want to see me, apparently. Those who stayed."

"Mm."

"If you're not going to voice your thoughts—"

"It's just interesting they sent the one more likely to fawn over you to get you. What if it's a trap?"

"Fawn over... Maria doesn't fawn over me!"

She laughs, low and dark. It reminds me of how she'd laughed the previous night as she taunted me to take her deeper, and my cock stirs.

"Sure."

"Elizabeta—" I move even closer. My knees hit the side of the bed.

"Stop. You can wipe that smirk off your face."

"What smirk?" I ask as innocently as I can, even while being unable to do as she asks.

Her tone is even more accusing when she grumbles, "You act like you're enjoying this."

"Okay."

"Okay? *That's it*?"

I chuckle. "Yep. Just okay."

And because I know exactly how big my bed is and where she is now, I reach out for her. My fingertips catch her jaw, tilting her face up to me. "You're jealous," I breathe over her lips.

"I am not."

"Mm," I return, and she smacks my chest. "That'll leave a mark."

"Now there's an idea..."

And before I know how, she's tackled me on the bed and straddled me. Her hair tickles my face, even as I chuckle.

"Elizabeta..."

And that turns into a groan when she trails her lips down my neck, my chest, and lower still. My traitorous dick is now at full mast.

She impatiently pushes the sweatpants off me—just enough to free it. And then she takes me so deep into her mouth, I arch off the bed with a loud, "Fuck!"

I can feel her smiling against my skin, and I'm a fucking goner.

Much later, I exit the apartment and find Maria's still there. "I, uh, sorry. Had to take a shower." Heat creeps up my neck, and I rub it uncomfortably.

"Okay," she says, then her footsteps patter ahead.

I clear my throat. No way she didn't hear me when Elizabeta had me climax within minutes, a few walls removed from her, but I refuse to let the awkwardness linger.

"How have you been doing?" I ask.

"Oh... you know, it's been... I guess about the same. Dull. Fairs and tarot reading and all. Bringing in the money Liviu wants—want*ed*, I guess."

"You know, with Liviu gone, you can do whatever you want now."

"I have nowhere to go. So I guess my happiness will depend on the next leader's plans." There's bitterness in her tone but also acceptance of her fate.

We finally reach downstairs and I know the moment I step out of the elevators that we're not alone. A buzz of murmurs greets me, then quiets down. Surreptitiously, I shift my wrist enough for the tip of my athame to slide out of my cuff and dig into the skin. The bit of blood is enough for darkness to rise to the occasion, confirming a big blob of auras is facing me.

I tense slightly, recalling Elizabeta's words. "How about some introductions? Since you all called me here."

One by one, they do as I ask. Their tones falter between wary and hopeful, but none are hateful. A mix of men and women seems to have stayed behind.

"We buried the dead," one—Anton—says. "Wiped all traces of the fight and started rebuilding the area. We, uh, don't know what to do about Liviu's house. Do we leave it as is?"

"I guess it depends on if any of you wants it."

One of the females, Cassandra, murmurs, "We could turn it into a sparring area for the women. Somewhere we can train in private, maybe catch up with the men?"

I nod, a soft smile on my lips. "That's a great idea. But why are you all asking me? You can do as you wish. I'm not Liviu."

"Well, that's the thing." The man, Anton, speaks again. "There isn't anyone else we'd rather lead us. We took a vote and.... You're it. If you'd like to, that is."

My jaw drops a little at that.

"And we don't have an issue with Elizabeta," Maria says by my side, though her tone sounds sad. "We understand the magic binding you."

"I.... Thank you. I don't know what to say."

"Say you'll do it. We don't really know how to put ourselves to use otherwise. And.... Direction would be appreciated. If it hadn't been for Liviu, you probably would've led us after your father's passing."

"I suppose so," I mutter. The thought never even crossed my mind, and I'm not entirely sure I want to dwell on it just now. I clear my throat. "Again, it depends on what you want to do. We all know there's trouble brewing. Liviu was making a mess of the territories, pushing us in the middle of it with hunters and other vampiri clans moving against the Draculs."

"They're really back, then?"

Another female interrupts. "My mother used to tell me stories about the heirs."

"Oh, they're back." I can't hold back a smug grin at that. "But, like I said, this isn't your fight. All I ask is you don't contribute to the mess by joining the hunters and clans."

"We won't," says Anton. "We swear it."

Mutters of assent follow his words.

"Then," I say, "let's take it day by day. I promise I won't ask you to fight. That is my battle alone. But, where we can, we may intervene to smooth over issues."

"About that..."

I turn to the voice, unable to place it despite the earlier introduction. "Yes?"

"The, um, the god. I was close to the fight, and heard what Liviu said. And he's wrong. Zalmoxis' prison *can* be reinforced."

"...How!?"

"I used to do research for him. He sent me far and wide for...a lot of things. And the way he learned how to get to Zalmoxis? It's similar to how to reinforce his prison. We only need a funnel."

I frown. "I'm not about to sacrifice anyone."

"No! It doesn't have to be a sacrifice. It just needs to be someone with a link to something Zalmoxis wants."

"Hmm." All I can think of is Silviana. "Find me that information, please, and come by later tonight." Quickly, I correct myself. "Uh, tomorrow morning." I have plans tonight.

To my surprise, no one objects.

"And Liviu's house, then?" Maria asks. "We... you're okay with the females taking it?"

"Da, absolutely. Sell what you can from within it, take what you want. If you come across any old scrolls, please bring them to me. Otherwise, it's yours to do with as you please." Impatience has me close and open my fist, the urge to return to Elizabeta something fierce. "Is that all?"

"Yes, Grand Ma—"

"No. None of that. I'm your equal, not your superior. You've known me as Ştefan all my life, and that won't change."

Their excited murmurs follow me all the way to the elevator.

Elizabeta

I lean against the counter, watching Ştefan cook himself dinner. He'd started by pulling out some pre-sliced pork loins from the fridge, letting them sit in some milk—to make the meat more tender, he'd said. He then moved on to a salad—a pre-mixed bag of veggies that he washed, added some condiments to, and massaged to let them sink in. Now he's taking the meat cuts out one by one from the milk and adding spices to them. His kitchen is extremely organized, with each spice container having a label in braille over it.

He's been buzzing with smugness and easiness since he returned from his meeting with the Dacians, and it looks hot as sin on him. Not that I'll tell him that. Bad enough he can't see that woman ogling him. I had to mark him, didn't I?

"You sure you don't want anything?" he asks over his shoulder as he flips a piece of pork over to spice the other side. "I'm almost done. Just going to toss them in the air fryer to cook on their own after, and then they'll be ready. Twenty minutes, tops."

I chuckle. "I'm good. The weakness has passed, and I'm better off just finding something to feed on later. On the way home."

He freezes for a moment. "You're going home?"

I move closer to him, hugging him from behind. "Only for a few days. I need to pack a few things, then I'll come back and help out."

He sets aside the meat, turning to me. "Help out? With what?"

"Your Dacians said you need a funnel to try and get to Zalmoxis. If you do that, you can find him, and potentially reinforce his prison bars, right?"

He tenses further. "Elizabeta—"

"I can be the funnel. Or my blood, anyway. Come on, it's not like you didn't think of it. I'm the choice that makes the most sense. Cezar himself said he needed the Dracul line to finish the spell for the portal, you know."

He's shaking his head before I'm even done. "Not going to happen. First off, I'm not Cezar. And second, it's bad enough Silviana is tainted by Zalmoxis. Do you really think I'll let you put yourself in danger?"

"I won't be in danger. You can oversee the magic."

"*Oversee* it? Absolutely not. I won't take a chance with this—with you. I refuse to put you in danger."

"What is it you're afraid of?" I ask, though I soften my delivery. "I want to help. And you can either take the help, or I'll go to Tytus and work alongside him and his brother instead."

Ștefan grips my shoulders at my words. "That's out of the question."

"Careful, Ștefan. That almost sounded like an order. And you know how badly I take those."

His grip on me tightens. For a moment, he almost seems like he's seriously considering a punishment—and my core clenches at whatever he's got in mind.

Then, his expression eases and he drops his forehead against mine. "I'll have conditions, if you're to do this."

I grin at him. "You can think them up while I'm gone."

I make it a point to find some hikers and feed off them quickly before heading home. The castle comes into view, and for the first time in my life, I'm apprehensive.

Elizabeta Dracul fears nothing. Fuck apprehension and all its cousin cowardly feelings. I walk through the doors, my head held high.

A butler appears by my side, dressed impeccably. "Your Highness, please allow me to take your coat."

I glance over my shoulder at the shredded, barely-there jacket I've got on. Then shrug, take it off, and toss it to him. "You might as well burn it. And I'm assuming someone can order me new clothes?"

"Yes, of course."

"Good. I'll leave a note with my siblings for where to send them."

I head up the stairs and run into Mirabela on my way up.

"Well, well. Look who shows her face finally." She tilts her head to the side. "You seem…weird."

I laugh, and her puzzled expression only deepens. "I'm fine, Mira. What's with the five-star welcome I just got?"

She glances down at the butler. Another servant comes by, takes the coat I'd given him, and scurries away. "If we're to be taken seriously, we need to play the part. Finally act our level, no?"

"Uh huh…"

She shrugs. "After the ball, Nico and I talked and made a few additions. We're going to slowly start reaching out to influential humans, too. Politicians, the like. Entertain them here, and…wine and dine them."

"To what purpose?"

"Extend our influence. Make sure we have powerful allies." She frowns. "After the attack, it became clear we need to send a better message that we're not to be fucked with. And that we *will* retaliate."

"Right. And you think the vampiri will be afraid of a few human politicians?"

It's her turn to laugh. "Oh, my dear sister. We're looking to do so much more than make them afraid." She steps closer, lowering her voice. "They'll understand that if they want to do anything in this country, they bow down to us. Else, suffer the consequences." She winks. "You'll see."

I shake my head, and move further on, to my room. I grab a duffel bag and quickly toss in some jeans, shirts, a couple of dresses, two jackets, bras, underwear, and my makeup kit. I glance around, taking in my room and the view one more time. I'll miss it, not going to lie. I'll miss the comforts this place has, the plush carpet under my feet, and having my siblings close. But I know I can't have Alex around my consort—not yet. So, time away is the best choice...for now, at least.

By the time I zip the duffel bag closed and exit my room, I find Nico blocking my way.

His eyes widen with surprise. "Liza. You're back? Vlad told me about—"

I pull him inside my room and lower my tone. "I need to tell you something."

And then, as quickly and efficiently as I can, I explain everything, starting with what I feel is the most important bit—our sire. By the time I relate the conversation with Father and Zalmoxis, Nico looks beyond shell-shocked.

He runs a hand through his hair and moves to my bed, as though in a daze. "He's... You're serious? You're not fucking with me, as some sort of payback?"

"Nico, come on. I may be many things, but I'm not cruel."

He arches an eyebrow. "I'm not blind to what you're doing with the hunters' descendants, Liza. You've been hunting them down, eradicating their whole lineages."

I shift on my feet. "Okay, fine. I *am* cruel. But not to you guys. I may stomp my feet and throw tantrums, but at the end of the day, we're Draculs. We have each other's backs, right?" He nods. "Well, I'm serious. Everything I'm saying is truthful. Father is stuck in limbo, and Zalmoxis is purposefully keeping him there. And there's nothing we can do...for now."

"For now?"

The rest of the story comes out then. The bond with Ștefan, my role in saving Silviana, Tytus, and Lucrezia and their visit, and why I'm basically moving in with a man I'd hated less than two weeks before.

When I'm done, Nico blinks at me. Then, he bursts out laughing.

I can't help it. I slap the shit out of him, cutting him off. And then he starts off again, louder and more uncontrolled still. Since violence didn't work, I roll my eyes and wait him out.

A few minutes later, he finally calms down enough to wipe his face. "Ah... Damn. To think, I'd always thought you'd be the last one to fall..."

I narrow my eyes on him. "You knew I'd fall?"

"Liza, we're *all* falling. That's how the curse works." He shrugs. "And, it's not so bad. I've tapped into parts of myself I didn't know existed."

"Ew."

"Not like that! Get your mind out of the gutter. My point is—as the humans say—you gotta do what you gotta do. But have you told Alex?"

I look away. "No. Can I... Could you?"

He nods. "Sure. But don't be surprised if he doesn't believe me, and comes to get you himself."

"Yeah...I figured as much. Thank you." I hesitate, then reach for him and hug him quickly. "I'll miss you."

"It's not like you're leaving forever. But, Liza? Be careful." He frowns. "I don't like the thought of you doing this, though I understand it's needed. Especially if it'll get us answers about Father." He pauses. "Should I tell the others about him being stuck in limbo?"

"Yes, please." I leave shortly after.

No sooner do I exit the castle, than a figure emerges from the shadows. Alex's face contorts with fury as he levels an accusing glare on me. "Leaving without saying goodbye?"

Fuck. How much does he know? And how?

He takes a step closer, sniffing. "I didn't want to believe it when I heard you talking with Nico, but you even smell like that Dacian." He shakes his head. "Never thought I'd see the day you betray your own kind."

"I'm not betraying anyone."

"No?" He moves in more. "Then what the fuck do you call what you did? Spreading your legs for a human?"

I scowl at him. "You had no issue with me sleeping with humans before. We've hunted and fucked them for ages."

"But we don't *fall in love with them,* Liza! *FUCK*!" He tugs on his hair in frustration, then drops his hand by his side, clenching it into a fist. His voice drips with venom. "I expected this shit from

Nico and Vlad. But you?"

"Alex..." I step closer to him, something in me breaking at his tone, and the hurt in his eyes. I've never seen this level of vulnerability from him. Because underneath all that anger, that's what's hiding. "I didn't do this to hurt you. The curse—" I shake my head. "I can't blame it on that. Maybe it started like that, sure. But Ștefan has shown me another side of me, something I didn't think existed anymore."

"Oh, fucking great. He showed you. I bet he *showed you* plenty."

"Watch it," I warn. "I'm not going take shit from you."

"TOO FUCKING BAD!" He screams, getting up in my face now. His voice echoes through the night, each word punctuated by a shove that threatens to push me over the edge. "YOU—WERE—SUPPOSED—TO—BE—UNFALLIBLE! Like me!"

"I DIDN'T BETRAY YOU!" I yell, shoving him right back.

Now we're both panting, fuming, ready to tear each other apart in a way we've never been. I'm not sure how much everyone in the castle is hearing, but they're definitely getting an earful. He's always been the solid one, my biggest supporter, my greatest fan. And now? He's looking at me like I'm no better than Nico and Vlad. It *hurts*, leaving a dull ache in my chest.

That only increases tenfold when his words sink in. "What do you mean, *like you*?"

He sneers, saying nothing. I've seen that expression aimed at everyone else *but* me, and it stings more than I thought it would.

"Alex, what did you do?"

"Nothing. I did fucking *nothing*, that's the whole point. Because unlike what they're all telling you, it's entirely possible to do nothing. Curse or no curse."

The smug expression on his features makes me want to wipe it. Even as I remember Tytus and Lucrezia's warning, that one of us...that one of us caused this. Started the downfall of the curse.

"Alex...I'll ask again. What are you talking about?"

His expression is stormy, his eyes cool like when he's talking to Nico, when he finally confesses. "You all act like there's no way this curse can be undone. It can. By us not complying. Which is exactly what I did. Easily, I might add."

"You...*what*!?" And then it hits me. "Oh, by all the gods. We never found out which one of us sparked the curse. It was *you*? All along, it was you? And you knew? But didn't tell us?"

The sneer gets more pronounced. "Why should I? My business is my own. As it should be."

I'm in his face, shoving him yet again. "Violeta suffered because of you! We all did! Vlad, me! Nico. You think this shit would've started if you hadn't—*damn it all to hell, Alex*! And you talk about betrayal? What the hell is wrong with you?"

He looks me in the eye. "You have no business looking down on me. I've stood by you when the others judged you for all your sleeping around, for all your kills, for the sheer impulsivity that rules you most days. But I *stood by you* because I understood." He looks me up and down, as if only now seeing me for the first time. "Or thought I did."

The dull throb expands, and if I were human and needed to breathe, it would've cut off my oxygen. "Alex, I'm still me," I whisper, hating how my voice trembles. Hating that he's getting to me, and I'm letting him see it.

"No, you're not. The Elizabeta I knew would've snapped a human's neck before ever allowing herself to fall in love with him. The

Elizabeta *I knew* would've stood her fucking ground, like she promised me, instead of being a damned hypocrite. *The sister I had* would've never debased herself this way." He takes a step forward, lips curling, body tense with unleashed rage. "Get your shit and get out of here, Elizabeta. You're no sister of mine."

Shoving his shoulder into mine, he walks past me. I stumble back, watching him go, my heart in my throat.

And then I turn away, blinking away tears, and run.

And run.

And run some more.

Because I'll be damned if I let this crumple me. Alex has no leg to stand on, having hidden his involvement in the curse from us all. He could've stopped it from getting so bad. But he chose to let his hate for humans get in the way. He'd do anything to maintain that, even if it meant killing us all.

I'm not willing to do the same.

And if he never comes to his senses, so much for Dracul loyalty.

I'll be fine. I've got Ştefan, and that's all I need.

Ştefan

I'm on the couch, reading a book, when Elizabeta returns. I know the moment she enters my apartment that something happened. Not just because of how she slams the door behind her, but because she's actually walking—stomping—rather than using her vampir speed to get across the small distance between us.

I set aside my book. "What happened?"

The stomping stops. A small pause ensues. Then her footsteps come nearer, until she's straddling me. Her hair falls around us like a curtain, tickling my cheeks, my nose. Her lips press against mine, a kiss meant to seduce—to distract herself.

I move my hands to her waist, indulging her. I'll never deny her any kisses, but I also won't let her use them to avoid communication as she's wont to do.

After a few minutes, I shift one of my hands to tangle in her hair and use the leverage to tug her gently. "Elizabeta..."

"I don't want to talk about it," she mutters, and presses closer. "Just give me this, right now. *Please.*"

It's the pleading in her tone that's my undoing, and all my good intentions fly out the window. I tighten my grip on her hair and instead of pulling her away, I bring her closer. This time, I lead the kiss—soft, cajoling, hoping my actions, if not my words, will be enough to get her to realize she's safe here, with me.

And for once, Elizabeta lets me. She gives in, submitting in a way that's so unlike her. I release her hair and cup her jaw instead, tracing every line of her cheekbones, her scar, down to her throat, her collarbone.

She gasps when my hand reaches the valley between her breasts—she must be wearing one of those dresses she loves so much. The fabric my other hand rumples is soft, silky, like butterfly wings.

"Ştefan... *Please.*" Again, that plea.

I'm a servant to her needs, to her desires. I lean in, pressing my lips against her collarbone instead. She pulls back for a moment then, after some movement, leans once more against me. This time, my hands touch bare skin—she must've removed her dress. I intend to take my sweet time, but she grips the back of my head, leading me to her breasts.

I chuckle against her soft skin. "Impatient, are we?"

For all answer, she rolls her hips against mine, and I groan. I'm already so hard, I doubt I'll last long once I'm inside her. Which is pretty much what Elizabeta wants, if I know her at all.

Sure enough, while I busy my mouth sucking on her nipple, she reaches between us and tugs off my shirt, then reaches for the waistband of my sweatpants. She pushes the fabric enough past my hips to free out my cock, and then she positions herself over it, taking me inside her in one fell sweep.

"*Fuck,*" I hiss, dropping my head between her breasts, even as my cock throbs at her tightness.

Elizabeta pauses, and her hands come around my shoulders, holding me to her as though enjoying the sensation as much as I am. Then I turn my head to the right and reach for her breast again, kissing every spare inch I can get my mouth on, while flicking her other nipple.

Elizabeta moans, and starts moving over me. Her entire body is taut like a bow, ready to snap. In the few times we've been intimate, I've enjoyed experiencing that control slip from her, and knowing I'm the reason behind it.

I drop my hands to her hips, pushing her harder onto me, knowing she needs that extra friction to explode. When her moans and her pace increase, I reach between us and circle her clit, as she demonstrated for me last time. I'm nothing if not a good student.

She tightens around me one last time, and I feel the tell-tale pulsing of her orgasm even as my name leaves her lips like a mantra. It only takes me two thrusts into her to come, my face buried in her chest once more.

Exhausted, I drop my head back against the sofa, taking Elizabeta with me. She rests her head on my shoulder, presses a kiss to the side of my neck, and lets out a soft sigh. Not that long ago, I'd have wondered at the sanity of having a vampir's mouth so close to my carotid artery. Now? I fully enjoy the electrifying tingle that races through me at the touch.

"Thank you," she whispers.

I run a hand over her back, enjoying the shivers I'm inducing. "I'll always give you what you need, princess. Always and forever."

Night falls and finds us entangled on a sofa, a blanket spread over us. Elizabeta hasn't moved, lost in thoughts, and I've given her the space to do whatever processing she needs to, in the hope it'll lead her to open up without me probing.

To my surprise, it does, shortly after my watch buzzes to announce it's past nine o'clock.

"When I went back, I told Nico everything—about Father, Zalmoxis, what Tytus and Lucrezia told us. The whole bit. I also told him about us."

I draw in a shaky breath. That she admitted as much to her siblings is... My heart swells. In her own way, Elizabeta's letting me know she's in this, all of this, with me.

I kiss the top of her forehead, and whisper, "How did that go?"

"Oh, he had a good laugh, you know." Some mirth fills her tone at this, but it's gone in the next sentence. "Alex overheard. He intercepted me once I was leaving." She shifts over me in a way that makes me think she's looking at me. Her fingers trace my nose, my lips, my jaw. "I'd intended to tell him, but not now. Alex is... He's volatile, and he hates humans."

"As do you."

She shrugs. "Maybe not *all* humans." Again, all levity leaves her tone. "Alex does, though. And we got into it. He said some things, I said some things, it escalated."

I turn my head to the side, kissing part of the hand that's been caressing me. "The pain in your voice tells me it was more than 'some things,' Elizabeta."

She's quiet for a moment, then shifts once more and presses her face into my chest. I feel the tears bathing her cheeks, falling onto my skin. The silent sobs rocking her body.

My arms come around her, pulling her tighter against me. "I've got you. No matter what, I've got you," I whisper.

It takes her a long time to calm down. When she does, she sniffles, and rests her chin on me instead. "You're pretty good at this consoling stuff, you know?"

I offer her a tentative smile. "Yeah? I guess raising a sister pays off."

Elizabeta's quiet again. I don't understand why until she says, "I'm sorry. For being so mean to her, and to you. I..." She trails off, at a loss for words, but the remorse in what she said tells me everything I need to know.

"Vengeance has a way of warping the mind, princess. It's normal you associated every human with the fuckers who took you captive and experimented on you. It'll take a long time for you to learn not to judge everyone for those hunters' actions." I raise a hand and she nuzzles her cheek into my touch. "I'm grateful to have the opportunity to show you that not all of us are alike. And as for my sister? She's the most forgiving person there is. All she needs to see is you treating me right, and she'll get behind us." I can feel more tears bathing my palm, and I frown. "What's wrong?"

"I just… I wish I could say the same for Alex."

I'm quiet for a long moment. The pain in her voice kills me, and I wish nothing but to take it away. I also know I can't. Her and Alexandru are as tight as me and Silviana, and that kind of bond comes with its downsides—like when you're fighting.

"In all the centuries we've been siblings, we've never fought like this," she whispers. "I don't think he'll ever forgive me for falling in love with a human."

Despite the weight of her words, I can't help a smile. "Is that what you've done, then? *Fallen in love* with me?"

She ducks her face in my palm and kisses it. I can sense the hints of a smile when she says, "You know full well I have. Just because I only said it the one time…"

I give up all pretense then and sit up, reaching to cup both her cheeks. "I'd say you've gone and made me the happiest man on earth, princess." And I kiss her with all I've got.

I can't take away her pain, or her wounds, but I can give her new memories. And in time, this newfound happiness of ours will consume the darkness of her past, hopefully freeing her from it—once and for all.

Epilogue

Lucrezia returned to her village, her mind still whirling over the vampir's revelations. To think, all along they'd thought whatever was coming could be easily controlled and prepared for. And now, to find out it was more than that?

She turned to Tytus. "You still think it was a good idea to move us here?"

"I have no doubt about it. And especially given what's coming."

"I won't risk my family, Tytus. We've been through too much."

"And I wouldn't ask you to." He glanced at the skies, then checked his watch. "I should get back to Fiona. And Declan and Constanza, fill them all in on what we're up against."

"You think Constanza could reach out to her parents? As

Hades' old guards, surely they can help keep us all safe?"

Tytus shook his head. "They'll have bigger fish to fry, if what I fear happens will happen. No. The best way to handle any of this is to get the first leg up on Zalmoxis. The gods will be unearthing every weapon in their arsenal to deal with him. We'll do the same."

Lucrezia nodded and hugged him. "Have a safe trip, then. And maybe shift a bit farther away than last time. It took us nearly a month to clean up the last forest you ruined."

Tytus chuckled, his chin resting above her head. She knew it still struck him as odd that she, a tiny human, thought to lecture him on *where he could shift*. "Fine."

He was releasing her from the hug, pivoting to leave, when a cry in the distance stopped him. His arms froze around Lucrezia.

"Mom!"

Lucrezia turned, gasping at the sight awaiting her. "Luca?" Her son was running to her, a wild look in his eyes, his features taut with tension. "What's going on? Are you okay?"

Panting, he nodded, but the panicked expression stayed. He seemed near tears. "I'm fine. It's not me, it's Dad. He's been acting off since I came back from dealing with those hunters. And earlier, he said he was going to check out something by the waterfall, that he wouldn't be long. But it's been ages and I went to look and… I can't find him." He lifted his hand, palm facing toward her. "I only found this."

Blood. His hand was covered in it.

Tytus had barely a moment to tighten his arm around her waist, holding her when she swayed. "What do you mean, you can't find him?" the zmeu asked.

"He's not…" Luca met her gaze. "He's gone. No trace."

Lucrezia's knees gave way for good at that and she welcomed darkness gladly. Anything was better than the thought of being without her mate.

Want to dig into Lucrezia and Dom's past? **Find out how everything started with *First to Fall.***

The events of this epilogue continue in *Angry Addiction*, Book 5 in the Lost Royals of Transylvania series., and *Vârcolac Legacy*, Luca's werewolf romance series. **Sign up for my newsletter to be in the loop when it releases!**

And as for the gods? **Dive into *Immortal Rogues* for more on Hades, Zalmoxis, Artemis and Fenrir, & so much more...**

And if you enjoyed Elizabeta and Stefan's story, please consider leaving a review at your choice of retailer. Even a line or two makes a huge difference to an indie author!

Have you read them all?

ROGUES EXTENDED UNIVERSE – READING ORDER

Moonlight Rogues

Flaming Rogues

Immortal Rogues

Lost Royals of Transylvania

Vârcolac Legacy (Coming Soon)

Coming up in *Lost Royals of Transylvania*

Alex has one rule—no humans. He'll fuck them. He'll drink from them. But he'll never see them as anything other than tools. Which is why two years ago, when he first felt the pull of the curse, he fought it. But fate is fickle, and his past is catching up to him. Will he let the curse work the second time around—and fall for Irina as he's fated to—or will he fight it to the death...and drag his siblings into Zalmoxis' expecting hands alongside him?

Sign up for my newsletter to get first dibs on new releases, including sneak peeks at Alex's first chapters when they're ready! In the meantime, enjoy this scene (keep flipping!) that may or may not be a deleted one

Scene from Angry Addiction

Alexandru

Rage fills every molecule of my body at Liza's betrayal. Out of everyone, I didn't think she'd ever do this. Fists clenched, I know there's only spot where I can go and unleash it. And I'll be relishing every second of it.

I change course and instead of going back inside the castle, head through the gardens, for the back exit. Leave it to my siblings to fucking annoy me.

Mirabela and Nico step in my path. "What the hell was that about?" Mira asks. "You and Liza went at it like you'd lost your minds!"

"*She* lost it. Not me."

Nico narrows his eyes. "You sure about that? What was that about you and the curse, and hiding stuff from us?"

I roll my eyes. "So I felt the pull of the curse before all of you. At least I was smart enough not to give in to it."

Mira gapes. Nico scowls. "*You* fucking started this?"

"Don't test me, frate. Not today. Not after Liza."

As he moves toward me, Mira lifts her hand to his chest, holding him back. "Let him go. We'll talk to him when he's calmed down."

I fake a curtesy bow, then speed away. And because I don't trust them not to follow me, I zig-zag through the trees for an hour, until I'm utterly sure I'm alone.

Only then do I slow down, and retrace my steps. Far on the grounds of our new palace, I'd found an underground wine cellar.

And I very quickly determined the best use for it.

So I push away the leaves, and lift the hatch. Then step inside, climbing down the stairs.

In a corner, tied to a chair with silver chains, a blond head hangs limp. At the sound of my footsteps, slow and purposeful, he lifts cool blue eyes to me. In another life, we could've been brothers. We sure look close enough.

"Dominic, Dominic. How do you find your new quarters?"

He spits out a mouthful of blood, blinks his good eye at me—unlike the swollen black eye—and scowls. "You're a stupid fuck, thinking you'll get away with kidnapping me. The vârcolaci in my pack have the best sense of smell. They will find you. And when they do—"

I laugh. "And yet, it's been a full twelve hours, and no one's knocking on my door. Funny, no?"

"Fuck you."

"Nah. But you will give me information."

He stares me, unmoved. "Information about what, you dumb idiot? I'm on your side!"

"No, no. See, I've seen who you hang with. That dragon shifter? Tsk. Add to it that when I came to ask you about those hunters that attacked your mutts in the woods—"

"You didn't came to *ask*. You *demanded*. Excuse me if I don't take kindly to attitude from a bloodsucker."

I narrow my eyes on him. "I'll pretend you didn't say that. Point is, you were less than forthcoming. And *I* have issues with liars. There's more to this, and I intend to get to the bottom of it." I kneel in front of him. "My siblings seem to think you're entirely trustworthy. But since you moved here, we've been attacked by vampir hunters, Dacians, and other clans. Someone's talking to them."

"It's not us!"

"Good. Then it should take no time at all for you to convince me, after which you can return home. But in the meantime..." I reach for his hand, and grab the thumb. "Tell me about this dragon shifter."

When he glares at me, refusing to let out so much as a growl, I snap the thumb. And move to his index finger.

He says plenty then, even if it's all curses.

Love my books?

Want to get your hands on them and review them first, before anyone else?

Sign up for my ARC team now

And you'll get to read and review everything first....

Including the next *Lost Royals of Transylvania* novel!

Vampires, sibling rivalries and mysteries continue.

About the Author

Alexa Whitewolf is a fiction writer, newspaper columnist of daily issues and author of the critically acclaimed ***Moonlight Rogues*** shifter series.

Alexa has been a lifelong writer and first began creating other worlds and characters at the ripe age of 12. Growing up in the Transylvania region surrounded by epic mountains and a never-ending stream of legends and stories was bound to create an overactive imagination. This shines through Ms. Whitewolf's writing by creating worlds filled with unique folklore, life wisdom and plenty of furry creatures.

An avid traveler, Alexa writes under a penname and spends her days between an office job and writing in Canada's capital, when she's not flying somewhere with lush landscapes and plenty of hiking trails.

Her series focus on strong heroines, kind yet sexy men, fights of good and evil and the never-ending learning curve of humanity's strong—and weak—points. Romanian folklore is intertwined with her writing, more notably in her shifter romance series, the Moonlight Rogues. Her other series draw on world mythology, such as the Avalon myth and Arthurian legend (***The Avalon Chronicles***) and Ancient Egypt (***The Sage's Legacy***).

You can follow her blog at www.alexawhitewolfauthor.com or on social media. Her column in Observatorul also tackles various issues, including health, technology, and a writer's life.

If you want up to date releases, make sure you sign up for her newsletter. For new releases notifications, you can also follow her on Amazon and Bookbub.

ALSO BY THE AUTHOR

Rogues Extended Universe

Moonlight Rogues series

Moonlight Rogues: Origins

First to Fall

Second to Surrender

Third to Tumble

Last to Love

Exclusive inside look inside the series

Flaming Rogues series

Fanning the Flames

Igniting the Ice

Exclusive inside look inside the series

Immortal Rogues series

Secret Shadows

Archer's Arrow

Dead Dilemma

Fickle Fate

Exclusive inside look inside the series

Lost Royals of Transylvania series

Immortal Illusion

Cracked Casualty

Deadly Deceit

Sinful Salvation

Angry Addiction

Primal Protection

Exclusive inside look inside the series

Demoni Sancti Extended Universe

Standalone

Blazing Ashes

Demoni Sancti series

Fallen

Broken

Unshackled

Risen

Ascended

Exclusive inside look inside the series

The Avalon Chronicles series

Avalon Dreams

Avalon Wishes

Avalon Nightmares

Atrox

Exclusive inside look inside the series

The Sage's Legacy – YA series

The Dragon Medallion

The Dragon Manuscript

Relics of the Underworld

Exclusive inside look inside the series

Standalone novels

Blood Ties, Love Binds

Unconditional Love

Exclusive inside look inside the novels

www.ingramcontent.com/pod-product-compliance
Lightning Source LLC
Chambersburg PA
CBHW020926020726
47495CB00002B/359

9781989384237